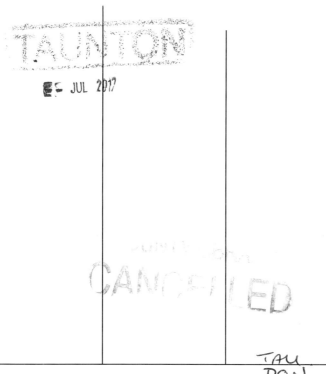
Please return/renew this item by the last date shown on this label, or on your self-service receipt.

To renew this item, visit **www.librarieswest.org.uk** or contact your library

Your borrower number and PIN are required.

Libraries**West**

Hearken to Avalon

Bright Blessings,
Arianna

Arianna Alexsandra Collins

1 3 1670015 8

ISBN: 1517115167
ISBN 13: 9781517115166
Library of Congress Control Number (LCCN): 2015915386
CreateSpace Independent Publishing Platform
North Charleston, South Carolina

Dedication

To the Gods & Goddesses who held my hand and walked me through this
land and who created the conditions to make sure this story was told.

To the Divine Masculine and the Divine Feminine within each of us.
For truly, as an integrated, whole being, whether male or female,
if you cannot find your true love within yourself,
you will never find it without.

To all who believe in a deep and trusting love that knows no bounds.

"I do not at all understand the mystery of grace — only that it meets us where we are but does not leave us where it found us." ~ Anne Lamott

Things are not always as they seem when stories lost in the mists are reclaimed ~ who is to say if the retelling is any less true than the story we knew.

Acknowledgements

First, I would like to thank the actor Richard Armitage for this story's inspiration. In his rendition of Guy of Gisbourne on the BBC Robin Hood series, he was an admittedly damaged character. In an interview, Mr. Armitage discussed his character's flaws. It made me wonder: if this character had love returned to him, if his prayer had been answered, would he be different? If love were given to him freely, could a villain who clearly has a heart and a tender spot for love, change? Could a villain rise up and become a champion? It made me question what defines a villain or a hero, and how love can affect a person on deep and mysterious levels.

And this novel would not have commenced if it were not for my friends Eve and Elizabeth who listened to that first fantasy about Guy and Morgaine and thought it was so hot that I should write it down. In fact, I should create a whole story from it. And so I did.

A big jump-up-and-down-hug thank you to all my friends and family who patiently listened to me tell the tale or a scene and looked forward to reading the novel in its entirety. To Nicole, Jessica, "Sarah the Seamstress" and the many friends who served as role models for character development; some of you even have cameos in the novel. And to all my friends on Facebook who responded to my quirky queries and answered them honestly and sometimes with great humor.

To Sharon and Gabrielli for inspiring me with their Infinity work; to Starhawk for her work on the concepts of power; to Jerry Jud for his concept of adoration; and to Barry Lopez for his concept of what constitutes a man versus a boy. I found beautiful, healing ways to incorporate these principles.

To Sarah and her husband Kevin for providing me with a role model of a completely adoring couple who communicate with each other in love and compassion and without arguing. They are a rare breed of coupledom and I hope to initiate the masses to a gentler way of being with a spouse.

To Heather and Lyle for their extensive knowledge of the medieval period and being willing historical consultants at any given moment. And of course, I thank all the researchers who put countless hours into cataloging events and important personages and places for me to review and incorporate. I will admit to a hand-shaking distance of facts in this work of historical fantasy. I also want to thank Marion Zimmer Bradley for her beautifully written *The Mists of Avalon*. Her novel was an inspiration for me as well as fodder for creating this "Into the Woods" version of colliding legends.

To Apple & Oak, and particularly to Laura for her inspiration of the food blessing and in helping set the tone for the Great Rite chants. To fellow writer Susan for her counsel and inspiration during our weekly story-shares in 2013. To Frank for his assistance with character development of Rodney and Wild Herb as it related to wilderness living skills, and for his assistance in describing specific maneuvers. To John, Malachi, Molly and Kathy for their expertise, debate and dialogue over a translation into Latin. Who knew one sentence could be so complicated? To Sarah and Malachi for translating dialogue in a scene into French for me. And to Jessica, Margaret and Beth for their council on translating horse body language and vocalizations into text.

To Laurel Thorndike for taking my vision and illustrating the cover of this novel. To Margaret Green for editing the first two rounds of the story. To Jennifer Wilhoit for copy editing. To Julia Blyth for proofreading the final draft. To John P. Buryiak for proofreading and editing the revision. To Evelyne Elie-Eisele for editing the French translation for historical accuracy.

To Gus Ganley for his enthusiasm and inspiration during the editing phase and gifting me with his skills as a videographer for my Indiegogo campaign to raise funds for this publication. And many thanks to all the individuals who contributed to the Indiegogo campaign so that this novel could manifest in the world! Deep gratitude to my mother MaryAnn whose financial support gave me the time to focus on writing this book. And to my father David and Mama Laura for all their love, patience, compassion and support.

To John, for walking into my life as if out of the pages of my novel. You are a wonder, my Love.

Cast of Characters

Characters of Glastonbury

Aelred — a castle guard

Anwen — daughter of Gwenyth and Bran and sister to Owain

Asher and Leah — horse breeders

Brighid — a cook at Glastonbury Castle

Col — musician in the Avalon household

Elizabeth & Wild Herb — elders

Evelyn Avalon — Morgaine's mother and Duchess of Glastonbury

Gareth Avalon — Morgaine's father and Duke of Glastonbury

Grace — an Avalon Guardian

Gwenhwyfar — Morgaine's childhood friend

Gwenyth — a servant a Glastonbury Castle; mother of Owain

Father Hale — a town priest in Glastonbury

Sir Hammond — former Master of Arms of Glastonbury

Sir Harry — a soldier

Jack — a foundling, Avalon Guardian in training

Lorrac — Morgaine's first love, the youngest of Gwenhwyfar's older brothers

Megan & Owain — townspeople

Meggie — Morgaine's companion

Morgaine Avalon — descendant of Morgaine, the half-sister of Arthur Pendragon

Mouse — Guy's servant

Nichole — Morgaine's childhood friend

Raven — an Avalon ancestor

Rainer — an Avalon Guardian

Reeve — Gareth's servant
Rhiannon — Morgaine and Guy's daughter
Rindill — an Avalon ancestor
Robbie — coach driver
Monsieur Rochefort — a French dignitary
Sarah — daughter of Asher and Leah, childhood friend of Morgaine's; wife to Kedem
Sarah the Seamstress — Morgaine's seamstress
Sophie — Evelyn's servant
Father Stephen — High Priest at the Glastonbury Abbey
Taharqa — Master of Arms
Tana — Taharqa's mother, servant of Evelyn
Viviane — Morgaine (the first) and Merrek's daughter

Characters of Nottingham and Surrounding Region

Sir Auguste of Gisbourne — Guy's father
Beth — a bar maid
Brin — servant of Guy at Locksley Manor
Caron — a woman from Locksley Village; Guy's childhood friend; wife to Robert
Sir Charlton — Marian's Father, a knight, served in 2nd Crusade
Delphine — Guy's sister
Dylan — Mary's son and servant of Guy at Locksley Manor
Sir Grigor — Guy's second in command
Hazel — a healer in Locksley Village
Jessica — silversmith f Nottingham; wife to Jeffrey, a baker
Marguerite — Guy's mother
Mary — servant of Guy at Locksley Manor; wife to Henry
Matthew — resident of Locksley as a child; Black Knight
Mock — a prison guard
Baron Robert Locksley– Robin's father
William Boxer — Wyatt's eldest son
Baron Wyatt Boxer — Robin of Locksley's mother's cousin

From the Robin Hood Legends

Allen a Dale — a member of Robin Hood's troop
Arthur — a member of Robin Hood's troop
Guy of Gisbourne
Marian — Robin Hood's love
Much (the Miller's son) — a member of Robin Hood's troop
Robin Hood
Will Scarlet — a member of Robin Hood's troop

Characters Heralding from Elsewhere

Ann — confidante of Guy's in London
Bartholomew — Delphine's husband
Darnell — friend of Guy's in London
Gwenhwyfar and Rufus' children: Julius (Juwelin), Rodney (Green Rod), Neirin
Hamelin — Guy's grandfather on his mother's side
Lane — Black Knight
Marie — Guy's grandmother on his mother's side
Merymaat and Yeturow — Tana's parents
Nasrane — Tana's lover; Taharqa's father
Nichole and Will's children: Godric, Rowan
Payton — Black Knight
Roderick — Chancellor to King Richard and to Prince John; Black Knight
Rufus — Gwenhwyfar's husband
Lord Thomas Winter and Lady Edwena Winter — supporters of King Richard
Will — Nichole's husband
Wyvern — Black Knight

Animal Companions

Cream — Morgaine's cat
Crown — Guy's first horse
Ink — Julius' crow
Merryweather — Morgaine's horse
Midnight — Guy's horse
Prometheus — Gareth's dog

The Faie (Fay, Fey, Fairies)

Cynewelew
Dewlynd
Merrek

From the Arthurian Legends

Accolon — said to be the lover of Morgaine
King Arthur — son of Igraine and Uther Pendragon
Gorlois — Duke of Cornwall; first husband of Igraine, father to Morgaine
Igraine — mother of Morgaine and Arthur; Priestess of Avalon
Merlin or The Merlin — a magician and counselor of kings and the Lady of the Lake
Morgaine — daughter of Igraine and Gorlois; Arthur's half-sister; Priestess of Avalon
Uther Pendragon — King of England; father to Arthur
Viviane — Lady of the Lake during King Arthur's reign

Historical Personages

Count of Anjou (Geoffrey V) — grandfather to King Richard and Prince John
Isabella of Gloucester — Prince John's first wife
King Henry II of England — father to King Richard and Prince John
King Richard I — Richard the Lionheart, third son of King Henry II by Eleanor
Prince John — youngest son of King Henry II by Eleanor of Aquitaine
Savaric fitzGeldewin — The Bishop of Bath and Glastonbury
Lord William de Wendenal — the High Sheriff of Nottingham, Earl of Derby
William Longchamp — Lord Chancellor to King Richard

Where to Begin?

THE YEAR WAS 990 when Morgaine, a creature of myth, stepped out of the mists and back into Glastonbury. It had been over four hundred years since she had seen the place she had made home. When the Saxons invaded, she had fled this Land. She buried her dear brother in Avalon and then retreated deeper into the Faie Realm. There she grieved all the losses: her brother Arthur, her mother Igraine who decided to stay with the nuns even though the Saxons were pillaging the Land, her aunt and mentor Viviane, her other aunt Morgause, her lover Accolon, her friend Raven, Lancelot. Her son, Mordred. All dead. She had no one left.

Morgaine looked around. The Tor was still standing and great oaks still lined up like sentinels on the pathway to that hill. The Lake was now receding. The Apple Orchard on the far side of the Lake from which she emerged was shrouded in mist as if it still hadn't made up its mind which world to live in. The castle was there, still bright and shining in the sunlight. Though a magnificent feat of 6th century building, she was surprised it was still standing, that the spell had held so long. "Ah, Camelot. The years have been good to you, haven't they?"

Had anyone from her lifetime actually been around to see this Lady of the Lake emerge from the mists, they would have been dumbfounded; she appeared not to have aged a bit in her four hundred year absence. But no one had, and so it was not until she reached the castle that the overseeing occupant noticed the approach of the small-framed, dark-haired, pretty lady in a long silvery-blue gown. She gently patted her abdomen. She was not yet visibly pregnant and so her secret was safe for the time being. She would eventually hear the stories others told about her: of Morgaine the Sorceress, Morgaine the Enchantress, Morgaine the Fairy, Morgaine the evil half-sister of King Arthur. She could ignore them all as she went about her new work in re-securing this castle for her family to be.

By the time it was the year 1191, Camelot was strictly and only called Glastonbury Castle. No sense in stirring the pot now that this place was not the seat of power. And besides, Cadbury Castle was now thought of as the old Camelot, even though the large round table was nowhere to be found and Cadbury was built for an army, not a family and council of brotherhood. This castle was small, quaint even, but beautiful and sparkling when the sun hit the quartz embedded in the bricks. Walls were patched and replaced, beams were propped up in places, but even the castle, had it had thoughts, couldn't understand how it was still standing with all it had been through, including the wars, the sieges, the long period of being forgotten. The ages told it to lie down but it refused. Had outsiders stopped to consider the age of the castle they would have said that only sorcery was holding that building up — and they may have been right.

The few castle occupants didn't bustle much in this magically-imbued dwelling. There was a calm, sweet temperament to the air, like a slow-moving hive of bees. But on this day, there was a disturbance in the hive. The Duchess, Evelyn Avalon of Glastonbury, the hive's queen, was of strained composure as her servant Sophie entered to deliver news from the Abbey on the hill. The Duchess was an elegant woman with high cheek bones, long brown hair braided ornately, spiraling up around her head, and deeply penetrating brown eyes. And though her physical stature was not large, her presence filled the room and she appeared statuesque and much taller than she actually was. She was a Priestess to the Goddess and she carried herself thusly.

"Why now?" The Duchess was annoyed and a bit exasperated upon hearing the news. Someone at the Abbey claimed to have discovered the tomb of King Arthur and Queen Gwenhwyfar in the old cemetery. It was bad enough to have all these monks swarming around, still twittering about while observing the reconstruction of the monastic buildings that had been destroyed years ago. But it was not Arthur's bones in that tomb; this she knew. Arthur was lying in the Isle of Apples where her ancestor put him centuries ago. Evelyn wondered whose bones those were. Probably a pair of priests or nuns or one of each. She sighed deeply, "Now watch the hordes come." She did a banishing sign as if to keep the outsiders at bay.

CHAPTER 1

$$\text{——} \ll \text{——}$$

November 1191 Introductions

THOUGH PRINCE JOHN did not spend much time at the Tower of London, while his brother was away he did occasionally take up residence in London as a way of snubbing King Richard's power. It was just the month prior when, after a brief stand-off with Richard's Lord Chancellor William Longchamp, he gained complete access to the castle. And so just to put the Lord Chancellor in his place, Prince John moved his annual party, a gathering of friends and allies, to London the year Richard departed for the Holy Lands on his idiotic mission to conquer and Christianize the Moors.

The castle was grand and still expanding though John stopped production of the inner ward in preparations for his party which he held in the White Tower's grand hall. This completely vexed the Lord Chancellor, King Richard's appointed man in charge, as clearly he was *not* in charge while the Prince stalked the halls.

Prince John sat on the throne in the grand hall listening to the names being called out as his more loyal subjects entered. "The Duke and Duchess Avalon of Glastonbury and their daughter, The Lady Avalon of the Lake." His eyes brightened as the Lady Morgaine came to him directly, not just bowing but holding her arms out and collapsing into his lap kissing his hand.

"Oh, my Prince, it is good to see you!" It did not matter, her drama; John loved it! He reveled in being so revered.

"Lady Morgaine, it is always a pleasure seeing you. And, Your Graces, thank you for coming." The Duke bowed and the Duchess curtsied. Both had secretly relieved smiles upon their faces as their daughter rose to a curtsy.

1

More people were announced and came in but not before Prince John caught Morgaine's hand, "I shall have a dance with you."

Morgaine replied respectfully, "It would be my joy."

The young Princess Isabella, John's wife, looked visibly annoyed but said nothing. She knew it was unlikely John would actually take Morgaine to bed — not yet anyway, as it would not please her parents who she was sure must be still trying to marry off the aging girl. And they were allies after all.

Morgaine looked at Isabella purposefully, "Your Royal Highness, you are looking absolutely radiant this evening. It will be lovely to watch you and his Royal Highness dance."

Princess Isabella looked surprised and then smiled, relaxing.

As Morgaine walked away from her friend the Prince, she looked for a retreat, someplace to be alone, if only for a moment. Her eyes scanned the grand hall. Everywhere she looked there were people. Their thoughts pressed upon her. Her mother, sensing her daughter's distress, took hold of her hand and gave it a gentle squeeze. They looked at each other. Evelyn took a slow, deep breath. Morgaine mimicked her mother's actions. Her mother took another slow, deep breath, encouraging Morgaine to do the same. Morgaine then heard mother say, quietly, in her mind, "Focus on the task at hand."

Morgaine nodded then said silently, "How do you keep this press of voices from completely overwhelming you?"

Evelyn looked upon her daughter with such compassion. Morgaine heard her mother's voice in her head, "It is not easy to cope with the barrage of so many grieving and fearful souls. Let them flow like water away from you. Keep your focus. It will help."

Prince John took the Lady Morgaine by the hand and led her to the dance floor. He knew well that she loved to dance. Being a relatively short man, John liked dancing with Morgaine as she was at least a little shorter. Isabella was not. But then Isabella's purpose was not to dance or even to be overly visible. He married her for her inheritance though dutifully showed her off at his functions. She was his shining jewel after all. John glanced over at his princess. Though she was no beauty, not like this dark gem he danced with now, with her long dark hair and glistening eyes. Isabella was comely enough and she did have fine long wavy blond hair. Still, it was this slight fairy dancer he liked having his hands on.

Morgaine smiled into the Prince's eyes giving him the perception that he was ever so important. She had collected herself and now felt a bit calmer being amongst so many people she did not know. She could appear vivacious in the Prince's presence because they were on friendly terms. But the people he surrounded himself with were guarded and fearful. Some were even vicious, a characteristic she did not understand and did not want to. Too many thoughts pressing in on her mind. It was so hard to turn off the noise that was like a swarm of flies. In Glastonbury, it was easier. She knew everyone and, for the most part, life was content in her town. But here…there was so much to take in. She reminded herself to focus. The family was here for a reason. This was no time to dwell on feeling overwhelmed.

As the pair danced, the Prince's hands roamed a bit which made Morgaine uncomfortable; but she knew that to stay in his good graces, she had to play along. And he wasn't all bad. He was quite intelligent and a curious strategist. But he had a most loathsome temper and one never knew when it might strike. John, though short, was a decent-looking man, with a powerful, barrel-chested body and dark, wavy red hair with a well-trimmed beard. Lots of jewels. He enjoyed his wealth: the monies he acquired from the populace that he liked to think was his. And so it was.

As they chatted about nothing and everything, a raven-haired knight suddenly drew Morgaine's eye. "Oh, he is splendid," she mused to herself. To the Prince, Morgaine asked, nodding in the direction of this ever so handsome specimen of the male persuasion, "My Prince, who is that?"

"That is Sir Guy of Gisbourne and Lord of Locksley. He is the right hand of Lord William de Wendenal, the High Sheriff of Nottingham and Earl of Derby. Would you like to be introduced?"

"Yes. Would you do the honor?"

John smiled slyly at the idea of such a match. He thought secretly, licking his lips, "Two beautiful creatures aligning houses loyal to me. How delicious."

At the end of the dance, they sashayed up to a melancholy and slightly bored gentleman who was darting his eyes around the room. The Prince immediately commanded the Lord's attention with his voice. "Lord Guy Gisbourne."

The Lord bowed and then kept his eyes on the Prince.

Prince John continued, "I would like to introduce you to the Lady Morgaine Avalon, the daughter of the Duke and Duchess of Glastonbury."

Guy turned his head and caught the eyes of a darling woman smiling unabashedly at him. He blinked and sucked in breath through his flaring nostrils. Time seemed to stop. Then Guy remembered his training in etiquette and took Morgaine's outstretched hand and kissed it as he bowed, keeping his gaze upon her.

John placed his hand on Guy's shoulder, stating, "My faithful knight, I must dance with the Princess or she will complain. Will you entertain this lovely lady for me?"

Guy nodded, trying desperately to remember the English language that suddenly seemed foreign; was he that tongue-tied? Words. Words… "It would be my honor, Your Highness," Guy breathed as he glanced at the Prince while still eyeing this enchanting creature of womanhood.

The Lady Morgaine leaned toward Prince John, giving him a peck on the check and whispered, "Thank you."

John blushed. Morgaine overstepped her bounds of familiarity with him but he never seemed to mind. He turned to face her, bringing his hand up under her chin, looking her in the eyes, "You are welcome." Morgaine curtsied deeply. John smiled, peering into her cleavage, then squeezed Guy's shoulder and looked at him meaningfully with a nod, turned, and walked off.

Guy watched the Prince walk away and then turned to Morgaine who was looking at him expectantly. I don't dance, he thought. I will look foolish. I… Guy managed, "Would you like to dance?" Morgaine beamed at him. He took her by the hand, did a mental sign of the cross, and prayed he would not step on her feet.

Morgaine and Guy danced, each of them doing rather well for being out of their own element — Morgaine being so far from familiarity and home and Guy — dancing. Internally, Morgaine was feeling more at ease. The din of voices subsided as she focused on this handsome man before her. And for Guy's part, occasionally he would look down at his feet, in awe they were moving to the music and he was managing to lead them around on the dance floor. Though Guy avoided dancing he found himself asking Morgaine, "Would you like to have another dance, My Lady?" He did his best to keep the pleading sound out of his voice while not wanting to give up this unexpected opportunity.

Morgaine responded, "If it pleases you, My Lord, as I am quite enjoying dancing with you." She gazed into his striking blue eyes that could be likened to the color of a kingfisher. She felt ready to dive into those captivating eyes like that bird of the water. As she stared at him with slight wonder in her eyes, Guy noticed how warm he felt. It was as if he was experiencing his own personal summer, right here at the fall into winter. He felt his face flush. He wasn't used to such attention; but he recognized he liked it! As they continued to dance both felt a heat brewing in their bodies that could not be attributed to the warmth of the room.

Prince John, upon finishing his obligatory dance with his wife, drew her back to the throne. As he perched his arms over his ornate chair, he watched the charming dancers with a hint of mischief emanating from his eyes. Prince John motioned to Duke Avalon of Glastonbury.

Gareth Avalon was a robust, middle-aged, rosy-skinned man with an easy smile, a salt-and-pepper curly beard to match his whitening locks of hair that used to be more black than white, and a flock of crow-feet imprinted at the corners of his piercing dark blue eyes, vaguely reminiscent of paintings of the

Roman God of Wine. This sweet Bacchus of a man kissed his wife's cheek, moving her head with his to face the Prince. The Duchess nodded slightly as she understood that her husband was being beckoned. Evelyn watched her beloved walk directly to John. She sighed and shook her head as she felt her place diminished in this culture. At least she knew she could trust Gareth to represent them well. It brought the slightest of smiles to her lips as she resolved herself to act like a mere wife instead of her station as Lady of the Lake: a title which passed on to her daughter who she could tell was the subject of discussion between Gareth and the Prince.

Gareth bowed and then followed John's gaze. "What do you think?"

Gareth, not knowing the man dancing with his daughter, responded, "Is Your Highness pleased?"

"Oh yes. That is Sir Guy of Gisbourne, Lord of Locksley."

At the last title, Gareth raised his eyebrows slightly, but he said nothing.

The Prince continued, "He is England's son, a loyal servant to Our Royal Highness and the right hand of Lord William de Wendenal, the High Sheriff of Nottingham and Earl of Derby. He would do right by your daughter, I think. His is a family of French dignitaries who have lived in and served England well. And he does share our bloodline — distantly. His grandmother on his mother's side is cousin to the Count of Anjou, our father's father. Would you entertain such a match?"

The Duke carefully considered his words knowing that ultimately the wellbeing of Avalon and Glastonbury would be determined not by stately alliances but of spiritual ones. "We take care in the considerations of our daughter's happiness in marriage. If she were to accept such a proposal we would be predisposed to consider it."

"Excellent," stated the Prince with slight excitement in his voice.

Gareth eyed John cautiously from the corner of his eye, then turned his attention back to his daughter who was happily dancing with this topic of conversation.

Gareth and John watched the couple, each in his own thoughts.

On the other side of the room, Lord William de Wendenal, the High Sheriff of Nottingham, a mean-looking grizzled man, a man one would be hard-pressed to say anything pleasant about for there was so little pleasant about him, was also watching the couple; one could almost feel a visceral chill surrounding Lord de Wendenal.

Finally, John saw an opportunity to change the pace of the party. He raised his hands and parted the crowd. He called out to Morgaine and asked her to dance.

She smiled and nodded. She quickly leaned into Guy and asked, "Will you stay and watch me?"

"Yes, of course."

To the crowd she announced, "I dance at the pleasure of His Royal Highness Prince John and I dedicate this dance to the land and all the promise it offers." As the musicians started, she danced, hands serpentine in the air, hips swaying, her long dark brown hair cascading around her form.

Guy watched her intently; he could not take his eyes off her. Her lithe body seemed to be created especially for dancing. He was entranced as she swirled and swayed around the room in her gown comprised of russet, gold, and burgundy fabrics which gave her the appearance of autumn leaves falling in the breeze. He looked upon her with desire…and wonder. She had looked upon him with such intensity. But she, the daughter of a Duke, surely would not be interested in a knight only recently elevated to baron. Surely she would set her sights higher than he. Guy tried in vain to prepare himself for the inevitable coy farewell that he knew he would receive. But his heart would not allow him to steel himself against this dancer. Instead, he felt his heart swept up in her dance.

Morgaine nodded to the musicians to pick up the pace and she swirled her way to John and Isabella, ending on her knees bowed before them with her hands raised to them. Everyone clapped appreciatively. Both John and Isabella brought their hands to Morgaine's and she raised her head to kiss their hands in turn.

"Well, I think this may have inspired our appetites," Prince John announced loudly, chuckling.

With that the partygoers funneled into the grand dining hall. A small herd of men slowly stampeded toward Morgaine. But as she rose and turned, she sought Guy's eyes that were still upon her. She directed one thought to him, "Come to me."

Without hesitation, as if he heard her call, he came to her side and offered his arm, "May I escort you into dinner, My Lady?"

"Oh yes, thank you my gallant knight."

They sat together eating each other's bodies with their eyes. They rarely noticed there was food on their plate and yet they did manage to consume food and drink as well.

Then Morgaine said thoughtfully, "I think it would good of us to toast Prince John. He would like that."

"You think so?"

"Yes."

"What shall we say?"

"You start and I will finish."

Guy wasn't used to giving toasts but as he had witnessed Morgaine on John's good side, her counsel must be wise. He rose and she followed, "A toast to His Royal Highness Prince John."

Everyone rose and shouted, "To Prince John!"

Morgaine followed, "Summer's End has passed, the cattle who have been fattening in the fields have come in, and we thank His Royal Highness for his generosity in holding this annual feast to celebrate the land's wealth."

Everyone chimed, "To Prince John."

The Prince was visibly pleased. He enjoyed feeling appreciated. It gave him the sensation that he was loved. He nodded and smiled and the people all sat, returning to their meals. The Prince then caught Morgaine's eyes and as he raised his cup to her, she bumped Guy's forearm lightly with her elbow and motioned for him to look at the Prince. They both raised their cups in return.

"That went well," she mused.

Guy responded, "Yes. How did you know? It is as if you look into people to see what they need and then provide it."

Morgaine paused thoughtfully, then answered, "Well yes. But I only provide it if it is within my means and for the people I care for."

Guy was intrigued, "You care for the Prince?"

Morgaine was blunt, "Yes. He is our sovereign leader. The King left us and John remains. He should be our focus."

Guy, in slight shock at her brazenness, could only say, "Indeed," as he drank his wine.

They sat, eating in brief silence, and Guy mentally returned to Morgaine's last statement. Guy was curious and questioned this lady on her premise, "How did you come into the Prince's favor so?"

Morgaine chuckled, "I think I have enchanted him with my dancing." She continued, "Two years ago, he visited my parents. While at dinner, my father requested I dance for the Prince. He seemed quite appreciative. He lingered a few days." Her voice dropped and Guy had to lean in to hear what followed. Morgaine shared her secret, "We walked and talked together. He confided how much he needed approval and how he has always felt unloved by his parents and how acutely aware of this feeling he was when he saw how much my parents adored me. I told him that he is loved and that sometimes parents do not always know how to show their child affection, especially a boy who would be ruler. They want their sons to be strong and sometimes people forget that even strong men need a gentle hand and kind words."

Guy was nodding. Yes, he knew that feeling, that keen need to feel his parents' love. All he was told was to be strong like stone, to be a man, to not cry.

Due to their close proximity, Morgaine could feel Guy's nod as unruly wisps of midnight hair tapping gently on her forehead. She continued, "Last year..." Morgaine briefly faltered, considering her words. "I could not attend this party and so John stated he would come for a visit again. Every night I danced for him and his young wife, Isabella. Then they would retire. Perhaps I inspired them," Morgaine giggled. "Anyway, I think that is why John is fond of me." She paused then, in a surprised whisper, "Goodness, I believe I have over-shared. I trust your discretion."

Guy nodded, "Of course, My Lady." He took note of her pause and knew she was wondering how much to say, and yet he noticed she had already given much away. But he was already on to a completely different line of thinking. "Has he..." Guy wasn't sure how to put it.

But Morgaine immediately got his meaning and searched his eyes, continuing to whisper, "He came to my family to ascertain my parents' disposition toward Richard. At the time we remained neutral and polite and supportive of the King. Given that we are unhappy with Richard's decision to invade a country with which we had no quarrel, and to enforce such animosity toward other religions and matters of spirit, I am sure now the Prince sees us as allies. I am not a lady-in-waiting at court so he has little opportunity to engage in...." she flipped her hand up and away and refused to say the words but the action was obvious enough.

Guy held in a laugh; he hadn't been prepared for Morgaine's thinly veiled, bold answer.

At Guy's smile, Morgaine sighed, "We do not know each other, Sir, and yet I feel completely at ease with you. Are you trained in such things?"

Guy's eyes widened and she knew her answer but he put her mind to rest, "My Lady, I am trained both to ease and to put one at ill-ease but for my part this evening, I am, in truth, thoroughly enjoying your company and would be nowhere else."

Morgaine smiled and allowed herself to feel his truth. Though she realized she had to ask, "And do you enjoy your work?"

It was Guy's turn to sigh. He shook his head and felt he could say nothing.

She searched his eyes and he did not turn away. She could sense he was guarded and not wanting to be so. She saw a wish in those eyes, "I want to trust you too."

Evelyn caught her daughter's eye and was looking at her purposefully. Morgaine could hear in her mind, "Well done, Daughter. You play the Prince well. Just be careful. Come, introduce your new friend to your parents."

Morgaine took in a deep breath. She could hear her mother's cautiousness. She sees too many paths, Morgaine thought. Turning to Guy, "Come, meet my parents." Not giving him *no* as an option she stood and held out her hand. It was he who now took in a deep breath, placed his hands on his thighs, and rose. She led him to her parents who were still sitting and eating. Morgaine knew better though. They had been waiting for her. "Mother, Father…" Morgaine announced. Her parents turned, "I would like very much to introduce you to Lord Guy of Gisbourne. My Lord, these are my parents, the Duke and Duchess Avalon of Glastonbury."

Guy bowed to each in turn, "Your Grace. Your Grace."

Gareth started, "Are you enjoying the festivities?"

Guy responded without thinking, something he rarely did, "I am now that I have met your daughter." Whoa, Stallion, that was forward! Right out of the paddock and into the open field at a gallop. What possessed him to say that?

Gareth chuckled and raised his glass to Guy.

There was small chitchat, but without chairs to be at the same level, the filler space came to its natural conclusion within a short time. With that, Morgaine felt they were being dismissed. She took Guy's arm, "Come. Take me dancing some more." A very relieved Guy smiled at Morgaine, bowed to the Duke and Duchess, and then escorted Morgaine back to the dance hall.

Morgaine and Guy were dancing, anything to be as close as possible. Morgaine looked upon Guy with such purpose, scanning his face, almost surprised at herself as she remembered. She stated dreamily, "You know, we have met once before. You were at Asher and Leah's choosing a horse."

Guy searched his memories for Morgaine. He must remember her! Four years prior he was in Glastonbury choosing a new horse. Guy recalled, "I heard Asher of the Lake was the best horse breeder in the region."

They both searched inside themselves for the memory —

Guy came by carriage having recently lost his beloved steed while doing work for the Earl of Derby. A lance caught his steed in a joust and he couldn't be saved. The whole time in the company of the King, Guy felt like his horse: mortally wounded, dying on the inside. The life of a spy was a lonely one. He couldn't trust anyone at court even as he did his best to appear trustworthy and gather secrets for the Earl. He grieved the loss of his goodness, mangled in service to the Black Knights and Lord William de Wendenal.

Though he was headed to Derby in disgrace, Prince Richard having dismissed him for his grief over his horse, he felt drawn down a western road when no available carriages were headed northward. His good friend and mentor, Ann, had suggested he take a detour as surely word to William would travel ahead of him. Best to let him calm down. But Guy knew there would be no calming down with William. And Roderick, one of the King's counselors, and a fellow Black Knight, counselled Guy to be patient. "Disappear for a while. Go unnoticed. All will be forgiven or forgotten in time. Remember our place is in the shadows and it is from there we do our work."

For comfort, Guy held the pelt of his dead horse to his face. It may have been an odd request, but Darnell, his only other confidante in London besides Ann, agreed to help him. Guy just couldn't leave Crown there; he wasn't ready to lose him. So Guy did the next best thing he could think of: they skinned Crown and prepared the hide. In the privacy of the carriage, now that he was temporarily the only passenger, Guy wore the pelt, Crown's face sitting atop Guy's head, as a badge of honor and protection as Crown had taken the deathblow, saving him.

In his westward travel Guy grew wearier. But after hearing positive remarks about a Glastonbury farm that bred beautiful, fast steeds, Guy decided to make this stop before heading north to Derby.

Guy remembered riding in the paddock, only vaguely aware of soft giggling.

Two young women approached. A slight dark beauty in a blue gown the color of a starling's egg jumped up on the rail stating, "That one is Midnight. He is a fine stallion, is he not? I think you two were made for each other."

Guy nodded but was too self-absorbed to make conversation.

The taller athletic blond, who more clearly lived at the farm due to her brown work dress, stood up on the railing with the dark-haired one. They both had recently-made crowns of wildflowers accenting their hair. They watched him and then the blond tugged at the dark-haired lass, "Come on, and let the man decide."

The young ladies departed and Guy continued riding. He called to the horse, "Midnight" and the horse responded, nickering softly. He enjoyed the feel of this horse. He allowed himself to relax, appreciating this one connection.

After looking at a few other horses he returned to Midnight. This was the clearly the horse for him. He agreed to a price with Asher, paid the man, and swung easily back up onto the large, powerful steed. Given Guy's own stature, he came out on Midnight looking formidable: a black-clad man with sheathed sword on black stallion, a warrior ready for battle. Guy grabbed his few belongings from the carriage, including the rolled up pelt, and sent the driver on his way. At that moment, the dark-haired lass came riding up to him on a gorgeous white and golden dappled mare. Between the girl's gown and the mare, it appeared he was gazing at a blue sky on a sunny day. She still bore the wildflower crown on her head and had the look that she should be off to some mid-summer festival.

She asked forthrightly, "Are you looking for a place in town to stay for the night?"

Guy nodded affirmatively.

"Come on then. I am heading home so I will show you the way and recommend a good place to bed down."

They were quiet as they headed into town. He could feel her eyes on him but he was unsure where to begin a conversation. He refused to allow himself to be drawn to look at her, though it took quite a bit of effort to ignore this strange pull he was feeling.

As they came into town he was aware that people were bowing as they passed and he could not fathom why. Did he look like royalty? Nevertheless, he stood up straighter in the saddle. That solicited an amused smile upon the maiden's face. She brought him to the Mutton and Mead Tavern and Inn.

The innkeeper came out to greet her, bowing and then kissing her hand. "What have you brought me, Lady? A wayward traveler?"

"He is a knight come home from some adventure and needs a place to rest."

"I shall give it to him gladly."

She inclined her head in acknowledgement, "Thank you." She turned to Guy, "Good day, my Black Knight. May our paths cross again when you are in gentler spirits."

Bewildered, Guy responded, "Good day, Miss. Thank you for showing me the way." He paused then added, "Here, wait, for your troubles." Guy fumbled in his money pouch and tried to hand the young woman coin.

But she shook her head, smiling, "It was no trouble. Keep your money."

Guy shrugged, thinking her a bit plucky to turn down money. He watched the lass ride off toward the castle and then realized they never exchanged names. How did she know he was a knight, indeed — a Black Knight — returning from traveling?

He was interrupted by the innkeeper, "Come, Sir, let us get you settled in."

Returning to the present moment, Guy asked, "Where were you?"

"I was on the hill with their daughter Sarah." Morgaine slyly smiled as she continued, "We were giggling over the handsome black-clad stranger in the ring."

"Ah. Well, I am glad I could provide such amusement."

Morgaine shook her head, "Oh no, Sir, it was not amusement that I felt but the blush of attraction."

Guy was now the one to blush. "You flatter me, My Lady."

Morgaine slanted her fertile brown eyes, "I only speak the truth."

At that Guy turned a deeper shade of red, his cheeks aflame as he smiled wonderingly at her. All his training and tactics in slyness and detachment were swept right out the castle door and he could not seem to help but be completely himself with this bold lady. "It was you who rode back with me showing me to the inn. You must have thought me so rude. I am sorry."

Morgaine reassured, "I could see a deep sorrow in you. You seemed turned inward. I let you have your peace and simply enjoyed the ride and view."

Remembering the town's people, Guy said with new awareness, "It was you they were bowing to. I had no idea who I was with…" Guy then remembered what he would have been wearing. What else but black? She was merely making reference to the color of his clothing and not his station. "And I was wearing black…"

"As you are now," Morgaine interjected. Adding, "Would you have been in any mood to act differently? Nay you worry. Let it go. Now is the appropriate time we meet. All is well."

Guy dipped his head to her as acknowledgement of this truth.

They danced several more dances. Looking flushed and radiant, the couple retired to a quieter anteroom. They gazed at each other, both felt such elation. Guy suddenly thought about how different he was feeling around Morgaine compared to Marian. What a tortured relationship that had been. He was so used to disappointment he couldn't imagine actually getting what he wanted in the realm of love. He felt he might be reaching too high to think he could have the daughter of a Duke.

Morgaine interrupted Guy's troubled thoughts, "Are you staying the night?"

"Yes," replied Guy, hopefully.

"Then I shall like to spend more time with you. Would you take me for a ride in the morning?"

Guy's hope turned to joy. "I would be most glad to, My Lady, but it will be chilly."

Morgaine's voice was breathy and full of promise, "Your smile will keep me warm."

Guy's heart swelled; she said the most perfect things, he mused.

Guy walked Morgaine to her room. Looking into her eyes, he took up her hand and kissed it tenderly. They held each other's gaze. "Until tomorrow," he managed, his voice quivering more than he thought it would as he spoke. He stepped away feeling shaken to his roots by a power and pull likened to gravity, only he felt pulled up and into something ancient and unbridled.

After releasing Morgaine to her chambers, Guy walked straight for his room and to bed. He dared not stop to check in with the Sheriff. He figured it best to stay happy as long as possible. And as the Prince did not indicate he was needed, now was as good a time as any to just enjoy a moment's peace.

CHAPTER 2

The Ride

I T WAS EARLY when Guy boldly rapped on Morgaine's door. The morning had not come soon enough.

A woman, possibly in her mid-twenties, with stormy-sea-blue eyes and ringlets of honey blond hair, in a rich dark brown gown with cream-colored accents, opened the door and peeked out. She had been waiting for the gentleman's knock as Morgaine had asked her to stay behind and wait for Guy's arrival before she came to breakfast. "The Lady is breakfasting with the Duke and Duchess." The woman pointed to the next door.

Guy nodded to the woman he took for a more-than-well-dressed-for-her-station servant. He then turned and proceeded to what he thought would be a wolf's den. On this door, his boldness fled, and he rapped more hesitantly than confidently. A servant opened the door. Sophie, Evelyn's servant, a comely lass with a long light-blond braid down her back, announced the stranger to the family. Guy stepped across the threshold, a bit nervous, but he couldn't stop himself now and was quite glad for it as Morgaine turned from the table, stood up, and practically glided to him.

She embraced him while inquiring, "Have you eaten?"

"Yes, My Lady."

"Well, we are ready then." She turned to her parents, stating in a love-struck, breathy voice, "I shall return after my ride."

Gareth and Evelyn smiled at the younger pair and nodded. As the two left the room, the woman in the brown dress smiled knowingly at Morgaine from the other door. Morgaine caught the other woman's hand, saying quickly as she passed by, "Thank you, Meggie." Meggie nodded, then closed the door and headed for the Duke and Duchess' room.

Morgaine was almost bouncing down the steps of the castle toward the stables with Guy holding her hand, tethered close behind. As they reached the stables Midnight nickered to Guy. "Hey there, Friend," Guy responded as he came up to Midnight, rubbing his horse's large black neck.

Morgaine then came up to Midnight, saying, as she slowly put out her hand, "Do you remember me, Midnight? It has been a while. It is good to see you again. You are missed in Glastonbury." Midnight let Morgaine pet his muzzle. He remembered the word "Glastonbury" and his ears perked up. The lady smelled of apples and he remembered Avalon's Apple Orchard; but this human was not an apple. Still, he breathed in her sweet scent. Morgaine continued to pet Midnight while Guy saddled up. "You are being a good horse for Lord Guy, are you not?" Midnight nickered affirmatively with a nod of his head. "Good horse." She patted him gently and then went to attend to her horse, Merryweather. Guy helped Morgaine with her saddle and when they were ready, they rode off.

As Guy continued to unravel his feelings, one stood out pure and burning. He had to have her! He reined in Midnight and stopped. Morgaine looked behind her, tilted her head as if in question and then turned Merryweather around and brought her up alongside Midnight and Guy. Guy looked at Morgaine with such intensity. Grabbing hold of that pure, burning feeling, he did something that surprised the both of them — his palm came up to cup Morgaine's cheek to bring her face to his. He looked into her eyes, "May I be so bold as to kiss you, My Lady?"

Morgaine's eyes flew up in momentary astonishment, then her whole face seemed to light up she breathed out the words, "I would be overjoyed."

As their lips touched, Guy felt he was in the grasp of something ancient, dangerous, and — yet — too powerful to turn away from. Not that he wanted to; he was utterly entranced by the Lady Morgaine. Kissing Morgaine was magic. And oddly freeing. It felt like the rest of the world burned away and his only purpose was to love this lady.

Their hunger grew with a rapidity that could only be likened to a fire being plunged into oxygen. Sparks flew up in their hearts as they kissed. Passion ignited their souls. When they broke away they were visibly breathless. Or breath-full. It wasn't that the other took their breath away; they gave it back in full.

"Did you feel that?" she asked in awe.

"I…" Guy gulped at the air to taste Morgaine's sweet breath; it reminded him of apples. "Have you ever seen eagles court?" He continued without waiting for a response. "When eagles court, they lock their talons together and allow themselves to plunge earthbound. But before they fall so utterly, they release their hold and climb the sky — together. It is a courtship committing to nest and nerve."

Morgaine took in Guy's poetic words. She began to allow herself to rise up in this feeling called love. She smiled warmly and Guy, too, felt his heart rise on the currents of love. All thoughts and feelings of his tortured love for Marian, a woman of Nottingham who had spurred his advances time and again, fell away. In fact, everything else fell away in that moment. His soul soared and he could feel Morgaine's soul beside his as they blissfully ascended the thermals.

Morgaine tilted her head, saying in quiet mirth, "You're a poet."

Guy snorted, "Not that I would ever admit." He was still looking deeply into her captivating eyes and felt compelled to add, just above a whisper, "To anyone else."

Gareth came up behind his wife as she stood on the balcony looking out in the direction her daughter had gone earlier in the morning. "Where are you, Beloved?"

She smiled and placed her hand over his as it came up on her shoulder. Evelyn replied, "I am just listening for Morgaine's happiness."

"And do you hear it?"

"Yes. I feel her elation with this new fellow. We must learn all we can for he may come to be part of the family."

Gareth chuckled. "Well, we know the Prince likes him which probably means that King Richard does not."

Evelyn responded, "I hate that we are being drawn into politics. If Richard had not been so stupid in leaving his country we would not feel pulled to choose sides for the immediate well-being of our people. I am feeling an undoing..."

Gareth rubbed his wife's arms, hearing her unspoken fears. He could feel the tenseness in her and wished he could ease her troubled thoughts. She sees so much, knows so much, holds so much together. He kissed her cheek for he knew no words would console her concern about their future.

As Morgaine and Guy drew up to the gates and walked their horses through, she could feel her mother's presence pressing upon her mind. "Would you share a meal with me? I am not ready for you to leave my side."

Guy beamed, "It would be my pleasure and honor, My Lady."

She loved seeing how his eyes lit up at her request. She giggled, "You make it so easy for me to want to be an eagle."

Guy blushed in silent satisfaction.

They brought the horses to the stables and then walked the castle steps. She looked up knowing she would see her mother. She smiled and waved. Guy looked up. Morgaine pulled at him, "Come." He nodded but felt his stomach tighten. He felt as if he was being drawn into another life entirely. If his life was a story, he felt he was being pulled into a completely different one with an unknown plot and mysterious characters. Something about the feeling enticed him and another part gave him dread as if he was walking into a misty forest at twilight, muffled sounds and shadows pulling at his psyche.

Gareth captured his petite daughter in a great bear hug, "Ah, Daughter, how was your ride?"

She relaxed into the safety of her father's enveloping arms, "It was delightful, Father!"

Guy bowed before the Duke and Duchess, "Your Grace. Your Grace."

"Come, share some food with us," Gareth said, taking Guy's arm, leading the way back to the Avalons' guest chambers.

Morgaine took hold of her mother's arm, rubbing it gently as if in reassurance that all would be well.

In the guest chambers of the Duke and Duchess, the servants laid out a bounty of food before them, compliments of the Prince. Evelyn dismissed the servants with a wave of the hand; she did not want the Prince hearing of the conversation. The four of them sat relishing the delicacies set before them. "Lord Guy, what is your vocation?" Evelyn figured she would be direct as she didn't really know any other way of being and was trying to dismiss the feeling that her world and her future were being undone. She suddenly caught an interesting thought bumping around in Guy's head as he worked through how to respond to her. Now she was more curious as she caught, "being pulled out of one story into another." She scrutinized him, thinking to herself, "What story about yourself are you willing to walk away from, Guy?"

Guy finished chewing, giving himself a moment to collect his thoughts, then stated, "I work for Lord William de Wendenal, the High Sheriff of Nottingham. I am his...personal attendant in all stately matters."

Evelyn nodded, then continued her questioning, "Who is your family? I am not familiar with Gisbourne."

"My father was Sir Auguste of Gisbourne. His father was a French dignitary who came to the English Court and married an English woman. My father grew up here, served England, and was knighted by King Henry the Second for his devotion to God and England. Upon his knighthood, he became known by his mother's father's name — Gisbourne — to legitimize the family's standing in England."

Evelyn interrupted with a sly smile on her lips, "So your father took the name of his mother's side of the family?"

Guy nodded, "Yes."

"He didn't mind giving up his father's surname?"

Guy shrugged, "I do not know. It is our English family name." Guy wasn't sure why that mattered or why the Duchess was so curious about his family name. He hadn't given it much thought until now.

Evelyn nodded, "Continue."

Guy inhaled and exhaled through his nose as he contemplated the Duchess' inquisitiveness. He continued, "My mother Marguerite, her father, Hamelin, was also a French dignitary who rose up upon marrying Marie, a cousin of the Count of Anjou."

"The Earl of Surrey?"

"No, Your Grace, not that Hamelin." Guy held Evelyn's gaze as she continued to look at him with interest. Guy tilted his head as if the memory of his grandparents' titles would somehow drop from his left hemisphere into his right. It did not. Odd. Guy was usually fairly well-versed in titles and connections and these were family members. To not remember seemed peculiar to him. He remembered there was some secrecy surrounding them and he rarely discussed his parentage. He could only respond, "My apologies. I am not recalling their titles in this moment."

"Do you see or correspond with your grandparents?" Evelyn was now quite curious about Guy's family.

"No, Your Grace. I honestly do not even know if any of them are alive. The last I heard about Marie was that she took vows at a convent many years ago."

Gareth interrupted, though he knew the answer because Prince John had told him, "But you are related to the Crown?"

Guy brushed off the association as it appeared to have done little to help him, and only served to make him and his sister pawns. "Distantly. Aren't so many of us related to some royal somebody by birthright or bastardy?" That got a chuckle from the family, though he was not entirely sure why. He then continued with his original line of thought, "My parents met at some event and fell in love. My mother stayed in England to be with my father. They married and had me and then my sister, Delphine. A few years after my parents died I was taken in by Lord William de Wendenal, the Baron of Derby. He spoke for me and I was knighted. I have been thankfully in William's good graces ever since."

Evelyn paused at Guy's loss, "I am sorry for your loss."

Guy brushed it aside, "It was a long time ago."

Though Evelyn could see the hint of sadness about his eyes, she pressed on, "And you live at the castle in Nottingham?"

"No, Your Grace. His Highness, Prince John, made me Lord of Locksley as I was Lord Robert Locksley's ward after the death of my parents. The Prince thought it was fitting that the title fall to me with Robin Locksley away."

Gareth chimed in, "Ah yes, Lord Robert died some while back while his son was in the Holy Land."

Evelyn continued, "So the Prince elevated you to Baron."

Guy nodded, simply stating the obvious, "Yes."

"Robert's son has returned though," stated Gareth as he wondered how Robin would cope with Guy usurping his lands and position.

Guy wasn't sure he was being judged but all this musing was uncomfortable. "Yes," Guy replied, "Robin of Locksley has returned from the Crusades. Apparently he only recently heard of his father's passing which is why he came back. Meanwhile someone had to take up his estates as there were no other kin on Robert's side. The title of Baron was only recently confirmed. Before, I was merely holding Robin's estates on his behalf. However, Robin, after only a fortnight being home, caused enough trouble for himself that he is now considered an outlaw by the Sheriff and the Prince and therefore his holdings and lands are forfeit."

Gareth chuckled, "Yes, well robbing from rich or poor is still robbing, however righteous the cause. There were other tactics he might have tried."

"Oh, he did, Your Grace. He did appeal to the other barons upon his return in open council. But the Sheriff has his ways of being persuasive. The cards were stacked against Robin."

Evelyn could detect the subtlest hint of fear in Guy's voice. She gathered that Guy was certainly among those who had been "persuaded." Instead of tackling that subject at this time, she tilted her head with a slight smile and good-naturedly offered, "Well, it is good to know that you were deemed fit to rule Locksley."

Guy was not sure if Her Grace was jesting or offering a hand. She was so hard to read, like the surface of a deep pool; there was no way to gauge where a foothold might be or how far he'd have to go to reach it. He wondered if he was making a decent impression. He knew so little of this family; he wasn't sure what to inquire about to better engage in conversation. He looked to Morgaine who had been silent all this time. She took his hand and squeezed it reassuringly.

Morgaine decided to give him a hand out of her parents' musings, "Guy has actually visited our lands. He purchased a horse — Midnight — from Asher and Leah four years back."

Gareth nodded approvingly. "So you know horses?"

Guy smiled, "Well I certainly know where the best are." At that, everyone chuckled.

Parting felt painful to these new lovers. They kissed and kissed again. They held each other tightly, not wanting to feel the chill from the lack of the other's bodily warmth. Finally they released and Morgaine stepped inside her family's carriage.

Gareth took Guy's arm, looking him in the eye, "It was good to have met you, Lord Guy."

"Yes, Your Grace. Thank you, Your Grace."

Guy sat in silence as the carriage ushered him and the Sheriff away to Nottingham, wishing desperately that he could simply ride Midnight instead of following some bizarre pretense of riding in the confines of a carriage just because he was now a baron and had to make a show of it. To distract himself, he thought about Morgaine's cascading brown hair, like a spring freshet, tangling in his fingers. Oh, to pull at that hair and lay her head back, her mouth opening in acceptance of his. He dreamed and swooned. Contentment lay across his brow. Most unmercifully, with a swift snap of the back of William's hand upon his thigh, he was back in the carriage looking at a man he loathed more with each passing second. Guy suddenly felt like a caged wild animal. A part of him wanted to run screaming from the carriage. Another part of him wanted to lash out and claw William to pieces. He had to calm this frantic energy in him. He clenched his jaw and all the muscles in his body tightened. William glared at him and then looked out the window. Guy fumed and then did the same. In the silence between them, it was dawning on Guy that he had had to put down some part of himself long ago to become the man he was now, to cope with the bars across his mind. He had allowed himself to become a prisoner of circumstance. But now he saw those bars cutting him off from his love, severing him from his destiny. It was like waking from a nightmare only to be confronted by another one.

Within days of returning to Nottingham, Guy wrote to Morgaine. Sitting in the privacy of his home at Locksley Manor, looking out the window into the courtyard, he counted his blessings, thinking that as much as he liked being close to those in power, it felt more powerful to be autonomous; to have his own home, his own bath, and his own writing desk where he could sit and write, using his better writing hand behind closed doors where no one could see him. He could think and feel and not be interrupted. Though he had a room at Nottingham Castle, he rarely used it. Now, as he sat at his small writing table in his sparsely decorated bedroom and swooned at Morgaine's image that was just behind his eyes, he poured out his affections into his letter to her. He sealed it, walked downstairs and into the kitchen where his servant Mary was working on the next meal, and informed Mary to see that the letter went out with the next carriage south. She nodded silently and continued her preparations for her mutton and vegetable pie, a dish she knew Guy liked. Guy watched Mary work for a few moments and then realized what she was making. He smiled, "Mutton pie?"

Mary nodded, a thin smile touched her lips as he turned around and walked out. With the pie bottom made, she added mutton, chopped onions and carrots. She then sliced her secret ingredient, Guy's favorite fruit, and placed the apple wedges on top to slightly sweeten the dish. She poured a bit of wine over the concoction, laid out the dough, rolled it out, and formed it on top of the pie. She then set the pie in the bread oven to bake. It was these simple pleasures she knew could soften his disposition and make him more pleasant to work for.

Brin, Guy's other servant, came into the kitchen with more wood. He saw the sealed letter on the counter. "I'll take care of that for you, Mary," Brin said good-naturedly.

Mary turned her head and watched as Brin picked up the letter. "It needs to get onto the next southbound carriage."

Brin nodded affirmatively, "I can get it to the carriage man."

"Thank you, Brin."

But before Guy's letter made it to the appropriate carriage, it was intercepted by the Sheriff who read the letter and then threw it into the fire. "Don't want Guy distracted." There was a look of wickedness on his face and the messenger shuddered inside. The Sheriff paid the man who brought the letter and sent him on his way. William had no idea that Prince John rejoiced in this possible union. He saw it only as a threat to Guy's servitude to himself and an instrument toward Guy's possible uprising in status beyond his birth and William's control.

Meanwhile, Morgaine walked the halls of Glastonbury Castle as it had been called for the past few centuries. Her heart wrote so many letters to the thick-thighed demi-god with rook hair and arresting blue eyes but nothing on paper would suffice. She had hoped to receive a letter from him, something she could respond to. She brooded, a feeling quite unfamiliar to her. Also, quite annoying. She did not feel centered in herself at all. Could she write him first? Did that matter? Perhaps his work was so consuming… Enough! Morgaine decided it did not matter who wrote whom first. She decided it was best to just be herself and write the man who set her heart and body aflame. In her letter to Guy, she proclaimed her affection and hoped they could see each other again.

Alas, all her efforts were for naught as her letter, too, was intercepted by the Sheriff of Nottingham. In reading the potential correspondence, William threw the proclamation of love into the fire. The burning embers grew more irate at a passion being so ignored.

CHAPTER 3

1192 February
A Dubious Invitation

GARETH AND EVELYN reviewed the invitation from Nottingham Court:

"To his most devoted subjects of the realm, his Excellency, Prince John…"

The official seal was that of the Earl of Derby, not the Prince. "I suppose we must be counted among those attending," Gareth stated flatly as he looked disapprovingly at the invitation.

"I smell a trap," stated Evelyn measuredly.

Gareth gave his wife a wan smile, "You always smell decay hidden beneath the bouquet."

Evelyn tilted her head slightly, "Perhaps." She then grew more thoughtful, "I agree though. I suppose we must make an appearance." But her face was dark with concern.

When the reply came back to the Sheriff, it stated that, the Duke and Duchess of Glastonbury would be in attendance, with their daughter. "Well, well. So many sheep lining up," the Sheriff mused.

Guy hated when William schemed, even more so now that he knew the Duke and Duchess were coming — and Morgaine. Morgaine was coming. But he hadn't heard from her in all this time. She had not responded to his letter. Why was she coming? His initial excitement faded hastily as he regretted not calling upon her. Perhaps he should have written again or visited. But was that all a dream? Would she really see him as a suitor? He reminded himself she had never responded to his letter. He tried not to focus on his elation that she was coming to Nottingham. But he could not help it. He found himself distracted by thoughts of Morgaine, the taste of her lips, the intense look in her eyes, her sweet smile. Some part of him must have thought to warn the family away, to make an excuse not to attend. But the love-struck Guy wanted so badly see his heart's desire again that the secret letter never was written, never sent.

Morgaine could hardly wait until she saw Guy again. She felt like a hive of bees buzzing all around the sweetness within, communicating by a dance and a shake where the most brilliant flowers had been. She thought she might even take flight, but nay her spirit was tethered tightly to the castle.

"Igraine, why do you return?"

Morgaine's dream-self responded to the feminine voice as she lay sleeping in her bed, "To call forth the Pendragon." But this dragon was red, blood red. He roared and he spit fire and then covered the Land in mist. And though she was in the mist, she did not feel lost. She was still at home and she felt safe. "Dragon's breath," she whispered. The dragon roared in response. Still, she was unafraid, for those piercing blue eyes held such familiarity.

The feminine voice whispered back, "He must have royal blood. The oath demands it."

Morgaine replied as she stared into the mist, "He does."

The voice said, "He must be of the Old Ways."

Morgaine replied, "He is."

CHAPTER 4

Two Stories Collide

THE AVALONS HAD been travelling for days to reach a place they had never visited — Nottingham. The carriage door opened and Lady Morgaine was the first to tilt her head out and breathe in the air as if she were deliberately attempting to pick up some scent. It was late March and too soon for blossoming flowers. But some floral spray was not the scent she was seeking. She stepped down off the carriage looking around. Then she saw him and waved. Guy was standing on the balcony in the shadows. "How did she see me?" Guy thought as he came out of the shadows, waved, and almost bounced down the stairs.

Morgaine was already making her way with haste to the stairs as her parents were getting out of the carriage. When the lovers met they embraced with no thought given to appropriate behavior for the meeting. Completely ignoring the Sheriff and Lady Marian standing on the stairs, Morgaine pulled at Guy, "Come greet my parents. Oh I have missed you. Why did you not call upon me? I wrote you but did not receive a reply."

Guy sounded shamed and surprised, "You wrote? I never received a letter. And I did write but I never received your response so I made myself believe that our time together was some spectacular dream and it was only when I heard you were coming that I regretted not calling upon you. But you are here, here to see me?"

Morgaine smiled and nodded, "Some mischief is afoot for each of us not having received the other's letters," and she then turned, "Mother, Father, you remember Lord Guy of Gisbourne."

Gareth took Guy's outstretched arm, smiling broadly, "My daughter has appeared to greet you with much enthusiasm, my son."

"Yes," was all Guy could manage at the moment. He was still dreaming; he must be. My son? These people did not hold to much formality or distance — though he was forced to reassess when the family greeted the Sheriff. There was much more formality. He liked how William was forced to bow his head before royalty. The Sheriff! I must confront the Sheriff, Guy thought and then he motioned to Marian, "And this is the Lady Marian..."

William interrupted, "...who will be showing you to your rooms."

Guy felt bad for Marian. As much as he felt wounded by her rejection he did not enjoy seeing her brought low.

Morgaine took Marian's hands in hers and looked her in the eyes, "I am sure we will be fast friends. I am grateful to the Sheriff for being so conscientious in asking that you be our guide. Thank you for agreeing to the task, Lady Marian."

Marian managed, "It is my pleasure, My Lady."

Guy covered his mouth as he almost allowed a laugh to escape. Morgaine seemed to have an uncanny ability to lighten any situation and he enjoyed knowing that William was not going to get away with treating Marian as a servant in front of Morgaine.

Morgaine turned to Guy saying sweetly, "My Lord, though I know the Lady Marian is completely competent in showing us to our rooms, will you also accompany us?" She slipped her arm around his as if to show that she would not take *no* for an answer.

"Well Sheriff, with no other carriages in the waiting, may we borrow your esteemed companions," stated Gareth, making sure that it did not sound like a request.

"Yes, of course," replied William flatly. To Guy he stated curtly, "Gisbourne, do come straight back; we have business to attend to."

Guy gave a quick bow of the head and then turned back to head up the stairs, Morgaine relinking arms with Guy so that she was now sandwiched between Guy and Marian.

Though Marian walked with a certain rigidity and guardedness, Morgaine's effervescent disposition got under Marian's skin and she became a bit chattier as they traversed the hallways. Still, Guy could tell that Marian's speech was very cautious. He sensed she didn't know what to make of this family and if they could be trusted. That disappointed him more than he wanted to think about.

Marian stated demurely, "The Duke and Duchess will be staying in this room. Your Grace. Your Grace," she curtsied to each after she gestured to their room with her extended hand.

"Thank you, Lady Marian. What time do we dine?" Evelyn asked as she walked past the threesome into the room.

"Sundown. I will make sure to have you called upon if it pleases, Your Graces. There will be an informal gathering in the grand hall beforehand."

Evelyn simply nodded and then inquired, "Has everyone arrived?"

"No, Your Grace."

Guy bowed to the Duke and Duchess and turned to Morgaine. "I will see you at supper then? Will you sit with me?"

Morgaine practically quivered, "My Lord, I would be most delighted to."

Guy fervently kissed Morgaine's hand, tantalized over her addressing him as "My Lord;" it sounded exquisite the way she said it. "Aye," he thought, "and you are My Lady." He came up from his bow, looking directly into her eyes, saying breathily, "Until this evening then." As he came to a straight stand, Morgaine couldn't help herself; she leaned in and up on her toes and planted a kiss on Guy's cheek. Guy flushed. There was a long moment of just taking each other in, then a movement caught his eye. He glanced at Marian, who stood there fidgeting. Guy took a quick bow, "Marian," and turned to go. He smirked knowing that Marian had witnessed the display of affection Morgaine bestowed upon him, feeling some poetic justice. "Ha! See? Someone sees me as a worthy suitor," he thought.

Morgaine caught Guy's smirk as he left and she turned to Marian, swooning, "He has the most adorable lopsided smile. It looks conspiratory and confident and sly and…ah…lovely."

Marian looked at Morgaine questioningly, "Are we looking at the same man? You think his smugness is adorable?"

Marian said nothing aloud but Morgaine cocked her head as if she had heard what Marian had thought and was contemplating it. Morgaine responded silently, "No, it's not arrogance. He is showing confidence. But in his need to show that confidence he lets a vulnerability slip in." The women gazed toward each other while in their own thoughts. Marian just stood there sorting out her feelings. Why did it bother her that Guy was so happy? And letting her know it. "While my father sits rotting in a cell…of course that would be my fault," Marian thought and shook her head.

Morgaine caught the action and touched her hand, "Marian, are you all right?"

Marian responded, shaking her head slightly, "Oh, I am well; just clearing the head of unhelpful thoughts." Marian wondered to herself, "Now why did I say that?"

Morgaine smiled compassionately. "Well, let's find something helpful for you to do to occupy your mind. Would you show me around the castle?"

"Yes, I think I can manage that."

"Mother, Father, I am going to take a walk with Lady Marian. I shall see you at dinner?"

Evelyn responded, "Yes."

Morgaine took Marian's arm and Marian led Morgaine on a tour of the castle. Both ignored the castle guard who followed them at a mildly discrete distance.

Meanwhile Guy returned to the courtyard to find William looking out at the wall as if he could see the horizon. "William," Guy started, as he strategized how best to confront William about the letters, then relented. He will not give me a straight answer, he thought. William ignored Guy's start at a conversation, and instead looked out into the distance beyond the gate, hoping for a better distraction.

Scrumptious scents of supper were wafting through Nottingham Castle. All guests who had arrived found their way down to the Great Hall for dinner. Morgaine was content, seated between her parents and Guy. Movement caught her eyes, a comely young woman with mid-length wavy brown hair shuffled retiringly out of the hall doors. "Guy, why is Lady Marian under guard?" Morgaine watched as Marian left the hall with the guard. She hadn't paid much attention to the guard before when he was skulking behind them on their tour. She had figured it was either for her protection or to make sure Marian did not allow Morgaine to go into certain wings or rooms.

Guy turned to watch Marian as well, replying, "Marian took a bold action to protect me but in so doing gave the outlaw, Robin, the upper hand. William became quite vexed and punished her by putting her under house arrest. Though I have argued on her behalf, he is still suspicious of her true motivations. She can move about freely as long as she has a guard with her. To make matters worse, her father, Sir Charlton, came out against the Sheriff and was thrown into prison. So now she is here under house arrest because she couldn't bear to be away from her father. It is all so…unpleasant."

"You love Marian?"

His mind went back to when he first felt the stirrings of love and what that love could inspire him to do. But for Marian it was for naught. She could not be patient and she did not believe. He remembered the last rejection —

Guy came up the steps of the castle. He caught sight of Marian to the left of him on the balcony and he realized she had seen him turning away the poor…again.

Marian met him with crossness in her voice, "Guy, how could you? You turned those people out. They have nothing."

Guy was already upset for doing the deed and it didn't help to be scolded. She didn't see the hidden loaf of bread he passed to them as he gruffly sent them packing, didn't know he had caught sight of the family and stole bread from the kitchen before he went to the gate. He couldn't shield Marian from all the things he had to do to stay on William's good side. He didn't even see the point of telling her what he did; he couldn't risk her announcing his kindness before the Sheriff in defense of feeding the poor. Their relationship, if he could even call it that, was strained. It always had been as they budded into maturity and left the innocence of childhood. He wanted to show her he could be kind. But it was never enough. "Marian, I…"

"Guy, I have seen your kindness…"

He was exasperated, "Then why do you reject me?"

She shook her head, "Guy, you are like a cat: affectionate one moment, a cold-hearted killer the next. You purr with sweetness for me, only to lash out when I do not please you."

He looked at her perplexed. It was not like that. He took her by the arms, "Marian, I love you. You are what is important to me. I do what I do to gain power so that I can be a better protector and provider for you."

She rolled her arms out to get away from his grip and stopped his advances with her hand, "And I care for those people, our people. The people of Nottingham. And if you cannot show compassion to your own people, I cannot love you in return."

Guy closed his eyes and clenched his jaw. He had good work. Money. He was aligned with powerful men. He could protect her. She wouldn't ever be one of them, on the other side of the gate. Couldn't she see that?

"Ah, what a painful subject." Guy put his hand on Morgaine's to assure her it was alright to have asked. "Yes, I suppose I still care about her, but my affections were met with disinterest and I had to come to terms that she did not want me."

"Well, thank the Gods for small favors," Morgaine teased as she walked her fingers up his arm to his chin to brush it ever so slightly with the back of her hand. Her smile caught Guy before he could utter another word and the sadness drained from his face as a lighthearted smile opened and then slowly, as one side often did, tilted higher than the other. Morgaine laughed.

"What?" asked Guy, caught off guard by the outburst.

Morgaine chuckled more as she brought her hands to cup his face. "It's just you. Lovely you. I love your lopsided smile. That smile. When I see it, I see a confidence and vulnerability about you that is very alluring."

Guy's eyebrow raised. "Truly? I have been told I have a contemptuous smile."

Morgaine shook her head, letting him know she disagreed with that assessment. She then got up slightly so she could reach up to kiss him on the mouth. It didn't matter who saw or the appropriateness of their closeness; he returned her kiss and the lusciousness of it made them both quiver.

The next morning Guy took Morgaine riding so he could show her Nottingham's natural beauty. As they soaked in the landscape, they turned and reached for each other, kissing. Guy moved his mouth to her ear and whispered huskily, "I want to show you something. Will you go with me a bit further?"

Morgaine nodded, feeling his lips brush her ear ever so gently. She shivered in delight.

They rode to a thin finger of the forest and out into a field. "There," Guy pointed to a large apple tree in the middle of the meadow. They rode up to the apple tree. Guy jumped down off his steed and came to Morgaine's side. She slid into his arms, their kisses more ardent. Guy explained, "I come here to be away from my life at the castle. To think, to read, to just sit and dream."

Morgaine nodded dreamily. "I love apples," she cooed as she gently shook a branch as if she were shaking a hand in greeting.

Guy agreed, "So do I."

Morgaine tilted her head, saying slyly, "If I were to invite you to Glastonbury would you come and taste my fruit?"

Guy chuckled, his mouth forming an O, his eyes narrowed in mirth. There was definitely a double meaning to her invitation. "Morgaine, do you tease? Could I reach so high?"

"If you feel that low then take my hand, rise up, and soar with me. We are eagles remember?"

Guy felt his heart take flight into his throat. He swallowed in an attempt to put it back in its place.

Morgaine added playfully, "Will you do something with me?"

Guy looked at her with lust, "You have but to ask, My Lady."

Morgaine knelt down and put her hand on his leg. "May I?"

Guy was certainly perplexed but he nodded with an eyebrow raised. Morgaine, confident that Guy kept a hidden dagger sheathed at his ankle, reached down, patted the right side but found nothing. She had remembered many years ago seeing her father strap a dagger to his right ankle when he went travelling. "Just a precaution," he had told her. She figured Guy might do something similar.

She looked at Guy and he was simply watching her with an amused question on his face. She tilted her head in contemplation and then reached down his left leg. Morgaine had a satisfied look on her face as she found the dagger sheathed on the outside of his left ankle. She took his dagger out from its sheath by the hilt and pricked her finger. Guy merely watched and only momentarily questioned how she would have known about his hidden dagger. He then squatted to be eye level with her, having an inkling of what might come next. His elbows rested on his knees and he offered his hands, palms up. She took his right hand in her left, kissed his forefinger lovingly, and pricked it as well. She then kissed the grind of the dagger reverently, eyes closed. Guy watched, fascinated. Morgaine opened her eyes, returning his dagger to its sheath. She looked at Guy, brought their hands up, and pressed their pricked fingers together. "The blood knows," she said mysteriously.

He looked at her wonderingly and then he felt a rush. He recognized her as if he hadn't fully before, as if some veil just fell away. "What am I feeling?"

The blood cast its spell on both of them.

"It's our blood mingling, recognizing like for like. We are a pair. My namesake devised of a way for couples to recognize each other; we are meant to be together. Do you feel it too? I sensed it and had to be sure."

Guy was in awe at the sensation he was feeling in his body and mind. "Yes. My whole being shouts 'yes.' I do not think I have ever felt surer of anything in my entire life. But, Morgaine, is this witchcraft?"

She cocked her head and asked seriously, "If it is, would you turn from me and deny our love?"

Guy's eyes were wide but he shook his head slowly, "No, I could not. I will not. If this is magic, it is the most blessed kind for I have never felt so happy or so sure. I don't care how quick or sudden this all appears. I want to be the man you desire."

Morgaine sighed in relief, "You are, Beloved." And she really did feel relieved. "It worked. It really worked," she thought silently. Her intuition was right. Now, no more searching. No more waiting. This one would stay and not run away from the blood bond.

The pair spent the rest of the morning embraced beneath the apple tree in a dream-like state. It was not until Guy noticed where the sun was in the sky that he realized he must attend to his duties. He kissed Morgaine on the forehead and helped her rise to standing. They stood gazing at each other.

Guy started, "Please forgive me Morgaine. I must return to the castle. Would that I be given leave, I would spend the day with you."

Morgaine nodded, "We each have our roles to play. We'll ride back and then dine together this evening, yes?"

"Yes."

While Guy returned to his duties, he told the guard who was following Marian to keep a more discreet distance to allow the women more freedom. "Consider it a reassignment. You are protecting our guest, the Lady Morgaine. Just stay back more." The guard nodded. As long as he didn't get in trouble with the Sheriff for not breathing down Marian's neck, he'd watch the pair however Lord Guy wanted him to.

Marian and Morgaine walked through the town. Though Marian could tell there was a castle guard behind them, he kept his blessed distance and she felt a bit more free and comfortable. Morgaine was proving to be an entertaining companion. She seemed to take delight in the smallest things, and her sweet disposition was infectious.

Though the town of Nottingham was a bit overwhelming to Morgaine, it was not the same as the press of Prince John's party before she met Guy. She realized, when she had something else to focus on, the din of voices in her head was kept at bay. Having a companion always made it easier. But Meggie was busy pretending to be a servant and slinking around the castle to gather information from the castle servants for the family. It was good that Marian was content to be in her company and show her around. Perhaps she was simply used to her own town and the internal musings of her own people. But both London and Nottingham were an assault of fear and mistrust. So many voices crying out for help.

As the ladies walked and talked, a silversmith caught Morgaine's eye and Morgaine tugged at Marian, pulling her in the direction of the stall. She dreamily tried on a few rings.

The silversmith, Jessica, asked, "Are you dreaming of a wedding, My Lady?"

Morgaine looked up with a wide smile, chuckling, "I suppose I am." The braided silver ring she coveted did not fit, but another ring did, and she sighed at the thought of a ring upon her finger.

Marian sorted through her feelings as she watched her new friend falling in love. Morgaine's presence certainly brought a smile to Guy's face and with his attention elsewhere, it only suited Robin's cause. Still, even seeing the goodness within him, Guy was villainous and she wondered how to warn Morgaine. She deliberated silently, "But then what manner of woman was Morgaine if her family was here in support of Prince John's campaign?"

Marian's thoughts were distracted as the pair came across a wayward trio of children sitting, leaning up against one another against a building.

"What matter is this that has eyes so downcast?" Morgaine questioned, approaching them.

The children looked up bewildered but respectful. "Our bellies are hungry Mum and we haven't seen Father in days," replied the tallest of the set.

"Oh dear, that is serious. We must remedy at least what we can for the moment," Morgaine replied. Turning to Marian conspiratorially, she questioned, "Did we not walk by a bakery?"

Marian smiled at the plot, "Yes, we did."

Morgaine reached her right hand down her right side into the hidden slit between the folds of her gown to her purse hanging on a cord. She brought up some coin and handed it to Marian. "Allow me to watch over these dears while you fetch something hearty for them to eat."

Marian winked, "I am up to the task." While Marian went on her errand she realized whatever Morgaine's stance on the royal brothers, she did care about those in need, same as her, same as Robin.

Meanwhile Morgaine, in her clean and gorgeous sea-green gown, took a seat next to the children and began weaving a story together with prompts from them as to who the characters were and what they set out to do. When the food arrived the children looked up ravenously. They remained polite as Marian handed a meat pie to each in turn.

Morgaine and Marian simply enjoyed the children's excited chatter and lip smacks upon their food. But more pressing matters of where the children were to go vexed their thoughts.

"What does your father do that he is still away?" asked Morgaine.

The children looked to one another and it was apparent they felt uncomfortable to say. "Never you mind. What were your plans for this evening if he did not return?" Again distressed looks passed between the children. Morgaine gently probed into their thoughts to see if any were willing to open to her.

The middle child looked pleadingly into her eyes, thinking, "If she only knew. A royal lady like that; she wouldn't help us."

Morgaine caught an image of the father and started piecing together the life of a thief. Interesting that he gave some care to his children though.

As Morgaine considered a course of action, a sweaty, small-framed man came panting toward the group.

He spoke out with mistrust, "What are you doing with my children?"

The children lit up at the sight of their father but then cringed at the food in their hands realizing their father may not be pleased.

Morgaine attempted to diffuse the situation, "Ah, there you are," she said to the father, "your children have been waiting patiently for you. They appeared quite hungry, though, so we took the liberty of providing them with supper."

"We don't need handouts from the likes of you," he spat.

"Indeed. I would dare suspect what you need is an honest job and the children occupying their time more productively. But as that is not your current situation, you can at least manage a thank you. And if you must insist I was in error to give your hungry children food, I am sure I could find something for you to do to repay me," Morgaine replied with authority.

The man looked down. "Thank you," he managed. "You were kind to my children. I should not mind."

"I am a stranger; of course you have every right to mind. Still, my friend and I meant well. We shall be going." Turning to the children, Morgaine added — as she looked each one in the eyes, "Please do enjoy your supper. It was a gift given in gladness as I enjoyed sharing a story with you."

The women were quiet as Marian looped them around back toward the castle.

Morgaine, second guessing herself asked her new friend, "Marian, was it wrong to provide those children with a meal?"

Marian's eyes widened, "Why would you think that?"

"Well, the father just seemed so displeased and perhaps my good intention only made matters worse for them."

Marian boldly, yet with mild trepidation for the difference in their station, placed her hand on Morgaine's shoulder, "No, My Lady, do not second guess your desire to do good. Whatever the father's reaction, it was the children you were attending to, not his pride. He should be glad that there are people willing to look after the well-being of his children."

Morgaine was pensive, "In Glastonbury, we all look after one another. I don't see children hungry on the streets. I don't know how we manage differently; perhaps it is just a matter of numbers or…" Morgaine's voice trailed off thinking that this was the work of the Sheriff.

"Or?" Marian waited for Morgaine to finish her thought, then decided to be brave and finish it for her. "Or it is a matter of state and who is ruling and how they treat their subjects."

"Yes, that is it," Morgaine agreed, furrowing her brow.

There was a feeling of relief in Marian's mind. "Ah, she does see the problem at hand. Then why is her family here?"

Morgaine caught Marian's silent thought but was not sure how to respond. She could tell her friend was aligned with King Richard while her family felt it more immediately prudent to align themselves with Prince John. And where was the Prince?

As the two ladies came up the castle steps, Guy spotted them and became much more animated than Marian was used to seeing him.

He practically pranced down the steps to greet them. "Ah there you are, My Lady. Did you enjoy your walk and tour of our town?"

Morgaine embraced his hug with her whole being, "Yes, My Lord. The Lady Marian is a most delightful companion." She turned to Marian and held her hand, smiling at her and then at Guy.

Both Guy and Marian felt the awkwardness of the moment, but only for a moment. It was actually work to feel awkward around Morgaine. She had a way of putting them both at ease just by taking their hands.

As they walked into dinner, Morgaine between them with her arm in each of theirs, she asked Marian to join them.

Marian shook her head, "I must attend to my father."

Guy surprised himself by blurting out, "I will see to it. Come, sit with us and then you can visit with him."

Morgaine could see tears welling in Marian's eyes. "Take a breath, dear. You do not need to feel guilty for enjoying a meal with friends. Come. Let us fix your father a plate. Guy said he would bring it to him. After dinner, you can go to him." Morgaine looked tenderly into Marian's eyes, knowing she could not fathom what it would feel like to see her parents imprisoned.

Marian and Morgaine put together a delicious plate of food and Guy promised to return promptly after delivering it directly to Charlton. Though he felt slightly odd at the errand he had set himself to, he was glad it brought a smile to Marian's face and pride to Morgaine's.

The dungeon guards opened the gated iron door for him, quizzical about the one plate. "Hey, where's ours?"

Guy snapped, "It's coming, you know that."

"Well then what is this, a meal?"

"No," stated Guy somewhat exasperatedly, "it is a mission of mercy."

"You? On a mission of mercy, Gisbourne?" The men chuckled.

Guy scowled. "Open Sir Charlton's door."

The men knew Guy carried a torch for Marian but with his mood they didn't dare tease further. Mock, the guard who had teased Guy, opened the cell door and bowed slightly. Guy walked to Charlton.

"What's this?" Charlton asked dejectedly.

"Your daughter sends her love. She is dining with the Duke and Duchess of Glastonbury and the Lady Morgaine. She was willing to reject the offer to come attend to you but I bade her stay and promised I would bring you the meal of her choosing. She will be along in a little while."

Charlton just looked at Guy and did not take the plate. He would do nothing to encourage this rogue's designs upon his daughter.

"Come on man! For the love of your daughter, eat!"

Charlton turned away in silent despise.

"Suit yourself. I will leave it here. But for your sake, and hers, I hope you will have eaten every morsel or your daughter will weep." Guy left, pulling the door closed behind him.

Mock, a burly ruffian, stood mutely, overhearing the exchange. He locked the door and followed Guy to the stairs.

Guy turned, commanding, "Leave the man alone. Let him eat in peace."

Mock and the other jailer just nodded.

Charlton sat alone in his cell, the smell of food tantalizing his belly. It grumbled in protest at a stubbornly prideful mind. After several minutes, the belly won the argument. Charlton picked up the plate and began to eat.

By the time Guy arrived back in the hall, everyone was seated and eating. Marian looked content as she chatted with the Duchess. He smiled in relief and thought, "Good, she needs a mother figure to distract her." He spied an empty seat next to Morgaine with a plate of food already set. He came up to Morgaine and the empty chair, "For me?" His heart simply melted as she nodded and patted the seat.

It was a night of odd festivities and had the sense of disjointedness. To Gareth, it felt ill-conceived, as if little thought had gone into to the organization of it. He sensed his wife's discontent as she stood next to him, her mind in a dozen places.

She sighed and leaned into him, whispering, "I think I will retire, Love. As the Prince is not here, I am not feeling compelled to make a show of it."

"I understand. I will be along shortly. I have been eyeing our new friend and I think he is going to approach me with a request."

Evelyn smiled with a twinkle in her eye, "Then I will leave you to it. I think to have to approach us both in this moment may be too trying on the man. But he'll get there. For some reason I have faith in him."

Guy approached Gareth who appeared only mildly interested in the show of musicians and fools. "Your Grace, may I speak?" Guy's heart was racing as Gareth nodded. "I will be forthright. I am in love with your daughter and I wish to court her."

A smile widened across Gareth's face, "Yes, I can see that. It is the way with Avalon women; when they set their hearts on their lover, you are theirs. It was and is with Evelyn and me. Yes, we give you permission to court our daughter. And you passed the blood test…"

"The what? Oh yes! That was odd and mysterious and gave me such clarity as I have never had."

Gareth chuckled. "Guy, I can tell you are as sincere as my daughter says you are. There is more to discuss, but not now. Though I do want to say that we heard you both made attempts at correspondence but have been thwarted. You have to ask yourself what someone would gain by not allowing the two of you to receive the other's letters."

Guy internally winced, though spoke plainly, "I can think of no reason, Your Grace. Nonetheless, I am vexed to discover that someone has been so devious."

Gareth probed, "Do you know who might have done such a thing?"

Guy was more than annoyed to not know who might have betrayed him. He replied, "I do not yet know who, but I am dismayed to consider who gave the order."

Both men grew silent, preoccupied by a variety of considerations.

CHAPTER 5

The War Room

GUY BREAKFASTED AGAIN with Morgaine and her parents. But this morning there was tension in the air as they dined. Guy's eyes darted back around the room. He could see no escape from William's plot. What could he do? Why had he waited so long?

Evelyn felt impatient, wondering why they were called here to Nottingham. She decided to just confront the situation. Breaking into Guy's thoughts, she asked, "Guy, where is the Prince? Why have we all been called here?"

Guy shifted uncomfortably, wondering, how he could protect this family without tying his hand to that of the Sheriff. Evelyn watched Guy's restrained body language. Though it was clear he had training to mask his thoughts, it was equally clear that he was withholding something. She recognized that he was in a quandary. Patting his hand she stated quietly, "Say nothing, just nod. Is the Prince coming?" Guy shook his head slightly. She implored, "What should we do?" Guy looked pained. He had been so elated Morgaine had come, while ignoring the consequences of their stay.

Though his tone was soft, Gareth became gruff, "Out with it man!"

Guy pursed his lips as his eyes looked at each one of them in turn. He said quietly and with great care, "You will be asked to sign a document. I do not think William has planned what to do if someone decides not to sign it. You were each chosen for your apparent loyalty to the Prince." His eyes implored not to be asked more. He was traversing a dangerous line.

Gareth's eyes narrowed in consideration, "What are his intentions?"

Guy closed his eyes and swallowed. He couldn't say. He wanted this family to trust him. He wanted to see this family ride off safe and unharmed. And

45

he wanted to be by Morgaine's side, but he couldn't tell them the purpose of the document.

Evelyn watched Guy as she probed his thoughts. She had little care for invading his mind as her family was at risk. She could tell he meant them no harm. Good. His thoughts were very guarded regarding the document but it was clear he was afraid about signing it; she just couldn't glean why. Not good. She probed further. "Will you help us?" His subconscious answered "yes" and she withdrew.

With her hand under the table, Evelyn touched her husband's thigh and gave it a light squeeze. Gareth placed his hand on hers and returned the squeeze, imbuing his love and trust in her.

Guy opened his eyes, stating in a hushed voice, "No harm will come to you. I will find a way, whatever you decide."

His wife and his daughter trusted this man and there was something within this fellow that felt like kin, so Gareth nodded measuredly with pursed lips and a furrowed brow.

Evelyn spoke quietly as she looked intently into Guy's eyes, "We will all get through this together."

Guy nodded in a silent promise. "Together," he thought. "They trust me. I cannot break their trust. I must find a way to keep them safe." And somewhere deeper in his mind, on the edge of his subconscious, he added, "And to leave with them."

As they prepared to go to the meeting, Guy caught Morgaine by the elbow, hissing fervently, "I don't want you in there."

Morgaine looked hurt but nodded. She had fallen so quickly for this man and though her willfulness wanted to make her indignant, her intuition agreed it was best to be elsewhere.

Gareth overheard Guy's command to his daughter, agreeing that there was no need to have her in this stately meeting. If this was Glastonbury she would be expected to be present at all such affairs as the future duchess and ruler of the realm.

Guy had moved his hand from Morgaine's elbow to her hand. She allowed him to bring it up to his lips. He kissed her hand tenderly as he looked at her with a slightly haunted gaze. She nodded to him. He stepped back and bowed to the family. And then he departed.

Morgaine watched him close the door and continued to stare at it. She whispered, "He didn't warn us away."

Evelyn came up to her daughter, stood next to her, wrapping her arms around her. "A man in love rarely thinks well with his head. Besides, his correspondence is being watched. Not that this is an excuse. Still, we sensed a risk and chose to come."

Morgaine contemplated, attempting to look at the paths before her. "Why can't I see what is before me in this castle?"

Evelyn had experienced the same disconcerting thing.

Morgaine turned her head to look at her father. "Could we just leave?"

Gareth knew that would be suspicious and, though they could possibly make it to the forest and vanish within it, they would be making a powerful enemy without knowing if such an action was warranted. Gareth closed the gap between himself and his daughter and rubbed her cheek with the back of his hand. "Daughter, why not spend some time with Marian. All will be well." She looked at her father knowing that he did not necessarily believe that last statement. His hand came down from her cheek and he squeezed her arm. She nodded in agreement. While unspoken, the family knew they were preparing for a trap of unknown magnitude and would have to see how it played out before they could discern which course of action to take.

Morgaine and Marian were indeed becoming fast friends. Marian was delighted that Morgaine had decided not to attend the council but instead spend more time with her before the family departed. Marian could tell that her friend seemed less than her cheerful self and wasn't sure of the cause but decided not to press the matter. Quietly they walked along Nottingham's streets and out onto the King's Road that wound its way through Sherwood Forest. Each, without saying anything, felt eyes upon them. It was more than just Marian's guard. Marian knew Robin was watching her; whereas Morgaine, in her searching, sensed two individuals guarding themselves. After a moment attempting to discern who the watchers were, she decided to leave it be as she sensed no malicious intent and continued her walk with Marian.

Morgaine then felt a presence in the forest that did bring her some comfort. She wandered off the road and leaned her back against a grand oak, closing her eyes.

Marian followed her. "Morgaine, is something wrong?"

With eyes still closed she replied, "I am not sure why we were requested to come. I was so happy because it meant I could see Guy again." She opened her eyes, looking at Marian intently, "I love him. And I do trust him. I do not think he would want harm to come to me or my family."

Marian sucked in her breath and could not help but say, "But just because he does not intend harm does not mean he can or will stop it."

Morgaine blinked and tears began to form.

Marian came to her new friend and took her hands in hers. "Morgaine, I can see he loves you as well and that is a blessing in so many regards." She paused in contemplation of how different and sweet an "in love Guy" could be when he felt equally well loved. She continued, "It seems to have happened so fast for both of you..." Marian hesitated then. How could she formulate the hard words she felt she had to say? She wrinkled her nose in an effort to not shed tears. She whispered, "Guy is the Sheriff's man."

Morgaine shook her head. The forming bond that was made manifest with their blood connection could not be denied. No, not again. This one would not abandon her.

Marian pressed, "Do you know why they are in there?"

Morgaine looked haunted. "Something about a document to sign."

"What document?"

"I don't know. Guy wouldn't say more. But he seemed worried."

"Why didn't he tell you to leave?"

Morgaine shook her head and laughed through her tears, "Because a man in love rarely thinks well with his head."

Marian eyed her friend quizzically then chuckled slightly, though her expression was pained. "That was selfish. He should have warned you away if he was concerned."

"Someone intercepted our letters."

Marian's eyes went wide. She was hardly surprised that the Sheriff did not even trust his own man. "That would be the Sheriff," Marian replied angrily.

"Why?"

"The Sheriff is a mean-spirited man. He keeps everyone, including Guy, on edge. And I cannot imagine he would want to see Guy rise above him. He must see you as a threat."

"Me?" Morgaine was deeply troubled that someone would see two people in love as a threat. She knew her spiritual beliefs could be seen as a threat and that is why the Avalons cloistered themselves away in Glastonbury and rarely ventured out of the safety of their realm. But for someone to think love was a threat? That seemed insane.

"If the Sheriff thinks Guy is in love with you and you with him and he cannot use that love to his advantage, he will strike at it in any way he can."

Morgaine looked dismayed, "But that is so cruel."

Marian's tone, though not directed at Morgaine, was harsh, "That is the Sheriff."

The company assembled in the war room, a darkly ornate chamber accented in crimson, dark brown, and black. It was a strategic move on William's part. He wanted his sheep to feel that war between the royal brothers was imminent and that it was vital to choose the winning side. He laid out his argument. "And the good King Richard, where is he? He demands his war taxes but does not see what it is doing to his people. For the Crown Prince also needs taxes paid to keep this country running. And he has dutifully stayed behind to keep his brother's affairs in order. Prince John loves his country and its people. And whether King Richard returns or not, the Prince needs to know that he has your esteemed support." Holding up the document, "This pact proclaims your loyalty to Prince John. With your signature, he will know that he can count on you in council." He paused, but only enough to sweep his eyes across the room to gauge his audience. "Lord of Locksley, as the newest Baron come. You do the honors first." William hoped that would promote a bit of jealousy among the other barons and royal families.

Guy stood up, knowing his part to play and hating every moment of it. He could only pray Prince John would understand he was just following orders, but somehow he knew that would not save him. He signed the document and stood by William's side, arms folded, looking fearsomely around the room. Though he avoided eye contact with Gareth and Evelyn.

Evelyn, for her part, invaded Guy's thoughts again. She was not willing to be blind in this situation. But she could tell he had no idea, ultimately which was worse — to sign or not sign — and he felt lost in how to navigate this course for the Avalons. He was in mental anguish, wishing they had never come and put themselves in this dilemma while at the same time thankful he now knew Morgaine loved him. But for how long?

One by one, the barons and other dignitaries who were assembled signed the document that outlined their allegiance to Prince John. For one reason or another, they had thrown their fidelity to the Prince, many thinking that the King might never return. It was rumored that he had been injured in battle and could die in the Holy Land.

Gareth came up to review the document. He looked it over and then looked up at William. "Where is the official seal of the Prince? If he wants our loyalty, I want to know that this document comes directly from him. And why is he not here, beseeching our loyalty himself?"

This threw William into a rage. Though he had no good excuse, he shot back, "Your Grace, with all due respect, truly, how dare you question the Prince."

Gareth retorted, "I do dare because I do not see the Prince's official seal. I will not hand my name or my arms to a proxy."

William could hardly contain himself, "Guards, seize the Avalons. They are no friends of the Prince!"

The guards came up behind both Evelyn and Gareth.

Gareth eyed William, "This is dangerous business you do. We have no quarrel with the Prince."

Guy's eyes were darting back and forth, unsure of what to do. He swallowed hard, praying reason would diffuse the situation. He put his hand on William's arm, saying with as much calm as he could muster, "Sire, surely, you know the Avalons to be loyal subjects of the Prince. You remember seeing them at the Prince's party in November. You have seen that their daughter is in the Prince's favor…"

William practically ripped his dagger out from its sheath at his side and put it to Guy's throat. "Do not come to the traitors' aid just because you fancy a pretty skirt. Get out of my presence before I throw you in prison! NOW!" William nicked Guy's neck with the dagger's point.

Guy drew up his hand to put pressure on the wound. "William…"

"NOW!"

Guy backed away from William and the dagger.

"Get out!" shouted William to Guy.

Guy bowed slightly, turned and left the room, glancing at Evelyn, mouthing, "I'll get you out." He could only hope she understood. He would see what he could do about getting them released.

Evelyn did understand what he said but she wasn't sure how he could help. There was another recourse she could take, but that, too, would be dangerous.

William turned back to the crowd after watching Guy leave the room. He felt quite aggravated that Guy had dared to put his plan in jeopardy just because of his infatuation with the Avalon girl. "Anyone else?" As the crowd watched the guards take the Avalons away, more followed suit and signed the document despite those now signing noticed there was no seal of the Prince.

Still most felt that the Prince must have given leave to the Sheriff to act as his proxy and was that not good enough? The Baron Thomas Winter and his wife, Lady Edwena, stood in the back, hoping not to be noticed. The Baron Winter was realizing he had played his part as spy to the counselors of King Richard all too well. Now his hand would be tried. There was no way he could sign that document, seal or no seal, as his true loyalty lay with King Richard.

William narrowed his eyes and searched the group. Everyone had either signed or been hauled away to the dungeon. All except Baron Winter. He dismissed the group, thanking them for their duty and oath to Prince John. As they filed out, he called out, "Lord Winter, pray stay a moment. You have yet to sign."

Morgaine sucked in her breath in shock. "No! This cannot be happening!" She hadn't heard a word Marian just said after her mother invaded her mind, practically screaming in hysteria, "They are taking us to the dungeon!" She had never known her mother to be so undone. She could feel her mother's fear, palpable, like claws digging into her brain.

"Morgaine, what is it?" Marian's arm and worried voice caught her new friend who she thought was leaping away and about to charge into a run back to the castle.

"My parents!"

"What about them?" Marian sounded confused. She did not understand what brought on Morgaine's sudden fright.

"I must get back." Morgaine ignored the voice in the forest pleading with her not to go back to the castle. They needed a plan.

"Wait," said the voice. But Morgaine gathered up her skirts and ran down the road with Marian chasing after her.

The castle guard who had been watching the women was about to give chase as well. Though he hadn't heard what the women were saying, by Morgaine taking off at a run, he instinctively reached for his sword, considering her act to be of grievous concern. But before he took a step, he was knocked out from behind, his body dragged off into the bushes. If anyone had actually seen what had just taken place, it would have appeared a buck had knocked the guard in the head with his hoof and pulled him into the shrubbery.

Marian caught up with Morgaine and grabbed at her arm. Out of breath and whispering loudly, "Remember your station. Do not run. I do not know what you think is wrong but you mustn't run."

Morgaine stopped. Marian was right. She caught her breath but continued to march up through the castle gates, pretending everything was alright now. She pushed one thought into the castle guards' heads, "Ignore me." Thankfully, they complied.

Meggie, Morgaine's companion, had been watching for Morgaine and Marian in the shadows. She stole up to the women silently and put her hand on her mistress, saying in a hushed voice, "My Lady, the Sheriff has imprisoned your parents!"

Morgaine nodded, her eyes wide and bewildered. She was still trying to get her bearings. She hadn't thought through any of this. She shouldn't have returned to the castle without a plan.

Marian spoke to Meggie, "Do you know if they are searching for Morgaine?"

Meggie shook her head. She didn't think so; she hadn't heard either way.

Marian looked up and around as if searching inside her head for what they could do. "The guards allow me access to see my father. Meggie, you stay here and I will bring Morgaine." Meggie looked frightened and untrusting. Marian was reassuring. "We'll be careful." Meggie nodded and rubbed her friend's arms.

Morgaine followed Marian as they stole down into the dungeon. The guards did not know Morgaine and let her pass through with Marian to see her father. Morgaine's father was pacing and her mother sat stony-faced. Morgaine knew better though. She could hear her mother desperately trying to calm herself while at the same time reaching out into the ethers to glean what path to take. Too many futures. Everything was jumbled and cloudy. Evelyn hated it here. There was hexing magic at work in this place.

"What happened?" exclaimed Morgaine as quietly as she could as she came upon her parents and reached through the bars to touch them.

"That fool Sheriff thinks he can imprison us for not signing a document. It doesn't even have the seal of the Prince. This is some scheme of William's, not the Prince's."

"Where is Guy? Did he not try to stop this?"

Marian shook her head in pity at her friend, as Morgaine asked what Marian knew to be a stupid question.

Gareth replied, "After confronting the Sheriff, he was ordered home at knife point. I do not think he can help."

Evelyn gathered her wits and spoke up, "He told me as he left that he would get us out. I could see he was earnest but I am not sure what he can do." She paused, "There is another option."

Morgaine nodded slightly, "I will go to Guy first and implore him to help us get a message to Prince John...and if not him then...."

Gareth nodded, knowing of whom else his daughter spoke.

"Don't get caught, Daughter; we can't have you in here too," implored Evelyn.

Marian spoke softly with her father and then she and Morgaine left. They met Meggie back at the stables. The three women conferred about next steps. Marian said she would look after Morgaine's parents. "My father's in there too."

"We'll see about that," Morgaine reassured. She was gathering strength, pulling it to her from the very ground, and felt more centered, though she still wasn't entirely sure what her plan was yet. She then turned to Meggie, "Where are Sophie and Robbie?"

"Robbie is in the tavern, I think, and Sophie is in your parents' room."

"Find a safe place to hide. They may not torture royalty but they would not hesitate in using the three of you to get at Mother and Father."

Meggie nodded gravely. The two women embraced and then Meggie departed to search for and gather up Robbie and Sophie.

Morgaine saddled her horse Merryweather herself as Marian left her in order to discreetly look for someone to lead Morgaine directly to Locksley Manor. While Morgaine appeared alone, a shadow slid up behind her. "Thank you," Morgaine whispered. "It is good to know you are here. I am sorry I did not listen to you before. Please do nothing as of yet. I want to try something else first before we give ourselves away in this way."

The shadow nodded slightly, "As you wish, My Lady. We are ready when you have need." With that, the shadow withdrew.

CHAPTER 6

Morgaine Appeals to Guy

THE SUN WAS going down as the young man who was heading back home to Locksley Village led Morgaine to her destiny. When they got to the manor she practically jumped off Merryweather. "Thank you for your help and your discretion."

The young man looked startled by the gratitude but simply said, "You are welcome, M'Lady."

"Would you please take my horse to the stable and have her secured?"

"Of course, M'Lady."

"For your troubles and your held tongue." She dropped a coin into the young lad's hand looking into his eyes with a regal air.

"Thank you, M'Lady. I promise not to breathe a word of this."

Morgaine nodded and gave no further thought to it. She knocked rapidly at the door. A squat middle-aged woman answered it. "Is the Master at home?" Morgaine asked in a hurried voice.

"Yes, M'Lady," answered the surprised servant. Guy was not known to receive regal ladies. In fact, the servant couldn't remember a woman ever coming to the manor to see Guy.

"I need to see him right now."

"He's indisposed, M'Lady."

Morgaine looked pleading yet commanding and the servant bowed her head, opening the door wider. She didn't know why, but she couldn't say no to this noble lady. Morgaine stepped across the threshold and put her hand to the woman's cheek. "Thank you." The servant nodded bewilderedly. Morgaine asked, "What is your name?"

The servant replied, "Mary, M'Lady."

"Mary, please show me in and bring me to the lord of the manor. It is of grave importance I see him immediately."

Mary welcomed Morgaine in and shut the door. "As I said, he's indisposed, M'Lady. But I will go and tell him you are here. Who shall I say is calling?"

"The Lady Morgaine."

Mary left the room to take the news to the lord of the manor. But Morgaine didn't feel she had time for formalities and instead followed the direction in which Mary went. She heard their voices and walked through the house into a side room where she saw a fire burning and there was Guy — in the bath. Morgaine's voice was aflame, "You are taking a bath at a time like this?"

Mary started, "M'Lady, please."

Guy, still sitting in the bath, was sheepish. "I...I think better in the hot water; it's calming."

Mary started again, "M'Lady, please."

Guy waved Mary away. She curtsied and left the room. Morgaine walked toward Guy and put her hands on her hips. She was visibly stressed. But as she looked at Guy she could see he was too.

"I am sorry. I failed you and your parents." The rims of his eyes looked red but tears refused to budge further than a possibility as he clenched his teeth, a habit he used to force his emotions down. He felt ashamed. But an unknown force compelled him to be completely honest with her, "I was not brave enough. I let him bully me. I always let him bully me."

Morgaine saw Guy's anguish then noticed the cut at his throat, "You are hurt."

Guy waved away her comment, hand dripping with water. "Just my pride is injured."

Morgaine started walking toward Guy with concern in her eyes but the closer she got, the more distracted she was by the fact that she was gazing at a very handsome, naked man in a washtub. She collected herself, then spoke. "I need your help. My parents are in prison and I am unsure what I can do." What she left unsaid was her private secret.

Guy looked up at Morgaine, overcome by a need to help her, to be her champion. "I have been thinking about a rider; we need to get a message to the Prince."

"That is what I was thinking too. Do you think he will help us?"

Guy continued to mentally chew on the likelihood that Prince John would intervene. Knowing his fondness for Morgaine, it was possible. But then the Sheriff was a stronger, more known ally. He shook his head, muttering, "This will ruin me."

She came to his side, kneeling by the tub. Though Morgaine was not entirely sure what he meant by that last statement, she recognized that he had put himself in danger by questioning William and might therefore be of little help, and in fact, might be in need of help himself.

They held each other's gaze. Some part of each of them recognized the absurdity of the situation. Both were clearly upset by the circumstances that brought her to his house and yet, in spite of their heightened fears, they also both felt a longing to be close to the other. "We will get through this together," Guy said, praying she could still love a man who calculates his odds before leaping into the fray. He looked into her eyes, imploring her love. And then he leaned over and kissed her. He wanted to console her but, the moment their lips touched, they sought each other hungrily. Guy took her in his arms, pulling her into the bath. Their kisses stirred their passion and they could hardly control themselves in their ardency.

Mary peeked into the room but was unsure what to say or do. She waited for direction from Morgaine, wondering how she would handle this extreme act of indiscretion. Then she heard Morgaine laughing, "Oh Love, you have soaked me through." They both sighed and Guy let Morgaine up. On that, Mary entered the room and Morgaine, seeing her, smiled, "It appears some men simply cannot stop themselves."

Mary replied, "That is what tends to get us all into trouble, M'Lady."

Guy ignored the comment and instead beseeched, "Morgaine, stay for supper. We'll talk and figure this out and you can stay the night. I have another room. Mary, get her one of my robes." Mary did a quick curtsey and left the room. The two lovers gazed at each other as Morgaine's gown dripped onto the floor.

Mary returned a few moments later, bringing in a red silk robe. It was a gift from Prince John that Guy had never worn. "Here, let me help you out of your garment, M'Lady. M'Lord, please turn your head."

Morgaine stood shivering by the fire as Mary helped her out of her gown, toweled her off, and wrapped her in Guy's robe. Guy had briefly turned his head out of some sense of decency but refused to be completely complacent, eyeing Morgaine as the robe came around her frame. He bit his bottom lip and could feel himself swelling further with desire. Oh, emotions were running hotter than the water in this room!

"M'Lady, let me hang your gown by the fire and we will see if we can't get it dry by morning."

"Mary, thank you. I appreciate your help."

"Of course, M'Lady." Mary was not used to being thanked in this house. She liked Morgaine already and wanted to make sure no rumors of indiscretion came to Morgaine. "M'Lord, shall I help you…"

"No, just fetch dinner," he said still ogling Morgaine who eyed him as if he was missing some point. "Please," he added, hoping that was the word Morgaine implied with her look that he was missing something. Morgaine nodded once with an approving smile.

"M'Lady," Mary curtsied and handed Morgaine a cloth and the robe for Guy. Mary left the room to the kitchen, happily surprised that Lord Guy said "please."

Morgaine looked at the cloth as if it was some foreign object. Guy lingered a moment more and then decided to just stand up. Morgaine's eyes widened as she looked up from the cloth to the incredibly gorgeous and very naked man before her. There was some part of her that wanted to shout out to Mary to "never mind about food, I have a feast right here." But surely she would not say such things. Guy looked at her ravenously as if she were the feast to be consumed. Her body then grew hot as if she was a cauldron and his eyes a blazing fire.

Guy stepped out of the tub and onto the floor. So close to her. Morgaine remembered the cloth in her hands and that it in fact did have a purpose. She patted his body with the cloth watching the water bead on his skin, the water droplets running down his torso, his chest expanding and contracting with his breath. She had never been a servant even to the Queen or Princess, as she never was a lady at court. But she willingly brushed the water off his muscular frame. She then gingerly placed the robe onto his back. When he turned again to face her she felt his manhood hard against her. He smiled at her with satisfaction, that adorable lopsided smile she loved so much. Morgaine grew amused; she sensed he felt powerful in this moment, that by her act of patting the water off him, he felt he had accomplished something. Her shoulders shrugged absentmindedly and she smiled up at him. She teased, "What did you win? You have the look of accomplishment."

There was a pause between them as he considered the blunt question. "You. I hope," Guy responded, a tad embarrassed.

She leaned into him and wrapped her arms around his torso. He enfolded her in an embrace and kissed the top of her head. She whispered into his chest, "Yes, you've won."

He squeezed her tighter, feeling a sense of relief. His feeling of accomplishment quickly returned and his hands slowly roamed her back.

As they caressed each other, Mary called from the kitchen, sounding reminiscently like a red fox's yip, her voice high pitched and fast. "Supper is hot." She was embarrassed to disturb them though at the same time concerned for the Lady's reputation.

The pair sat in the kitchen in their robes, eating and talking, scheming about next steps, while Mary sat in the corner as if merely a fly on the wall. But Guy became distracted with thoughts of family ties and the idea of marrying Morgaine. He finally asked, "A man who marries you, what becomes of his titles?"

Morgaine, though surprised by Guy's complete redirection of focus, explained, "The man takes the name of the Land. The Land is what matters. That is why we are all Avalons. When my father married my mother, he released his surname and took Avalon, as will my mate. For this country now only recognizes the man's right to land, and so our men must be married to the Land as well as to us so that we retain the Land."

Guy nodded and prodded further, "Why were you introduced as "Lady of the Lake?"

Mary overheard and quietly gasped. Could it be true? Those weren't just fairytales?

Morgaine afforded Mary a sidelong glance, making mental note of the woman's excitement but directed her answer to Guy. "Though my mother still carries the right to the title as well, she relinquished it to me a few years ago. Our family has kept it a custom that the daughter of the duchess carries the title when she reaches maturity and until she has a daughter who reaches maturity. It is a much smaller lake now than when my ancestors were called by that title. Still, I am honored with that recognition of an older time when a woman's station was more upheld."

Guy took in Morgaine's words. He vaguely remembered stories of the Lady of the Lake and Arthur's sister, the Sorceress, Morgaine. Was his love, the Sorceress' descendant?

"Yes, I am Morgaine's namesake and the descendant of the High King's sister," Morgaine replied to his unspoken question.

Mary, overhearing this, was beside herself with elation. "I have stumbled into a legend," she beamed to herself.

Guy's mind raced with questions of how it would have been possible that the descendants of a sorceress, High King's sister or not, had been able to keep titles and lands. But instead, Guy, overcome by some powerful force he could not yet begin to fathom, responded by taking her hand in his. "Lady, you have enchanted my heart. I am yours. Use my hand and sword as you will."

Morgaine offered a welcoming smile, "Guy, I am pleased by your openness to my ancestry and I am honored at your willingness to be my Champion. I accept."

As if a veil had fallen away, his trance-like state cleared and Guy was suddenly perplexed at what she was accepting. But he was too happy to care or contemplate the weight of the words he felt compelled to speak. They returned to their scheming of how to free Morgaine's parents.

As they talked, Morgaine finally broached a subject that needed clarification if she was going to better understand where Guy stood with regard to William. "Guy, I have been sensing hesitation in you with regard to any action against the Sheriff. What power does he hold over you?" Guy looked physically pained. "I am sorry. I did not want to pry, but it is important. You say your sword is mine but you allow this man to intimidate you."

Guy clenched his jaw in an effort to quell his anguish. He stated as calmly as he could, "You do not understand the depth of William's schemes. And I…I fear his wrath. I used to love him as a father. Sometimes I still do, even though…Morgaine, he took me in, gave me purpose, and treated me like a son." He sighed, "At least in the beginning. But he allows no one to get close to him. And as I grew more attached, he grew more detached. I have become merely his weapon to wield as he wills. To lose one father was painful enough. But Morgaine, he will kill me and anyone I love if I cross him." Guy swallowed hard and mentally slapped the tears that threatened to well up.

Morgaine laid her hand over his, and with a secretive voice whispered, "Well then, for now, we mustn't let it appear you are crossing him."

They had exhausted all thoughts and knew their plan for the next day. Morgaine yawned and Guy noticed how tired she was.

Mary had been sitting slumped near the kitchen hearth but opened her eyes, stretched, and crouched next to Morgaine, whispering, "Do you want me to stay, M'Lady?"

Morgaine yawned again, whispering back sleepily, "Do you have a husband?"

"Yes."

"Then no, Mary. I appreciate your concern for my virtue and I promise that, as much as I am taken with my gallant knight, I shall allow no indiscretion to transpire. Go home. Rest." Morgaine put her arms around Mary and hugged her close. Mary felt the warmth and light of the Lady of the Lake, and after she was released, wearily wandered out of Locksley Manor to her home across the courtyard to fall into a blissful sleep, feeling held by the Lady, the Great Mother.

Brin, Guy's other servant, finished emptying the washtub and cleaning up the hearth room which, during the winter, served as Guy's wash room too as he loved to spend any free moment immersed in steaming water by the fire. Guy, on more than one occasion, thought it one of the better perks of being a baron: a warm bath of one's own.

Morgaine eyed Brin as he warmed his hands by the fire, but Brin pretended not to notice. She wondered how much he had heard but allowed herself to be distracted by Guy taking her hand and leading her up the stairs to show her to her room.

The lovers paused in the doorway. Candle flame between them, Guy reached out with his other hand, caressing Morgaine's cheek and then turning his fingers, stroked down her chin to her throat, then down her chest, forcing the robe to release its cling at her breasts. His enchanting blue eyes danced in the firelight. He bit his bottom lip, exhaling forcefully through his nostrils in excitement and continued to stroke her body with his hand in a downward trajectory until he reached the robe's knot at her navel. He took hold of the knot and pulled her more closely with one hand while raising the candle up with the other. She reached her hands up around his neck and they kissed. Teeth gently tugged at bottom lips. Tongues hotly touched. She felt him hard against her and she shifted her hips to press into him further.

Oh she could give in to their lust so easily. But no, she mustn't. Morgaine whispered heatedly into Guy's ear, "My Lord, I do not reject your advances in the least. In fact, I would give myself to you willingly. But I need to remember my station and that as a daughter of a duke I cannot…"

Guy sighed. How did Morgaine know exactly what to say to ease his fear of rejection? He knew he was pushing her. It was so hard to keep his hands off her. "I know," he said hotly, "Bed then?" He motioned her into her room, gave her the candle, and then stoked his hand up from her pubic bone to her chin, carrying her chin to his face to give her one final, fervent kiss goodnight. Guy then retreated into the darkness and into his room after watching Morgaine turn and walk into her room.

Morgaine placed the candle down on a stand next to the bed. The room was mildly warm with the fire roaring downstairs. Even though it was a baron's house, it was on the small side and was built so that the rooms upstairs were open to the downstairs and the warmth. She pulled back the covers and sat down, stroking her legs against the silk robe. She blew out the candle and moved her body back and forth along the bed to feel the silk against her skin. Oh how this man inspired her to feel so alive and beautiful and desirable. She lay there touching herself, fantasizing that she was still in the hall with him and that he opened her robe and stroked her, feeling her mound pulsing and her nether lips wet with desire. Her body was cresting in rapture.

Suddenly, and most unkindly, her mind felt under attack by a multitude of winged, angry thoughts. She shook her head, attempting to clear the mad beating of wings and met the visceral complaints with calm, "One way or another, you will be free; I promise." The haunting left her and she knew her mother would rest more easily knowing she was working through how to free them. The moment was broken for Morgaine though, and she could not return to her blissful state. She sighed and willed herself to sleep.

Brin heard the house quiet from his small room off the side of the hearth room. He crept up, went for the door, and stole outside. Guy, who hadn't been able to fall asleep yet, heard the floorboards creak and went to the window to watch Brin sneaking to the stable. "Where the devil is he going at this hour?" Guy wondered. He followed him, wearing only his robe and instinctually grabbing his blade on the way out of his room.

Brin was about to get on a horse when Guy stalked into the stable, blade drawn.

"And where are you off to at this hour?" Guy's face was a fury.

Brin gulped. "Nowhere," he stated meekly.

Guy nodded then added, "I have been wondering how it is that Morgaine's and my letters had not reached each other. Simple love letters shouldn't cause a fuss. There would be no gain to intercept them. And how would one know that there were letters?" Guy eyed Brin menacingly. "Nothing to say for yourself?

Not: 'Please, My Lord, I did not do it'? Not: 'The Sheriff made me'?" Brin felt as caught as he was. He knew he was damned whatever he said. A pretty coin was not going to convince his master that he had no choice but to betray him. Guy pounced on Brin like a cat, snarling, "Where were you going?"

Brin stumbled over his words, "The Sheriff. When you got back in November, he told me he wanted any letters coming to or going from this house. He said it was for your own good. He gave me coin for my cooperation. Please, Sire."

"And were you going to alert the Sheriff of my plans for my own good?"

Brin nodded then shook his head.

"You have betrayed me for the last time," Guy whispered in Brin's ear as he plunged the sword up under Brin's ribcage into his heart. Brin slumped down and bled out. Guy shook his head, annoyed. He smirked, this being a contemptuous smirk, the type Marian accused him of, "Hard to get good help these days."

Mary came scurrying into the kitchen horrified at what she had just seen in the courtyard. Guy was already up, in fact had never been back to bed or sleep. Mary spoke with grave concern, "Sire, did you see Brin?"

Guy didn't turn to face her but merely continued to gaze out the window. His monosyllabic response sounded callous. "Yes."

"But, M'Lord — he's lying..."

Guy's face was grim, hard. "Yes, you are right, he is lying. He was lying. He was the traitor who gave the letters to William, who was riding out of here late last night to tell the Sheriff that Morgaine and I were planning to rescue her parents. So, yes Mary, Brin is lying face down in the dirt because I put him there. I didn't want the blood to spook the horses. Get someone to clean that up, will you." Mary quickly curtsied and went back out to get help burying the body. Guy looked deadly.

It was only a short time later when Morgaine waltzed down the stairs looking for Guy. She looked through the house and arrived in the kitchen.

Though her mood was sweet, she started as she caught Guy's stance and hardened face. "What has happened? Are you alright?" Morgaine came swiftly to Guy's side. She then looked past him through the window to the courtyard. There were two men removing a body. "Is that your servant?" she questioned.

There was merely a hint of a nod from Guy. "I caught him leaving last night to warn the Sheriff of our plan. He was the one who intercepted our letters for the Sheriff."

"Hmmm," was all Morgaine said. As if picking up on a thought in the air, she added, "You did this for us, to ensure our plan's success."

"Yes. I was hoping to use Brin as our rider but, as you can see, that won't work." Guy felt cautious. He was not sure how Morgaine would take him killing someone, even if it was for their cause.

But Morgaine merely watched Brin being removed from the courtyard, eyes narrowed, lips pursed. Still looking out, "Who will be our rider?"

Mary walked back in hearing that question. She ached seeing the Lady of the Lake in such distress. Without thinking, she exclaimed, "Allow me to help, M'Lady."

"What can you do?"

"I will go get my eldest, Dylan. He will be your rider." Mary left without allowing for a response.

Morgaine looked after her, holding her breath and only finally letting it release slowly when Mary was out of sight through the window.

Guy watched Morgaine with concern and dread and cautiously asked, "Morgaine, what are you thinking?"

Morgaine was lost in thought, hating that a man just died but also hurt that someone who did not even know her would betray her. Her emotions felt jumbled.

"Morgaine?"

She could hear Guy's voice pleading and she knew he was fearful of her judgment. Morgaine wasn't sure what to say. She was not sure what she would have done if it had been she who discovered Brin. Was there a choice to allow him to live and what would those consequences have been? She knew she could not place herself in Guy's boots. He was a swordsman after all. And why leave Brin's body in the dirt? That must have been calculated. So cold. But Guy was hot with emotion. What to say? Instead she reached her hand up to Guy's cheek. He took her hand and kissed her palm and then placed her hand back on his cheek with his hand over hers. He sensed that whatever her mixture of emotions was, she was letting him know that she was still there and that her love for him did not diminish because of what he did.

He exhaled, his thoughts directed at her, "My Lady, I am the sword in the darkness and I will protect you at all costs."

Morgaine cocked her head as if she could hear him. "My Dragon's Breath," she whispered.

Guy furrowed his brow, not knowing the reference. Was this a good thing or a bad? Their thoughts were interrupted as Mary came through the door.

Mary returned with a bewildered Dylan who had only heard part of the story and knew only that he was being enlisted to get a message to the Prince whom he despised. Morgaine turned from Guy to face the pair. Mary introduced Dylan to Morgaine, "Dylan, this is Lady Morgaine, the Lady of the Lake, and she needs our help."

All he heard was "Lady of the Lake" and his mind went to his mother's stories of King Arthur and the sword Excalibur that was given to Arthur by the Lady of the Lake. Dylan dropped to his knees, asking fervently, "What would you have me do, M'Lady?"

Guy watched on, bewildered at the sudden act of devotion for someone the boy did not even know. It was the title, Guy realized. These two were acting in devotion to a story, a myth, a legend. He shook his head in amazement and yet realized he, too, was caught up in the story and in his devotion to this lady, his lady.

Morgaine allowed herself a relieved breath. She then placed her hand on Dylan's shoulder, who she now remembered as the young man who brought her here, and stated, "Gallant Dylan, it is my pleasure to make your acquaintance though I wish it were under more pleasant circumstances. The Sheriff of

Nottingham has captured my parents. Lord Guy is going to escort me back to the castle in an attempt to talk my way into freeing them. If I am unsuccessful, I need someone who is a fast rider, someone who can stay hidden, out of the Sheriff's prying eyes, and get word to Prince John that we are being held unjustly at the hand of the Sheriff. Not knowing me, not being beholden to my family, will you do this for me?"

Dylan looked into Morgaine's eyes and knew he could not refuse. He was amazed that she, a highborn, was asking. Not demanding, not pleading. *Asking.* He felt compelled to help her. "M'Lady, I will do this for you. But how will I know to ride to the Prince?"

Morgaine shifted her hand to touch his forehead. He smelled the scent of apples in the air. All tension left his body. He then heard her command, "Dylan, ride!"

He jumped, and was about to leave the room when she caught his arm. He looked at her, "I heard your command."

Mary looked anxious, "Dylan, she said nothing."

"I heard you, didn't I?" Dylan implored not wanting to think he reacted wrongly.

"Yes Dylan, I called out to you with my thoughts and you heard me. This is what you will hear if I need you to ride."

"I heard you in my mind," he said wonderingly. "What magic is this?"

Mary took a deep slow breath realizing that she just placed her son in a dung heap of possible danger; but the thought of helping a legend was just too strong to ignore.

It seemed as if Dylan had just now noticed Guy in the room watching the scene take place. He looked at Morgaine thinking, "Can you hear me?"

Morgaine replied back into his mind, "Yes."

"M'Lady, forgive me for being so blunt. Lord Guy is not a kind man. Please be careful. I fear you are misplacing your trust." Dylan tried hard not to look at Guy as he silently relayed his thoughts to Morgaine.

Morgaine felt the fear in the young man and his desire to do good. Morgaine replied, "I thank you for your boldness and your bravery. Please, do not worry yourself about me with regard to Lord Guy. Trust me in this matter," Morgaine looked at Dylan with compassion and understanding.

To Mary and Guy it appeared as if the two were staring at one another though both knew that they must be communicating.

Dylan bowed, saying out loud, "I wish you God's speed M'Lady and await your command."

Morgaine put her hand back on his shoulder, "Thank you, brave Dylan."

Morgaine and Guy readied themselves to leave for the castle. Guy did not want to intrude on the apparent conversation between Morgaine and Dylan but he was curious as to what information had passed between them and how she was able to do what she had done. He was about to ask her when Mary ran to Morgaine's side, "Oh sweet, noble Lady of the Lake, please stay safe…" There were more words but Mary wasn't sure how to say them.

Morgaine touched Mary on the cheek, "Thank you. Bless you."

Mary sighed. After watching them leave she walked purposefully back into the manor, lit a candle, and prayed for the rest of the day.

Morgaine reached out in her mind to another, a shadow in the forest. "Watch this house. If a young man by the name of Dylan leaves, escort him to Wallingford. Make sure he gets there alive." She knew Rainer, her shadow so to speak, would not want to have to go into more populated areas or visit with the Prince, as in some ways he was less equipped in that environment. But she also knew he would do whatever it took to make sure the Ladies of the Lake were safe.

CHAPTER 7

Confronting the Sheriff

MORGAINE AND GUY walked up the steps together, each breath being more re-solved. They had already agreed how to play this out and to trust each other, knowing that they were on the same side no matter what they might have to say. They had made this promise as they looked into each other's eyes.

As they walked the corridor, Guy heard a "psst" sound coming from his left. He turned his head and there, in the corner, was one of the guards who was usually assigned to Marian. He stopped, which made Morgaine stop, and tilted his head indicating for the guard to approach. Morgaine recognized the man as Marian's guard. She had a feeling about what must have happened to him and was hoping that the part of her that was glad to see he was still alive would continue to feel that way. That would depend on what he said next.

"Sire?" said the guard as he came to stand in front of Guy.

"Yes?"

"I see that you have the Avalon woman."

"Yes," said Guy plainly. He wasn't sure the purpose of the conversation and was annoyed by the man delaying him and Morgaine.

"My apologies, Sire. The Lady Morgaine and the Lady Marian..." The guard wondered how to explain himself. He could see Guy wasn't feeling overly patient. He fumbled over his words. "They were running back to the castle. I do not know why. I was about to follow but was...knocked out."

Guy eyed the man incredulously. "Knocked out?"

"Yes, Sire. I only revived a short bit ago." The man had no idea he had been drugged. He only knew he felt groggy. "I don't know by whom. Perhaps Robin Hood's men?"

Guy looked at the ceiling impatiently. "Why Robin Hood's men?"

The guard shrugged. What he didn't want to say is that he thought he saw a stag standing over him before the bee stung him and he went unconscious again.

Guy considered what the motivation might have been to knock out Marian's guard. As he contemplated, he turned his head to assess Morgaine's expression. She appeared to be studying the floor. If Robin's men were going to steal from the women then perhaps they'd knock out the guard. But to knock him out after he witnessed the women running away? That did not make sense.

The guard broke into Guy's thoughts. "What do you want me to do, Sire?"

Guy sighed. He thought about the time. Marian might be with her father in the dungeon. Or in her room. He didn't think she would try to leave the castle without a guard, as she knew the consequences. Guy spoke softly to the man, "Be discreet. Look for the Lady Marian. I am sure she will be somewhere in the castle. Her room or with her father."

The guard nodded, considering his good fortune. Lord Guy appeared to be letting him off the hook. All he had to do now was find his charge and he would not get into further trouble. He bowed and departed.

Guy shook his head as he thought to himself, "Knocked out?" But as he had more pressing matters, he didn't want to consider who knocked the guard out or why.

Though it didn't show on Morgaine's face, internally, she was smiling. She knew what must have happened and was thankful Rainer was there protecting her. And that he had managed to incapacitate the guard this long without killing him or doing lasting harm.

The castle guards watched as Guy and Morgaine approached and opened the doors to William's receiving room. Guy was, after all, a baron, and there was no reason not to admit him to the Sheriff's room as Lord Guy often came at this time of the morning to confer with the Sheriff. It mattered not that he had some fancily dressed lady with him.

Morgaine confronted William with all the refined fury of a snowstorm slowly piling up against the eaves, the weight forcing the bricks to slowly give in. "Sheriff de Wendenal, what is the meaning of this?"

William looked up from the pile of papers on his desk, addressing Guy, not Morgaine. "Yes, Gisbourne, what is the meaning of this? Why is this daughter of traitors not gagged and in some dark cell?"

Guy replied calmly and honestly, "She came to me in the night."

William spat back, "And you didn't have her bound?"

Guy made his voice sound condescending as he gestured dismissively in Morgaine's direction with his hand, "She is a woman. What could she have done? And where could she have gone dressed like that?"

Morgaine smoothed her gown as if distracted by the comment. As her sweeping long sleeves brushed against the fabric of her gown, William could swear he heard the soothing sound of waves lapping at the shore. It was slightly hypnotic. He shook his head as if he could force the sound out of his ears.

Impertinently, Morgaine continued, "What will the Prince say when he finds out that you have imprisoned two of his loyal subjects?"

William shot back, doing his best to ignore the strange lulling sound in his ears, of waves rolling across the sand. "If they are that loyal, they should have no problem signing a document proclaiming their allegiance."

Morgaine retorted, "Does this document carry the official seal of the Prince?" She could see by his expression that it did not and so she continued, "But if your so-called proclamation of allegiance does not have the Prince's seal then how do we know it came from him?" Morgaine's gaze was icy, ready to stab.

William chewed on the inside of his bottom lip behind a pursed mouth but refused to be outdone by a woman. Instead, he turned to Guy, "Gisbourne, control your woman," he spit out.

Guy placed his hands lightly on Morgaine's shoulders. They knew they had to play this delicately so that they could protect one another and the family. Morgaine took a breath as she heard Guy's thoughts in her mind, "I am here for you, Lady." Her hand reached back and lightly touched his thigh so that he knew she felt his commitment to her. And in that moment, Guy felt something more keenly then he ever had before. Protective. He suddenly realized if this plan didn't go well for Morgaine, he would not allow his love to be carted off to the dungeon. Terms like "hero" or "villain" meant little as he considered killing the guards, and even William, to protect Morgaine.

Meanwhile Morgaine continued to play her role; she looked down, acting beaten, sighing resolutely. Underneath her lashes she could see William standing taller, thinking he had won the argument already. Her devious smile would betray her if not for the fact that William was so sure of his manly superiority.

The color drained from his already pale face as she derailed any thoughts of his supremacy as a schemer.

Morgaine carefully laid out her intentions while Guy secretly appreciated her spiteful behavior toward William. "Sheriff de Wendenal, if you are so resolute in detaining my parents for unsubstantiated transgressions, then I have no option but to turn to my patron, Prince John, to resolve this matter. I am sure he will be annoyed at this bothersome account for it will appear we Avalons are childish in our actions. And yet I will implore him to see reason that we are acting in sole loyalty to him and not any proxy. I wonder, what will he say to your document, demanding loyalty, without his seal?"

William felt caught. He didn't like being trapped in a lie. That document was his weapon to pit highborn against highborn, to bring chaos to the realm. The bitch had him and he knew it. He considered killing her right then and there. Perhaps he should just kill the whole family. He realized he should not do that here, that would only bring the Prince down upon him. He would have to bide his time. He looked at Guy, thinking, "And you will be my weapon whether you like it or not." To Morgaine he stated, "The Prince would not appreciate being bothered by such trifles, I agree. But I can be patient. You all can sit here and rot until you sign."

Morgaine responded, "I will not rot until after I die. I anticipated your reluctance and so have already sent a rider. If I do not meet up with this individual, he will continue on to Wallingford Castle, where I know the Prince is staying. Did you really think I would be so ill-prepared walking in here?"

Yes, thought William; you are but a woman. Scowling, William spat, "So what would your family have to say for itself by not signing?"

Morgaine countered, "We will sign any document, proclaiming loyalty, provided it contains the Royal Seal and it is in the presence of Prince John."

William breathed heavily. Without the seal he had nothing, only the ability to prey on the weak minded, but the Avalons were proving more solid than he wanted to believe. His aspirations of tearing a country apart into complete anarchy were disintegrating. To maintain this one card against both brothers, he could only hope that Morgaine's threat was empty.

William begrudgingly agreed to release Morgaine's parents on the stipulation that no more would be spoken about this document that they hadn't signed. Morgaine agreed on behalf of her parents, hoping that they would hold the peace and let the disjointed pieces fall as they may. They both knew it was only a matter of time, though, before William would have to find a means to do away with anyone who knew of his plot.

Figuring she would take as much as she could get in the moment, Morgaine added an additional request, "Sheriff de Wendenal, in addition to setting my parents free, you will release Marian and her father into our care. She appears to be a distraction to this..." Morgaine sought a word that would convince William of the need to let Marian go, "castle's occupants," she ended lamely.

William's eyes slanted in mistrust. But then Marian was a distraction, mostly to Guy, but still, having her disappear could simplify his life and bring Guy back to him. Also, two fewer mouths to feed. Well, if Morgaine wanted the added complication and possible competition that was her business. "So be it. You can have Marian..." Morgaine eyed him meaningfully and he added, "...and her father. But I don't ever want you to step foot in Nottingham again. You have proven yourself adversarial and I don't want you meddling in Nottingham's affairs."

Morgaine stiffened but agreed, with one clarification, "I agree never to return unless it is by the request or command of our ruler." William nodded, secretly fantasizing the family's demise so that there would be no chance for a return.

Guy looked broken-hearted and William grinned. "So that will be the end of that," he thought. As the couple started to walk out, William gave Guy an icy stare, clipping, "A moment, Gisbourne." Guy paused and then faced William full on. William, who had stood up and stepped away from his table, motioned Guy to come to him, to which Guy obeyed. William took hold of Guy's arm and hissed loudly toward his ear, "Do not betray me for that skyrta!" Guy yanked his arm but William held fast. William looked at Guy tellingly and Guy said nothing, looking down. Morgaine, who was just outside the door watching the two, tried to appear as if she didn't care what William said. William then eyed her and quipped, "You are just a means to an end for him. He only thinks he is in love with you. He seeks power and he thinks you may have access to it. You are nothing but a title and a pretty distraction." Morgaine glared at William but said nothing. The words stung but she willed her herself not to ingest William's venom. She decided it was more important to poultice herself with Guy's love and wear his words like bandages against William's cutting remarks. William let go of Guy's arm and dismissed the two with the flick of his wrist, sending them away to prepare the prisoners' release.

Guy and Morgaine glided down the dungeon steps. Guy was in front of Morgaine holding her hand and squeezing it with a gentle firmness to let her know he appreciated her trust in him.

Gareth, pacing, appeared to have never ceased this activity while they were away.

"The Sheriff has agreed to release all who have not signed the document provided that, should the Prince directly request such an oath, it is given, and that this document is never mentioned to anyone." The six prisoners looked at Morgaine forlornly but recognized this was a simple matter to gain their freedom. Evelyn, Gareth, and two other gentlemen stood up to leave. Lady Edwena then stood as well. She wanted to get out of this cell. But her husband, Lord Thomas Winter, was resigned to his course out of loyalty to King Richard and stayed seated. "You will rot in here," Morgaine proclaimed to Thomas and his wife. The woman sobbed. She didn't want to stay locked in here. She looked to her husband but he just folded his arms.

Morgaine and her family went to their rooms but both were empty. Fearing the Sheriff had relieved them of their possessions, all they could do was wait until Marian got her belongings. Meggie slinked up the stairs staying in the shadows until she saw it was in fact just the family and made herself more visible.

Morgaine sensed Meggie and turned. "Meggie, it's you! Are you and Sophie alright? Is Robbie?"

"Yes My Lady, we are all alright. When you didn't come back last night, Sophie and I grabbed all your belongings and brought them to the carriage for safekeeping. The three of us have stayed in the stables out of sight waiting for news. I decided to sneak around and come back up here and then I saw you. Are we leaving then?"

Morgaine smiled at her faithful companion, "Yes, Meggie, we are leaving now. Thank you for anticipating our departure and keeping our belongings and yourself safe."

Walking down the steps, Morgaine reached out in her mind first to Rainer, "If you have not noticed yet, we are leaving. Prepare." She heard the response, "We are ready." Then she reached out in her mind to Dylan and Mary. She sensed that though he was trying to busy himself, Dylan was taut and ready to spring into action. Mary bent in prayer. She delicately entered their minds, whispering, "All is well. We are all safe and on our way home. Thank you both." Then she withdrew, feeling their relief. Mary and Dylan both inhaled the scent of apples in the air.

As the family came down the stairs to the waiting carriage Guy noticed there were no guards with the carriage. He hadn't noticed that when they arrived. "Where are your men?"

Gareth merely patted Guy's arm and winked as he escorted Evelyn into the carriage. Sophie came to Sir Charlton's aid to help him down the remaining stairs with his daughter on the other side of him.

Morgaine leaned into Guy whispering, "They are about. Our guardians are hidden. If our attempt had not worked, they would have rescued us."

Guy wasn't content with her explanation. "How?"

"Guy, my love, all will be explained in time. Just know that they are men of the forest," she paused as she could feel his hackles rise up, "No, not outlaws. We have guardians who can blend in well with the forest, though not so much within the town. They watch us wherever we go. We are as safe as we can be. And now we have you." The last sentence was more of a question as she looked up at him hopefully.

"My love, I will escort you as far as I am able, but the Sheriff will not give me leave. I will take the rest of the day so that I can be by your side as long as I can."

Morgaine sighed, "Then allow me to ride on Midnight with you." Guy brought Morgaine into a tight embrace. He felt he would almost weep. He could not lose this woman.

After Marian escorted her father into the carriage and was mentally preparing herself to leave Nottingham, she turned from the carriage and walked back toward Guy, noticing the intense emotion on his face. She waited, looking down. Guy noticed Marian, kissed the top of Morgaine's head, and took a deep breath, clearing his thoughts. "Yes, Marian?"

"Guy, this could be the last time my father and I see our home. Could we make a short detour to the manor?" Guy looked pained and Marian asked, now concerned, "What is it?"

Guy broke from Morgaine, took Marian's hands and explained, "Marian, your home was burned down by order of the Sheriff."

"What!?"

Charlton overheard and his nostrils flared and his face reddened but he refused to shed the tears.

Marian beat on Guy's chest. "How could you? Why didn't you tell me? When?"

Guy took the beating of her small fists. What else could he do? Morgaine came to them and placed a hand on each of their backs, holding a space for peace. "A few weeks ago, Marian. It was reported that Robin's men were roosting there."

Marian had spoken with Robin only days ago. He hadn't told her. Marian couldn't allow herself to be angry at Robin too. She focused all her rage on Guy. As she pounded on him, he cautiously, gently, enveloped her. She didn't want his arms but eventually she sagged toward him and, as she felt Morgaine close herself into them, she leaned into her new friend. Charlton just looked on while Gareth and Evelyn watched in silence as their daughter widened a path to peace that these two could enter. Everyone's breathing slowed, Marian's sobs quieted as she resolved herself to her fate. She looked at Morgaine whose eyes, now opening, held her so delicately. Both women breathed together and Guy joined in. Morgaine kissed Marian's cheek and then Guy's arm and brought their hands together in hers.

CHAPTER 8

On the Road to Glastonbury

GUY'S FACE WAS a reflection of the afternoon light through the sun-dappled forest. Morgaine sat sideways on Guy's steed, his arms around her holding the reins as they traversed the road through Sherwood Forest. She leaned into him feeling his warmth. He kissed the top of her head, and caressed her ear with his lips, whispering, "How did you do it? I felt something back there when you had your hands on our backs. What did you do?"

Morgaine turned her head slightly so her lips were closer to his chest and murmured, "I prayed peace into you both. I held a question, 'Do you really want to be this way with each other?' Neither of you want to hurt the other. She was able to let go of her anger against you."

Guy remarked endearingly, "You are a remarkable woman."

Morgaine upturned her head, smiling, "Thank you."

Marian was anxious, peering out of the carriage, her heart hopeful of glimpsing her love, Robin, in the forest. She knew not if she would return to Nottingham again. Evelyn watched the younger woman, curious as to why her eyes were darting back and forth, watching the woods. She didn't appear afraid, more in anticipation of seeing something…or someone. Marian felt eyes upon her and turned to see Evelyn watching her. Marian fidgeted and looked down, knowing there was no way to explain herself.

"Who's that there?" proclaimed Robbie as he was forced to pull the reins and stop the coach.

Guy looked up from Morgaine and realized how dangerously unaware he had been. Two men were blocking the road.

Robbie, more forcefully inquired, "Here now, what is this?"

The men looked nervous as they eyed behind the carriage and noticed Guy on horseback. They hadn't expected Guy to be an escort to a carriage. But they stood their ground. "Pay the toll. Your contributions feed the poor."

As Guy rode up past the carriage, Morgaine deftly pulled out her sword from a hidden sheath in the top corner of the carriage and pointed it at the men. The sword may have been thin and small, like its wielder, but that didn't make it any less of a threat. "How dare you stop us," Morgaine stated angrily.

One man spoke, with less conviction than before, "See here, we don't want any trouble. Just give us your purse and we will let you pass."

Morgaine retorted, "Our purse cares for the people of Glastonbury. Let us pass."

Marian looked out of the coach and caught the glance of one of the men. "What are you doing with the Lady Marian?"

Morgaine looked momentarily perplexed but then responded honestly as she saw a pattern emerging in Marian's watchfulness, "Not that it is any of your business, but we have just set her and her father free and are taking them with us to start a new life in Glastonbury."

The two men looked at each other and realized this was not going to be an easy score. Robin would not be happy, but then it would be more important to live and let Robin know where Marian was going than to fight Guy. They turned and ran.

Guy was about to kick Midnight into a gallop but then realized he had Morgaine sideways on the horse with him. Midnight kicked up and came down but did not bolt forward. Guy shouted after the men, "That's right, run back to your master, Robin of the Hood." He then muttered to himself, "Damn outlaws."

Morgaine just chuckled.

Guy looked at her sharply, "You find this amusing?"

Morgaine ignored his tone. "I find your reputation curious. Did you see them run? You didn't even have to do anything and yet they fear you. And they were completely taken aback by a maiden defending her carriage." Morgaine chortled again, amused with herself.

Guy relented, chuckling slightly. He would give Morgaine that — yes, it was amusing that the pair of them had done so little, yet the two would-be-robbers ran away. He was just annoyed that the outlaws continued to get away. Then his attention turned to the bushes around them. Where were her guardians, as she called them, Guy wondered? He looked around with a predator's eyes. Then his gaze softened and he took in the whole of the woods. Morgaine watched, knowing what he must be doing. There, he saw something, someone. The man had just silently, slowly closed the bow that had been aimed where the-would-be robbers had run. The man turned his head and gave a slight nod to Guy. Guy whispered to Morgaine, "How many?"

Morgaine whispered back, "Five."

"Still, I do not think it would be wise to spend a night on the road."

"Whatever you think is best. You know this area and what problems could arise." Guy sighed at Morgaine's confidence in him. "To be honest, I would not put it past the Sheriff. And he would have more men. He doesn't take well to being outdone. Better to be in a town where it would be too obvious for a troop. He wouldn't want it getting back to the Prince that he had anything to do with a plot against your family. I know a place where the inn is on the outskirts so that your men can watch from the forest while all of you can get some rest."

As the company came into the small town, Guy navigated them to a tavern on the other side. Guy swung off his horse and then helped Morgaine slide down into his arms. She smiled at him and looked completely content in his embrace. "God, I could get used to feeling this good," Guy whispered to himself. Morgaine's smile turned into a bemused secret as Guy looked ahead to the tavern door. The carriage pulled to a stop and Guy motioned to Robbie to have everyone wait.

Guy handed Midnight's reins to the stable boy before he and Morgaine walked hand in hand into the tavern that also served as an inn. They had made decent time, though it was late in the day when they reached the inn he thought would serve well enough. He didn't want to see the family continue their journey into the night if he could help it. Too many ruffians on the road. And then of course, the Sheriff had to be considered. He hadn't liked telling that to Morgaine, but he also didn't want her thinking that a campout so close to the Sheriff's domain was a safe bet, regardless of her odd guardians.

Even with Morgaine on his arm, Guy looked formidable, and only partly because he was so recognizable as Nottingham's Sheriff's right-hand man. The barmaid ran back to get her father and the innkeeper came out to greet Guy. "What can I do for you, Sir Guy?"

Guy momentarily ignored the erroneous title, stating, "I need rooms."

"Yes, we do have rooms available. Just one?"

"No, I need four."

"We have three."

"Alright then, three." Guy reached with his left hand to his purse and laid coins on the bar, "One room for two dignitaries, a room for the daughters, and one for a gentleman. I will sleep in the stable with the carriage and horses."

"Oh Guy, no. There is no need for that," Morgaine pleaded.

Guy shook his head. He was firm, "I will stay in the stable."

Beth, one of the inn's wenches, overheard and stated, "That's right Guy, no need for that. You can stay with me." She smiled, but as she came around to face him she saw his hand in this other woman's hand. "Oh, you got yourself a real lady now. Don't you?"

Guy turned to her exasperated, "Oh Beth, let it be."

Beth eyed Morgaine coolly only to feel dismissed by this greater woman as Morgaine looked at her with a quiet, regal air that commanded the woman back down. Beth shrugged and then sauntered away, like a cat pretending nothing had just happened.

The families settled into their rooms. Morgaine and Marian looked about in their room as Sophie brought in a bag. Morgaine stated, "Two beds." She looked to Meggie, who had followed Sophie in. "Meggie, you and Sophie will take that bed and Marian and I will share this one."

Sophie started, "Oh no, My Lady, you shouldn't…"

"I will not have any of us bruised come morning. We can all make do."
Meggie considered, "What about Robbie?"

"Well, here is where we ladies can fey being more delicate creatures than men," Morgaine mocked as she put the back of her hand dramatically to her head. The women all laughed. "He and Guy can rough it in the stables for one night."

Everyone came back downstairs for supper. It was not an overly rough and tumble place but it also did not see royalty in its midst either. Guy had already grabbed a table and stationed himself with his back against the wall so he could watch the room. He motioned for the company to join him.

Evelyn sized the place up as she sat down at the table, saying, "Guy, it is very kind of you to have us put up for the night after our ordeal."

Guy nodded, still watching the room, then turned to face Evelyn, replying, "I just wish it could be someplace more suitable. But I knew there wasn't anything else for miles and I didn't want you on the road after dark."

Evelyn nodded to him approvingly. Then she caught sight of something, an image superimposed on him: a stag. She blinked and then the ghost image was gone. Guy looked as though he was about to ask her something, but then he caught sight of movement behind her. It was Morgaine coming over to plant herself next to him. Evelyn looked at the two lovers willing herself to see the image again but it had been pushed aside for the moment, lost in new love.

The Avalons, plus Guy, Marian and Charlton and the woman, Meggie, who Guy was beginning to understand was not a mere servant but served the family in some other capacity, all dined together and chatted about non-essentials. Before Guy could pick up his utensil though, Morgaine reached over and swirled her fingers on his hand. Guy could sense the tactile question, "Will you hold my hand?" Guy gingerly switched to eating with his left hand, wondering if anyone would take offense. But no eyebrows went up, so he happily accommodated Morgaine as they held hands and ate.

Charlton, Marian's father, occasionally glanced over at the display of affection between Guy and Morgaine. He was uncomfortable with it; it was unbeseeming a lady of her station and yet her parents gave it no mind. He wondered if the family knew who they were actually dealing with. Hadn't they ever heard of Sir Guy of Gisbourne? Guy had not been known to be a kind fellow. And yet he remembered his daughter considering an alliance with this villain to protect them both. And now, here was the Lady Morgaine, seemingly sweet, attaching herself to Guy as if he were someone of merit. He wasn't sure what to think, though Guy apparently did help them get out of prison and he did pay to put them up at the inn. What was his game? Charlton's eyes narrowed and, though Guy did not seem to notice, Evelyn did.

Guy bid all a goodnight and a safe journey in the morning explaining that he must be on his way at first light back to Nottingham Castle. His eyes lingered on Morgaine and with hers she implored him to stay. They finally broke their hold on each other's hands, Guy kissing the back of her hand with a promising look and then sweeping himself out the door.

Morgaine looked longingly after him. The thought of not being in his arms for some unknown period of time seemed too unbearable. She excused herself, murmuring something about seeing to Merryweather and walked swiftly to the stable.

Robbie watched Morgaine leave, thinking, "Well, I suppose I will just sit here. There is no way I am going out there to possibly interrupt something."

Beth was also watching Morgaine slip out and then she noticed that a man at the bar was watching too. Beth slinked up to the cute, chubby man, saying, "Buy me a drink?"

Robbie replied, "Sure, why not. I am Robbie. For whom am I buying this drink?"

"Beth."

"Hello, Beth." He motioned to the innkeeper who poured a mug of ale for Beth, handing it to her, barely rolling his eyes at her change in focus; but then that was Beth, easy come, easy go, easy come again. The innkeeper then refilled Robbie's mug. "Cheers," offered Robbie, holding his mug up toward Beth. She held up her mug in cheers as well. They both gulped at the brew. Robbie was starting to feel a bit warm and lightheaded. He gave a sidelong glance to the buxom lass, considering to himself, "Well, this could all work out."

Inside the stable, Morgaine peered into the darkness while whispering Guy's name. Guy, his eyes already acclimated to the darkness, could see Morgaine better than she could see him. He slid up behind her, grabbing her in a tight embrace. Her alert lithe body immediately recognized his frame and relaxed into him. His hands roamed her body as his lips kissed her neck. She turned her body to face him, tilting her head up to feel his breath on her face. Their bodies pressed into each other. There was an urgency between them that was almost too painful to bear as they knew they must part for a time. But not now, not in this moment. She wondered to herself what she would allow Guy to do to her. Her body was on fire for this man. She wanted him to touch her, to reach down to her pulsing mound with his fingers and slip inside between her nether lips and feel how wet he made her. She felt as if her whole body was a heart beating in anticipation of his touch.

Their lips found each other. This wasn't the soft, tentative kiss of new lovers cautiously exploring the boundaries; this was hunger feeding on itself. He pulled her in tighter as his lips tasted hers, sucking and pulling on her bottom lip. It made her shiver in delight! Oh, to surrender to her lust, to allow herself to be captivated by his caress. "Oh, please touch me, touch me there," she beckoned silently.

As if Guy heard her call and her permission, he propped Morgaine up against the railing, her feet finding their footing on the bottom rail. His right hand reached up to cup her breast while his left hand reached down, gathering her gown so his hand could slip in underneath it. He felt her skin, the hairs on her legs; everything about her felt alluring. He caressed upward and felt her thighs open slightly to receive him. "My Lady of the Lake, I intend to take a dip," he murmured in a muffled chuckle as he buried his face against her stomach. Morgaine moaned. He petted her nether lips, then strummed them like an instrument.

"Oh my," was all Morgaine could utter breathily. Oh, this felt exquisite. Her body was humming. She moaned again.

Guy gently opened her two-leaved gate and began to swirl his finger just inside her dark rose, caressing her moist velvety petals. He found her hooded jewel and swirled his finger around it, then stroked it. She shuddered. He smiled to himself. He played with her, enjoying this power to give her pleasure. "She is so wet," he thought to himself as he slowly pulsed his forefinger inside her. He imagined unlacing his breeches and sliding her glistening rose onto his cock. He willed himself to slow down. He couldn't do that with her, not yet. But soon.

Her scent was intoxicating to him. He propped her up higher on the railing and lifted up her gown further, burying his head into her earthy rose, tasting her sweet and salty nectar.

Kissing, licking, sucking, probing — the sensations were so intense for Morgaine. She'd never felt anything like it. "Oh...please...yes," she whispered, her voice trembling and heaving in ecstasy. She could feel Guy's mouth smile as he continued devouring the petals of her dark rose. "Oh...oh...my," Morgaine exclaimed as the sensations grew more penetrating. Her body began to shudder uncontrollably. She felt herself explode as if she were the ocean spray reaching for the heavens, again and again.

Guy nuzzled his nose against Morgaine's mound after he felt her come. It thrilled him to hear her fast breathy exclamations of "Oh" as he had pleasured her. Now, as her body slumped into him, utterly spent, he withdrew slowly. He gently helped her down off the wooden planks of the horse stall. He chuckled softly as she continued to lean into him, her legs obviously unsteady from the strain of keeping herself propped up while he dined on her. She looked up at him, her eyes glimmering, as if drunk on her own ecstasy. He took his left hand and brought it to her face so that she could smell her own scent. He whispered a command, "Taste."

Morgaine kissed his hand. She took in her own scent. It was earthy and smoky, salty and reminiscent of ripe apples.

"Taste," Guy softly commanded again, his eyes sparkling in excitement. He stroked his middle finger against her lips. She opened her mouth and tasted his finger with her tongue. He lightly moved his finger in and out her mouth. She closed her mouth around his finger and sucked.

As she sucked his finger, pulling it in and out her mouth, she watched Guy's face. His expression told volumes of the euphoric sensation he was now experiencing.

Guy's breathing was quick and shallow. He then exhaled forcefully and gently removed his finger from her mouth, then pressed it against her lips. He brought his hand to his face and breathed in her scent. They were both intoxicated by their passion. He looked at her purposefully and sucked on his middle finger, tasting her.

She shivered in delight, remembering his tongue swirling her hooded jewel. "You can do that to me forever," Morgaine whispered breathily.

He chuckled softly again and pulled her into an embrace. Morgaine felt his impassioned cock against her. She longed to give him such pleasure and release as he had given her. Though Guy could not hear Morgaine's thoughts, he somehow sensed her longing and inner conflict. He was reassuring, "Soon, my love, soon."

She nodded into his chest.

He brought his hand up under her chin so that she would look into his eyes. As she did, he smiled warmly at her, whispering, "My love, I wanted to give you such a sensation that you would not forget. And as much as I would love to bed you right here and now I will honor your maidenhood."

Morgaine sighed contently and again leaned into him.

Guy felt Morgaine's body relax into him and he realized what he said was exactly what she needed to hear. It excited him to know he could find the right words to say and give her ease, that somehow he had the ability to make her happy.

Morgaine quietly mounted the stairs and crept into the room she shared with Marian, Meggie and Sophie. She pulled off her green gown and the light long-sleeved cream-colored dress with silver embroidered cuffs that accented the long, sweeping sleeves of the gown and carefully lay down next to Marian in her white shift.

Marian stirred and turned toward Morgaine. "Happy?" Marian asked sleepily.

"Yes, very much," Morgaine practically giggled.

"You love him," Marian said, trying to keep the surprise out of her voice. She was still shifting through her feelings of how the Guy she knew could be loveable. Still, she recognized he wasn't all bad. She had even considered accepting his marriage proposal while Robin was away. But it wasn't out of a feeling of romantic love; it came from feeling the pressure of her father wanting her to marry a man of lands and title, to be under another man's protection. But she couldn't do it. She had longed for Robin and prayed every day for his return. But now that he was home, they still were not husband and wife. It was maddening.

Morgaine interrupted Marian's thoughts with a giggle, "Yes, very much so."

"Then I am happy for you," Marian whispered sincerely.

"Thank you."

The women snuggled together for warmth. Despite neither being used to sharing a bed, both felt a sense of comfort and security by the other's soft breathing and warm body.

Meanwhile, Guy was settling into the Avalons' carriage, doing his best to make himself comfortable. He had finally found a slightly comfortable position when he heard the stable door creak. Guy silently drew his sword and when the carriage door opened, poor Robbie was met with a sword pointed at his nose.

"Hey, no need for that," Robbie snapped, his words only slightly slurred from the ale he had been drinking as he passed the time at the bar with Beth.

Guy shook his head and dropped the point, apologizing good naturedly, "I am sorry, Robbie. I forgot that we'd be sharing the stable."

Robbie, now feeling a bit more alert than a moment before, cleared his head, and shook off the shock of being met with a sword in his own carriage. Still, Guy was a knight and a lord, and he a servant, so he realized he must apologize, "No, Sir, it is my fault. I am sorry to disturb you."

Guy chuckled softly, replying, "Well now that we are both over the disturbance, let's get some sleep."

"I will sleep upstairs in the hay, Sir, if you want to stay here to protect the carriage," Robbie said as he closed the carriage door.

"Good enough," replied a very tired Guy. He yawned and tried to settle back into the position that offered some semblance of comfort. As he drifted off to sleep, he wished he was beside Morgaine, feeling her body next to his. He hoped she was sleeping soundly in her bed in the inn. Still, he wished it was he that was sharing the bed with her instead of Marian.

"Damn," was the first thought that popped into Guy's head as he jolted himself awake. It was pitch dark but he could sense that someone close by was up to no good. And in these parts, he was supposed to be the one up to no good as the labeled villain, meting out hard times on behalf of the Sheriff. And as he had not authorized anything, nothing should be happening. "God, all I want is to sleep." Guy sighed exhaustedly. Silently he got up and crept out of the carriage. He slinked toward the barn door. As he passed Midnight, he put his forefinger to his mouth. He hoped his trusty steed saw the motion. Quietly he opened the door, slid out, and closed it behind him. He scanned the inn but saw no movement. He turned around slowly, watching and listening. There was a quiet scuffle in the brush ahead of him. Guy drew his sword. Behind the brush there was a standoff: three of the Guardians against six of Guy's own men, the Sheriff's men. Guy walked into the mix with an arrogant air as he sheathed his sword, "Ah, gentlemen, what seems to be the trouble?"

Sir Grigor, though completely shocked at seeing Guy, did his best to maintain his composure, responding, "No trouble, Lord Guy. Just taking care of some bandits."

"A bit far out for patrol though, eh," responded Guy, who then added with more than a hint of annoyance in his voice, "and a bit late."

Grigor fumbled for a response, failed, and merely shrugged. Guy was not supposed to be here. He was supposed to be home. The Sheriff was specific in stating that Guy wasn't to know of this plot, and he didn't know or care why.

Guy eyed his men menacingly, "Do you realize who these men are that you are facing off?"

His men shook their heads.

"These are the Duke's private guard. They are purposefully concealed so that you don't know how many are out there. And there are more, believe me. I found that out this afternoon when Robin's men attempted to rob the carriage."

The men looked from one to another. This was unexpected.

Guy demanded, "What is your business out here on the road so late?"

The men shuffled their feet. No one wanted to go up against Guy... except Grigor; he was the competitive sort. "We were told to find a carriage and kill the inhabitants, enemies of the Prince."

Guy tried to remain calm as he seethed inside, "Why?"

Grigor shook his head, "Didn't say. Didn't ask."

Guy was gruff, "Well I haven't seen any other carriages except that belonging to His Grace, the Duke of Glastonbury, whose carriage I was escorting. And you men certainly would not be looking for the Duke's carriage."

They eyed one another. They hadn't been told who; they were just told it was an unarmed carriage heading south.

Guy continued, "Well, I cannot allow you to follow through on your instructions. The only southbound carriage you are following bears royalty. It would be treason. It is my duty to look out for you and for them." He waited while the men pondered this, taking in the idea that Guy was looking out for them too. Guy then demanded, "I want you all to turn around and go home. When you stand before the Sheriff, you can say with honesty that you did not find the carriage. And all you met was me returning, who gave you the order to return to your posts."

Grigor exclaimed, "We can't lie to the Sheriff! He'll have our heads!"

Guy scowled, his voice threatening, "If you say what I told you to say, you are not lying. Do you see a carriage?"

More shaking of heads. At that, two more Guardians came out of the forest with bows raised and arrows at the ready.

Guy continued, "The Duke of Glastonbury is an ally of the Prince. And we all want to stay friends with His Majesty, the Prince, do we not?"

His men this time nodded.

"Go home. I will be behind you shortly," commanded Guy.

His men bowed and retreated into the dark.

Guy made sure they heard him apologize to those they were told were the Duke's guards. "My sincerest apologies for my men. They knew not what they were doing."

Rainer played the role, sounding angry and sarcastic, "Oh, I am sure they did."

Guy was earnest, "We wish no quarrel with the Duke or the Prince. I am sure it was a misunderstanding."

As the Sheriff's men withdrew, three of the Guardians backed away down the road until they were enshrouded in darkness. Then they quickly and silently headed toward the inn to check on their charges. Rainer looked Guy up and down. There was an odd veil masking Guy's being. Still, the Lady trusted him, so he would too. As Guy's men drew out of earshot, Rainer whispered, "We could have handled that."

Guy pursed his lips then exhaled, also speaking quietly, "I am sure you could have. I just didn't want any dead...on either side...that could lead to more... complications."

The Guardian in the strange garb nodded, then questioned, "How did you know?"

"Which? That something was amiss or what to say to diffuse the situation?"

"Both."

"I am a light sleeper. I knew my men would be surprised that I sided with you so I reminded them that a duke trumps a sheriff." Guy shrugged then, thinking to himself, "Weakness. Strength. I find what I can use to my favor."

Rainer nodded, hearing the silent thought.

Guy turned to who he figured was the lead Guardian, which was Rainer, "The family should be safe from the Sheriff's men...for now. But this isn't over." Guy looked glum. Why couldn't falling in love be easier? Why did he have to deal with a master who wanted his sweetheart dead? It wasn't fair. Maybe he was just tired.

Rainer patted Guy on the shoulder. "Try to get some sleep."

Guy nodded, "Thanks." Guy returned to the stables.

Neither the Guardians nor Guy got much sleep before morning.

Though Guy had said he was a light sleeper and currently that was true, it was not always that way. As he settled back into the carriage hoping he could fall asleep again, he wondered restlessly when he ever had gotten a full night's rest. He might have thought he hadn't been a deep sleeper since watching his mother die. But after that pain had subsided, there were times when he had slept soundly through the night. No. What might have been the true marker for his habit of light sleeping was the night his comrades abruptly woke and dragged him before judgment to ultimately initiate him into the Order of the Black Knights. Since then, some part of his brain commanded itself to stay on guard, warning him of potential threats.

The Sheriff's men walked the road to their horses who were tethered a short distance away at a quickly made camp in the woods. They had figured to set up camp and scout the area in the dark, assuming the carriage would be either camped in the woods or in the town. They had not expected Guy to come from the town but perhaps he had watched the carriage off and it was too late to head home. There was the inn.

"A pretty set of tits is at the inn. That's where 'e is," said one of Guy's ruffians.

They muttered amongst themselves.

"If the guards came from the woods, the carriage would probably be there," stated another.

"But you heard Lord Guy," replied a third.

"The Sheriff is not going to be happy," commented the second.

"The Sheriff is never happy," retorted the first, adding, "Guy said there is no carriage. Let it fall on him."

"You mean the carriage or the blame?" asked the second.

"Both," sneered the first.

The group's laughter was fiendish and Rainer's stomach churned as he listened in from the darkness of the woods.

Meanwhile, as the men went back and forth and finally agreed to say they found no carriage, only Guy, Grigor was furiously thinking how to manage the situation. He didn't actually know he had been sent to kill a duke, only an enemy of the Sheriff. And that he was searching for a carriage without guards and to kill all the inhabitants. Where did his loyalties lie? With the Sheriff? With Guy? With the Prince? At the moment, he was second in command to Guy. But that could change. He could circle around. No. Those oddly dressed guards were alert and would be ready for him. No. Better to say that they found no carriage. Or...what would happen if... Grigor's mind continued to grind as he worked through what would ultimately put him on top.

It was early morning when Guy reined up and swung onto Midnight. He took a last look at the upper windows of the tavern knowing that Morgaine slept above him. Then he heard her voice, "Wait!" His eyes scanned the windows but he saw no sign of her. Yet he waited. Meanwhile inside, Morgaine awoke with a jolt, feeling her lover leaving. She threw off the bed covers, apologized to Marian, and scooted down the stairs and around the corner to the tavern door. She opened it and saw Guy waiting for her on his horse. "One last kiss goodbye," she smiled and opened her arms to him.

He reached down and scooped her up into an embrace. "You are in your shift, Love."

"I…sensed you leaving and I wanted to see you one last time before you left."

Guy smiled triumphantly; he'd never felt so desired. The mirth in his eyes turned serious as he said, "I need to get back to the castle. I don't want to be missed by the Sheriff especially with all that has transpired. But I am so glad you came out to me." Morgaine touched his cheek with her palm and he turned his head to kiss it. His voice was suddenly grave, "Morgaine, the Sheriff's men were here last night. They didn't expect your Guardians or me. I sent them home. But this won't be the end of it. The Sheriff is a schemer. He'll try again."

Morgaine nodded. "I'll let my parents know. I am grateful you were here looking out for us."

He smiled. He felt appreciated. When was the last time he ever heard gratitude spoken for him? She reveled in his sweet smile and offered her own in return. All thoughts but this moment dropped away as he thought to himself, "She came out here to see me. To kiss me. She really does adore me." Guy realized he'd longed for this woman his whole life. He'd never been anyone's priority and here Morgaine was, in her shift, completely unconcerned with her appearance or behavior, all to have one last kiss from him before parting.

Morgaine kissed his neck and then looked into Guy's eyes lovingly, "I do not want some torrid affair. I want us to love openly, honestly and without shame." Guy breathed in the pleasure he was feeling from her uncompromising love. As she held his gaze, she added, "Though I do not profess to know all the choices you must make or understand all the deeds you do, know that I love you and that I trust you to do what you must to protect me."

Guy responded, his voice quivering, "Oh Morgaine, know that it means the world to hear you say that. I love you. My beautiful, sweet lady, I love you."

The lovers clung to each other. Then sensing he really did need to get back, Morgaine whispered, "I will yearn for your touch. Come to me soon."

Guy breathed into Morgaine's ear, "I will as soon as I can." He ardently kissed her again before releasing her gently to the ground and riding off.

CHAPTER 9

Contemplating Consequences

WITH SO LITTLE sleep Guy found the day overlong and it was just getting going. Guy arrived at Nottingham Castle in good time and the Sheriff made little complaint. He did inquire, "Any troubles seeing them off?"

Guy simply shook his head. He was not sure what the Sheriff's men may have said or if they had gotten a chance to speak to him first. He figured it best to say as little as possible until he knew more. And, he was not sure how long he could conceal his seething rage. As William droned on about something, Guy imagined pulling out his sword and skewering William with it. Stick it in his belly right up to the hilt. That would teach him. There was a look of evil satisfaction on his face and as William turned back around he caught Guy's expression.

"You approve?" William questioned mockingly.

Guy merely gave a slight nod having no idea what William had just said.

For his part Grigor made himself scarce as he continued his attempts to figure out how to handle the situation so that he came out on top, or at least not on the bottom...or on the rack. He shivered involuntarily. He knew the Sheriff would rage at him for not carrying out his plan; but then Guy had his means of retribution as well. The men had all agreed they had not seen a carriage that night; that they had met up with Lord Guy who ordered them back, and that they could not refuse his order, as their commanding officer. At least this way, it would be Guy to take the fall — which was fine with them.

It was the end of the day and Guy had left for his manor when Grigor approached the Sheriff.

"Where have you been all day?" The Sheriff was in a foul mood. Then, when wasn't he? He looked at Grigor expectedly, "Well, is it done?"

Grigor braced himself. "No, Sire."

"No, Sire?! Well what the hell are you doing here then?"

"Ordered back, Sire…by Lord Guy."

"Lord Guy? What the hell was he doing out there?"

Grigor wasn't sure why either and so, because he didn't want to surmise, he ignored that question while he explained himself. "Sheriff, we met up with some trouble. There were some strange looking guards who came out of the forest. Lord Guy diffused the situation."

William interrupted, "Guy diffused a situation?"

Grigor nodded. "He told us there was no carriage heading south except the one he had escorted and that the men we were having a standoff with were the Duke of Glastonbury's guards."

"The Duke's?"

"The one you had locked up, right?"

William's eyes narrowed in annoyed contemplation as he thought to himself, "So the Avalons did have guards. But I didn't see them. Where were they? Why would Gareth keep guards a secret? And why did Guy know and not tell me? What was Guy doing going that far south with them? That skyrta!"

Grigor stayed silent as he waited for new instructions.

William then remembered that Grigor was still waiting on him. He was non-committal, "No other carriage, eh?"

Grigor shook his head. He was wondering to himself, "If the Sheriff actually meant that carriage, then he is wondering if I am loyal to him?" To the Sheriff he inquired, "What would you have me do, Sire?"

William looked at the man. Grigor had come with him from Derby. He tended to trust the man. "Nothing more for the moment. You are dismissed."

Grigor bowed and left.

William sat down at his table, drumming his fingers, trying to keep his composure. He was disappointed in Guy. Very disappointed. He turned his thoughts to Grigor. Why hadn't he been more explicit with him? What more would he have had to say, "…and if you see Guy with them ignore him and run the family through?" Of course the Duke's guards were the added complication. That cagy bastard. Of course a duke would have protection. He wondered if the guards had been in the castle the whole time. Morgaine! That bitch! She said she had a rider. She had a guard disguised somewhere in the castle. And that guard would know if she was taken away and his orders would then be to ride to the Prince. That meant there were more people who now knew of his plot. Damn! William continued to drum his fingers on the table. He would have to bide his time. He'd have to wait for an opening. Then he'd kill them. Kill them all. Even Guy. His traitorous Guy.

When Guy finally arrived home, he found Mary in the kitchen.

She looked up, "Supper is ready, M'Lord. How are the Lady and her family?"

Guy never noticed Mary being interested in much of anything that had to do with his life. Then of course, he had hardly noticed Mary before. He replied, "The Lady and her family are safe as can be and continuing on the road to Glastonbury. They took the Lady Marian and her father Sir Charlton with them."

"Ah good," Mary smiled as she spooned out a bowl of stew. She ushered Guy into the dining area and after he was seated she served him the stew. She then handed the bowl in her other hand to her son, Dylan, who was sitting by the fire whittling what looked like a block of wood.

He smiled up at her, "Thank you, Mother."

She put her hand on his shoulder peering at his work.

He held up a wooden apple. "I was craving apples today. Couldn't get the smell or taste off my mind."

"So you carved yourself one," said Mary mirthfully.

Dylan nodded. "I know it was nothing practical but I just couldn't seem to stop myself."

Mary and Dylan both chuckled.

Guy looked over at them and then at the apple. Guy resumed eating, inquiring in a jovial spirit to Dylan between mouthfuls, "So Dylan, what brings you whittling into my home?"

Dylan, hearing Guy's friendly tone, looked at Guy with a knowing smile and stated, "Well, Lord Guy, as it appears you have no steward, I thought I would offer my services to you. What do you say, Sir, could you use another hand here at the manor?"

Guy looked perplexed as he had had the distinct impression that Dylan did not trust him and he wondered what Dylan was up to and said as much. "Change of heart, Dylan?"

"M'Lord, if you are the Lady of the Lake's consort and she trusts you, I will do my best to trust you too."

Guy was admittedly a bit offended by this young man's boldness, while at the same time refreshed by his honesty. And he could tell that both Mary and Dylan were earnest. It had been so long since he felt trusted by anyone here and so it was difficult to come to terms with this new tenuous amity, but he acted in good faith, rose, and put out his hand to the young man.

Dylan took it gratefully, "At your service, M'Lord."

Mary made up the bed in the servant's room that Brin only recently vacated, being dead and all. Now that it was settled that Dylan would serve as Guy's new steward, she grew concerned for her son. She had mixed feelings about the new arrangement but felt that this was one way that her family could serve the Lady.

As his mother fluffed up the pillow, Dylan walked in, whispering, "That worked well."

"Just be careful, you. We do the work for the Lady but I don't want the Lord of the Manor dragging you into any of the Sheriff's schemes."

"I am more concerned about the Sheriff. Brin was here most of the time and wasn't out with Lord Guy on the Sheriff's errands. It had to have been the Sheriff who got to Brin and made him do his bidding."

Mary and Dylan had talked about this earlier in the day, and they both knew that the Sheriff might approach Dylan. Of course, if the Sheriff found out that Guy had killed Brin having found out that Brin was working for the Sheriff, the Sheriff might not approach Dylan and might instead attempt to keep an eye on Guy through someone else. The two felt nervous, hoping they made the right decision and that by staying close to Guy they could help him remember his love and how she treated others, and that she would want him to treat others with kindness as well. And with that, they both knelt, Dylan placing his carved wooden apple on the table next to the candle his mother had placed in the room for light, and prayed to the Lady of the Lake.

In another inn much further south, Morgaine was reading by firelight. She looked up, feeling prayers directed toward her. She smiled as she felt Mary and Dylan's prayers wafting around her. She closed her eyes and could see them in a room with a candle and a wooden apple. She smiled secretly, having the perfect gift in mind for her new worshippers as the Lady Incarnate. Evelyn, in another room, also felt the prayer. Her heart warmed as she considered that even two brought back to the Goddess meant the world.

CHAPTER 10

Enchantment

THE GUARDIAN DOES his Lady's bidding, gathering apples for the villagers of another land. He does not question his Lady for he knows that those who are supposed to will return to Avalon and those who are not, will simply enjoy the kindness of a stranger.

His name is Rainer and he has been in the service of the Lady of the Lake for three generations, though he was just a boy when the first Lady he served died. He worked with The Merlin and learned his ways. Being a curious fellow he often read The Merlin Manuscripts when he thought The Merlin wasn't looking. But Rainer, a quiet yet playful fellow, was not cut out for court life. He preferred the forest. And so while he appeared often in the presence of The Merlin when The Merlin was out and about, no one paid Rainer mind that he might just be the next one. So without care or worry or the hassle of living up to a title, Rainer shadowed The Merlin, copying his spells and potions in the secrecy of the dark forest.

As Rainer works, the hood of his gray-green cloak falls back exposing a white-blond head of hair. The hair is long and pulled back with a strap of leather wound around several times and secured with a knot. The man's eyes are light blue like the color of a sunny sky and the lines around his eyes speak of mirth and merriment. Rainer is generally a content and happy man. He moves through life like an imp, casting magic by the fireside to embellish his stories.

As Rainer gathers the apples in the Apple Orchard for his trip, he allows himself to fall into trance; he sees the face of a black horse. He recognizes this horse. He senses this horse grew up here. He compels himself deeper into the vision picking up the strand as if it is a ball of thread he was winding. The horse leads him to another face, the face of a human, and this human, too, looks familiar. But he is not the same as the one bearing this face he met so many years ago; this face is human, or at least partially so. This human connected to this horse needs to come here, that much feels true. He winds the thread more and the human in his vision shifts until he is a stag.

Rainer awakens abruptly. The stag, the Stag King is coming home! And it's Guy! How did he not see it? Why did none of them see it? They were all in his presence. It was as if Guy were cloaked somehow, even to himself. But why?

Rainer reaches into a small bag at his side and draws out a bunch of little bones. He casts them upon the ground and looks at them inquisitively. The bones tell him nothing. They read shadows. But then that is something. Shadows. More than one. He picks up the bones again and casts them again. As he reads them, the thought forms — an order of shadows. Some kind of secret group. That would mean this would be a very old cloaking spell that not even Rainer could decipher. Only the original Merlin would know how this was done or undone. Either way, he must help Guy get home to fulfill his destiny; that much feels true. A cunning man after all is he, Rainer picks up one of the apples and sets an enchantment into it to be sure that the one who eats it has the ability to see Avalon's Apple Orchard and appear in it. Chanting over the apple as he swirls it in circles, mimicking a gentle whirlwind that gives no heed to time or space, Rainer casts his spell —

> *"Eat and remember sunny days in the Apple Orchard*
> *your back warmed by the sun*
> *the smell and taste of sweetness in your nostrils and mouth.*
> *There is nowhere else to be but here in Avalon.*
> *See Avalon's Orchard before your eyes and come.*
> *Step out of the mist and arrive safe and sound in the Isle of Apples."*

"This one is for you, Horse," smiles Rainer mischievously as he holds up the apple in the air. He knows not if Guy was ever here in Avalon, but he knows well that the horse from his vision was. "This will get you both here."

CHAPTER 11

Eating Apples

SEVERAL DAYS LATER, Rainer of the Lake, an emissary of the Lady of the Lake, having ridden northeast, reached the borders of Nottingham. He had been cloaked and avoiding the roads. As he rode through Sherwood Forest he felt eyes upon him. Though cautious, he was confident that no harm would befall him. Even as two men dropped from the trees, he smiled.

To the men, this stranger appeared eerie. They had quietly debated about dropping down but they convinced themselves that he was just a man, a man riding with a significant bag strapped to his steed. Now, down on the ground, in front of the man, they looked less sure, for the man atop the horse wore a face mask that made him appear stag-like. He wore gray and green, not so dissimilar from the-would-be robbers. But this man carried himself like a priest or royalty and was not in the least dissuaded from his direction though he was forced to stop with arrows pointed at him.

One of the men called out, "Who the hell are you?"

The man on the horse bowed in slight mockery, "No one from Hell. I am an emissary of the Lady of the Lake and I come bearing a gift to the servants of the Lord of Locksley."

The men were shocked on two levels: first, that the stranger stated his business so plainly and, second, that he was carrying a gift to servants, to Gisbourne's servants at that. The one on the right said, "Well, then that would be to the true lord, Lord Robin of Locksley."

The emissary shook his head, "No. This lord's name is Guy; Guy of Gisbourne, Lord of Locksley."

The forest man on the left responded, "You can't just ride up to Locksley Manor looking like that and bearing gifts to an enemy of the people!"

The emissary scoffed, "Lord Guy is not my enemy, nor that of the people I serve, so I can and I will ride…now."

The two men on the ground, one dark blond, the other a redhead, both of thin build, looked at each other and then raised their bows. But before they could let their arrows fly, the man on the horse vanished in a poof of smoke. They heard laughter and the sound of hooves beating past them. As the smoke cleared, they found two apples on the ground at their feet. Both shrugged, picked up the apples, sniffed them, shrugged again, and began eating.

As he finished chewing a most crisp and delicious apple, Much looked at Will Scarlet, aptly named for his dark red hair and ruddy completion, and said, "There is no way this is going to make sense when we tell Robin."

Rainer rode up to Locksley Village. It was an early Sunday afternoon and many of the villagers were home from church. People stopped what they were doing, staring. He and Morgaine had agreed there was no reason to be subtle on this mission and that, in fact, by being completely out in the open as to the purpose of the mission, it could potentially help their cause. And now that Rainer knew it was Morgaine's love that he would be calling out, he knew with absolute certainty that seeing him would confirm the truth of his vision. Rainer called out in a commanding yet soothing voice, "I am Rainer of the Lake and I am seeking Mary and Dylan, servants in the House of Gisbourne and Guy of Gisbourne, Lord of Locksley, who sheltered the Lady of the Lake in her time of need."

Guy, also home from his dutiful church attendance affair, heard a voice calling his name from outside. Mary and Dylan were working in the kitchen, and also heard Rainer's call. All three walked out the door to see a majestic gray-green clad man wearing a strange headdress addressing them. Rainer was glad he had his mask on to hide his delight at seeing Guy again; best to appear mysterious and impartial for the moment. He hardly had paid attention to the rook-haired, handsome man carrying Morgaine on his black steed on the road back to Glastonbury. So focused was Rainer on being watchful and protecting the family, he simply discounted the man as Morgaine appeared to feel completely at ease with him so obviously not a threat. Now he could take the time to look over Guy more thoroughly. He appreciated what he saw — a strong, confident, muscular man, hardened, but you could see in the mouth that he liked to smile. And those eyes, those bright blue Faie eyes, again with the smile lines creasing away from the corners of his eyes. Those were Merrek's eyes, the Faie he met so long ago when he was just a lad. How did he miss all this when he first saw Guy in the forest? He still couldn't believe this man had been so masked from him, why he hadn't seen Merrek in him immediately.

Rainer held up his hand and beckoned them forward. He spoke again, maintaining a loud voice so that all within earshot could continue to hear, "Lord Guy, Mary and Dylan, for your services and your prayers, the Lady of the Lake bestows this gift upon you." Rainer motioned behind him to the large bag, then to Dylan to retrieve it.

Dylan approached and bowed to the man on the horse, asking, "Who are you?"

"I am Rainer, one of the Lady of the Lake's Guardians and I am here on behalf of the Lady to thank you."

Dylan unstrapped the bag and hefted it to the ground. He opened it up and looked in. A broad smile crossed his face and he looked up to his mother, "Apples!"

Mary clapped her hands in delight and then curtsied to Rainer.

Guy just stood there smiling and shaking his head, looking around at his villagers. Morgaine played this one well, he thought. Mary held up two apples, her eyes asking Guy for permission. Guy nodded and Mary called to the villagers to come and get apples. Some approached immediately while others were more wary. This was just too strange.

Mary mouthed to Rainer, "Will there be enough?"

Rainer smiled and nodded.

Guy spoke out loudly to Rainer in his most magnanimous tone, "Please tell your Lady of the Lake that her gifts are well received here at the Manor and Locksley Village."

There were several heads nodding of the townsfolk gathered to receive the apples. None understood this odd fellow's generosity nor that of their new Lord of Locksley, but in this moment they did not care. If Lord Guy and this stranger wanted to be generous, so be it.

Rainer nodded approvingly.

Guy then came up to Rainer. Rainer bent down in the saddle to hear Guy whisper, "And please tell my Lady and my love, that I will personally come to thank her as soon as I can get away."

A faint smile crossed the masked man's lips as he whispered back, "I shall be sure to tell her, My Lord, for I know it will bring her much joy." There was a pause, then, "And Lord Guy — here, for your trusty steed." Rainer reached into the side of his overcoat, pulled out an apple, and handed it to Guy.

Guy held it up in gratitude. "Thank you. I know that Midnight will appreciate it. I think he loves apples as much, if not more, than I do."

"Ah, yes, Midnight; that is his name, of course," thought Rainer. "See that he eats it," was all that Rainer replied.

Guy nodded, thinking that last statement a bit odd, as if he were going to administer some tonic or remedy, but decided to ignore it and focus on the act of kindness. In showing kindness in return Guy inquired, "So, Rainer, is it?"

Rainer nodded.

"I would be honored to put you up for the evening, if you would like to rest yourself by the fire."

Rainer nodded and smiled. "I thank you for the invitation but I must get back. I will see you soon though."

Guy nodded then added, "Well, you are very welcome to gather food and water for your return."

Mary listened in to their conversation, pleased by Guy's generosity. "Yes, the Lady does him good," she assessed silently.

Much and Will, Robin Hood's men, ran through the forest toward Locksley Village. When they got there, panting and heaving, they saw quite a sight. There was the strange emissary, talking to Mary and Dylan, thanking them for their services to his Lady. Their eyes just about popped when they noticed Guy standing back and approving the distribution of the apples.

Much whistled softly, "Robin is not going to believe this!"

Will looked on in disbelief, "Guy has always confiscated food for the castle soldiers. What is he up to?"

Much was thoughtful. "Love?"

Will wrinkled his nose and said with some distain, "Guy? No."

Much nodded, his voice full of longing for love he had never known, "I think love. Robin said he was courting the daughter of a duke. Allen a Dale and Arthur stopped the family in the woods and Guy was there protecting them. She must be this Lady of the Lake." He paused, as if in a daydream, then with sudden alertness, Much added, "Hey, wasn't there a tale about the Lady of the Lake? Wasn't she in the legend of King Arthur?"

Will thought back on the story. Morgaine was King Arthur's half-sister and a sorceress. And the Lady of the Lake was some other relative to the two of them. An aunt? A grandmother? But she was also a magical being who rose out of the Lake of Avalon to give Arthur the sword Excalibur to defeat his enemies. He shook his head. None of this made sense. Unless...the lake in Glastonbury was also the lake that led to Avalon, the Isle of Apples. But that place was a myth. There was no island on that lake in Glastonbury.

Much waited for Will to complete his silent ponderings as he awaited an answer.

But instead, Will turned from the myth to the point at hand, "Much, Guy would get into serious trouble if the Sheriff heard of this."

Much laughed wickedly, "So we should tell him?"

Will jerked his head back in surprise, "Are you insane? All that would accomplish would be more suffering for the villagers. They are the ones that the Sheriff would punish — after he thrashed Guy within inches of his life." Will thought that would be poetic justice somehow but then shook his head realizing that, as much as he wanted Guy dead, letting the Sheriff hear of this would only make Mary and Dylan suspect to treason and they were good people who always helped their neighbors. They didn't deserve the gallows for helping this lady or accepting her gift. The villagers looked so happy biting into these apples. And the apple had been tasty. Will became disturbed as he realized the apple that the stranger had dropped at his feet shouldn't have been able to be dropped. It was too early for apples. Seasons too early for apples. How did the Lady come by apples in April? Most peculiar. Perhaps the Lady had a really secure storehouse that kept apples well. But why give so many away? Were not her own people hungry for apples as well? Why share with strangers? Will continued to be lost in thought as he and Much left the scene and snuck back to their encampment.

As the small crowd dispersed, Guy accepted an apple from Mary and bit into it. It was sweet and tart, crunchy and perfect, and he could not help but be swept into a state of euphoria between the perfume and taste of the apple. He thought about Morgaine as he licked the juice dripping down his hand: how sweet her smell and the taste of her lips. He was only vaguely aware of a few of the villagers whispering amongst one another wondering why an unknown lady was sending apples to this village.

One woman, Caron, a sweet-natured lass, approached Mary and whispered, "Why were you thanked? What did you do?"

Mary was not sure how to respond. It was a surprise that Brin had been spying on Guy. Were there others? Would the Sheriff be told of this happy occurrence and the Lady's generosity and of Guy allowing the distribution of this gift?

As Mary looked to Guy for guidance he became aware of her watching him. "Sorry, what?"

Mary repeated, "What do we say for why the Lady of the Lake gave us these apples?"

Guy recognized the deeper question. He was also now wondering if there were spies of the Sheriff who would get them all into trouble. He scanned the village. There was no way to be sure. He would have to take responsibility for this. He looked directly at Caron with a bit of sadness and hope that she would still well represent him, stating, "The Lady who gave us these apples is the daughter of the Duke and Duchess of Glastonbury. She came to us seeking shelter when her parents and the Sheriff had a... misunderstanding. I...could not turn her away."

Caron nodded with a perplexed expression on her face.

Guy could think of nothing more to say so he turned and walked away.

Caron and Mary both watched him, each in her own thoughts. Mary put a hand on Caron's shoulder, started to say something but stopped and shook her head. Best not to explain further, even to this particular woman whom she knew had once had feelings for Guy.

As Caron watched Guy walk away, she turned to the fascinating man who was filling his water bladders at the town well. She came up to him and stood at his side, waiting until he noticed her.

"Yes, my child?"

Though he sounded like a priest, he did not look like any priest she ever knew of. And he still wore his odd mask that made him look like a stag. Though she had thought she would start with another question, the one that came out was, "Why are you wearing a mask?"

Rainer turned and looked into her eyes with compassion and intensity. She saw the smile on his lips. It was kind yet full of merriment and mischief. He laughed. "Does it not lend itself to a sense of magic and mystery?"

Caron replied, "Well, yes. It just seems a bit out of place."

"And so it is. But then so am I. I am a forest dwelling creature after all."

Caron wasn't sure how to reply to that so she instead asked the initial question that was on her mind, "You came all this way to give us apples?"

"Yes."

"Why?"

"Because it was very important to My Lady of the Lake that she honor your kindness."

"My kindness? But I didn't do anything. I didn't even know she was here."

"If you had, would you have protected her as the Lord Guy did or would you have alerted the Sheriff?"

Caron first cocked her head in contemplation. Guy had protected someone from the Sheriff. Curious. Caron then shook her head. She said very quietly and cautiously, "I would protect anyone I could from that scoundrel. But he has his ways…"

Rainer put his hand on her shoulder in consolation, "The Lady knows your heart. Be at peace." Rainer then turned back to filling his water bladders, hitched them to his horse, swung up, tilting his head to Caron in acknowledgement, and rode back the way he came.

Mary came up behind Caron. "What did he say?"

Caron nearly jumped, so deep in thought was she. She then turned to Mary with wonder in her eyes. "He just said the Lady knows my heart."

At that Mary beamed.

"Do you know her?" asked Caron.

Mary replied, "I only met her the other night when she came to Lord Guy asking for his help. He took her in and sheltered her. She was gracious, sweet and kind and she smelled of apples. I trust her."

"And she would give us all apples?"

"She just did."

Guy held the apple Rainer gave him discreetly curled in his left hand as he walked to the stable. Midnight perked up at the approach of his human. "Midnight, I have a gift for you from a friend." Guy held up the apple and Midnight nickered softly and nodded. Guy then teasingly put the apple in his own mouth, biting down to hold it in place as Midnight's great black muzzle mouthed at the apple. The juice of the apple dripped into Guy's mouth. Midnight's whiskers tickled Guy's face and he laughed, releasing the apple into his hand and bringing it up into Midnight's mouth who gladly accepted the treat. As Midnight crunched on the Avalon apple, memories of the Apple Orchard flooded him. Reality seemed to waver for one brief moment. Guy blinked, his eyes saw mist and a vague image of an apple tree. "Midnight?" Guy petted his horse for confirmation of reality. The image faded for both of them. Midnight put his ears back, discontent that they were still in the stable. But now he remembered how to get back home to the Apple Orchard.

CHAPTER 12

✦

The Apple Orchard

MIDNIGHT WAS MORE restless than usual. He had been given the key to get back and he wanted to use it.

Guy found it challenging to ride as they traversed the forest back to the manor from Nottingham. He kept thinking he was travelling through some odd haze with an apple orchard superimposed on the scenery wherever he looked. He would shake his head but the haze kept reinforcing itself on his vision. As evening fell, he found himself lost in the woods. He didn't recognize anything. Pride and danger kept him from calling out. He wandered off the road and brought Midnight to a halt. "I think we are going to have to stay out here for the night, Friend."

Midnight nickered. He had other plans but shifted his weight patiently as his human dismounted.

"Too late to do anything. At least it is not too chilly. Come on. Keep me warm."

Normally horses do not want to lie down. It is not overly comfortable or safe. But Midnight trusted his human and so he lay down and Guy followed, leaning up against his horse. He petted Midnight which lulled him into trance and helped him drift off to sleep. He dreamed Morgaine was petting Midnight and telling him, "Good horse."

When Guy awoke early the next morning he was quite surprised to see that he was on the edge of an apple orchard that overlooked a castle. It was not Nottingham. It was Glastonbury!

Less than a fortnight after the lovers had parted, here was Guy, keeping his promise to come as soon as he could, riding up to Glastonbury. "I am here,

Love," Guy thought, not knowing that Morgaine could hear his call, "I don't know how I am here, but I am here." Guy patted Midnight's neck, "Look at this and wonder at it." But Midnight did not wonder, not with his belly contently full of Avalon apples.

At hearing Guy's voice in her head, Morgaine jumped up from her embroidery, and Marian and Meggie watched their friend leave the room in a cascade of shimmering, rustling blue fabric.

Marian shrugged, having no idea what made her friend leap. "Nature calls, I suppose."

The two women giggled and went back to work.

Morgaine went to the balcony and watched Guy ride up. She sucked in her breath, her eyes roaming his form. "He has the thighs of a stallion," she mused to herself. One could tell he was made for riding. She waved and he caught the movement from the corner of his eye. He raised his hand in salute and watched her disappear. Morgaine ran down the stairs and out onto the castle steps. She raised her hands up and then proceeded down the steps to him.

He scooped her up in an embrace. "I am here."

"You are here and my heart is brimming with joy!"

Guy caressed his love's face and felt such a deep content, feeling Morgaine's love. He then looked at her perplexed. "Morgaine, I do not know how I came to be here. I was in Nottingham last night; I am sure of it. Else I slept the whole way here or I am dreaming now."

"You are not dreaming. You are here."

"How? It should take days to get here."

"It does."

"Then how?"

"Ask Midnight."

At the call of his name, Midnight nickered as if in soft laughter at an inside joke.

"Blast. Forget reality for a moment. I am here and you are here and we are here together and that is all I am going to care about right now." Then Guy kissed Morgaine's ear and whispered, "Where to?"

Instead of responding to Guy, she clicked her tongue and said to Midnight, "To the Apple Orchard."

Midnight's ears pricked at the word "apple" and he did a swift turn around and led his human charges back to the Apple Orchard.

Guy chuckled, shaking his head, but allowed Midnight to lead, saying, "Oh, now I see who is boss."

Midnight nickered again.

"I was just here," stated Guy, overseeing the Apple Orchard and shaking his head. Morgaine just smiled, slid off Midnight, and held out her hand for Guy to join her.

While Midnight was left to his own devices, the lovers walked out among the apple trees to the heart of the Apple Orchard from where they watched Midnight munching on an apple. Guy called firmly to his horse, "Midnight, slow down on apple consumption. I will not have you colicky."

Midnight's ears went back at hearing the command. He then yawned, dismissing his human's concern.

Guy's brow furrowed. "Friend, I am serious. I will not have your hooves swell and ache. Slow down on the apples!"

Morgaine cocked her head as she watched human and horse in a peculiar standoff. She knew of colic in horses and that it could lead to founder, a most dreadful foot disease. Curiously, she had never known Glastonbury horses to become colicky after consuming Avalon apples. Still, she left the two friends to work it out for themselves.

After Guy's distraction bantering with his horse, he turned to Morgaine, asking, "How did Midnight know to come here?"

Morgaine shrugged. "Magic?" Her voice was a question but only on the surface.

Guy peered at her in a sidelong gaze studying her veiled composure.

She felt his eyes upon her and looked at him with a big grin on her face. Then suddenly she reached up right quick, gave him a peck on the cheek, and frolicked away.

Guy laughed and gave chase. After several near misses and much running about the trees, Guy captured Morgaine in an embrace. He backed her up against the crook of the tree and lifting her into it. They kissed hungrily.

Morgaine then laughed wickedly and threw her precious little weight onto him to topple Guy to the ground. She sat atop him and felt his growing hardness between her thighs. She smiled mischievously, "I feel something hard protruding into my thigh."

Guy swallowed and stared at Morgaine as if daring her to do something. He lowered his eyelids in sweet mischief, replying eagerly, "That is my passion growing in response to you."

Morgaine was wicked. "I would like very much to see what this passion of yours is that is growing between our legs."

Guy just stared at her, not sure how to respond other than ripping off their clothes and thrusting himself inside her. But that was not the request. And he learned long ago, he would get more satisfaction if he could actually please a woman, not just have his way with her. So he held his patience with every cell of his brain he could muster as Morgaine got off of him, eyeing him as she unlaced his trousers. His stiff rod in her hands, she smiled excitedly and began to stroke him gently with one finger. She had imagined this since she first saw him in his full majestic nakedness when he stepped out of the bath those many nights ago. Now she was finally allowing herself to touch him, to touch his manhood. Her eyes lit up with excitement as his cock responded to her touch.

Guy blushed and laid his head back against the grass. Looking up into the apple tree, a mosaic of branches was reflected in the bright blue of his eyes. He felt her breath upon him. She kissed his cock and his eyes widened. His mouth formed an "o" as he exhaled in excitement. He bit his bottom lip as he let her play with him. He was simply being present; simply allowing. His teacher should be proud, he thought momentarily before being swept away by Morgaine's touch.

He heard her purr, "Allow me to return your kindness." She kissed his staff again. "What would give you pleasure, a sensation you would not forget?"

Guy moaned. He wondered, was she really asking?

Morgaine responded audibly, "I am asking."

Guy craned his neck forward to look at her. In breathy excitement he commanded, "Take me in your mouth."

Though Morgaine had rarely been commanded to do anything, she felt compelled to comply. It thrilled her. As her mouth was full of him, she asked him mentally, "Like this?"

"Yes," he moaned. Then, as gently as he could, for he realized how pent up he had been feeling all these months waiting for Morgaine to touch him, he encouraged her head to move in an up and down motion upon him so she understood. She got it. Morgaine was making long slow strokes with her mouth and tongue. Guy's head fell back onto the grass. Oh the joyful agony of it all! He could barely contain himself as she sucked on him. It'd been so long. He could feel the climax building as he rode that edge. He rode it as long as he could, not wanting the sensation of her mouth taking him in to end. He allowed himself to lose control, immersing himself in complete rapture.

This being her first time, some part of his brain kicked in that she may not know how to or be able to, swallow his seed. He then moved his hand to his rod and started stroking himself faster. Morgaine released her hold with kisses and just watched him pleasuring himself.

Gazing at all his muscles working and the look of concentrated bliss on his face, she murmured, "You are magnificent!"

Well that just did it for Guy and he felt himself climaxing in a full body flush. As he came, he rolled his body over to spill his seed on the grass.

Morgaine chortled, "Christians see the spilling of seed as a sin..."

Guy finished her thought, "but we both know that is not true."

Her smile brimmed, "You give a gift to the Mother Goddess with your seed."

Guy smiled wonderingly at this sweet, wild woman.

They lay back in the grass and Morgaine tucked herself into Guy's arm. It felt so natural for both of them, and Guy, especially, felt the distinct sensation of the benefits of a man's role as protector. Curled under his arm with her head on his heart and one arm across his chest, Guy was saturated in the most delightful feeling of love. He laid there just basking in this moment and not waiting to break it.

As Guy stared into the branches, he blinked as if he was just waking up and still seeing a dream. He looked around in slight disbelief though some part of him recognized that the bits and pieces were coming together to form a most bizarre reality. He craned his neck around. The outermost trees circling the grove all looked appropriate to the season. Leaf buds opening and the distinct white and pink flower buds still closed. But here in the center of the orchard, something was very peculiar. There were trees in full flower with a few bees humming around. And there was fruit hanging from other trees. A few others appeared to be dormant as if it were winter. It all came together. The reason all those apples could be given to his villagers. Why Midnight was eating yet another apple.

Guy shook his head and called to Midnight, "Midnight! Stop!"

Midnight's ears went back, and if a horse could, this one had the distinct look about him that he was ready to aim and spit the apple at his human, knocking him in the head, as punishment for an unreasonable demand. But instead, he gingerly put the apple down. Only to pick it up again as soon as Guy's woman distracted him with her voice.

Morgaine had been watching Guy as he looked around the Apple Orchard. She drew him back to her with her voice, "Now you know our secret," she said seriously.

Guy kissed Morgaine's forehead and stated equally as seriously, "You have not misplaced your trust, My Lady, though either I am dreaming or we are on the shores of the Isle of Apples."

"There is no island anymore, but the Apple Orchard remains. The Land is still in flux and somewhat out of time."

"Out of time?"

"I am not entirely sure how to explain this phenomena in a way that will make sense. Because it really doesn't — make sense that is. But somehow when my namesake lifted the mists to wed Avalon back to the mainland, not all of the Land complied. Some of it, the Orchard in particular, is out of phase, even within itself." Morgaine paused as she watched Guy and his furrowed brow attempting to wrap his brain around this oddity.

He said, as if to himself, "Midnight and I ate Avalon apples...and now we are here in Avalon. Midnight grew up on these apples though, didn't he?"

Morgaine simply nodded. She was almost as surprised as Guy was at this miracle. It was rare to see an animal, or human even, pattern to a place enough that he could move in and out of time and space, especially without training.

Guy's head felt as if it were on fire as he continued to make sense of all this. Eventually he just shook his head; it did not make sense and he was just going to have to live in this mystery.

Morgaine made light, "It does work in our favor. You are here. And as you can tell, there are always apples. Did I not tell you, should you visit, you would be most welcome to taste my fruit?"

Guy laughed. He leaned over and kissed her, "Mmmm," he purred, then bit into the apple she offered him.

Evelyn gazed out at the Lake from a balcony. She could see the edge of the other shore and the Apple Orchard. She had felt Guy arrive, felt the magic that brought him here. There was more to that horse than met the eye. She knew Morgaine took Guy into the Apple Orchard. What would his reaction be to this most wondrous miracle, she wondered? Could they trust him with the knowledge of the secret of the Apple Orchard? If outside folks heard about the magic of the Apple Orchard it would either be overrun or burned or both. She had to make sure to protect the remnants of Avalon. Why was he so willing to walk into this story, as he called it, especially when he knew not the ending? This was no dreamy bedtime story. This was the real world too, just as surely as the story he wanted so desperately to walk away from. But could he? Or would he merge the two? Evelyn reached out in her mind to her daughter. All she could sense was the sweet perfume of love. She inhaled deeply and slowly, promising the Goddess she would trust the process past the end of time.

Having spent the day in the Apple Orchard, Morgaine was becoming aware of the time. "Come. We should head back." Morgaine held out her hand to Guy. The two got up and walked to Midnight who looked perfectly content and possibly intoxicated.

Guy scratched Midnight's neck where it met his back, saying. "I know I just got here, but how am I going to get back? Can Midnight do what he did in reverse?"

Morgaine leaned into Midnight, pressing her head into Midnight's neck, combing his mane with her fingers. "What are we going to do?"

Midnight's ears went back in annoyance. Even in his apple-drunkenness, all he knew was that he was again in the place of apples. He didn't want to leave. There should be no talk of leaving.

Morgaine responded to the horse's displeasure, "I don't want you to leave either, but Midnight, it would be dangerous for Guy to just disappear without given leave. He would be hunted."

Midnight saw an image of torches and flames and angry men. He shook his head as if to clear this thought.

"Rest here for the night, but Midnight, you have to get both of you back to Nottingham to keep Guy safe. Understood?"

Midnight was irritated, his ears flattening against his head in protest. He had just gotten here. Still, he blew air out between his closed lips as if in resignation of what needed to be done.

Guy was still puzzling over the Apple Orchard as they rode toward the castle. "Morgaine, what do you tell other people? Your gift? How do we explain it?"

Morgaine responded, "I would not ask you to lie. We do our best not to lie, though protecting the Orchard is paramount. You will find when people cannot make sense of something they will cling to whatever bit might make sense. I am sure if your villagers gave it any thought, as some of ours do who do not already know the secret, they decide to believe that the apples must have been in cold storage all this time. It seems overlong, it is true, that stored apples could make it through the winter with a whole town eating them, but you will find that is what people would prefer to believe."

Guy merely nodded, realizing that so many people choose not to see magic and miracles before their very eyes. Now that the veil was being lifted, he never wanted to live so mundanely again.

Evelyn called out to Rainer in her mind, "Meet me in the Knights' Room." She walked purposefully through the hallways, turning a corner to find herself in a very old room. It was generally unused and not many knew of it or how to find it, so it tended to serve her purposes as a secret meeting space. She kept her eyes off the large round table that took up the majority of the room in the center and instead focused above her on one of the few tiny windows surrounding the room. Rainer came in and bowed as she turned to face him. She reached out her hand and he kissed it on bended knee. He rose and looked intently into her eyes. "Rainer," she said with a quiet smile, "what have you done?"

His eyes were filled with mischief but his face expressionless otherwise. "Whatever can you mean, My Lady?"

"Rainer, dear, do not play with me. How is it that, one, you are back so soon and two, that Guy is here?"

Rainer licked his lips, then plainly said, "The trees that are in flux, if you eat enough of them, you can be too. We have found that we can hone into the Apple Orchard and return very rapidly."

"Rainer, it is not appropriate to use this magic so casually."

"My apologies, Lady. I just thought to save time by returning this way, though it took me five days to get to Nottingham to do Morgaine's bidding."

"Yes, it was a great act of kindness though I am not sure that was appropriate either."

"Lady, I understood why we did not use our abilities while we had our charges, but for any one of us to move more efficiently, I do not see the harm."

Evelyn pondered. She scanned her mind for the paths but did not see where this caused a problem. So she reverted back to her line of questioning, "Why did you do this?"

"My Lady, while I was picking apples I had a vision. I saw the horse and recognized him. I followed the thread that led to the face of who I now know to be Lord Guy of Gisbourne. It felt very important that he be here. I felt the hands of Merlin on me."

"The Merlin?" Though many years had passed, Evelyn still very much missed her confidante. "You think Guy is the boy Merlin was searching for?"

Rainer swallowed and nodded.

"When The Merlin left all those years ago to find the young man, he left many things unsettled and many unknowns. I have not been able to find his last journal explaining himself, only that note."

Rainer looked dismayed, considering how dangerous it would be for such a recording to fall into the wrong hands. It would have probably been on his person. The Merlin was always careful but, still, it was a magician's personal account. "Ten years ago. That journal is probably..."

She waved her hand in an arch, silencing him. "Never mind the past. Tell me the present."

Rainer told the tale, "The apple that I gave Guy to give to Midnight was enchanted, in addition to already being an Avalon apple. I wanted to be sure and it was easy enough, with his horse having come from this place. So I just gave a bit of a push."

"A push? Why would you do this?"

"Lady, you have seen it: the face of the Stag upon the man. I know this because I saw it too. And with Morgaine bonding to him I know that to get his seed into her we must act swiftly. She is not getting any younger and he was the one The Merlin saw all those years ago."

"Are you sure? He is foreign blood."

"No. I do not believe so. I think he is Merrek's."

Evelyn's eyebrow rose. "Truly?"

Rainer replied, "Goddess knows why it is he, as damaged as he is, but it is. So we must trust his path so that the circle becomes complete and he fulfills his destiny."

Evelyn pondered. She was not used to not seeing all the paths. As disorienting as it was, the fact that Guy's path had eluded her until now was perplexing. She closed her eyes to focus on Guy's face. Hmmm. Yes. He could be Merrek's; those eyes. How did she miss it? Oh what a terrible twisted road that man had walked to come to this point in time. Then he would have the blood, not tainted by so many human ancestors, but just half. A half-breed. And his royal human lineage would make him acceptable to the Land; to be the Stag King he must have royal blood. And to those in power, it would appear that houses were aligning. She smiled a secret smile, though Rainer could tell what she was thinking. He nodded to her as they shared this secret. "I must be sure."

"You will be." Rainer paused, then added, "My Lady, he's been deliberately cloaked. I am sure of it. Some old spell belonging to some secret clan." He bowed and departed.

Evelyn walked purposefully back to her room and went to her scrying bowl. "Show me Merrek." Her fingers swirled the water. As the water settled, Merrek's face appeared. A raven-haired, bright-blue-eyed beauty of the Faie. "Show me Merrek's children." Too many faces emerged in the water for her to have a clear sense of all of them. And by their varying dress, she could see that his legacy extended into the distant past and the distant future. "My, you are a fertile one aren't you, Grandfather," Evelyn said playfully. "Quite the busy old goat." She waved her hand again through the water. "Show me Merrek's sons in this lifetime." There was no doubt. She smiled. There was Guy's face staring back at her in the water. She stated to the reflection, "Well, you may not be happy with this news my son-to-be, it may cause you confusion and grief at first, but it is good news just the same. We are related. You will strengthen the line." She continued to stare into the water. "Now, about that cloaking spell." To the water, "Show me." The water rippled but all was dark, shadowy. She pondered to herself, "What would Merlin do?" The water rippled and showed the first Merlin with shadows. "That is an old spell." She continued to watch the water.

After securing Midnight in the stable, the lovers walked back to the castle. It was early yet for dinner but Morgaine heard Guy's stomach grumble. He looked at her slightly embarrassed. She chuckled, for even after the apple her man was still hungry, so she promptly led him to the kitchen. "Let us find you something to quiet your appetite." He looked at her and then raised his eyebrow. She laughed more as she got the double meaning. Morgaine was chuckling still as she pushed open the kitchen door. "Hello Brighid," Morgaine called to a fiery redhead standing at the counter working on a fish.

"Ah, M'Lady. What brings you to my realm?"

"Healing of hunger," giggled Morgaine to the other young woman for whom she teased as being the Irish Goddess Brigid incarnate for all her dedication to making the most delicious, nourishing meals. Morgaine continued, "Lord Guy, meet the mistress, Brighid, our head cook. She makes the most nourishing dishes and we are all the better for it."

"Ah, M'Lady. Thank ye." Brighid curtsied to Guy who nodded his head, smiling.

Guy considered how astute Morgaine was at appreciating people, for finding and stating their strengths; and he noticed how people, from Brighid to Prince John, responded positively to her praise. Guy was growing to truly appreciate how Morgaine approached people from whatever walk of life. She was respectful and sweet, and by her very nature, commanded the same.

"Well, Lord Guy, will a bit of bread and wine temper the pain of hunger as supper is not for a while yet?"

"That would be most kind," Guy replied. Ah, he thought, I can be polite too. He glanced at Morgaine who was eyeing him already with a great grin on her face. The three chatted in the kitchen while Guy ate his bread, and to his delight, Brighid produced a bit of cheese as well.

As they left the kitchen, they thanked Brighid again and watched as more workers came in to participate in the preparations for this evening's meal. Guy was amazed at how differently things were arranged and felt at this castle versus Nottingham. As he walked the halls, he felt as if he were in a beehive where everyone knew their job and was proud to do it. There was no bitter taste of backdoor scheming to do in another; this was very different than the stench of fear at Nottingham Castle. He looked at Morgaine as they walked and felt very protective of her, wanting her never to know or have to live the difference as he did.

Evelyn found her husband in his study. She came up behind him and put her arms around him, leaning down into him. Gareth reached up with his hands to give his wife's arms a reassuring squeeze. Then he pulled her around to face him. She sat down on his lap.

He looked lovingly at her with his merry eyes. "I know that look. What is on your mind, Wife?"

Evelyn started, "I feel energies are moving quickly."

Gareth chuckled, "You feel two impatient lovers."

She tilted her head to acknowledge his making light of this, continuing, "It is true they are bonding rapidly. Give him the talk."

"Do you know that he arrives?"

"He is here."

"Here? Now? How did he manage that?"

"Rainer enchanted an apple. And now I am certain, as well, that Guy was the young man that Merlin went after."

"Truly?"

"Yes. Please, Husband, give Guy the talk?"

"Now?"

"Yes. After supper."

"Of course, my dear, but why so soon?"

"Beltane is approaching. They should be married by Summer Solstice and with child soon after. I have seen the face of the Stag upon him."

"When?"

"At the tavern. I dismissed it because I was picking up on so many other thoughts and there was Charlton's keen mistrust of Guy."

"But you are now sure."

"Yes."

"Then perhaps it is not fair for Morgaine to marry him."

"She loves him already. And she has already lost one love without consummation; it would be cruel to make her wait further and dangerous for the family line. No. There is a reason it is he."

As Morgaine entered the dining hall she saw Marian and gasped, then came up behind her friend in an embrace. "I am sorry. Forgive me for abandoning you. Look who has come for a visit."

Guy came up quickly behind Morgaine and as Marian turned, her face brightened and she laughed, "Of course." Marian rose and the two old friends embraced.

As they parted, Guy said appreciatively, "You are looking well."

"Thank you, I feel well here." Marian then turned to Morgaine, "You are forgiven," she smiled.

Morgaine beamed and sighed.

Guy caught site of something out of the corner of his eye and did a double take when he saw what he was looking at. Entranced, he left Morgaine's side to study the large magnificent tapestry. Mouth open and in awe, Guy could hardly believe what he was seeing. It was almost identical to the small tapestry in his room in Nottingham.

Morgaine came up from behind him and took his hand, studying his face. "You like it?"

It took a moment before it registered to Guy that his ears heard Morgaine's voice. He turned his head slowly to look at her. Then he looked back at the tapestry. "Your family's crest is a dragon?"

"The Pendragon of old, yes. It felt more fitting to take up Uther's crest that became Arthur's when he was still aligned to Avalon, than Gorlois'."

Guy was still in awe but managed to ask, "Who?"

Morgaine responded, "The Duke of Cornwall, Morgaine's father."

Guy shook his head and began to laugh.

Morgaine had a combined look of perplexed amusement on her face. "What do you find so amusing?"

Guy looked at her again, entwining his fingers in hers, "Everything. Life. Coincidences. Fate."

He was about to say more when Sir Charlton came in, clipping his words, "Lord Guy. What brings you to Glastonbury?" The couple turned and faced the composed older man. He maintained his bearings but it was obvious that in addition to his ill health, his heart was ill with misgivings toward Guy.

The conversation about the tapestry set aside, Guy turned his attention toward Charlton without answering his question for there was no logical way to answer it. "Sir Charlton, the change of scenery appears to do all of us good. You look well."

Charlton nodded in agreement. "I am feeling better here, yes."

There was an awkwardness between them and neither was sure where to go with a conversation. Thankfully, Evelyn and Gareth entered and the household sat down to dinner in the formal dining hall, Evelyn and Gareth at the head of the table with Morgaine and Guy to their left and then Meggie and Marian and her father Charlton to their right. Servants approached and presented the food to which Evelyn and Gareth nodded their acceptance and the meal was served.

Evelyn turned to Guy, "Lord Guy, it is a welcome surprise to have you in our midst. How long are you staying?"

"Just the night, Your Grace. I must get back."

Evelyn nodded, deciding this was not the time or place to discuss how he came to be here.

Guy was feeling keenly aware that his time here had to be limited. Though he might be a baron in name and the title afforded him certain luxuries, William still saw him as his personal servant. The life of a baron was such that Guy could spend some time away from his duties at the castle without being overly missed but that was more up to William's whim than any actual sense of time or schedule. And it was one thing to be at home in the manor. It would be an entirely different matter if it was discovered that Guy had just vanished.

As they finished their meal, Gareth invited Guy to walk with him. It wasn't really a choice. They walked out of the castle and into town. Guy was amazed that Gareth only had one guard at a discreet distance behind him, that he seemed unconcerned about walking through his own town at night. He looked around for the secretive Guardians but saw none.

Both men were quiet as they walked. Guy wasn't sure where Gareth was leading him so he simply took in the night and the soft sounds of a content town. They walked down a side path which led them out into a field with the Lake in front of them and the Tor up on the hill to the right. Guy could sense it was no mistake that he was given this view.

"Guy, we can tell you have much passion for our daughter…" Gareth held up his hand at Guy who was about to interject and then continued, "We also see that you have the aptitude to lord over others. Do you have the fortitude to lead others and to serve those whom serve you? I do not expect an answer from you this night. The rapidity of the Quickening is to be expected and, though you may not understand, we are willing to accept it and you as Morgaine's consort. We accept that it is not your past that defines you and we urge you to accept the same. It is what you decide now, at this crossing that is important. If you feel that you can humble yourself, give up your name and title, lands and station and be reborn into this family, you will return on Beltane Eve and ask for Morgaine's hand in marriage. Then, as my father-in-law trained me, I shall train you how to rule and serve these lands as the Lord Guy of Avalon, future Duke of Glastonbury."

Guy was dumbfounded. He had not expected such a conversation to take place, certainly not so rapidly, and certainly not with the Duke initiating the direction of it. And it was he who was being asked to consider, not the other way around. But then they had already accepted his request to court their daughter. What an odd family this was. But the oddness only lent itself to further awe and Guy was ecstatic that he was being accepted so readily. And all he had to do was give up the life he led in Nottingham to become a future duke with Morgaine as his wife? There was little contest. In fact, none. A life here seemed immeasurably better and grander than at Nottingham. He smiled bewilderedly at Gareth as Gareth held up his hand again so that Guy would not yet utter his assent.

Gareth then turned his head to look out onto the Lake again. Guy did the same, though he thought he might just bounce out of his skin. Surely he was dreaming. He folded his arms and patted them. No; still awake. So he forced calm and looked out on the Lake. Gareth gave his future son-in-law a sly sidelong glance with the merest hint of a smile in his eyes. He couldn't read thoughts like his wife or daughter but, just by being around them for so long, he had ages ago picked up how to read people by their body posture and the look in their eyes. This man definitely had the look about him of a love-struck man who just heard all his dreams coming true: that he'd get his love and the castle.

Gareth continued to meditate on the Lake and Guy did his best to calm his racing thoughts. When Guy appeared more composed, Gareth turned and headed home with Guy following after, putting his footfalls in step with Gareth's.

As Guy and Gareth approached the castle steps, they saw Morgaine walking at a quick pace down with another woman. She looked up as they were about to pass, a satchel on her shoulder, and said, "Gwenyth just came to me. Her son Owain fell from a roof and broke his leg. I am going now."

Guy responded, "Could you use you my help?"

Morgaine was honest, "I am sure of it."

Gareth embraced his daughter and then clasped hold of Guy's arm as a parting, then walked up the steps alone. He turned to watch the lovers rush away with Gwenyth, thinking, "We hardly know this man and yet I feel compelled to completely trust my daughter in this matter. The Gods are at work here, I am sure of it." He shook his head slightly, "Whatever his past, it is his future that bears most importance."

Gwenyth led them down the cobbled stone street to Owain and his wife, Megan's, home. It was a small, thatched-roof house, lined up among other similar quaint homes that constituted the look and feel of Glastonbury town. Gwenyth knocked but didn't wait for a response, leading them into the dimly lit room. Candlelight illuminated the scene. The young man, Owain, was lying on the bed and in quite a bit of pain. The position of the leg did not look good.

Megan pleaded, "Mistress, tell me you can save his leg please."

Morgaine came closer and examined the leg. If she could get it cleaned up enough and set properly, he might be able to keep it. "First things first, Gwenyth. Let's get your son's leg cleaned up. Guy, will you please cut the breeches so we can clean the leg?"

Megan held her husband's hand as the occupants of the room bustled around them. Any touch felt excruciating to Owain and Guy tried to be careful as he unsheathed the dagger at his ankle and cut the fabric up the leg.

Gwenyth then came over and began washing the leg, feeling pained as she saw the agony on her son's face. She prayed as she worked, "Lady please do not let me lose him. I am not ready to bury a son so soon after I buried a husband." Morgaine picked up on Gwenyth's prayer and laid a hand on the woman's shoulder.

When the broken skin was thoroughly cleansed, Morgaine told Guy to hold down Owain's shoulders as she commanded, "Drink this," to Owain.

He took a swig of the strong brew, coughed, and took another swig.

"Now bite down on this," Morgaine directed, as she handed him a strap of leather.

He complied.

She laid her hands on his leg to find the right spot. When she was certain, she pulled and redirected the bone with all her might.

Owain bit down and then passed out from the pain.

Meanwhile, Morgaine went into a trance as she poured healing energy like golden honey into Owain.

Guy watched in fascination, considering — the daughter of a duke, a dancer, and a healer: a curious combination. He could sense Morgaine doing something but was not sure what, as she was so still and focused.

Megan and Gwenyth looked on, though they too, appeared to be in prayer.

When at last Morgaine stirred, Gwenyth came to her lady's side and helped her up. Morgaine looked tired and a bit shaky on her feet. She steadied herself even as Guy reached out his hand. She smiled at him and then turned to Megan. She took a packet out of her satchel and handed it to Megan. "Pour the contents of this into fish broth and have him drink it several times during the night. I will be back in the morning to check in on him."

Megan nodded, "Thank you, M'Lady. Bless you."

Morgaine allowed herself to lean into Guy as he drew himself closer to her.

Gwenyth asked, "M'Lady, would it be alright if I stayed here a spell with my son?"

"Of course, Gwenyth. I will see you in the morning."

Guy looked at Gwenyth and said, "Not to worry. I will see to it that the Lady Morgaine reaches the castle safely." To himself he added, "And if I could, I would even tuck her safely into bed."

Morgaine suddenly glanced up at him and he got the distinct impression she heard him. But neither said a word.

Guy helped Morgaine navigate the streets, content to feel her leaning into him and glad to be here to support her. He thought, "Whatever she did in there it seems to have sapped her strength."

Morgaine nuzzled into him closer, saying out loud, "Healing work can be very strenuous. I pour so much of my energy into those in my care."

He kissed the top of her head wondering how she knew to answer his unspoken question. As they cleared the castle steps, he realized he really was escorting her to her room. But nay, she had them pause in the hallway. They sat down on a bench. She leaned her head onto his shoulder and then he shifted so that he was holding her with her head on his chest. She spoke quietly, "I can hear your heartbeat."

Guy murmured, "You can also somehow hear my thoughts too, can't you?"

Morgaine looked up at him and with a tired smile said, "If I thought I could have you in my room I would love for you to tuck me safely into bed."

Guy chuckled, shaking his head at the apparent magic involved, "So you did hear me! But I know I said nothing out loud else Gwenyth might have knocked me on the shoulder."

"She might have at that. It is good you told her not to worry."

"Morgaine, you seem to know what I am thinking and I think you can even put thoughts into my head. How is that?"

Morgaine responded, "Your mind is open; you allow me in. Even that first time when I asked you to come to me after I danced in the hall, you responded; you came to me."

"Could you demand I do something?"

"I do not know. I wouldn't want to."

"But Dylan…"

"Dylan was open and ready for me. I didn't demand, though I was firm. It was an accepted command."

"Could you force someone?"

"Someone of weak mind who is weak-willed, yes. But I loathe to command another in that way. I would prefer that the person does my bidding willingly."

Guy thought back on the apparent conversation that Morgaine and Dylan were having and wondered what Dylan had to say about him. He had caught the side glance Dylan made as well as his wariness. He recognized it would not be fair of him to ask Morgaine to break confidence, but he was curious if he could trust this young man. He may have need of him as an ally at some point.

Morgaine heard Guy's unspoken question and responded, "Beloved, Dylan may have his concerns about your actions but he placed his trust in me. You can have faith in that as you deal with him. He will not betray the Lady of the Lake."

Guy closed his eyes, assessing and taking mental note of a possible — though guarded — new ally.

Guy changed his focus, "I must leave in the morning or else the Sheriff will miss me, if he doesn't already. He did not give me leave. I am not sure how to explain myself. I can only pray Midnight can do whatever he did to get us here and get us back. This is all so much to take in...but I will take it in, Morgaine. I will accept all this magic. I just want to be by your side. When... while we have to be parted...Can we talk even if we are apart?"

Morgaine rubbed his chest and said in her mind to his, "Yes, Love, we can. You may not have the Sight but you will be able to hear me and I will be able to see and hear you."

Guy tried it, thinking his thoughts to her instead of saying them, "You can see me too?"

"Yes. Just as I can see when Mary and Dylan pray to the Lady of the Lake. If you focus on me, I can see you and hear your thoughts."

Guy considered the benefits of this incredible gift, saying wonderingly, "You are truly a remarkable woman!"

Morgaine turned her head to look up at Guy, smiling as she said, "Thank you."

Anything else that might have been on their minds was interrupted by a large white cat who had been slinking up to them and now jumped up into Morgaine's lap. "Ah Cream, come to be introduced?"

Cream cocked her head slightly.

Guy sat still as Cream eyed him. She then stepped onto his lap and put her front paws on his chest.

Morgaine whispered, "Just stay still. She just wants to sniff you and determine if you are acceptable."

Guy held in a laugh and looked directly at Cream. "Well? What do you say? Do you find me acceptable?"

Cream reached her face toward his and sniffed him. Then she moved one paw up and onto his heart. Guy had the distinct sensation that this cat really was assessing him. He gently and slowly lifted one hand to pet Cream's back. Her tail went up and she began to purr. Then she looked at Morgaine, gave the appearance of an ever so slight nod of the head with a blink, and made herself comfortable in Guy's lap.

He kept gently petting the cat, shaking his head slightly, saying softly, "Will wonders never cease."

Morgaine smiled and leaned back into Guy, putting her hand gently on Cream's head and rubbing her soft ears. "She is a good mouser. She has lived with me for many years and keeps my room and the castle free of mice and rats…along with several other cats we house. But Cream, she's special. We have quite the friendship."

Cream purred more loudly hearing her name spoken by Morgaine.

Meggie came slinking around the corner. "My Lady…" she started slyly. Morgaine and Meggie both knew that Meggie was just checking on her because she was alone with a man at such a late hour, and to let her know that she would do whatever she was asked by her mistress.

"I am fine, Meggie. I will find my way to bed soon. My Lord and I were just talking. Sleep well, my friend."

"And you as well, Morgaine." With that, Meggie walked back down the hall from whence she came.

As Guy absent-mindedly pet Cream, lulled by her soft fur, he inquired, "Meggie is quite devoted to you. She is your shadow whenever you give her leave to be. How did you come by her?"

Morgaine leaned her head back and walked her memories back into time, recounting the story.

The Avalons were in London. The Merlin was still alive. While the Duke and Duchess were attending to matters of State, Merlin and Morgaine decided to explore the city. Morgaine, a girl of twelve, had never been to London, had never been anywhere before this, and she was excited to see the city. But as they walked the streets she grew more anxious. There was an overload of sights and sounds and smells.

Merlin placed his arm on her shoulder, quietly saying, "Morgaine, you must learn to take in the information without being overwhelmed by it. Just let it all pass through you, like water."

Morgaine nodded, attempting to comply. Still, it was all so hard to let in. And then she heard a plea. As the pair passed a side street, she saw that some young men were harassing a girl. She was compelled to turn the corner. Something in that plea arrested her heart and charged her with taking on the mantle of the Lady of the Lake. She walked briskly and purposefully to the scene. The Merlin watched Morgaine intently and followed swiftly behind; he could tell Morgaine must have heard a call. And given he was her protector as well as her teacher, he had to make sure to keep Morgaine safe.

With hands on her hips, in her most authoritative voice, Morgaine demanded, "If she is offering you services then you must pay her. And if she is not, then you had better move on."

The young men started, then all three turned their attention on Morgaine. There was name-calling.

The Merlin put on a glamour and appearing bigger and ominous, hissed, "You had better listen to the young lass. She is the Duke of Glastonbury's daughter and a guest in your city. You would not want to cause trouble and be brought to the attention of the King would you?" It was not actually a question.

The boys bowed and fled.

The girl, perhaps thirteen or so, looked feral but she was polite and curtsied, "Thank you, miss. I am not sure what I was going to do. All I could do was pray to God. And then you came. I am in your debt."

Morgaine looked compassionately at the girl. "What is your name?"

"Meggie."

"Meggie, I am Morgaine and if you called out to God, it is the Goddess who responded and put me before you."

Meggie's mouth dropped open. A goddess? There was a goddess who could save her? "Sweet Mother Mary," she whispered hoarsely.

Morgaine smiled, "I do not know Her by that name but if that is how you know Her, it is She who compelled me to come to your aid."

Meggie was not sure what to do with this information but what she did feel was a strong sense that this must somehow be fate. What could she do to stay with this young lady?

The question was answered by Morgaine approaching her, taking her hand. "Come back with me. Let's get you cleaned up."

Morgaine and Merlin took Meggie back to the castle. Morgaine had one of the castle servants draw a bath as Meggie looked around in awe. She had never been inside the castle. There was such extravagance. Now it was she who was overwhelmed.

With the bath hot and ready and smelling of rose petals, Morgaine and the castle servant helped Meggie out of her clothes and into the bath. "Thank you. That will be all."

The woman was about to protest but simply curtsied and left Morgaine on her own. Who was she to disagree with royalty, even if the young lady was but a child?

Meggie started to relax into the bath.

As she washed the girl, Morgaine noticed the bruises on her upper arm. "Who did this to you?"

Meggie shook her head and then quietly said, "A man."

"He would violate a girl?"

Meggie's eyes started to tear up even as their eyes met and they held each other's gaze.

Morgaine then had a vision: this girl would become a woman of Glastonbury. She saw the pair of them walking arm and arm. Morgaine spoke up, "Meggie, you have survived many abuses, I see that. You shall endure but be a victim never again. And if you choose, I would welcome you into my life and my home."

Meggie was astonished but managed to say, "It would be an honor."

Morgaine returned to the present moment, saying, after recounting the tale, "The rest is history. Having no family, she returned with us as my companion. It has been a blessing to have her around. She has been a dear companion to me and we have drawn especially close since my other two dear friends moved away. Meggie is a sweetheart, attending to my every need, and I adore her. I do hope that someday she finds love. Though I would miss her, I really do hope she gives herself to love."

Guy looked thoughtful, "Perhaps she has."

They both knew that the hallway was an inappropriate and entirely uncomfortable place to sleep but neither wanted to get up. Cream sensed this and stood up. Looking at both of them, jumping down from Guy's lap, she walked away then looked behind her at her human as if to ask, "You are following me, are you not?"

Morgaine sighed and nodded, "My cat makes for a most interesting governess. I must away to bed." They both rose and then embraced. "Come, I will show you to your room." Morgaine led him by the hand down the hallway and opened a door. The bedroom was elegant, yet simple, clearly created for royal guests of unknown dispositions.

Guy kissed Morgaine's hand, "Until tomorrow."

"Until tomorrow," she smiled back.

When Mary came into Locksley Manor that morning, she heard from her son, Dylan that Guy had not come home yet. As they chatted, there was a knock at the door. Mary peered out and saw that it was one of the castle guards. "What do you want?" Mary said behind the door. Her mind was racing. Guy was not back yet and she was not sure what to say. "Lady, help," she pleaded in her mind.

Morgaine heard her call and replied back, "Please protect him."

Mary swallowed. Protect him? She mouthed to her son, "We'll say he is sick."

Dylan held up his finger for his mother to pause, for he had heard the Lady's voice in his mind too. He quietly raced up the stairs to Guy's room.

"Here now, open up. I am here to check in with the lord of the manor."

Mary reeled. Oh, to lie to the guard could be the death of her and yet she knew that the Sheriff could not find out that Guy was missing. Where was he? Was he with Morgaine? How? But before she could reply to the guard on the other side of the door, she heard her son answer from upstairs.

In the gruffest voice he could muster, Dylan called out, "Good lord, cannot a man have some peace? I have been puking all night after eating something most disagreeable. Tell the Sheriff I am sick as a dog and I have sent for the healer." Then Dylan started hacking.

The guard looked up to the window where the voice was coming from and replied, "Yes, Sire." The guard walked off not wanting to argue with Lord Guy, "Nasty temper, that one," said he as he heard the gruff voice slurred with apparent sickness say, "And Mary, if you serve that slop again, I'll have you flogged."

Mary cupped her hand over her mouth. She was grateful that had been as easy as it was and that the guard believed that Dylan was Guy. But what if Guy was headed for the castle before returning to the manor? There would be no way to warn him that they had covered for him. She could only pray he returned to the manor first from wherever he was.

CHAPTER 13

Leaving Is No Simple Feat

THE LOVERS BREAKFASTED early as they had precious little time and wanted to make the most of it. Morgaine walked with Guy to the stable but Midnight was nowhere about.

"Where could he have gotten to?" Guy wondered.

"You have to ask?" Morgaine replied playfully.

"Uuhhh," was the only exasperated response Guy could make.

Out past the Lake Guy marched, with Morgaine following along, until they came upon the Apple Orchard. And there was Midnight munching quite contently on an apple. "Midnight," Guy called, trying to keep the harshness out of his voice. This was really too much for Guy. The stable door had been closed but here was Midnight, in the Apple Orchard. The horse had somehow simply willed himself to this place.

Though she was listening to Guy's coaxing voice as he encouraged his horse to come to him, Morgaine suddenly became preoccupied, no longer paying attention to the mental duel between horse and would-be rider.

More firmly Guy snapped at his horse, "Midnight!"

Midnight nickered in response as if to say happily, "Hey, there you are," and pranced up to Guy. Midnight certainly appeared in happy spirits.

"Midnight, I don't want to lose you. You can't keep eating these apples like there is no tomorrow!"

Morgaine laid a hand on Guy's arm, stating quietly, "Guy, Midnight is your horse and I will not tell you how to handle him. I just want you to know that I have never seen a horse with colic from eating these apples. But then I wouldn't want Midnight thinking any apple orchard was safe to eat as many apples as he has been eating."

Guy nodded in contemplation. Letting that thought go for the moment, he patted Midnight's head and neck. "Midnight, we have to go." He turned back to Morgaine, "Morgaine, how do we get back?"

Morgaine came up to the pair of them. "Oh Love, I am not sure. The Apple Orchard has its powers but the focus is here. I have never attempted to find myself someplace else."

"So you can do this too?"

"Possibly. I have never tried. There has never been a reason and I suppose I have not been curious enough to make the attempt. It is not magic to play with."

"Well then, how did it happen with me and Midnight?"

Morgaine was noncommittal, "I am not sure."

Guy put the halter he had been carrying around Midnight's neck. "Come on. We need to get back to the stable and saddle up."

Midnight started digging his feet in.

"Midnight, stop being stubborn. Come on."

Midnight heard that his human was annoyed but he was annoyed too. Still, his devotion to Guy won him over and he felt complacent for the moment, allowing himself to be led back to the stable.

Morgaine watched as Guy strapped the saddle on Midnight. She patted Midnight saying to Guy, "I think Mary and Dylan gave you some time. I heard a plea and told them to protect you. Whatever you do, go to the manor first."

Guy nodded to her and then turned to Midnight, "Ready to go back?"

Midnight neighed in protest.

"Aw, come on Midnight. You know we have to go back." He tugged at the reins and Midnight dug in, tensing his body, refusing to budge.

Morgaine spoke to Midnight reassuringly, "Faithful Avalon Steed, I thank you for your loyalty to this time and place. I see that something inside you has awoken. Guy needs you. Please, honor the tasks he sets before you."

Midnight held his breath, conflicted, sensing his human needed them to leave this place while also sensing that neither of them wanted to go. He released his breath and relented, allowing Guy to lead him out of the stable.

After a final embrace, Guy swung up onto Midnight. Reassuringly, he repeated what he had told Morgaine last night, "I shall return, my love."

Morgaine beamed, knowing what the words meant. She kissed Guy's hand saying, "Until then."

Though Midnight was not happy riding away, he allowed himself to be directed along the road that led north. As they travelled to Locksley Manor, Guy thought back to a conversation he had with Morgaine shortly before they parted.

"There was more to your playfulness in the Orchard then just setting me afire."

It was a statement, not a question, but Morgaine could hear the question behind it and responded, "Yes Guy. I wanted your seed on the Land. I want to anchor you here in Glastonbury. It is of course your choice. No seed, nor hair, nor blood will I use against your own will, but I do want the Land to take you in with welcoming arms as I am. I want to you feel the pulse, the sway, the beat of the Land and by spilling your seed upon Her, She can feel you wherever you are. This can be your home if you allow it."

Guy took in these words even deeper than he had before. He was on a Glastonbury horse riding away from Glastonbury toward Nottingham, and he could feel Midnight's desire to turn around just as he himself felt. He patted Midnight, saying, "I know that back the way we came is truly home, and I promise we shall return. But right now we have a job to do, so let us finish it and be done with the place we now walk toward."

Midnight softly whinnied and nodded his head as if he understood.

It was evening and they had been traveling in a northerly direction all day. Guy was exhausted but tense and awake. He saw the haze before his eyes that was the Apple Orchard but he could not allow himself to focus on it. Instead, he focused as hard as he could on the road ahead. But it was no use. He was tired and they both needed to rest. He dismounted and walked Midnight off the road behind the undergrowth. He sat down and pulled at Midnight's reins to join him. Midnight begrudgingly lay down.

"Okay Midnight, what do we do?"

Midnight just eyed his human slowly blowing breath from behind his lips. He knew what his human was asking, he just did not want to do it. He wasn't even quite sure how and he didn't want to return to where the Angry Man dwelt, who was always hissing at his human whenever he was around. He didn't want to return to a place his human mate feared.

Guy was facing Midnight, imploring, "Midnight, please. Focus on the stable at Locksley Manor. Remember Caron, the woman who feeds you carrots? You like carrots."

Midnight recognized the word "carrots" and the associated image. He nudged Guy's hand, sniffing and mouthing at Guy's hand.

"No. I don't have any carrots but Caron does. Carrots. Caron. Stable. Is this getting through to you?" Guy gently pushed his friend's muzzle away and then leaned against Midnight's muscular frame. He closed his eyes willing himself to think of the Manor. He opened one eye, peeking around, then closed it. After another moment, he slit both his eyes open. No haze. He closed them again and when he opened them he could see the Apple Orchard surrounding him. "Midnight!"

Guy angrily stalked around the Apple Orchard. He wanted to stay and knew he couldn't. He knew it was a long way back, just made longer. "Midnight, I could be flogged or worse. I may be a baron of a manor but I am also a servant to the Sheriff. Getting us back there will protect me until I can figure out how to leave there permanently. Do you understand?"

Midnight suspiciously regarded his human who was squawking and flailing about as he munched on an apple. Carrots just weren't apples.

"Damn it!" Guy stomped away, heading back across the marsh and toward the castle that would then lead him to the road.

Midnight watched his human leave and then whinnied to him.

"No, Midnight. We have to go. I have to go." Guy kept walking away.

Midnight looked at the apple trees and then at Guy. Something inside him grew fearful. His human was leaving, leaving him. As much as he wanted to stay, he saw that Guy could not. Midnight took one final apple in his mouth and held it there as he trotted away from the Apple Orchard and toward his human. As he came upon Guy, he nuzzled his neck into Guy's head and dropped the apple at his feet.

Guy picked up the apple, wiping off the saliva and put it in his overcoat where the belt held the apple up against his side. "For later," he said to Midnight.

They walked together in silence and then Midnight nudged Guy again.

"Yes, I love you too," sighed Guy in slight exasperation. But they were again walking in a northerly direction and Guy could tell that Midnight was ready to do what was needed.

The next morning Morgaine went to the Apple Orchard. As she walked amidst the trees she could feel Guy and Midnight as if they were also walking there. She closed her eyes, slowly opened them again, and could see a slight haze with the two of them travelling through. "They are caught between here and there," she thought.

"Yes, they are."

Morgaine chuckled slightly and turned to face Rainer. "How is it that you can still sneak up on me and know my thoughts?"

Rainer's merry eyes danced but he just shrugged his shoulders.

"How is it that Midnight is patterned to the Apple Orchard?"

"He did grow up here, Lady. And he did eat Avalon's fruit."

"But to have this unique ability."

"It is not entirely unique."

"Come again?"

"I spoke with your mother and told her what I did."

"What did you do?"

He smiled, "I enchanted an apple."

Morgaine's eyes widened. She tried to keep the annoyance out her voice, for she was also very glad to have had Guy visit. "Do you know that to be here without given leave puts Guy in danger?"

"No more than he ever has been. That handsome rogue will manage."

Morgaine gave a sly smile at Rainer's comment then paused in thought. "This means however, that Guy could get back here by Beltane if he chooses."

"Yes. And he will so choose. The blood knows like for like and it will not yield. He can feel his purpose coursing through his veins and he will not falter, My Lady. He will return."

Morgaine beamed. "I will write a formal letter of invitation and send it by bird so that he has proof of the royal request. Are there any places close to Nottingham we can send it so that it can get to him in time?"

"Close enough I am sure."

It had been four days since Guy went missing, Mary covering for him the whole time. A trip that should have taken him over five days just to ride each way, took a total of only four. He came in quietly and alert for trouble, as he knew he would have been missed. He secured Midnight and then came in through the servants' door, got some carrots, went back to Midnight. "Here, for your troubles," Guy stated with a mixture of amusement and sarcasm. "Now don't go anywhere without me. Agreed?"

Midnight just looked at his human. His place was by his human's side.

Guy patted Midnight. "Good horse."

They put their heads together for several moments, just feeling the surety of the other's presence. Then Guy nuzzled his horse's head and left. Guy came quietly back through the servant's door and into the main room. Dylan was waiting for him at the fire.

Dylan started, "Where have you been, Sire?"

"I couldn't say," responded Guy.

Dylan continued, "We covered for you. A guard came looking for you the other day and I pretended to be you, sick in bed."

"And did it work?"

"Yes. I sounded as gruff and sick as I could through your bedroom window."

"Well, I appreciate you doing that, Dylan. It is an unexpected pleasure to hear someone is on my side."

"Really?"

"Yes, Dylan. My line of work doesn't lend itself to friendship or easy camaraderie. Though I think the only reason you and Mary are giving me any assistance is because of your trust in the Lady of the Lake."

Dylan's eyes caught the reflection of the firelight as he responded directly, "That is true, Sire."

Guy's voice was grave, "Dylan, I cannot promise to appear a better man while doing the work of the Sheriff. You will probably still detest what I do for him. I am under obligations you cannot begin to fathom. Or perhaps you can because you heard the terrible choice Brin made. I understand Brin's actions. But that did not make them acceptable to me."

Dylan measured this man before him, recognizing there must be more to him than met the eye as he simply stated, "Yes, Sire."

"Good night, Dylan."

"Good night, Sire."

Guy sat in bed deep in thought. All he could think about was his decision. But it really was made already. He knew he would return to Glastonbury and take Morgaine's hand in marriage. This need to return to her was like fire coursing through his veins, consuming him, burning away all other desires. He would give up his surname, leave it on the road for his dead father to carry. He would be born anew into Avalon. God, this was so quick though. Could changes like this happen so quickly? Could he fall in love and have it so easy that they'd marry with this little courtship time? But that was what was happening, so of course it must be possible. Love could truly open up a door and one could simply walk through it without trauma. Tragedy can happen in the blink of an eye, why not a miracle? Why not something so exquisitely beautiful: a life transformed within the beat of a heart? Guy snapped his fingers, chuckling to himself as he said, "Happiness is mine. I accept this miracle in my life and rise to meet her." He chuckled again. Feeling quite invigorated, he slipped out of bed, down the stairs, and outside into the night. He prowled up the hill and watched the moon rise. And though it was nowhere near full yet, he let out a howl, opening his arms wide to let in the light.

CHAPTER 14

❧

Back in Nottingham

THE NEXT MORNING Guy could hardly contain himself. He was in the most blissful mood, grinning and giddy. This was an entirely new and very odd thing to witness and there was much shaking of heads amongst the village folk as he strolled to the stable. Dylan was readying Midnight when he saw Guy waltz in. Dylan, too, shook his head, but was smiling; he had watched Guy steal up the hill last night and had heard the howl.

Dylan handed Guy the reins, "Beautiful morning isn't it?"

Guy nodded smiling, "It certainly is! Thank you for reining Midnight up. I should be back by supper."

"Very good then, Sire. Take care…and remember you are supposed to be recovering from falling ill." He could see Guy's smirk from the side as he nodded his head in understanding. Dylan watched Guy ride off and actually felt a bit concerned for Guy, wondering how he would survive the day with the Sheriff, all happy like that.

Guy thought that nothing could disrupt his happy mood. Gareth was already giving permission and he knew Morgaine's heart, and the Prince was sure to give him leave to marry Morgaine. Everything would fall into place. Surely William would come around…wouldn't he? As Guy rode up into Nottingham, passing the townspeople marked by poverty and desperation, he felt his heart drop and then steeled himself for the day. By the time he got to William's receiving room he was stoic, but only on the outside. Inside he felt a crushing sensation on his heart just by being in the same room with William. Guy felt he was straddling a precipice: one foot in each realm and so far to fall if he couldn't negotiate the crossing.

"Feeling better, I trust, Gisbourne?" William questioned with only mild interest and much disdain for the man before him.

"Yes, Sire." Guy put his hand to his stomach and pretended to still be feeling a bit queasy. He ignored William's tone.

William continued, "Good. While you were indisposed Sir Grigor managed to capture one of Robin's men." William paused then added in a contemptuous voice. "I thought that, given how these criminals have managed to elude you for so long, you would want to do the questioning."

Guy did not want to do the questioning. But he could see when William was testing him, his loyalty, and he knew that his prior actions led to this test. "Of course," was all he said, with the pretense of conviction. William had a devious look on his face and Guy got the meaning loud and clear. He feigned a smile, nodded, turned, and headed for the dungeon.

As Guy made his way down, he felt the acute sting of doing the Sheriff's bidding. He had little trouble killing when he saw the need; it was a job. But he had no taste for torture. If he had to kill, he preferred it be over quickly. Cruelty for its own sake had little merit and was best left up to the sadists lording over the dungeon. Still, to save his own skin he'd stomach inflicting pain. Each step through these dank walls he thought to himself, "It's either me or them." He made damn sure it was always himself who came back out alive.

The guards let him in through the gates and led him to the prisoner.

Mock said over his head, "We got the minstrel in here. You gonna make 'em sing?"

As Guy approached, he saw that it was not Allen a Dale but Arthur who sat on the bench on the other side of the bars. The two looked vaguely similar so it was possible to confuse them; but no matter. "Hang him up," Guy barked at Mock and the other guard whose name he could never remember. They stripped Arthur of his shirt and cuffed his hands above his head; still he stared stony-faced at the wall. Guy slapped Arthur across the face to make a show of it for the guards. Arthur maintained an attitude of defiance. "Leave us," commanded Guy to the guards. They bowed and left, shutting the door. As they walked away they could hear the punch followed by a muffled moan.

Guy brought his face close to Arthur's and whispered in his ear, "Arthur, I have a proposition for you. Do you want to go free?"

Arthur nodded.

"I am not in the mood to torture you."

Arthur bowed his head weeping softly, thinking that mood or no, Guy was not known to be lenient. Only recently, he had killed his own servant, Brin, for some unknown transgression.

"Scream for me, Arthur." Guy's whisper was a hiss in Arthur's ear and as Arthur felt a dagger tip touch his side he complied. Upon hearing the scream, the guards looked to one another and shuddered, glad to be on this side of the barred door and not strung up alone with Guy.

"Scream again." The dagger was merely pointed into his side, it was not actually hurting or piercing skin. Arthur didn't know what Guy's game was but if all it took was to scream instead of actually feeling the dagger, scream he did. Guy whispered, "Arthur are you going to tell me where Robin's encampment is?"

Arthur shook his head.

"Scream again."

Arthur moaned as if in agony. Though he was in no physical pain, no one else knew that.

Guy continued his hissing, "So nothing will convince you to betray your people?"

Arthur shook his head and sobbed, turning his head to Guy. "I cannot. Though I do not wish this even on you Sir Guy, I cannot betray that trust. You really are going to have to just get on with it."

Guy could see the man was earnest, and though torture might actually work, Guy had never been convinced that a man would not say anything to stop the pain. But that anything still may not be the truth. Arthur would bide his time, praying for a rescue, leading the soldiers to an old encampment and then die when it wasn't the right place. No, Arthur would die in agony; that was clear. Guy whispered back, "You are an honest man, Arthur, despite your misguided belief that somehow stealing from those who you think have it better than you makes you a good man." Guy was annoyed that he wasn't going to get anything useful from Arthur. "Scream." Arthur yelped as Guy hit him in the back, shouting, "And it's Lord Guy!"

Arthur sobbed, "Lord Guy."

The guards outside looked to one another. Mock whispered, "He sure is touchy about his title." The other guard shrugged.

Guy really didn't want to spend all morning with this back and forth. He was functioning on no sleep and just didn't have the patience. How long did he have to be in here to be convincing, he wondered? Guy whispered, "You sure about this Arthur? Is this how you want it to end?"

Arthur shook his head. No, of course he didn't want it to end like this.

Guy asked, "Well?"

Arthur heaved a strangled sigh then shook his head again. "I can't. I…"

Guy was consoling, "I know." He paused, then hissed, "Scream again!"

Arthur complied, though he was confused. Both his confusion and screaming ended abruptly with the snap of his neck.

As Arthur slumped, Guy repeated in the dead man's ear, "I told you I was in no mood for torture."

Guy bowed his head and took a deep slow breath. He hated perpetuating this myth that he tortured prisoners. But it was this lie that helped keep him alive. He methodically cut gashes in the body to make it look as though these slices had eventually killed Arthur. The guards would ignore the snapped neck; this he knew. It had not always been this easy; not that this was easy. As Guy went about his work, he remembered when he was first commanded to torture a prisoner. It was the final part of his initiation into the Order of the Black Knights. He had to question a prisoner and he had to be willing to get the information in any way necessary. When the prisoner did not yield the answers the knights wanted, they demanded he proceed with greater force. When Guy stated he did not think that force would actually provide the accurate information, his choice then became, either do it to the prisoner with force or they would show him how it was done — on him. So with swords raised at him, he began first punching then resorting to cutting the prisoner. They got what they thought they wanted, but it wasn't because the poor man knew any more than he had offered. Guy was convinced it was only because the man was willing to say whatever they wanted him to say to end the pain. But he passed his test even as his soul shook in silent terror. He became a Black Knight, repeating words he did not fully understand in an English tongue that was old and laced with malevolent magic. And ever after, when he was told to question a prisoner, he made sure to do it in private and either the prisoner yielded up information or was killed and then cut. Guy's reputation was built on deception, and it was his mother's voice that spoke like a chant in his head, "You will survive this." She told this to him when he lost his father to the leper colony. And it was this phrase he held onto since then, whenever he had to do something he didn't want to.

There was an open grave on the edge of Locksley Village. No one usually went there, not even the children. But on rare occurrences some child would dare some other child and all would run to the open hole in the ground.

"It's just a hole in the ground," said Guy.

"Then jump in," said Matthew, who was older, daring the young Guy.

Robin shook his head at Guy. "It's bad. You'll bring death upon you and yours if you go in there. It's only meant for the sullied."

Little Caron who was always following Guy around, tugged at him. "Don't do it, Guy."

But Guy felt he had something to prove. Being just a child he really had no idea what there was to prove, but somehow it was important to show up Matthew. Guy jumped in, hearing all the children suck in their breath above him. "There are no ghosts down here. No death. It's just a hole. A hole where the Priest tells people that they are now dead to us; but they are not! You see them walk away." Leprosy was not a common disease in England but it did happen, and the inflicted were treated with much fear and hostility. Guy was only four years old the last time it happened in his village. He still remembered the man, a soldier, running away after he was told he was dead to his people.

"Wait 'til I tell Father," exclaimed Robin and ran off.

Guy looked down. Now he knew he would get in trouble. Robin, the Baron's son, was always the tattletale. He looked up at Matthew who had his hands on his hips and some awful smirk on his face. Guy realized he had been tricked. He was meant to get into trouble.

Matthew kicked dirt down on him, teasing, "It's your funeral."

Much, another village boy, had hesitated, not sure what to do. But as Matthew turned away, Much reached his hand down. He, Caron and Marian helped Guy out of the hole.

Guy dusted himself off, "Thanks," he said to his friends.

Guy trudged back to the village. His mother was already outside waiting for him with Robert Locksley, the Baron. While his father was away, the Baron was around much of the time. He would even share a meal with the family on occasion. The man treated Guy and Delphine like his own, sort of: more like they were prized, though unruly, possessions. Robin was there too, of course, arms folded, like he'd won some argument.

Though Marguerite had her arms out for her son and he was more than ready to fall into them, the Baron, standing at her side, said in a soft but commanding voice, "Come to me, Son."

Guy complied with his head down, barely glancing at his mother. She looked at him compassionately and with concern, biting her bottom lip in silence.

The Baron then took Guy, one hand on Guy's shoulder, turned, and headed to the church. Robin started to walk too but the Baron shot his son a look, "No, Robin. Though what Guy did was wrong and I thank you for bringing it to my attention that we show Guy the wrongness of it, this is no time to gloat. As my son and future baron of this land, you should have done better to keep it from happening."

Robin looked down, crestfallen.

Robert, seeing Marguerite's pleading look at him, shook his head, saying, "Marguerite, you stay too. I will handle this."

Guy's mother wrung her hands and simply nodded as she watched them walk away.

Marguerite was a beautiful woman. It may have been why the Baron fancied her so — that, and the fact that she was related, however distantly, to the crown. She had an hourglass form, wide in the bosom and hips and slim at the waist despite having had two children and two late miscarriages. She had long, luscious, straight dark brown hair and brown doe-like eyes. A giving mouth with full lips. Creamy skin. Though still just a little girl, her daughter Delphine was a perfect copy of her; it was like looking into a mirror of polished metal and seeing her younger self. The parents had hopes that they could marry her high and, thus, further their station. Guy, on the other hand, they figured would be a soldier, like his father. No highborn English woman would want a knight for a husband, and a French one at that, no matter how good-looking. And the Baron made sure to remind Marguerite that her children's relation to the Crown was a distant one and not to get her hopes too high for her children. He didn't want her setting her sights beyond him. He was determined to be the one to decide on the best matches for her children to help him rise further.

The Baron was also a handsome gentleman to behold — a tall, muscular, broad-shouldered man with sandy, blond hair and blue eyes. His wife, when she had been alive, was a sweet-looking lass with dark blond hair and brown eyes. The family resemblance in Robin was obvious. Interestingly, this was not so with Guy in his family.

Though he looked somewhat like his mother, Guy had black hair and brilliant blue eyes. Everyone said he must resemble Auguste's English grandmother's side.

The Priest punished Guy severely for disobeying and taking the dare. No one was to go into that hole. It was for the sullied only. "You bring a bad omen upon yourself, my child." Somehow the words stung more than the lashings. It felt like he was everybody's child except his father's — who was away, again, on the Baron's bidding. Everyone acted as if they were quite concerned about Guy, but he didn't believe it.

It was only three years later that the hole saw another human body. Guy was thirteen when he watched his father go in. The Priest and the Baron were there to see his father go and tell him he was dead to all of them. But he wasn't dead. Because there Auguste stood — in the hole. Marguerite wept and held her children's hands tightly, whispering, "You will survive this," over and over and over again. Guy looked at his mother and she looked to him continuing to re-peat those words. Her eyes were wide and haunted. Her lips parched and cracked. Repeating "you will survive this" was all she could bear to do. The Baron then ceremoniously wrapped his cloak around Marguerite and brought her away. Now, there would be no question; he could claim the baby growing in Marguerite's belly as his, and this child would help him rise further.

Auguste looked on in anger and despair. When he had returned home, his own wife looked on him with fear and revulsion. There was no time for goodbyes. He looked from his wife to his daughter, whose head was hidden in her mother's skirts, sobbing uncon-trollably. He could not console his own little girl. He then looked to his son. Guy was staring at him wide-eyed in disbelief. Auguste was pained but made a motion with his head, a slight nod for Guy to follow his mother as she began to walk away with Delphine and the Baron. But Guy could not.

"No!" Guy screamed and ran off across the field. He stopped at the grand apple tree that was his favorite place to be by himself and sat down and cried, his mother's voice still ringing in his ears, "You will survive this." He sobbed and pounded his fists into the ground.

It was hours before he was found. It was, of course, the Baron who found him. But Robert took pity on the lad; he was, after all, Marguerite's son and a good boy who had just lost his father. "Guy, it is time to come home. You are the man of the house now. I will always be here to help you, your mother, and your little sister. Your family shall not go without." Guy wanted to be hateful. He wanted to say, "It's because of you my father is proclaimed dead. It is because of you my mother is with child. It is because of you I have no father." But Guy was silent. He remembered all too keenly when he had been willful with the Baron just weeks ago. It was a simple shove against the stairs where he had been standing; but his back hurt for days afterward. And he was too grief-stricken to have the energy to do or say anything. So he walked home with the Baron in silence. He found his mother in her chair by the fire. Delphine laying her head in their mother's lap, quietly cried while Marguerite stroked her daughter's hair. Robert left the family alone and Guy came to his mother who outstretched her arms to him. He sat on the other side of his sister and laid his head down in his mother's crowded lap. She silently stroked both of her children's heads with tears streaming down her face.

It was only three months later that Guy and his ten-year old sister lost their mother in childbirth. She had let out a scream and her children came running to see the bed soaked with blood. "No, I cannot lose him! You cannot do this to me!" She looked and sounded half-crazed as she screamed at shadows on the wall. Guy yelled at his sister to go get Hazel, the village healer. Delphine scampered out the door crying, both out of fear for her mother and from being spoken to harshly by her brother. He hadn't meant anything by it. He was frightened and Delphine was just standing there. Guy went to his mother's side. Her breathing was quick and shallow. Something was very wrong. And the child wasn't due for three months at least. He was afraid to see his mother so distraught. He felt helpless as he stroked her hand. Then he thought he heard something. He looked back to the corner where his mother had been watching. He heard a voice as if inside his head, "She was not supposed to have another child, not another son. You will not be put down, nor cast aside." Guy looked at his mother in question. Did she hear that? Marguerite touched her son's face whispering hoarsely, "Never cast aside. You are my jewel." He looked back to the corner of the room but there were only shadows. The Baron burst in with Hazel and Delphine trailing behind. Guy cast a mean look at his sister, mouthing, "Why did you bring him?" Delphine shrugged helplessly. She hadn't meant to. The Baron called out to her. He must have seen her running across the courtyard.

The Baron came to his lover's side on the opposite side of the bed from Guy. Still, Guy felt cast aside. Neither Marguerite nor Guy mentioned the apparition in the corner of the room. Marguerite was crying, "Something is wrong." Robert considered that to be an understatement. The bedsheets were soaked with blood, his woman pale as the white sheets once were. "What has happened?" Hazel came over and now Guy really did have to physically move. He got up and moved to the bottom of the bed where his little sister was. He wrapped his arm around her and she leaned into him as she cried, fretful about what was happening.

Hazel checked Marguerite's pulse. Looked into her eyes, opened her mouth and checked her tongue. She moved quickly and thoroughly. Marguerite suddenly convulsed, her body wracked with pain. Hazel went around to the foot of the bed, shooing the children aside.

She pulled back the sheets and drew up the mistress' dressing gown. Everything was soaked with blood. But the baby was not out of the womb yet. She looked at the Baron, made a motion with her finger to come closer, and as he leaned in toward her, she whispered, "You are going to lose them both." He howled. The sound frightened both of Marguerite's children and they involuntarily stepped back. It would be the second woman he lost to childbirth. He drew Marguerite up and held her close, sobbing, "Noooo." She whispered in his ear, "Take care of them. Take care of my jewels as if they were your own." He nodded, but she persisted, "Promise me." He continued to nod, saying earnestly, "I promise you, Marguerite. I promise." And with that she convulsed again. But her sobs were cut short as she made a final, strangled exhale. Then her body went still. "Mother!" The children cried out in unison and charged at the bed, lying over her body sobbing. Robert, still at Marguerite's side, had one hand on her head. His other hand rubbed her children's backs in their grief. He did not know how to console them. He promised to look after them.

It was a hard and challenging change, one that would have come anyway a fortnight later, when Robert and Marguerite married. She had wanted to wait a few months to let the children grieve their father before the marriage. Robert begrudgingly agreed. Still, he had the servants make up the rooms and gaily decorate the manor in anticipation of his new bride.

He didn't allow the children to stay by themselves that night in the house. He bore them both into his own home even though they didn't want to leave their mother's body. All three were sobbing. His son, Robin, was not happy having to share space with the two interlopers. Guy was angry that Robert gave away his family's home to someone else; he felt like he was losing everything. He had run out into the woods in search of his father, screaming, "She's dead. My mother is dead. Your wife is dead." But there was no reply. He never saw his father again.

CHAPTER 15

Beltane

GUY RODE UP from the Avalon Orchard and the marsh to the hilly farm and grasslands of Glastonbury as the sun was setting. Though it was not a pleasant conversation, he had managed to convince William to give him leave to visit the family, stating that they had invited him and it would be unwise to turn them down, being friends of the Prince. And he would be sure to assuage any misgivings they may still have of the…"misunderstanding." It had taken him days to prepare and scheme and carry out, but it was over and now he was here. Midnight was practically prancing being back in Glastonbury again, smelling the heady scent of Avalon apples as he happily trotted up the road.

They had come by way of the Apple Orchard, Midnight again having managed to get them there by sheer will and a most perplexing magic. This time Guy had even been awake as it happened. It was the most bizarre sensation and quite disorienting.

Guy saw the bonfire in the distant field and the townspeople walking toward it singing. He rode past them at a distance and then headed toward the castle stable. There was no one about so he secured Midnight himself, deciding to trust that his bag would be safe with his horse while he investigated.

As he walked toward the castle, Robbie happened by. "Hello there, Lord Guy. I must say you are going the wrong way. Everyone is heading toward the fire."

Guy responded, "I can see that, but I was looking for the Lady Morgaine."

"She will be there too. Come on." Robbie linked elbows with Guy and steered him in the other direction. Guy complied. Anything to be going in the direction that would lead him to Morgaine.

At the fire, Robbie broke his link with Guy and meandered off toward the large keg of ale.

Guy meanwhile spied Gareth and walked purposefully toward him. "Good evening, Your Grace!"

"Good evening, Lord Guy. We are pleased that you have come. I trust you are still resolute?"

"Unwaveringly so, Your Grace. I gratefully accept the terms."

Gareth chuckled. "Grand! Then our plan is in action. You only need wait until you two jump the fire."

Guy beamed and then asked, "Where is my lady?"

"She will be coming along shortly."

The fire burned brightly as the Glastonbury townsfolk gathered around drinking and singing. The priest, Father Hale, came early from town to bestow God's blessings upon the fertile fields before retreating from this most pagan ritual. After a solemn blessing, he and his more devout parishioners departed, respectfully leaving the remaining revelers to their own devices.

The aging, silver-haired Father Hale knew he had remained at his station for so long because he and the Duke and Duchess had an understanding and so he agreed not to breathe a word to King Richard or even to other priests outside the town about these alternative ceremonies. And not even to Father Stephen, the High Priest of the Abbey, whom he thought might be aware of this. He knew that for any closed-minded Christians in power to hear of this ritual would mean the demise of these people, and he knew them all to be good folk even with this evening's revelries. Still, it made him happy that he did have his more devoted flock who did not partake in the remaining festivities and departed with him.

As Father Hale and his followers walked out of the field, someone started singing. Others joined in. Soon everyone in the field was singing praises of the Land's fertility. Suddenly, a horn sounded in the distance somewhere near the Lake. The crowd seemed to anticipate what was next, and parted. Guy noticed that Gareth was missing and Evelyn and Morgaine were still nowhere to be seen. Six Guardians with Gareth in the lead walked slowly toward the large circle and the fire while surrounding three exquisitely-clad and painted women. Guy's eyes widened as he saw that one of the women was Morgaine. The men looked primitive: wild, half naked, with antlered masks. He observed a white-blond braid and knew that Rainer was among them. Gareth was wearing a crown of new greenery whereas the women's crowns were woven with spring flowers.

Rainer, from behind his mask, projected loudly, "Behold the Lady of the Lake, Maiden, Mother, and Crone."

Guy did not recognize the older woman and wondered if she was part of the family. The circle widened until everyone in the field was part of it, with the Guardians flanking Gareth and the women.

The crone spoke, "Though I am old, I still carry the wisdom of the ages within me. Hearken back to a time when we knew this to be the Motherland and we clung tight to our Mother's breast and tasted her sweet cream. Remember a time of balance for both predator and prey. Hearken back to the wild lands and know that love made is not a sin; nor are you born of sin. You are bathed in the blood of the blessed womb as you enter this world. You are the embodiment of sacred life. You are a temple of the Holy Spirit and your love is a testament to that."

Gareth and Evelyn were each handed a pitcher. They faced one another and blessed each other, the people, and the Land. "Milk of Her breasts and the honey of His seed, bless the fertility of our fields and may hearts and hands join as one." Gareth and Evelyn took turns kneeling and accepting the contents poured from each other's pitcher into their own. When they completed their strange way of mixing the milk and honey, they passed the pitchers around for all to enjoy.

Guy took a sip; the flavor was most delightful and he didn't remember anything tasting so rich and sweet.

Morgaine came forward and she was given one of the pitchers. "May the richness of the Lord's honey and Lady's milk bestow fertility upon the Land." Morgaine poured the contents of the pitcher out in a sun-wise circle. As if on cue, everyone started singing.

> *The Maiden lies down in the grasslands.*
> *The Lord lies down in the grasslands.*
> *All join hands.*
> *For the Lady and Lord lie in the grasslands.*
> *Milk and honey, milk and honey*
> *And from their sweet union new life is born.*
> *And from their sweet union new life is born.*

Evelyn stepped into the circle and the chanting slowly came to rest. Evelyn stated loudly, "For all those willing to commit to hearth and home, for all those willing to release the past and walk anew, for all those desiring to walk the path with another, jump the fire." She spread her arms grandly toward the bonfire, which had thankfully diminished just enough that it would be possible to make a leap across it.

Guy sought out Morgaine and took hold of her hand. She was adorned in strange painted patterns upon her body. It didn't matter. In fact, it did. It made her all the more desirable: that she would openly be so strange and magnificent and never consider any other way to be. She accepted herself exactly as she was. It made him proud to know what would be coming next. "I would have you to wife. Will you have me?"

Though it sounded commanding, Morgaine could hear Guy imploring. She nodded smiling, planting a full-lipped kiss upon his mouth.

Guy and Morgaine took their turn leaping the fire. As they leapt the fire, Guy remembered Evelyn's words and prayed for them to be true. Upon crossing the flames, Guy swung Morgaine around to the side, went down on bended knee, and again asked for her hand in marriage. "Marry me, Morgaine? Marry me and make me the happiest man alive."

Morgaine's eyes widened in mirth and she nodded her head most vigorously before leaping into Guy's arms in a passionate embrace. "Oh, my sweet love! Yes Guy, I will marry you!"

Other revelers could see what was occurring and after everyone had leapt the flames, they gathered around the new couple, chanting —

> *"Sweet Lord and Lady*
> *Fertile Lord and Lady*
> *This Beltane Eve he promises to wed*
> *Solstice shall be their wedding bed."*

Gareth and Evelyn joined in the revelry and chanting. As the couple looked into the eyes of all who sang their praise, they gave special thanks to Morgaine's parents. Guy clasped hands with Gareth only to be drawn into a big bear hug by Morgaine's barrel-chested, proud father. Other men came around and playfully teased Guy, tousling his hair and slapping him on the back in congratulations. The men parted as Evelyn came forward. She held her hands out to Guy and he took them, kissing each one.

Guy went down on bended knee. "Lady, you know my heart. I see that. I am honored by the trust you place in me with your daughter's heart."

Evelyn clasped her arms around Guy and embraced him, his head buried in her belly. She felt the Goddess draw into her and heard her voice say, "Welcome home, my son." She could feel him shaking with emotion and could sense that too many had called him "my son" without really meaning it. She stroked his raven hair as a mother would, as the Great Mother would, and turned his face up to her. "Arise Lord Guy, son of Avalon. Arise and take our daughter's hand. Marry our daughter and be wedded to the Land."

The look on Guy's face was one of awe and relief.

As the formality of the moment was released, Morgaine guided Guy to introduce him to the attending Guardians. The five men and one woman lifted up their masks so that Guy could see their faces.

"Good to see you again, Rainer," Guy stated with mirth in his voice when they were reintroduced.

Rainer responded, "The pleasure is mine. I am glad you returned."

Guy nodded in agreement. He was glad he returned too.

Morgaine then drew him away and introduced him to an older couple. "Guy, this is Elizabeth and Wild Herb. Elizabeth and Wild Herb, this is Lord Guy, my betrothed."

Elizabeth, Guy recognized, was the old woman who spoke during the ceremony. He bowed to her, took up her hand, and kissed it.

Elizabeth blushed. "Oh my! What a gentleman!"

Now it was Guy's turn to blush. He wasn't used to being called a gentleman. But some part of him recognized the honor that must have been placed on her to participate in the ceremony, so he thought it best to treat her like a lady. Guy then shook hands with Wild Herb.

The night was long and the singing and dancing continued around the fire. Guy was caught up in the celebration, as he had never known such utter abandon and delight. Gareth and Evelyn finally bid the attending townspeople goodnight and the townspeople in turn sang farewell to their duke and duchess with sweet praises -

> *"Sweet Lord and Lady*
> *Gracious Lord and Lady*
> *This Beltane eve you bless this land*
> *We do our part with guiding hand."*

Slowly, the numbers dwindled until there was just a handful of Beltane attendees, Guy and Morgaine among them. The lovers lay down in the tall grass with other lovers surrounding them, each with their own slightly private spot. Guy and Morgaine caressed each other's faces and squeezed each other's arms and backs. They looked into each other's eyes and saw the reflection of the fire. There was a sustenance to their love; their love seemed to feed upon itself, continuing to grow and blossom. They lay together, soaking up that love and basking in a sensation that felt so natural to them both. Morgaine felt her body fit perfectly into his. Guy kissed the top of her head and held her close. Her ear was against his chest and she could hear his heartbeat like the beat of a drum calling her soul to dance with his.

In the morning, the lovers all awoke with hay in their hair as the sun crested the open field. Meggie, ever devoted to her mistress, came out into the field with food and drink borne by a few servants. All the lovers gathered around. Morgaine ceremoniously held up the bread and a goblet that Meggie had passed to her, proclaiming:

"Sweet Mother and Father of this Land, we thank you for this food and drink.
We thank the seeds and beasts from which it came.
We thank the air that caressed, the sun that warmed,
the rains that soaked, the earth that held.
We thank all hands, seen and unseen, who brought this delight before us this day
that we may be nourished and in return nourish all life.
May it always be so."

Those gathered, repeated, "And it is so." Morgaine then broke the bread and passed it around in both directions. She passed the cheese and the wine. Guy savored the taste. Guy noticed that somehow the bread and cheese tasted better than he thought food could taste. It was more than just hunger; something about sharing in this ritual brought out the true flavors. He added to the hum of "mms" that made the group sound like a hive of bees.

After breakfast, Guy and Morgaine walked back through the town in a glorious daze. So in love; beaming. The townsfolk smiled, just looking at them. Guy felt he could just be himself here. He wondered: either his reputation hadn't preceded him here, or the people just didn't care. They only saw a man in love with their darling Lady of the Lake. Either way, Guy felt at peace here, a peace that he had not ever experienced. And though it was unsettling not to have to feel on guard all the time, he allowed himself to be at ease and enjoy the moment.

Almost as if sensing a guiding hand pulling them along, Guy and Morgaine turned down one of the streets that led to the marshes and the Lake. They walked out along the shore and around to the Apple Orchard on the other side. Remembering the last time they were here together, Guy leaned Morgaine into an apple tree. This could become a habit. She felt him press against her and felt his manhood rising. Her hand impulsively reached down and around to his trousers to feel his stiffening cock. Guy's head tilted back in pleasure, and a soft moan escaped his lips. Morgaine smiled wonderingly, coming to realize the power she held in her touch, another kind of magic. She wisped her fingers back and forth on the fabric teasingly.

Morgaine knew that soon they would make love for the first time. "Guy, what will it feel like to make love to you?"

Guy's eyes widened in eagerness at the thought; he smiled confidently. He had waited what felt like an eternity to enter this woman and what had held him together was the surety of her love. He paused before answering. He had grown used to her blunt questions, gave some thought, and responded poetically, "Beloved, when I prick your maidenhood it will feel like a flash of lightning and a clap of thunder. I will bring you to such ecstasy that there will be no room for pain."

Morgaine's eyes widened in excitement, crooning, "I believe you!"

CHAPTER 16

A Robin Drops in on the Festivities

THAT NIGHT THERE was much revelry as it was officially announced that Guy and Morgaine were to be wed on the Summer Solstice.

Robin listened to the announcement in the shadows. He had been trying to get Marian's attention but she was happily caught up in the festivities. He did not know the family but still could not understand why anyone would marry that devil! Finally, he decided to walk up to Marian.

"Robin?!" Marian was overjoyed and did not think to keep her elation quiet as she embraced him with much enthusiasm. Heads turned and a hush fell on the scene. The couple soon realized they had become the source of curiosity. Robin and Marian looked around sheepishly.

Guy's eyes narrowed and he spit the name, "Robin" under his breath.

Morgaine, still holding Guy's hand, rubbed his arm with her other hand.

There was tension in the air as the men focused their mistrust of each other in a heated stare.

"Robin of Locksley I presume," announced the Duke in an authoritative voice.

"Yes, Your Grace," Robin broke from Marian to bow before Gareth and Evelyn.

"And pray tell, what brings you to our court?" inquired the Duchess.

"I…please forgive me; I do not mean to intrude on the festivities. I heard…that Marian and her father were taken in by you and I was inquiring after their health," replied Robin falteringly, realizing he was potentially putting Marian in danger by giving them away as a couple.

Amused, Evelyn continued, "And what business do you have with the Lady Marian?"

Robin fidgeted, wondering if the Duke and Duchess would have him arrested. He was a wanted man after all.

Evelyn could feel the man getting ready to bolt. Curious, though, that he hadn't thought how his actions could affect him or Marian. Evelyn waved her hand, "Come now, Robin. We have no quarrel with you. It is obvious you are love-struck or would not have placed yourself in such possible jeopardy. Go ahead; woo the lady if she will have you."

As Robin bowed and started to turn, Guy could hold back no longer. He left Morgaine's side, seething, pointing his finger, "This man wantonly flaunts the law. He has a bounty on his head in Nottingham."

Gareth eyed Guy curiously, "Guy, we have no quarrel with this man as long as he goes in peace."

Guy's mind was spinning. Robin came here for Marian. Marian was in love with Robin! Always Robin. She never loved him. She was saving herself for Robin. She was spying on him for Robin.

Suddenly he felt a hand touching his, "Forgetting something?" Morgaine whispered coolly.

He turned to her, astonished, "No. Forgive me. I am just shocked. Marian denied she had feelings for Robin. She was under suspicion for aiding the outlaws."

Marian felt quite caught now. First, Robin got her house burned down and now, because he came to her so publicly, she might be accused of aiding the infamous Robin Hood.

Morgaine could see her friend rabbit-like and frozen.

Robin though, incensed by Guy's comment, retorted, "You are one to talk. You are in league with a tyrant. You plot against the King."

Upon hearing that grave statement, Gareth interceded, "Robin, that is a dangerous accusation. This family will not be pulled into political spats. Are you prepared to cast that stone without looking first to yourself? I can see that there is more here than meets the eye. You both have some past pain with each other. Go settle it. We cannot have our countrymen fighting one another. Ladies, accompany your men and see to it that they work out their differences without bloodshed." Eying both men, "You will respect my court and my judgment."

A dark black man with the official bearing of a man not to be trifled with approached with two other guards behind him. Both Guy and Robin did a double take at seeing this dark-skinned man clearly as the man in charge.

Robin stated incredulously, "He is Moor."

Morgaine scolded, "Sir Taharqa is our Master of Arms and protector of this realm and he will be obeyed."

Sir Taharqa narrowed his eyes at Robin, stating firmly, "I am not Moorish. I am English."

At that, Guy made a mental note to inquire about this man's story later.

Morgaine led the three away into another room as she heard her father encourage the crowd back into merriment. As she ushered the men and Marian in, Taharqa stood next her, putting his hands out, "Weapons."

The two men looked at him and obeyed, handing over their swords to Taharqa. Robin handed Marian his bow and quiver as well as the dagger at his side to demonstrate his good faith. Morgaine took note that Guy did not reach down for the hidden dagger at his ankle. But she said nothing, trusting that Guy would not use it on Robin, that he merely didn't want to show his hand he had such a weapon. A look passed between Guy and Morgaine. He tilted his head ever so slightly to let Morgaine know that he was aware that she knew he was not giving away this secret. Meanwhile, Taharqa and the two guards removed themselves to the other side of the door, closing it behind them and blocking it with their bodies.

"Would you two please explain yourselves so that we can get back to the party? My beloved just asked me to marry him and we are supposed to be celebrating." Morgaine eyed Guy with a look of frustration on her face.

Guy looked down. Morgaine's cross look was wounding. He did not intend to hurt her feelings. If he could just have kept his mouth shut. He was here, with a woman who loved him and who he adored. He could start a new life, a life without Robin around.

Robin was edgy but recognized he was not going to have to bolt, that he did not endanger himself or Marian. He became bold and spoke, "My Lady, your parents are generous to allow me my freedom and to not hold my love for Marian against her. This rogue that you intend to marry is a traitor to the crown of England. He and the Sheriff plot against the King."

Marian winced and nodded in agreement.

Morgaine looked to Guy, "What can you tell me of these accusations?"

Guy looked at Robin with hatred, fearing he could lose the woman he loved because of Robin's words. It's one thing to choose a side. It is another matter entirely to actively plot against a side. He turned back to Morgaine, closed his eyes and exhaled; then opened his eyes and looked directly at her. "Yes, I have been helping the Sheriff with his plans. I could not do otherwise. I swore an oath to obey my duty to the Order of the Black Knights."

Marian interjected, "But why would you?"

Guy turned his head, glaring at Marian, and snapped, "Why would I not?" Seeing the injured expression on her face, he mustered all the calm he could manage and continued. "Marian, please keep in mind that after my mother died, Delphine and I had nowhere to turn. Lord Locksley did unwell by us. We were treated like game pieces. When Delphine came of age, the Baron agreed to a marriage to a much older man. She pleaded with me to save her. But how could I? I convinced myself it would be better for her but she hated me for it. I hated myself for it too. But then the Baron sent me away as well."

Marian nodded as she remembered that day. Guy had been so angry...and so lost, forlorn. He was taken away without notice.

"You will go, even if I have to shackle you."

Guy was angry, willful, but he could not disobey the Baron's command.

The Baron had already sent Matthew up to Derby two years ago and now he agreed to give the Earl another lad. In their communications, the Baron was specific to the Earl, "The man-child is strong and strong-willed. He is also related to the Crown. He could prove useful to both of us."

It suited William de Wendenal, Earl of Derby, to take in the young Guy.

Guy continued, "William took me in. He said he saw something in me. He trained me and vouched for me and that is how I came to be part of the Black Knights. I was impressionable then."

As he paused, Morgaine asked gently, "Would you continue with it now?"

Guy turned to Morgaine, again, looking directly into her eyes, "When I asked you to marry me and you said yes, you made me the happiest man alive! My first obligation is now to you, my Beloved, to this family, to this Land. You have seen what I am willing to do to protect you, right?"

Morgaine nodded. "I have also seen how tortured your mind is when you are around William. He has been like a father. Yet you know he has been betraying you and you feel you have nowhere to turn. It is like you have lost two fathers."

Guy clenched his jaw and closed his eyes for a moment to be sure a rogue tear did not have the opportunity to escape and give any tenderness away. No; not in front of Robin.

Marian watched Guy and her heart softened, reminding herself that she, too, had seen good in him. He had done good deeds.

Robin, however, would not relent. He could barely contain himself upon hearing Guy's portrayal of his father, but he redirected his focus to a more recent painful event. He accused, "You killed Arthur! You cut him and you killed him. Are you going to deny that?"

Guy heaved a strangled sigh, "Yes, I killed him and then I cut him."

Robin shook his head angrily, "I do not understand. Why are you playing with my words?"

Guy replied softly but firmly, "I am not. I am merely telling you the order in which it happened."

"Why does that matter?"

"Perhaps it does not." There was so much more he wanted to say, but it was for Morgaine's benefit, not Robin's. Robin didn't deserve to know his heart. He would willingly bear up his soul for Morgaine and wanted so desperately for her to love him even if others thought he was a monster. But to show his hand to Robin? To tell him his tactics in navigating this abyss so he could survive? No. He turned to Morgaine, took her hands, looking at her, imparting his thoughts only to her. "I did not torture Robin's friend. Please believe me. I do not believe that is the way to truth despite what the inquisitors say." Guy searched his lover's eyes and he opened his memory to her. Morgaine saw the scene that transpired between Guy and Arthur. It was hard to stomach, seeing Guy's tempered resolve. But she gave a slight nod, letting Guy know she felt his inner struggle of how far he would go to endure.

Robin was fuming. He felt Guy was deliberately ignoring him. He laid a hand on Guy's arm, pulling him toward him.

Guy grabbed Robin's hand and the two advisories locked eyes in a nasty stare down.

Morgaine stepped between them, firmly shouting, "No!"

Upon hearing the Lady of the Lake's voice, the Master of Arms opened the door to check on the party. Marian looked at Taharqa and shook her head slightly. He waited at the door, noting that the men were posturing at each other but no blows took place. Still he waited for his Lady's signal. Morgaine gave a slight nod of the head. Taharqa returned it and closed the door again.

Morgaine's hands were on the men's chests. She recognized she could not will peace into their hearts. All she could do was focus on Guy and ask him silently to remain calm. Her words filtered through all the anger into his mind, "Love, I heard your side. I saw it. That is what matters. I know you see Robin as the enemy and you do not wish to try your hand that he may use it against you."

Guy breathed a sigh of relief. He then stepped back from Robin. And Robin, begrudgingly, did the same. With as much calm as he could muster, and choosing his words carefully, Guy said to Robin, "I do what I have to in order to stay alive. And if it comes down to me or you, it's going to be me I choose."

Robin spat back, "You had a choice!"

"What would you have me do? Lay my head down for the Sheriff to cut it off? No. I have a strong urge for self-preservation." With that he turned to Morgaine, "And I pray you can forgive me for what I have done to survive this long. And I promise now, whatever my own desire is, I will live and die protecting you."

Morgaine had tears in her eyes as she nodded, understanding more deeply than Guy could explain in the moment, as she caught a memory of his: of him surrounded by men with swords drawn as he stood in front of a chained prisoner.

Robin too understood this choice of self-preservation as he had lived through it in the Holy Lands. But this did not make him any more compassionate toward Guy. He thought Guy had been at it too long to come back from it. But if one added up the bodies as Robin never would, it was Robin in the Holy Land who had more kills. Robin did all he could to blot out those memories, as fresh as they were, for if he could not, he thought no one, especially not Marian, could love him. He thought Marian could not understand his justifications for killing in the Holy Land. And he may have been right. Yet she still cared for Guy and she still saw good in him and that made him all the more enraged.

Morgaine picked up on his thoughts and then turned on Robin, "And what about you, Robin? What are your sins against others? How many did you kill in the Holy Land?" Robin just glared at her so she continued, "Would you return to the Holy Land to fight against a people we have no quarrel with?"

There was no hesitation, "Yes, for God and country and at the King's command. King Richard gave me leave to put my estate in order when I received word my father had passed."

"I am sorry for your loss," Morgaine stated, but then continued with her former line of thought, "Is this the same God who says 'turn the other cheek'? Who states, 'thou shalt not kill'? That God? You are saying the Christian God told Richard to go kill the Moors?" Robin was not sure how to respond. He hadn't thought of it that way. Morgaine continued, "So you are upheld as a hero in this land because you stand with a king who fights a people in a foreign land. Did you ever consider that to the Moors, you are the villain?" Robin was visibly taken aback but wasn't sure what to say. He certainly didn't consider himself a villain. He was nothing like Guy. Morgaine's eyes narrowed, as if she heard his thought. Then she said, "Perhaps you both are villains, killing your way through life for causes." Guy looked hurt and Morgaine softened, "What makes you a hero are the deeds you do from a place of love."

Marian chimed in, "Guy, I have seen your kindness and your cruelty. As much as you do ill by the people of Nottingham under the Sheriff's orders, I have also witnessed the good you do to remedy suffering and to protect those you care for." Turning to Robin, Marian stated, "Robin, I see you as an honorable man, a man of principle, a man who does what he thinks is right. Is it right, though, to have such venom toward Guy? He was once your father's ward and so like a brother..." Her voice trailed off as she added "to you," seeing the menacing look in Robin's eyes.

Guy's eyebrow rose. Though he was upset with Marian for lying to him, for being secretly not only in league with Robin, but in love with him as well, he saw she was throwing him a peace flag. He took it. "Thank you, Marian."

Marian turned from Robin to Guy and nodded slightly before turning back to Robin.

But Robin's heart still stabbed for what Guy said earlier and he turned on him, bringing up the past. "Brother? Never! And would a good man lie? How dare you say such hateful things about my father! He is dead and cannot defend his word."

Guy was taken aback by the redirection to Robin's father. He did not figure Robin was so vexed about the comment he made earlier but he responded, "Because it is true. Your father, I think, was troubled that my sister and I reminded him of our parents. It would have been a constant ache. He loved my mother..."

"Take that back! It isn't true."

"It is! Your father bedded my mother while my father was away on a mission of your father's design. She was with his child. We would have shared kin..."

"You lie!"

172

Guy sounded exasperated now at Robin's perceived childishness. "Robin, why would I lie? You might not remember, but how could I forget how round she was getting? How could I forget the nights she entertained your father? As much as I loved her, I hated her for coupling with him even if he was the Baron. I saw it. I saw the look in their eyes. There was love there."

Robin bit his lip and looked down. He had no idea what to say. As much as he despised Guy, he wasn't sure how to respond. He had successfully managed to turn the focus away from him in the Holy Lands but only by focusing on something that opened an old wound. It hurt to think of his father having relations with other women after the death of his mother. And Guy's mother? And they would have shared kin? Robin hadn't been privy to Marguerite's pregnancy. He only remembered that she died and that his father took in the two orphans, disrupting his household.

Morgaine's eyes were slit like a cat's. She could see this was a calculated redirection, but before she could pounce on Robin again, Guy spoke in tired irritation. "Robin, I am about to release any claim I have on the Locksley Manor so that I can join with the Avalons. I am about to break with the Sheriff and I have no idea what penalty may befall me should the Prince not grant my leave. Please, let the past rest. I would give it back to you if I thought that mattered. But we both know your life is forfeit and that you cannot reside in your home as a criminal."

"What are you saying?"

"When I ask Prince John to give me leave to marry Morgaine and live here with her family, I will ask him to allow me to hand over the land to Boxer. He has a son of age who could take care of the property. And you could go to your family and work it out directly with them should King Richard return."

"You would ask Prince John to name Wyatt Boxer as Lord of Locksley?"

Guy nodded.

"By name?"

Guy nodded again.

Robin mulled over the thought. He couldn't see any deception in such a plan. Of course, this was Guy so there must be deception. But then, when love entered the equation, Guy had always proved earnest.

Morgaine listened with pride as her husband-to-be laid out his plan to Robin. She felt he took a huge leap in his heart and mind to be able to make peace enough with Robin so that he could move on with her. She recognized that though love may not wash away sin, by its very nature, it could alter outcomes.

As they moved back into the hall, Morgaine took hold of Guy's arm. "You make me proud, Beloved." She leaned her head on his upper arm as they walked. She could feel his tense body relax a bit. He kissed her on the head and squeezed her hand, whispering, "My Love, you inspire me to be a better man."

Robin and Marian walked together behind Morgaine and Guy, both watching the couple ahead of them, overhearing their words. Robin glanced at Marian upon hearing Guy's words, but she was still looking ahead.

The couples rejoined the party and Gareth, in his big, booming voice, called out to them, "Though they have blood on their hands, do you, Morgaine still love your Guy?"

"Yes, Father! Very much," she exclaimed, squeezing Guy's hand.

"And, you Marian? Do you still love your Robin?"

"Yes, Your Grace, I do love Robin."

Gareth nodded and waved his hand in an arch, "The past may yet haunt you but do not let it define you. Your reward for rising above your past is not what you get, but what you become. Now, by Gods, let us enjoy the present moment we have. Shake on that." The two adversaries eyed each other warily but both reached out their hands and shook.

Sir Taharqa sided up to Robin, extended his arm, gesturing for him to head the way of the door. He nodded to the two guards who had been with him to escort Robin out of the castle.

Marian slipped away from the hall, keeping a discreet distance until Robin and the guards had cleared the castle steps. Then she hurried her footsteps and called after Robin. Robin turned, as did the guards. As she came to them, Marian asked if she could have a moment with Robin. The guards, knowing Marian was Morgaine's friend, nodded and stepped back, allowing a small amount of privacy. Marian decided to be brazen like she had seen Morgaine be with Guy. She reached up and planted a kiss upon Robin's lips. "I am glad you came."

Robin was quite pleased with Marian's brazenness and returned her kiss in kind. "I am too, though I am sorry if I put you in any danger."

"I am in no danger here, my love. Morgaine's family is looking after us. And once I feel secure that my father is settled here, then I shall go with you wherever you shall ask."

"It will be dangerous to live the life of an outlaw."

"I would live it, if it meant to live with you."

Robin smiled warmly to that. "I shall come for you after their wedding then."

"Yes." They stood embraced in the growing darkness. "Robin?"

"Yes, my love?"

Marian confided, "When Morgaine and Guy freed her parents and my father, there were a few other prisoners. Two other men went free who agreed to the terms that Morgaine and William agreed to, but Lord Thomas wouldn't agree and so he and his wife remained in the dungeon."

"On what exactly are they being held?"

"I am not entirely sure. While I was down there, Evelyn told my father and me that William was attempting to force them into signing a pact proclaiming loyalty to Prince John but that the document did not have the Prince's seal. They knew they were caught in a web of intrigue between the brothers. They knew that to protect Glastonbury now they would have to sign such a document, but — as it did not actually come from the Prince — they knew it to be a trap to cause more upheaval and chaos in the country. They did not sign it and neither did a few others, so they were thrown into prison. Morgaine threatened the Sheriff that she had a rider set out to beseech the Prince to resolve the matter, which of course William did not want. So a tentative truce was reached and those that agreed to keep quiet would be allowed to go free. Lord Thomas Winter would not agree to side with the Prince, though, so he and the Lady Edwena are still there...unless they have been quietly done away with. Robin, would you..."

"I will see what I can do to find out what has become of them. If they live, I shall find some way of freeing them and getting them to safety. They have dangerous information. Even the freed ones do. You all are in danger."

"Gareth knows this. He has stepped up security but no one wanted to hamper the festivities."

Robin redirected the conversation by asking, "Is Guy truly earnest in his marriage to the Lady Morgaine? This is not just a ploy to gain more power, is it?"

Marian was surprised and hurt on Guy's behalf, but responded, "Yes, Robin. Guy adores Morgaine. I truly believe he will do whatever is needed to be with her. As much as he has been diligent in his role as William's right arm, he is completely willing to set it aside to be here with her. And he risks breaking with his patron in a bad way. The Sheriff was very angry with him regarding the pact incident. Now, seeing them at Beltane has sealed it for me that Guy would live and die for Morgaine as he said. He pledged his heart and his arms to her as well as to this land."

Robin whistled low. Marian was a practical woman and not given to exaggeration. He had to believe that Guy would soon be out of the picture at Nottingham. Then he wondered, would that be better or worse for Nottingham? Even if Boxer got Locksley Manor, he would not be instated as the Sheriff's right hand man; the Sheriff would handpick that person. It would be unlikely to be a man of Nottingham again. The Sheriff would see his mistake there. Never have a local police his own people; it leads to compassion and complications.

CHAPTER 17

Make Friends

THE NEXT MORNING Guy awoke to someone in his quarters. Sword drawn, he snuck up on the youth and tapped him on the shoulder. Mouse, an aptly named slight, light-footed youth, nearly jumped out of his skin. He was used to being quiet, to being virtually unseen, hence his name. He turned to be face to chin with a rather impressive man; Guy had an intense yet slightly bemused look on his face. Still, not someone to be trifled with.

Mouse piped, "My Mistress made it clear to me to present you with these gifts as a surprise. I will have a bath ready for you shortly, My Lord." As Mouse held the clothes out for Guy's inspection, Guy felt the cloth. So soft. He could tell that Morgaine had honored the spirit if not the letter of a Black Knight's dress code. The pants were much softer than the leather he wore and the color was closer to the darkest of blues then pitch black. And the blouse was the same, except in linen. He nodded his head to Mouse who squeaked, "Very good." Mouse then placed the clothes down so he could prepare the bath.

Guy sauntered into the dining hall for breakfast feeling like a new man. He sat down next to Morgaine and lifted her hand, kissing it.

She reached her other hand out to touch his shoulder. "It suits you."

"Thank you. It is a very thoughtful gift. Who is your seamstress?"

"Sarah. She is the best in town. She makes all of my garments. If you like her work, I would like very much for you to consider a wider range of color options for your wardrobe."

Guy smirked. "Are you telling me I don't have enough color in my life?"

Morgaine giggled, "Yes! Though do not get me wrong; you are devastatingly handsome in black. I just would like you to consider expanding your palette."

Guy only heard the words "devastatingly handsome" — for him that was enough. He kissed her on the mouth and then breathed in her ear, "For you, my love, anything."

Marian stood just outside the door and she smiled as she listened to the playful banter of the couple. Then a sadness crossed her face. It pained her that she and Guy hadn't made up. She knew he was upset with her not only for being in league with Robin but loving him as well. She left the hall before being noticed by the pair.

After their meal, Morgaine and Guy meandered through the town. Guy pondered, "There is much celebrating in this town. You celebrate both the Celtic and Norse holidays. Why is that?"

Morgaine and Guy were walking through the field and she tilted her head in thought. "My great, great, great grandmother, Raven, married a man of Viking ancestry. Guess his name," she added playfully.

Guy shook his head, "Crow?"

Morgaine shook her head barely containing her humor, "Rindill!" she blurted out.

Guy pondered, "Wren? King of the birds?" She nodded as Guy offered, "Given your family history, I can see how that is appropriate."

Morgaine then added, "When they wed, they married their traditions as well and so it has been with all Avalons since that we honor the quarters and cross-quarters." She concluded mirthfully, "And what could be wrong with more celebrations?"

Guy chuckled at that. "Nothing wrong with that." He paused as he mentally scanned the crowds both at the Beltane celebration and their wedding announcement. "Morgaine, but not all of Glastonbury celebrate these, as some would say, 'heathen holidays.'"

"That is true. But there is a quiet acceptance here of all traditions. You know Asher, the one from whom you bought Midnight? He and his wife, Leah, their daughter, Sarah, and her husband, Kedem are Jewish. I know I can say this to you in trust, my love. But if Richard knew how many so called 'heretics' were here, he would burn this place to the ground."

Guy nodded, adding, "And yet the Tor is here. There is much romanticism about the Tor, and now Glastonbury Abbey, being heralded as the final resting place of King Arthur. I would imagine Christians are now flocking to it."

"That is true. And it is the vocation of this family to keep the peace. Think of all the religions as spokes on a wheel. Each serves its purpose in seeing the Divine. We are all turning toward God though I am sure none of us, no matter what anyone preaches, has the full picture of God."

Guy smiled thoughtfully at his bride-to-be. "You are so wise, My Sweet." Morgaine beamed as he continued, "Would that the priests understood that." He was hesitant, considering the misgivings he had of the Church. He paused, wavering on how much more to say. He settled on, "I suppose I have been a heathen since my parents died. I grew tired of listening to all the rules and the ways one could be bad or wrong or spoiled goods."

Morgaine touched her beloved's shoulder, "You are safe here, Love, for even as we live in the Light, we all live in the shades of gray as well." They leaned into each other, entwining fingers.

The evening meal, though happy enough, had the distinct flavor of wariness. It wasn't quite that Marian and Guy were actively avoiding each other, but there was a sense of unsettledness between them. Guy and Marian were polite but there was definitely an odd quiet to this meal, everyone doing their best to step carefully and allow the two to work it out on their own.

By the next day things were still tense and Morgaine wondered who would speak first to whom. But as neither appeared to approach the other, she took it upon herself to create an opportunity. "Guy, Marian, would you please accompany me?" Morgaine held out her hands and each rose from the table where they had finished their meal. She led them away and they all walked hand in hand down the castle steps and out to the field facing the Lake. Morgaine sighed and sat down. Guy and Marian both looked down at Morgaine and then joined her. They could tell that Morgaine had a plan and that they were somehow part of it; each were full of thoughts as to why Morgaine brought them out here to sit on the ground. Morgaine just sat there looking out onto the Lake.

Guy broke the silence, "Morgaine, why did you bring us here?"

"Isn't it just lovely to spend time with friends?"

They both shifted uncomfortably.

Then Guy stated plainly, "I do not believe that Marian and I are friends."

Marian looked at Guy, hurt by his words. She bit her lower lip and then looked down.

Morgaine responded, "Why would you think that?"

Guy heaved a sigh and then looked at Marian, "Because you lied to me, Marian. You said you did not love Robin. You said you did not side with him. I protected you countless times from the Sheriff and you lied to me."

Marian remembered keenly the backhanded slaps and harsh words Guy took on her behalf. Yet defiant tears moistened her eyes. She bit her words, "What choice did I have? You two are sworn enemies. I have always wanted to help the people and he and I agreed to do that. I do care for you. I did not want to hurt you or lie to you but I had to protect myself."

"From me?" Guy felt wounded.

Morgaine touched his shoulder, "Beloved, what would you have done if Marian had confessed her allegiance and her love?"

"I...I am not sure. It would have been a shock. I want to believe that I still would have wanted to protect Marian."

"But that would have put you in a dangerous fix, to have information, a potential spy for Robin, as you were protecting her."

"Yes, well, that is why I asked for her loyalty."

"Asked?" Retorted Marian, "It felt like a demand."

"Okay, yes. I demanded to know that you sided with me."

"And so what could I say otherwise?"

Guy looked down. "Nothing. You were protecting yourself and your father. I would have been forced to lock you up. William would have used you as a weapon to get Robin. I understand. It just hurts."

Marian reached her hand across Morgaine to touch Guy, "I am sorry. I do care for you, Guy. I always have and I am so happy that you have found Morgaine and that you are becoming the man I knew you could be."

Guy patted Marian's hand and then looked into her eyes, "As much as it hurt to be rejected by you and not know why, it hurts more to be lied to. Though now I understand why. I am sorry you felt you could not trust me. I hope to earn your trust."

"You being the way you are with Morgaine earns my trust. I see there is a strong bond and love growing between the two of you. It has been amazing to watch. You are changing, Guy. I want to be a friend to this person who is before me now." The tears were now streaming down Marian's face.

Morgaine kept looking out to the Lake but now there was a smile on her face.

Guy looked at Morgaine and then at Marian. "Yes, I would like very much for us to be friends."

With that Marian reached her arms around Morgaine and to Guy. And he reached back. Morgaine was caught in the middle and began to giggle. They each kissed her cheeks and then reached to kiss each other. The three of them rocked together and sighed and laughed. The tension drained away and they all knew they could move on from this.

CHAPTER 18

The Hunting Party

AT THE EVENING meal, Gareth told Guy to prepare to go hunting early in the morning. Guy smiled proudly at being included in Gareth's hunting party. He'd only been once before with Prince John. In Derby, William and the Black Knights went on hunting parties. It was stiff competition as they all vied to demonstrate their prowess with the bow. Guy was an excellent marksman and was looking forward to demonstrating to his future father-in-law that he could be a good provider.

Guy awoke again to Mouse in his room. From his bed he spoke out, "Do you make it a habit of creeping about in other people's rooms?"

Mouse again nearly jumped out of his skin. He thought he was being quiet. No one else seemed to notice him.

Guy picked up on the young fellow's nervousness. "Look, I am just used to having to be very aware and so I tend to be a light sleeper. Is it time to get up then?"

Mouse nodded in the dark and lit a candle on the table. He turned to bring Guy his clothes and Guy was already standing in front of him. Mouse involuntarily jumped, startled by how silently and cat-like Guy had moved from his bed to him. Mouse shook slightly as he handed Guy the new garments. The pants and blouse and over-shirt were dark browns and grays.

Guy ignored Mouse's behavior, inquiring, "Another gift?"

Mouse nodded, saying, "The other men will be in similar colors to blend in with the landscape."

182

Guy dressed by one lit candle, not even looking at himself in the polished metal mirror. He belted his sword and quiver, grabbed his bow, and moved swiftly outside to where the others were gathering. He nodded to Gareth who introduced him to the rest of the hunting party. The men did not ride out as Guy was accustomed to. They crept swiftly through the field that led away from the Lake and into the forest on the other side of Glastonbury. It was quiet and still dark. The dawn was only just blooming in the sky, the palest of light. The men were very still, all listening for movement. The group motioned to one another and two broke apart from the company to attempt to flush game toward the others. There was much waiting. Then movement. The wind was in the hunters' favor. Bows were raised.

Guy caught sight of a small herd of deer coming toward them. He took aim and breathed out slowly as he released the arrow. He heard other arrows make their mark as well. Three bucks were brought down out of the five that were seen. The men gathered together around the bodies of the dying deer. The men ended the suffering of dying animals and honored their lives, thanking them for the meat that their bodies would provide for the town. One man dipped his finger in the blood and marked each of the men in turn on their cheeks. No words were spoken about why this was done, but Guy recognized it as another way that the hunters connected with their prey. The deer were then tied up to sturdy limbs and the men returned to town as the sun rose a third of the way into the sky. The animals were brought in to the butcher and Gareth shared a list of recipients of the meat, in addition to the hunting party's men. The party all shook hands and returned to their dwellings. Gareth and Guy walked back to the castle together. Guy wasn't sure he should break the silence but he had questions.

As they mounted the steps he spoke up, "Your Grace?"

"Gareth."

"Gareth?"

"Yes?"

"Thank you for including me."

"You are most welcome, Guy. You are good with the bow. You made your mark."

There were a few meanings Guy could take from that; instead he just said, "Thank you." Guy paused, pondering how to ask his question. Then started, "Gareth, I am wondering about this hunting party. You were present more than just to hunt, but to give it legitimacy, following the letter of the Crown's law, yes?"

Gareth smiled slightly. "Yes. Though it is true, too, that I enjoy the hunt. The purpose of the hunt is to feed the people of our town and not simply for the King's sport. I cannot go out as often as needed, so it is good that you are joining our family and that you are a strong marksman. There will be more early mornings."

"I look forward to them."

"Good."

CHAPTER 19

Braiding Lives Together

GUY WENT BACK to his room, washed the blood off his face, and headed back to the dining hall. As Guy walked into the hall, he saw Morgaine speaking with Taharqa. She kissed him on the cheek and gave him a hug. Then she noticed Guy, and motioned him to come to her. He complied readily.

"How was the hunt?"

"We did well. I enjoyed it."

"Good." Morgaine put a hand on each man's arm, stating, "Guy, I want to formally introduce you to Glastonbury's Master of Arms, Sir Taharqa, son of Tana."

The two men shook arms.

Taharqa had a very curious accent even as he spoke impeccable English, "It is good to be introduced to you, Lord Guy."

"You as well," stated Guy.

"I am sure there will be time for better acquainting ourselves with each other but right now I have duties to attend to."

Guy offered generously, "Of course. I look forward to our next opportunity."

With that Sir Taharqa gave a bow and withdrew.

Guy eyed Morgaine, "You seem quite familiar with the Master of Arms."

Morgaine giggled and pushed Guy's arm. "We've grown up together. He is a good friend. Do not be jealous."

"I'm not. I am merely taking notice."

"Well then, take notice of this," Morgaine exclaimed as she planted an eager kiss upon Guy's lips.

Guy closed his eyes and breathed deeply, in utter happiness. After a moment he questioned, "What is Sir Taharqa's story? How did he come to be Glastonbury's Master of Arms?"

Morgaine responded, "He rose up like any young man with a keen aptitude for weaponry. He is a most deadly mark and so Sir Hammond, the former Master of Arms, took Taharqa as his apprentice." Guy nodded and Morgaine could tell that this only partly answered his full question. "You mean, you wonder how he, a dark-skinned man, got here, to England, in the first place?"

"Yes."

"Taharqa and I are very close in age. His mother was pregnant with him when she arrived, just as my mother was newly pregnant with me when she received her. Tana arrived with Sir Harry who had returned from the Crusades. He apparently had bought Tana to take her out of a most wretched situation. When he told her she could go, she stayed. She said she had no idea what Harry was saying to her. So she came with him, just followed him wherever he went. And so Harry gave her to the Duchess. My mother asked Tana if she wanted to stay or go home. Tana pointed to the floor and so she stayed. My mother sheltered her, gave her work, and helped bring her baby into this world."

"Where is Tana now?"

"Watch. You will see her."

As the family breakfasted together, Guy noticed a shadow behind Evelyn. But it was no shadow, it was Tana, the Duchess' dark-skinned servant. She was quiet, proud, and simply watching over her mistress. "How could I have missed her," Guy wondered to himself? Tana felt eyes upon her and looked at Guy. He smiled reassuringly and gave her a nod. Tana nodded back and then resumed her focus on the Duchess.

Guy leaned over and whispered to Morgaine, "Love, why I have not seen Tana traveling with the family? Clearly she attends to your mother."

"The people of Glastonbury are used to Tana and her son but we know there could be problems on the road if either were to come. There is much prejudice against the Moors and those who look similar to them though it is we who invaded their lands. And Taharqa's place is here; as Master of Arms he is needed here, protecting Glastonbury. Besides, Sophie looks after my parents as well. But it is Tana you will find when you enter my mother's receiving room. She was a temple priestess in another land and she serves in a similar way here, attending to my mother as a priestess to a high priestess."

Though Guy was not entirely sure what that meant, he nodded in contemplation as he considered the various roles people served in this castle.

After the meal, Evelyn nodded to Sophie as she left the room. Sophie approached Morgaine and Guy. "My mistress asks that you follow me."

Evelyn was already ahead of them and as they entered the Duchess' receiving room there was Tana, behind Evelyn, who was seated in her chair. The couple approached her. "The full moon is tonight. Prepare yourselves."

Morgaine could hardly contain herself with glee. She clapped her hands and rushed to her mother's lap. "Thank you!" Though her mother hadn't told her what was to transpire, she knew what had to be coming. There was nothing else she could think of that would warrant her mother's bemused smile.

Guy observed that Evelyn's eyes had the look of merriment about them. He figured since Evelyn was a direct woman, she wouldn't mind directness. "What am I preparing for?" Guy asked.

"Your lives together, of course. Tonight you will weave your Handfasting cord and commit your lives to each other. Into the cord you will weave what you bring to the marriage: your qualities, your promises. After this night, you will be recognized as handfasted and you will treat each other as husband and wife. On the Summer Solstice you will then be formally married before the town, your family, and your friends, and the Prince."

"You know he will give me leave to marry?"

"He will give you leave, yes."

As the full moon rose, the family and Guy gathered at a small white dwelling, partially hidden by shrubbery at the edge of the Lake. It looked like a small open-air chapel with high open windows. In design it looked like those in ancient Rome, like a miniature colosseum; it was an oddity among the other Roman, English and French architectural feats in town.

Evelyn took their hands in hers and briefly explained the Handfasting tradition, that it is meant to bind the couple together emotionally and spirituality as well as to prepare them for their combined life together as husband and wife. "This tradition takes place over the course of a year and a day to be sure the couple is uncompromising in their devotion to each other. However, as we have seen energies aligning and the firmness of the bond, Gareth and I are predisposed to speed up the process provided you both are resolute in your commitment. Are you so determined?"

Both Morgaine and Guy responded in unison, "Yes."

Evelyn nodded with a gentle smile upon her face as she wrapped the strands of colored wool around the couple's interlaced hands. She then kissed each of their cheeks in turn and gestured for them to walk into the chapel.

Gareth winked at them as he closed the doors, leaving them alone inside.

Guy and Morgaine retreated into the small dwelling by the Lake. The place was made up beautifully for the occasion. Scents of fresh herbs wafted in the air. Both inhaled and looked around observing that much care went into making this night special for them. Even food and mead awaited them on the small table.

Guy lightly rubbed his upper lip with his forefinger in contemplation, then waved his hand in the air back and forth, "What is this place used for, normally?"

Morgaine responded, "It has not had any other use for years, except for small ceremonies."

"Small ceremonies like this one?" Guy asked slyly.

Morgaine just laughed. As they had walked in, she pulled the woolen strands from their hands and now had the cords draped around her neck. She looked down as she fingered them.

Guy noticed and touched the cords as he grazed her breast, "What do we do?"

She looked up at him shyly and whispered hotly, "Let's sit on the cushions." They sat facing each other. She took the long strands of colored wool, remarking, "This is what we shall braid together. As we do so, we shall say what we want to bring into our marriage together."

Guy looked slightly dubious as he cocked his head to the side, "I have never braided."

"It's easy. Here, you sit behind me and I will guide our hands." They shifted positions and she knotted one end then braced it under her foot. He placed his hands over hers and they began to braid the strands together. "I weave in our strong bond to each other. May our love grow and thrive like the Apple Orchard."

Guy followed suit, "I weave in trust. May we always trust each other."

They continued to weave and state what they hoped for their marriage. Morgaine giggled, stating, "May we spend much time kissing."

Guy smiled and kissed her ear, then nibbled at it, adding, "Yes, kissing — kissing everywhere." They rocked together as they wove the long cord. Guy wondered at the length of the cord and if it was meant to be a specific length. He stopped her hands from braiding for a moment so he could ask the question. "Morgaine, is there a reason for the cord's length?"

She chuckled, "Are you fingers getting tired?"

He laughed, "Well, a bit. I am not used to braiding. But the question is legitimate. I am curious."

"The cord is fifteen hands long by my mother's hand. The number five represents the five Elements — Earth, Air, Fire, Water, Spirit. The number three is something we call 'the three-fold law.' At the first level, we speak the prayer, chant the spell. At the second level, Spirit takes over and the prayer is heard, the spell is cast. At the third level, our prayer, our spell, manifests."

Guy listened intently, taking in this curious power of three. He wondered if it related to the Christians' power of three — the Father, Son, and the Holy Spirit.

Morgaine responded to his silent ponderings, "There are many similarities between religions and the value we place on specific numbers."

Guy rubbed Morgaine's head affectionately with his cheek, "It is such a wonder you can hear my thoughts. I am still getting used to it."

"I am sorry. I don't mean to pry. Hearing you just seems to come naturally."

"I am not offended, Love, just in awe of your gift."

It took some time, but they completed the braid and Morgaine knotted it off. "We will be tethered together with this cord when we are married in ceremony. When we leave this place, we shall also wrap this cord around our hands and walk through town, showing that we are a couple." Meanwhile, she draped the completed braid around her neck and let the ends fall over her breasts.

Guy turned his thoughts and body to the other part of the ritual, the part he had been looking forward to since the moment he understood he was being given permission to finally consummate this relationship. Guy kissed Morgaine gently. He wanted her first experience to feel wonderful. He pushed the thought out of all the times a woman's pleasure was not his primary purpose as he fucked so-and-so's wife to gather information for William. It was all just the work of a pretty spy. But, by God, this time he would take absolute care to give his woman a pleasurable experience for her sake and not merely for his own ends. He knew a woman's first time could hurt and, unfortunately, Morgaine knew it too. "What do you know of the first time?" Guy murmured into her ear.

Morgaine sat up straight and turned to look at him, "My friend Gwenhwyfar told me how it hurt. Her husband was not overly gentle. Actually, he is a brute. Nichole vaguely remembers it being uncomfortable, but she told me that she and her husband have such delightful romps that, whatever the first time felt like, every time since has been wonderful. My mother said to relax and focus on our breathing, and that if you had any sense it would hurt little at first and none later."

Guy chuckled, "Well I hope to have more than enough sense." Guy took his time in caressing Morgaine and feeling her body relax into his. As their fingers slowly swirled along each other's forms they both felt their passion build. He reached up through the folds of her gown to caress the petals of her dark rose and feel it moisten. She moaned, "Oh I love this part. This feels so good!" Guy smiled and kept rubbing her, knowing that — by giving her more pleasure — breaking her maidenhood wouldn't hurt as much. Then, as he knew she would, she could tell her mother that Guy had much sense.

A woman's voice echoed unbidden in Guy's head, "No, start slow. I know you want to just throw yourself about but that does nothing for your lover. Slow. Listen. Feel your lover's body. Touch here..." Ann circled in his head. "Go slow. Tease. You want a sweetheart who will yearn for you, do you not?"

> William had paid Ann, a prostitute of some stature, to lie with Guy for his first time. But she also took an interest in the lad; her focus was to make this pretty boy an attentive lover. "Do you know what to do with that thing?" she teased the young, beautiful Guy.
> "Yes," he stammered, "I stick it in you. We fuck."
> "Oh heavens, I think I shall swoon with your poetry," she mocked. Ann then took hold of the young man-child and taught him the ways of lovemaking. She was an older woman: a big, buxom blond. William had chosen her because she was known for her specialty in teaching young virgins, both males and females, how to be good lovers. A useful skill for the spy William was training Guy to be. William also knew she'd show Guy a good time. And the lad was so tense. William figured Ann was exactly what Guy needed. It was actually one of William's more intelligent decisions.

Guy came swiftly back into the present moment. This night was for Morgaine. He kissed her and caressed the length of her body. They helped each other remove their clothing. Guy then kissed his way down the center of Morgaine's body and when he reached her mound, he opened her two-leaved gate gently, tasting her nectar. She moaned in delight. He smiled and then kissed, licked and gently pulled on her nether lips. She writhed and swayed, all the while making short breathy sounds of "ah" which were music to his ears. Guy kissed his way back up to her lips and their bodies moved together.

As her entered her, Morgaine felt a searing pain like the lightning he had described to her once. But then an odd feeling remained, yes — like the rumbling of thunder, it was building and felt like a wave of reverberations inside of her. It was just as he had described. And the pain subsided and the rocking together felt exquisitely good and right and perfectly natural. She felt as if their bodies had been made for one another. She felt him rocking faster and she joined to keep up with him. Suddenly she felt a flood of warm liquid rushing inside her. As odd as it was, the sensation also made her shudder in delight. She couldn't keep quiet, "What is happening? I feel I am being flooded."

Guy, surprised to hear a question that sounded like something he was supposed to answer, tried to come back from his altered state of euphoria. "Are you okay? Did that feel good to you?" Guy was suddenly concerned he was misreading her and that she was not having a good experience.

She quickly relieved him of any concern, "Oh Guy, this has felt as you said it would and more. I am going to enjoy making love to you for the rest of my life!"

He practically glowed at that compliment and she added, "It is just, I am so wet!" She giggled. "It's more than just my juices in here. You have soaked me." As they moved slightly apart, she could feel the sensation reverse itself. "Now the flood is coming out. What an odd sensation."

Guy watched her merry eyes dancing with a mixture of questioning and excitement. She looked down to see a bit of blood from her maidenhood; her mother had told her to expect this.

Guy reached over her and brought back a bit of cloth and gently rubbed her thighs and mound as he looked at her lovingly. He was slightly in awe she was finding such amusement in the act, but was also overjoyed that she wanted to make love to him for the rest of their lives. They laid back and gently caressed each other, allowing themselves to float in a blissful state.

In the morning, Morgaine rose and sauntered naked to the back door that faced the Lake. She opened it and walked through. He suddenly heard a splash and an exclamation. He chuckled to himself and rose to join her.

"I-eee! This water is cold," exclaimed Guy, after he surfaced from his plunge off the rickety, small dock.

Morgaine laughed exuberantly, "Ha! Nay, the water is invigorating!"

Guy's body shivered uncontrollably as he rolled his eyes at her description of the water's temperature. Still, not to be completely outdone by his bride-to-be, he performed a few strokes through the water then headed for shore. Standing naked on the ground he shivered again while Morgaine continued to swim and twirl in the water. He shook his head, "For all that is holy, woman, how do you stand it?"

Morgaine continued to roll her body in the water enjoying how the chilly water penetrated her skin. She responded with mirth in her voice, "I am part otter."

Guy left his part-otter betrothed in search of a blanket inside the dwelling. He returned a few moments later wrapped up in one and holding Morgaine's shift in the other, calling teasingly, "Come on out, Otter."

They returned together to the small dwelling and lied back down on the bed, caressing the water droplets on each other's bodies.

At some point, they realized their stomachs were grumbling for food. Guy chose fruits, cheese, and bread, placing them on a plate. He grabbed the bottle of mead, too, and brought it all to the bed. They fed each other, smacking their lips, and swigging the mead. Morgaine wiped her mouth, smiling mischievously, and proceeded to pour a spot of mead on Guy.

Guy jumped at the liquid being poured on his loins, only to laugh seductively, thoroughly enjoying Morgaine's tongue as she murmured, "Oh, oops, let me lick that up," as she licked and sucked on his cock. "Make love to me again," she crooned as her tongue circled his shaft of delight.

Guy moaned as she continued to play with him. Sensations were building, but he was not yet ready to come. He surprised her by dumping her backwards on the bed. He took a swig of the mead and went down on her. She felt his tongue and the alcohol on her nether lips and circling her hooded jewel. He licked and sucked on her and she moaned loudly pulling his hair to get his head closer to her. She rocked and continued to moan in ecstasy. Guy rose up on his knees, pulling her legs up around his torso and thrust himself deep inside her.

"Oh, you are so deep inside me," she exclaimed breathlessly! Her "ohs" echoed in the room, in his ears and he was in heaven.

Entirely spent, they laid entangled together, breathing peacefully.

Morgaine was lying in front of Guy with her body up against his and his arms around her breasts. Morgaine's eyes, though looking ahead, saw the past. "Guy?"

"Yes, Love?"

"How did you do it?"

"Do what?"

"How did you do all that you had to do under the Order of the Black Knights?" She could feel Guy suddenly hold his breath. This was not a question he wanted to have to respond to. Still, she pressed on, "I saw something; men in black had you surrounded with swords drawn as you cut a chained man. It was horrible!"

Guy held her more tightly and she let him. He kissed her ear. In a voice only slightly above a whisper, Guy strangled his words, "I cannot say with any clarity whether it was courage or cowardice that allowed me to get through that ordeal. I promised myself to survive. At times I have not been entirely sure it was worth it. I steeled myself against it all." He started rocking gently with her. "But then you came into my life and everything changed. I have had to tell myself everything was worth it, that I made it this long so that I could meet you and find love with you. Tell me it was worth all the pain I felt, all the pain I inflicted. Tell me, and I will believe you."

Morgaine did her best to review his path and see the forks in the road of his choices. Many led to an earlier death. Certainly, the one in the dungeon with the Order did. Her silence was agonizing to Guy. But he held his tongue, waiting, holding his breath. Finally Morgaine spoke, turning to face Guy as she did, "I cannot see all the choices you made and all the paths you may have taken. There were many circumstances that led to an early death and we never would have met. So, though I cannot absolve you of your sins and it is painful to see images from your past where you hurt others, I am ever so grateful that you are alive and in my arms and in my heart."

Guy finally exhaled.

She brought her hand up to his cheek, "Beloved, the past is what it was and cannot be altered. You may never be forgiven by those you wronged. By some, you will remain the devil; by others, you are a hero; to others still, you are just a man. It is rare that any one person can be seen as one thing by all people."

"But surely, Morgaine, people love you. I see them adore you."

"Not William de Wendenal."

"One person."

"Still, Love, do you see? There will always be someone who sees the devil. No one is ever seen or remembered as only one thing or another. Even monsters have mothers."

Guy chuckled.

Though there was more to say, each felt the pause in the conversation and allowed it to grow. Guy stroked Morgaine's arm, feeling the ground they had covered in accepting Guy's past as the past. He felt loved by her and decided for the moment not to care whether he thought he deserved it or not.

Another night came and went as they reveled in each other's bodies. But in the early morning Guy's thoughts returned to yesterday's unfinished conversation. Because Morgaine wanted to know about his past, he wanted to know about his future. "Do you think everyone is redeemable?"

Morgaine responded, "I am not sure. I would like to believe that."

"Even William?"

"Hmm."

"What do you believe brings about redemption?"

"Love. And not just love from another but also self-love. You have to look at yourself in a pool, see the surface and the distortions from the waves and the depth, and decide you are lovable."

With that, Morgaine got up and reached out for Guy's hand. He took her hand and stood up. They were naked and Guy felt slightly self-conscious, but he let her lead him outside. They walked to the shore and knelt down, looking into the water. Guy looked at himself, really looked at himself. He could feel his emotions draw to the surface. He clenched his jaw to fight back the welling of emotion.

"Why do you do that?" asked Morgaine, as she watched his reflection.

"What?"

"You know what. I see you clench your jaw, getting frustrated with yourself for showing emotion."

Guy smirked, only half believing what he said, "Men aren't supposed to cry."

Morgaine countered, "That is horse dung! It is unhealthy to disconnect yourself from your emotions. I am sad that so many boys grow up being told such nonsense. One would think that in this day and age we could learn from one another better. We are about to enter a new century after all. We are not in some barbaric period of the five hundreds. This is eleven-ninety-two."

Guy shook his head with a thoughtful smile, "You are such a wonder, My Love. Sometimes it is hard to believe you are real." He reached over and pinched her bottom. "But you are."

They both laughed.

"Look," Morgaine said tenderly, pointing to the water. Guy looked again. "Guy, I love you! And I want you to love yourself for all that you are." Morgaine was thoughtful as she continued, "I want you to love that tender, emotional little boy. I want you to love that sour, impressionable young man. I want you to love that gallant knight. I even want to you love that villain and show compassion for how he got to where he was. And I want you to love the man you are becoming, the champion. Can you do all that?"

Guy was silent as he gazed into the Lake taking in all that Morgaine said.

They spent the rest of the early morning just gazing at each other's reflections in the water. When Guy felt some resolution in accepting himself for who he was, he took a deep breath, expelled the air, and watched the force of his breath create ripples in the water. He nodded and decided it was time to move on. Morgaine loved him and that was enough for now. And besides, he was hungry.

He drew her up and she did not question him. She recognized this interlude went as far as he was able to go for the moment and that was enough for her was well. They walked back into their little sanctuary and sat down to eat, both preoccupied in thought. Both got dressed, as Morgaine said she had a special place she wanted to introduce to Guy. As they left the small dwelling, Guy took Morgaine's hand in his. They smiled sweetly at each other. Morgaine then took the Handfasting cord that she had still draped around her neck and wrapped it around their held hands. They walked into the town like that, with many heads bowing and faces smiling at the recognizable pair. Seeing their acceptance, Guy's sense of belonging grew and he smiled back at the townspeople.

As the couple walked to the stables, Morgaine felt a familiar and slightly uncomfortable feeling in her abdomen. She squeezed Guy's hand, saying, "I will be back shortly. I have a matter I must attend to first." She untangled her hand and left him with the cord. Guy lazed on the steps soaking up the sun's warmth. In her room, Morgaine lifted up her gown and pulled down her undergarments. She noticed the blood on her undergarments. This was not her maidenhood's blood. Her Moontime had come a day earlier than she had expected. Morgaine sighed, "Well, this could alter my romantic plans." But there was nothing that could be done, so she shrugged off her disappointment. She took off her undergarments, put new ones on with her Moontime rags, and set her soiled undergarments in a basin to soak. She then readied herself for her ride with Guy.

She came back down the steps and they re-tethered themselves with the cord, walking hand in hand to the stables. Guy then unwound the cord and placed it around Morgaine's neck, caressing her breasts as he smoothed the strands down the front of her body. She shivered in delight.

Midnight nickered, letting his human know it was high time that Guy pay attention to him. Guy chuckled, came closer, and patted Midnight's neck. Guy and Morgaine saddled up and rode off. Guy could tell Morgaine was preoccupied, but he was fine with the silence. Morgaine was now re-considering what she had in mind. She still wanted to bring him to the waterfall though now her plan of a romantic afternoon might have to be altered with her bleeding. She wasn't sure if men made love to women during their courses. And would Guy? She did not remember hearing that it was unwise to have sex during this time so there certainly shouldn't be any reason not to. She just wasn't sure if either of them would want to; it might be rather messy.

Morgaine led the way past the Lake and into the woods. Though Guy could tell there was a foot trail, this certainly was not a horse trail. When at last they came to a small clearing, Guy whistled low; the sight he saw was divine. A waterfall tumbled into a small pool. They were surrounded by forest. Morgaine dismounted from Merryweather, leading her to a patch of tall grass. Guy did the same with Midnight. Morgaine took Guy's hand and led him to the waterfall.

Midnight was not as interested in the grass. He nickered to Guy. Guy eyed his horse. Midnight stood still watching Guy. Guy responded, "I know, I don't see an orchard either. What are you to do? I suppose it is grass for you."

Midnight neighed slightly in protest. Guy chuckled and shook his head. "You are fine, Midnight. Keep Merryweather company."

Midnight continued to watch his human. Merryweather then made an inviting sound from where she was grazing and Midnight responded and pranced over to her. Grass was certainly not an apple, but Midnight was over his disappointment within moments.

Morgaine chortled as she listened to rider and horse banter. Then she tugged on Guy's hand. "Come." Pointing, she said, "See the lip? I love standing there and feeling the water pound on me."

"What are we waiting for then?" Guy started stripping.

Morgaine giggled and then explained, "I am on my Moontime."

The meaning was lost on Guy. "And?"

"And, well...I am not sure. Blood may drip down my leg."

"And you of all people, after pricking our fingers to join our blood together, are embarrassed by a little blood?"

"No!"

"Then..."

Morgaine pulled the cords and let her gown fall. The waves of sumptuous green and golden fabric fell away. She then dropped her undergarments, turned swiftly, and made her way to the mouth of the shallow cave. Guy followed suit. They stood under the very cold water, feeling it pound on their bodies. They turned to one another and embraced the warmth wherever their bodies touched. Guy then lifted Morgaine and she wrapped her legs around his torso. Despite the cold, his cock was hard with desire and he slipped inside her. They began moving together. He heard her moan in his ear. Then she leaned back and the water pounded her breasts. Guy tried to compensate for the weight displacement but it was over much and they tumbled into the pool. Both came up sputtering and laughing. They swam and played in the water for a while, enjoying the invigorating sensation of the cold water on their skin. As their body temperatures cooled, they decidedly swam for shore and lay down in the grass.

As their bodies warmed in the sun, Guy turned over and watched Morgaine. She was rubbing her abdomen slightly. "Are you in discomfort, Love?"

"A bit. I actually think our lovemaking distracted me."

"Oh I am ready to oblige, My Lady," Guy chuckled heartily.

Morgaine giggled in response. "You don't mind the blood?"

"Let's have a look."

"What?!"

"Come on, spread your legs. Let's see."

Shyly Morgaine complied.

Guy pretended to be studying her with several "hmms" and "ahas" as his fingers probed the petals of her red-stained rose. She moaned. Watching him, she could tell by the smirk on his face that he was having fun with it all. Then he started fingering her hooded jewel and she swooned as she fell back and let him play. Her hips bucked in shivering delight as he entered her, thrusting repeatedly with blissful abandon, each ecstatic "oh" echoing in his ears. When they finally pulled apart, they were both covered in sticky blood.

Guy snorted, "Well, they say love can be messy."

Morgaine chortled, "Oh you are terrible…and absolutely wonderful!"

Guy helped Morgaine up and they washed each other in the pool.

"Guy?" Morgaine began shyly.

"Yes?"

"Have you had sex with a woman during her courses? I mean before me." She could see he was about to answer and changed her mind, "No, wait. I do not want to know your sexual prowess. It is enough to know that you know how to please me so well."

Guy grinned and sighed, "Lady, I believe I can answer you honestly and to your liking." Guy turned more serious. "No, Morgaine, I have not had sex with a woman while she has been on her courses. It's you. You bring out this playfulness, this curious spirit in me."

"But surely you know about women and what pleases them."

"Yes, Ann taught me well."

"You had a teacher?"

"A teacher? Hmmm. Yes, you could call her that I suppose." Guy inwardly chuckled at a prostitute being called a teacher; but that is what she was. "When I was younger, William, who was then the Earl of Derby, saw fit to have me instructed. He thought, given my looks, I would make a good spy and what better way to spy than to be in the company of women."

"Why?"

200

"Women are known for being more prone to talking about life and love and incidentals. If I could be a good listener, my benefactor would learn much about the dealings at court."

"Did you enjoy this life?"

"Hmmm. No. It was a job I had to do. I did enjoy my time with Ann. She was prone to fits of laughter which made her quite amusing. She was blunt with her instructions which were sometimes hard to take, but she made me fit for William's services. Sometimes I would go back to her just so I could feel more myself. Though we were honest with each other, it was she who taught me how to lie. It has been lies that have kept me alive so long." He looked at Morgaine with longing, "Sometimes I feel I must still be dreaming that I could feel such love given to me so freely. Truly Morgaine, I cannot imagine what I could have done to deserve you."

Morgaine took Guy's hand reassuringly though she was not sure what to say in response; she felt such deep love and did not understand what deserving had to do with it.

After a pause between the two of them, Morgaine returned to her thoughts about Ann. "Is she still alive?"

"It is certainly possible. I lost touch with her when I left London. And with William wanting me at his side when he became Sheriff of Nottingham, I hardly went back unless to do his bidding."

"What would you say if you saw her again?"

Guy was thoughtful, "Hmmm. I would thank her for her lessons as now I can employ them upon my true love with revelry."

Morgaine, liking his answer, gave him a big a squeeze. "Then I should very much like to meet this Ann to thank her myself."

CHAPTER 20

❧

Putting His House in Order

GUY WAS USHERED into Prince John's receiving room at Wallingford. The castle itself was of Norman design, a stone stronghold which John had seized just last year. Of course, it was within his right. His brother, King Richard, had granted the town to him, so why not the castle too?

"Ah, Lord Guy, what brings my most magnificent stallion to me this day?" John chimed melodically.

Guy's eyes narrowed; he was a bit perplexed by John's tone, but decided to dismiss it as he had more important matters to attend to. He bowed deeply, "Your Excellency, I have come to ask for your blessing for the hand of Lady Morgaine Avalon. She has agreed most exuberantly, to my utter joy, and her parents have given me their blessing to marry their daughter." He stayed bowed.

"Come." At John's command, Guy approached and knelt to kiss John's outstretched hand. John caught Guy's chin so that Guy had to look up at his lord. "Yes, Guy, I give you my blessing to marry the sweet Lady Morgaine." John then bent forward and kissed Guy on the mouth. He rose back swiftly and added, "I am quite pleased by the match. We are related after all...distantly. When is the wedding?"

Guy, still feeling odd about such an intimate kiss from his Prince, shook his head to clear his thoughts, then smiled, "Mid-Summer, Your Excellency."

Prince John looked slyly over at Guy, "That's quick!"

Guy nodded, his cheeks beginning to flame.

The Prince added, "Well, I promise to be there to celebrate you both."

"Thank you, Your Highness."

"Come. Let us talk." The Prince rose and Guy followed. They entered another room where food was being served. The Prince motioned to Guy to be seated. They sat and chatted and ate.

Guy realized this was his opportunity, "Your Excellency, I would like to request that you allow me to live on in Glastonbury. The Duke has agreed, that upon his death I can bear his title and name. With your permission, of course."

"Ah, coming up in the world are you? A bit unconventional, but then — as they have no male heirs…I think it is a splendid answer and I approve. I shall relieve you of your post at Nottingham immediately so that you may take up your duties at Glastonbury."

"Thank you, Your Excellency. There is the matter concerning…" Guy was not sure how to put this delicately. He knew William would not be happy and then there was how to get the title transferred to Boxer, the man Robin and he had agreed to.

"Yes, get on with it."

"The Sheriff will need to be informed properly. And then there is the matter of who shall take over my duties as Lord of Locksley. I was thinking Wyatt Boxer's son, William."

"Hmmm; you do think of everything, do you not?" There was a pause and Guy did not want to interrupt John, not when everything was falling into place. John continued, "I will write a letter to William giving you leave and instructing him to pay you your wages in full through the end of the week of your return, while you attend to putting your house in order and acquainting William Boxer of his new station. How does that sound?"

"Most generous and wise, Your Excellency."

"Splendid!" John ordered his royal notarius to take dictation and draw up the documents while Guy waited. The Prince signed the documents and handed them to Guy. Guy was impressed he could have this all done within the day. This was more than he expected and was deeply touched at the Prince's indulgences.

"Thank you, Your Excellency. I appreciate your kindness."

John chuckled seeing how star-struck the man was. "You do right by me, Lord Guy," he said seriously.

"Yes, of course, Your Highness."

John raised his hand out and Guy kissed it.

John chuckled again and dismissed Guy.

Guy walked back through the doors an entirely happy man. He did not even have to stay the night. It did not matter he rode all that way and was not taking respite. He walked to Midnight and swung up upon his back, saying as he patted his horse, "We'll sleep under the stars tonight, Midnight. But we have to keep going — to Nottingham. Do not put us back in that Orchard until we are done with our mission, understood?"
Midnight turned his head slightly and yawned.
"Midnight, please."
Midnight chewed his bit then dropped his head as if nodding.

As they travelled toward Nottingham Guy reached out to Morgaine with his thoughts, "Beloved, Prince John has given us his blessing. I ride to Nottingham to give William my papers, relieving me of my services to him. All is well." He could almost sense where Morgaine was in the castle back home. Back home. His new home. His home with his Beloved. He could feel her response in his mind, feel her smile, her adoration.

Lord Roderick, Prince John's Chancellor, watched Guy ride off. He had listened in secret to the conversation between John and Guy. Roderick, a tall, sinewy man, like an old Hornbeam tree, if one could see that beneath his sumptuous robes, drummed his long fingers on the ledge. His eyes narrowed at Guy. A new scheme would be set in motion with the traitor Guy as the pawn. No Black Knight did anything without consulting the Order...not without consequences.

Back in his private chambers, Chancellor Roderick sent for Sir Wyvern, one of his most trusted allies and also a Black Knight. Wyvern entered Roderick's chamber, bowing his head slightly. He was not one for giving pleasantries. Roderick ignored the man's rudeness as Wyvern had other talents that were more important to the task at hand. He motioned for the thick brute of a man to come forward. The air between them was devilish.

"Was that my dear friend Sir Guy leaving the castle?" inquired Wyvern in a sarcastic tone.

"Lord Guy now. And yes, it was. We need to bring him back into line, teach him a lesson he appears to have forgotten."

"I would be pleased to accommodate."

"I knew you would. I need you to ride out and get ahead of him. I can't risk sending a bird and having any misunderstandings."

"Understood. And what shall our lesson be for the wayward son?"

"I trust you will come up with a good one that will leave no room for confusion."

Wyvern's face twisted menacingly and if anyone had thought there was a kind bone hidden somewhere on that man's face, that individual would back away quickly and realize it was not so.

Midnight was having difficulty travelling any faster than a normal horse when it came to getting anywhere except Glastonbury. There weren't any apples waiting at the other end and, besides, he had never been to Wallingford, and Nottingham was simply not enough of a draw to get him to just magically appear there. Guy tried a few times because Midnight had managed with enough coaxing the first time; but now he thought it was perhaps just luck. And it was dangerous to keep at Midnight because the haze of the Apple Orchard had started to return. Guy could not afford to start all over again. So on they trotted. At night they would get off the road and camp. Guy liked being out under the tree branches and stars. It was soothing. But this night, while in dreamtime, Guy was not soothed by the experience.

"Whatever made you get into this line of work?" Robin asked, as Guy fed a ground squirrel part of his breakfast.

Guy looked up, embarrassed, and then angry that Robin caught him being gentle with some woodland creature. "You!"

"Me? How can you blame this on me? You're the one feeding them with one hand, cutting them down in the other."

"That's not true. I am not like that."

"Oh, but you are. Everybody knows you are the cruel one. You have no heart."

"I do. In fact I am a hart."

"Nah. I don't believe it for a second."

"How dare you…"

Guy woke up slashing at the air with his sword. Midnight had caught the shine in the moonlight and immediately got up, backing away from the blade. He whinnied to his human, concerned. Guy shook himself awake and looked at Midnight sheepishly, "Sorry. Bad dream."

Guy arrived at Locksley Manor as the sun was setting. Mary saw him approaching, wiped her apron, and called out to him from her own dwelling across the courtyard. "M'Lord, come in for a meal. I did not know when to expect you. We have supper ready." Guy was surprised and pleased by the gesture.

While sharing supper with Mary's family, Guy told the tale of his proposal to the Lady Morgaine. Mary was entranced, so pleased she had actually met the real Lady of the Lake. She then realized the Lady of the Lake would not leave her home. "Where will you two live?" she asked.

Guy responded, "I am being adopted yet again. The Duke and Duchess are taking me in and I shall be the next Duke of Glastonbury someday." He paused in thought, shook his head and smiled, saying, "It can be a far off 'someday' as far as I am concerned. I will just be happy with my sweet lady…" He trailed off as he thought to himself, "and away from William."

Dylan and his father, Henry, looked at each other. There was a mental shaking of heads but they held their opinions to themselves. The change they were seeing in Lord Guy was over much and quite perplexing. And it was getting more challenging to simply cast him as some lovesick villain. That was too simple. Henry, several years older than Guy, remembered Guy from when he was a boy in this village. He remembered the sensitive crybaby who grew more brooding after the death of his father. And he only returned worse, after being up in Derby those years.

"Who will take over your duties here, M'Lord?" Mary pressed.

"I have a document from the Prince. He has agreed to have William Boxer, Wyatt's eldest, perform the duties as Lord of Locksley."

Mary and Henry looked at one another; this was most excellent news, indeed, for Boxer to be allowed to carry this title.

Henry could now not keep quiet, "Prince John agreed to this?"

Guy turned to Henry. "Yes. All will be as well as I can make it here." The finality of the statement let the family know that they should ask no more questions regarding this issue. And all that really mattered, after all, was that the Boxers were an even-handed family.

The next morning Guy rode out to Wyatt Boxer's home. He was ushered in very politely and came to the matter at hand swiftly. Wyatt and William were most pleased at the honor and gladdened that, though neither had done anything to receive good graces from the Prince, neither had they given cause to the contrary. Guy then carefully outlined what would happen if Richard did return. Robin of Locksley was sure to have his lands and titles reinstated by the King and Guy wanted them to be aware that this agreement with John could be revoked. The men nodded. They knew there was nothing that could be done about that and they would be sure to keep the peace as best they could and give Robin no cause for animosity toward them. Little did they know that Robin was well aware of this agreement and that he was trusting them with what he perceived to be his lands.

"Lord Guy, what about your station at the Sheriff's side?" Wyatt was a bit nervous. He did not want either himself or his son to have to be saddled up to the Sheriff.

"Those are separate appointments. It was the Prince who bequeathed me my station as Lord of Locksley, so it is his to bestow or remove. My title is of little consequence to me now as soon I will be a Lord of Glastonbury. The Sheriff will be permitted to hand pick my replacement as his right hand. I honestly have no idea who that might be though it would make some sense in rank for it to be Sir Grigor. My advice to you both is to stay out of politics as much as you can. William, you will be required to attend any meetings whereat the Sheriff requests your council. It is not your council he is seeking so I would suggest discretion. Stay in the Prince's good graces; that will help."

Both men were thoughtful, considering how they must tread. Again Wyatt pressed for more information, "Lord Guy, of all your choices, why did you recommend this family?"

"Lord Wyatt, it made sense. You are cousin to Robin's mother so the holdings are kept in his family. You are known to be even-handed and the people appear to genuinely like you. And because you appear neutral, neither brother should take issue with you."

Wyatt was duly pleased and honored at Guy's assessment. "Again, thank you for your confidence in our family, Lord Guy. It is a very generous gesture."

Guy tilted his head in recognition of the compliment. The men shook hands. Guy left with father and son looking on in silent contemplation and slight astonishment.

As excited as Guy was to be done with the Sheriff and his scheming, he was not excited to be bearing the news. He knew William disliked Morgaine. He also didn't know how William would take his leaving. Guy recognized William liked having people under his thumb and Guy had just gone above William, to the Prince, to get permission to leave William's side. He wrung his hands and avoided going to the castle for the whole rest of the day. Instead, Guy walked the streets of Nottingham for what he felt may be the last time. He looked at the vendors whose names he had never bothered to learn, whose wares he had rarely made time to glance at. A silversmith caught his eye. He hesitated, but then drew in to review the merchandise. He eyed a ring and as he touched it he could almost feel Morgaine fondling it.

The smith, Jessica, interrupted his thoughts, "There was a lady eyeing that same ring a moon or so back. I always thought she would return for it but I think she had hopes of someone buying it for her."

Guy looked at the smith, "What did the lady look like?"

"Slight. Long, dark hair. Not from here. She was walking with the Lady Marian."

"Morgaine," Guy whispered heatedly.

"Pardon?"

"My Lady Morgaine was with Marian. Tell me, did this ring fit her?"

"No, My Lord, but this one did, I remember. I could make you the ring she desires. It will not take me long. Come back tomorrow."

They agreed on a price. Guy walked away beaming, as if the sun had cast its glow upon his whole being.

The smith looked at Guy curiously as if seeing him anew. And then that glow caught her too. It was as if she was infected. As if Guy had infected her with a strong need to be joined with her beloved. Jessica was not the first to be infected. Only last night, after Guy had left Mary and Henry's dwelling, had they reached for each other in a tight embrace, remembering the love that had drawn then together all those years ago. It was a curious magic, working its way through these couples who spent even just a brief period of time with the love-struck Guy.

That afternoon after Jessica, the smith, closed up her stand she practically glided into the bakery. Her husband, Jeffrey, was behind the counter selling the last of the bread. She watched him adoringly, arms folded on the counter, her head set atop her arms, as she grinned from ear to ear at him. After the customer left, Jeffrey looked over at his wife, eyebrow raised as he could tell his wife was quite pleased about something.

He sauntered over to her she and placed a lusty kiss upon her mouth. "You have happy news, Wife?" He suddenly felt feverish; a warming glow penetrating his whole body.

Jessica nodded vigorously. "I have made a significant sale today."

"That is wonderful, my sweet; you are such a talented artist." He kissed her again and maneuvered her into the back room, keeping his arms around her as she walked backwards. Enveloping her in a floury embrace, he nudged her onto the table. He looked at his wife and felt such love for her. "You are so beautiful," he said as if in awe.

Jessica smiled in wonder. In between kisses, she pondered, "What if a customer comes in?"

"We'll hear them," Jeffrey murmured as he kissed his way down Jessica's torso.

"What about the children?"

"They are around."

Jessica sighed, letting herself be swept away in the moment, in love with her husband and her life.

The next morning Guy rode back to the castle, having no idea of his effect on Mary and Henry or Jessica and Jeffrey. No idea he was touching couples' hearts as if with Cupid's arrow, deepening their love and devotion for one another.

He approached William in his office.

The Sheriff barely looked up from his writing, "Where have you been?"

Before answering, Guy placed the document in front of William.

"What is this?" William spit out as he noticed the official seal of the Prince.

Guy's elation faltered as he spoke to his mentor and boss, but persevered. "I have proposed to the Lady Morgaine and she has accepted. I have been granted the blessings and permission by both her parents and his Royal Highness, Prince John. I am to relocate to Glastonbury immediately. Sir William Boxer, by order of the Prince, shall take over my duties as Lord of Locksley." There, he said it, and all in one breath. He could see the venom in the Sheriff's eyes.

He suddenly felt quite miserable that William thought Guy was betraying him. He really was not. He was just following his heart. "William…"

"Don't! Do not say another word. Leave."

Guy opened his mouth and then closed it. There was nothing he could say. With William hatefully eyeing the papers before him, Guy turned and walked out. He wandered the castle for a short time wondering what to do or say but realized William had cast him out.

Meanwhile, back in the Sheriff's office, a man in black stepped out from the shadows; it was Wyvern. "It is as I said, is it not." It was a statement of fact, not a question.

"He is ultimately the Prince's to decide what to do with," William grumbled.

"Though a lesson is in order, is it not." Again, a statement, not a question.

William considered menacingly, "Well, if a duke he wants to be — then a duke he shall be. And he shall be ours!" William spat, "Get the others."

Guy left his wanderings remembering he had a very important item to pick up. His step lightened as walked to the smith, and there she was, smiling confidently at him. She presented the braided silver ring to him and he whistled. Happily shaking his head, he said, "Thank you. This is beautiful work. I know she will love it!" Guy then presented Jessica with the coins. It was a bit more than they had agreed to.

Jessica nodded her head, "And thank you," she responded proudly.

Guy returned to the manor to pack. There was nothing left to do here. He noticed how few belongings were his. He carefully removed the dragon banner off his wall above his bed and wrapped it. An old book that he thumbed through so many years ago, that he was not even sure why he had kept but still had, he also counted among his belongings. He stashed his jewels and money in two large satchels. Clothes. Weapons. All his belongings took up the bed; but there was nothing more.

In the morning Guy sensed the band riding up before he heard them. He quickly dressed and went outside. There they were, his sworn brothers in arms, four of them, plus William.

William threw a pouch of coins at him, which Guy caught. "Your wages," William sneered, adding, "You will do more for us. You swore an oath."

Guy looked at the men in turn, feeling quite nervous, but said indignantly, "William, I thought you could be happy for me..." William held up his hand commanding Guy to stop talking. But Guy, letting go of his speech about how this marriage was a good thing, instead stammered, "I have helped you play the brothers against each other. And I have gained Prince John's confidence. What more do you want from me?"

William spelled it out contemptuously, "We only want to help you attain your elevation to power. Sir Wyvern and Sir Matthew will accompany you back to Glastonbury. Shortly after your marriage, you will become the new Duke and our plans will continue accordingly."

"No. I will not allow you to have the Duke and Duchess killed. You do not understand. They support the Prince."

William responded with cool cruelty, "I do understand. Now you understand that you do not get to walk away from us. We will help you to live or die by your oath." William's voice was quiet but deadly as he continued, "You ride out tomorrow."

"Why tomorrow?" Guy asked.

William turned his horse and shot back, "Because you are not fit to ride today."

At that William rode off and the four knights leaped off their horses and approached Guy. Before he could even reach for his sword they were on him. They beat him most unmercifully. Though villagers saw, they did not dare go outside to save him. Though he might be the lord of the manor and baron of the village, he was still just another villain after all.

Back in Glastonbury, Morgaine and Marian were walking down the steps together when Morgaine heard Guy cry out in pain. "Guy!" was all she called out before collapsing on the stairs.

Wyvern spit at Guy who was down in the dirt and his own blood, "Be ready to ride tomorrow, Duke!" The four left, heading back toward Nottingham castle, confident that Guy wouldn't be going anywhere without them.

Guy could not get up. He felt Morgaine's presence but even she could not help him.

Morgaine called out to Mary and Dylan, penetrating their minds, "Please help the Lady's consort."

Immediately, Mary and Dylan rushed out of their home to Guy's side. Another couple came to his aid as well. The young men lifted Guy and brought him back to the manor. Mary picked up the pouch of coins and followed. They placed Guy on the table while Mary looked for clean rags to dress Guy's wounds. Dylan ran for the village healer. That left the couple alone in the room momentarily with Guy. Guy moaned in pain and the young woman came to him to hold his hand.

"I am here," said the woman with kind eyes and an enduring love for her childhood playmate.

Guy looked at the woman from behind a blackened eye swelling most dreadfully. "Caron." He looked at the young man behind her and vaguely remembered her marrying. "Why are you helping?"

She smiled faintly, "Because you need help."

He could feel Morgaine holding his head. He knew she was in his thoughts. He moaned again.

"Try not to move," Caron said.

Still he looked at her. He remembered her and how she looked that night, how she wanted to be everything to him but she was nothing. "I did wrong by you, Caron. I am sorry. I can see that you care. And I was not kind to you… before."

Caron looked at him and then at her husband. She preferred not to dwell on the past. "M'Lord, it is in the past."

"No. I was wrong to…" He looked from her to her husband and recognized how awkward this could be.

Caron smiled with tears in her eyes. She could sense what he was trying to say. "Robert, would you please give us a moment."

Robert hesitated but nodded and begrudgingly left the room, stating, "I will be right here, Caron."

She nodded, then shook her head, "I will see you at home, Robert. I will be along shortly. I promise."

Though Robert looked quite unhappy, he did not want to argue with his wife in front of the lord of the manor, especially this lord, even as beat up as he was. He kissed his wife on the cheek and left.

Guy gulped at the air, winced and continued after Robert left, "I know you liked me…"

"From the beginning," Caron whispered.

"I should not have betrayed your affection for me."

She exhaled and shook her head slightly, surprised that he would apologize. She gently squeezed his hand, "I forgive you. And I am a happily married woman now. I know I carried a torch for you as you carried one for Marian. I know it was Marian you wanted to be with that night. I know I wanted to make you love me. I did not imagine it would go so far."

"Still, it was my responsibility," Guy managed to say through his pain. Oh, everything hurt. Still, he pushed on because he knew it was important to tell her. With labored breathing he added, "I am glad to hear you are happily married."

"And soon you will be too, I hear."

"Yes, if I make it through the day."

"You will. You cannot step onto a road to redemption and not see it through to the end."

"Is that what I am on?" He could hardly smile as he bore the pain.

Caron touched his face gently and simply nodded.

Hazel, the village healer, arrived. An older woman, with soft curves and a thick graying bronze braid running down her back, touched Guy's arm to let him know she was there. She began her assessment as Mary delicately started cleaning the blood off him.

Caron looked on; she felt in the way. And this was so awkward, after all. She wasn't sure why she had run out to him. Though, now that he had apologized, she felt better. "Maybe that was all I needed," she thought. Caron gazed at his battered face, willing herself to see his beauty beneath the blood and bruising. Behind his closed lids she could imagine his mesmerizing, bright blue eyes. She fell back into memory when they were all younger. When she was little she followed him around like a puppy. He was her hero. When he smiled at her, the world appeared brighter. He saved her from the river. They were all playing by it and she lost her footing and fell in. Guy was the one who went in after her. And he protected her when Matthew was bullying. And he hugged her when she cried, sometimes tearing up right along with her. She never wanted to believe he was bad. "Someone with those eyes could not be all bad," she thought. Even when he was unkind to the villagers as an adult she kept telling herself that her hero was still in there somewhere. That hero had just come out; even in his own pain, she could tell it was important to him to apologize for his rough behavior with her. She smiled, bent over his body, kissed his cheek ever so gently, and left.

Mary and Hazel barely noticed Caron leave.

Hazel wrapped Guy's ribs as she could tell two were broken. Then she tested them again because they felt different as she finished wrapping them. Broken? Not broken. She could have sworn the ribs were broken. Bruised? She kept working on him. She placed a poultice on his many cuts and bruises. As she worked she felt a strong presence around her. "Lady?" She called out to the Goddess in her mind.

It was Morgaine who answered. "I am here. I am here pouring energy into this body that he may heal. Continue your good work, Sister."

Hazel nodded, in slight awe of the Goddess responding.

Guy kept moaning and calling out for Morgaine. To Hazel, he sounded delirious. "Morgaine, I love you. I promise to honor you and treat you kindly. Oh, please sweet God: let me live. Let me live to touch Morgaine again."

"Love, I am right here," Morgaine called gently in his mind. "I am with you. Stay with me. Rest."

Guy felt the brushing of wings that was her spirit and he fell into sleep.

As he drifted off he could hear Hazel say, "The gods smile upon you, Lord Guy. There is a power at work here beyond the two of us mending you."

Dylan sat by the fireplace, watching and listening. "Or the devil," he thought, remembering all the times Guy was harsh and unpleasant. "Unless…could it be the Lady of the Lake? After all he has done, does this man deserve so much?"

Morgaine heard Dylan's frustration and her spirit brushed him. It felt like feathers delicately brushing his cheek. The air smelled of apples. Dylan heard the Lady's voice in his head, "We have need of him. And know that there is more to this man than you see before you. Trust us."

Dylan sighed and nodded, whispering under his breath, "Very well, M'Lady."

Meanwhile, in the stable, Midnight was going mad. He was beside himself, disturbed by hearing Morgaine's voice calling out to help his human. He could not see any of them but he smelled blood: his human's blood. His eyes were wide, whites showing. He was completely spooked and needed Guy's reassurance. But he wasn't getting it because Guy was not there. Midnight began to neigh nervously and stomp around in his stall unsure of how to get out. His ears swiveled, attempting to locate where Guy was, listening intently for his human's voice. All he wanted was to be close to his human. He strained against the wood of his stall. He whinnied; the sound was mournful, lost, and afraid.

As Caron left the manor and headed back toward her home she heard a horse whinnying and a commotion coming from the stable. Without thinking of her safety, she rushed in and stopped short and wide-eyed at who was causing all the fuss. Her voice was scolding, "Midnight, what are you up to?"

Midnight was pacing and stomping, neighing loudly. He eyed the woman who gave him carrots, at first with suspicion, then with pleading as he whinnied at her.

"Midnight, what is wrong? Are you upset? You seem upset. Do you know that Guy is hurt?"

Midnight's ears went back at her questioning but Caron went to Midnight anyway and put her hand out, touching Midnight on the lower part of his forehead. But he would not be consoled. All he knew was that he must see his human, but he didn't know where Guy was so he didn't know how to get to him. His tail swished angrily.

Though she could tell this horse was angry and upset, Caron found herself reaching for the stall door. She felt compelled to unlatch it. And once the rope was lifted off the post, Midnight pushed the door open and was out. As he trotted out of the stable, Caron shook her head and then ran after him, realizing if he ran away Guy would be completely vexed at her for allowing his horse to get away. But as she watched Midnight, she saw that he was heading toward the manor. She followed after him and watched as he pawed at the door.

Caron laughed and cried at the same time as she saw Mary open the door, stating, "Well, look at you. What the devil are you up to?"

Midnight pushed passed the squat human, just enough to force her out of his way, but without hurting her. Then he was in the house and out of sight as Caron followed him in.

Midnight heard his human moaning and followed the sound.

Hazel looked on in shock but was dumbfounded about what to do. Horses did not usually find their way into houses.

Midnight nuzzled Guy.

"Ow. Ow. Ow." Guy opened one black eye carefully to see his horse standing there. "Oh, hey there, Friend, how did you get in here?"

Caron approached, "It's my fault, Guy...M'Lord, I let him out. I don't know what I was thinking. He was so upset. I just wanted to comfort him. But all he wanted to do was to get to you." Caron then looked down, unsure of what else to do or say.

Midnight gently placed his cheek next to Guy's. The action gave them both comfort.

Hazel looked at the pair, "Will wonders never cease?" She smiled and then slowly approached Guy again with the bandaging.

Mary put her hand on Caron's shoulder. "Not to worry. Leave him to us."

Caron nodded and then left again. This time she went straight home, whispering, "Good bye, Guy."

Back in Glastonbury, Marian rushed for help. Taharqa lifted Morgaine off the stairs and bought her to her room. He laid her down while Meggie went in search of Evelyn. When she arrived in Morgaine's room she gathered a very scared Marian into her arms and asked urgently, "What happened?"

Marian recounted that the two of them were just walking down the stairs when Morgaine called out to Guy and collapsed.

Evelyn looked down at her daughter. "You are not here, are you?"

Marian looked perplexed, "What do you mean she isn't here?"

"I mean that her spirit flew off to attend to Guy. Something must have gone terribly wrong for her to allow herself to just collapse to the ground without preparing the body. It's dangerous."

Marian was still reeling from the statement that somehow her friend had been able to separate her soul from her body without dying.

Evelyn stroked her daughter, sighed, and then said to Marian, "Please watch over her. There is nothing else we can really do."

"Should we not call her back?"

Evelyn shook her head. "We will know more when she returns. Not to worry, she will return." With that, she turned to Taharqa, "If something had her attend to Guy in this way, then something is wrong. Make preparations for his return; he may not be alone."

Taharqa nodded. Gareth, Evelyn, and Taharqa had discussed the possibility of Guy falling to the Sheriff under some plot to silence the family. They had to be prepared to either rescue him or deal with whomever he might be forced to bring back with him.

Marian sat with her friend on one side of the bed while Meggie had gathered herself up on the other side of Morgaine, sitting with her in silence and praying over her body. While Meggie appeared not to be paying attention to what was being said in the room, Marian was listening to the three talking in hushed voices. And now she was worried for both Morgaine and Guy.

Later on that evening, Dylan kissed his mother who had stayed to watch over Guy and told her he would return soon. He stole away to relay a message through another villager so that Robin Hood would hear what had happened. He returned quickly with more bandaging so that his mother wouldn't wonder.

The next morning Mary and Dylan helped get Guy ready for his ride. Guy gave them a pouch thanking them for their services. Then he gave Mary another one and asked if she would please give it to Caron and Robert as a belated wedding gift. She promised she would. "Take care, M'Lord."

Guy winced as Dylan helped him up into his saddle, then turned to Mary, "I will. I promise, no harm shall come to the Lady of Lake or her family."

Mary nodded reassuringly. Saying "good luck" seemed meaningless.

CHAPTER 21

Return with the Black Knights

THE RIDE BACK to Glastonbury was wretchedly painful for Guy. The men wanted him to go faster but he just couldn't. And really, it was their fault. Beat up a man and crack his ribs and then expect him to be good for riding a day later. Guy winced again. Sir Wyvern and Sir Matthew had him sandwiched between them, with Wyvern in the lead. And as much as Guy wanted to allow Midnight to just have the two of them disappear, Guy was afraid to risk it, not knowing where Matthew and Wyvern would go or who they would tell before he could get help to deal with them appropriately — which would be killing them, of course. Guy definitely had plans to kill them. Sword-through-their-bellies killing. Or throats-slashed-open killing. Even in the extreme pain, killing was on his mind. At the moment, though, the rest of his focus was on just getting through this and holding Midnight in check. He could see the haze and he knew Midnight was thinking about the Apple Orchard. "Stay with me, Midnight. Don't go," Guy whispered, patting Midnight's neck. Midnight kept walking, but Guy could tell that his friend's body was tense and his ears were flickering back and forth. "Don't endanger the Orchard." This time Guy's whisper was a hiss, firm and commanding. He could only hope Midnight would obey.

Glastonbury's men were prepared for the party. And instead of pulling ahead as Wyvern and Matthew might have expected, Guy fell behind. He had done it a few times during the trip so they hadn't thought much of it, and being in the pain he was in, they did not expect him to be able to make a run for it. The men in the forest awaited Taharqa's signal as the three rode through with

Guy trailing behind. Thankfully, it made the two in front easier targets, and Glastonbury's men took Wyvern and Matthew down with poisoned darts. The process went without much mishap, though Wyvern needed several darts, as he was most reluctant to go down. As the castle guards were tying up Wyvern and Matthew, Guy rode by, looking down at them with a smirk on his face and that is the last thing Wyvern saw before he was unconscious. Wyvern and Matthew were both flopped unceremoniously back on their horses. Though each horse had also sustained hits, it wasn't enough to bring them down, just make them groggy. The company made their way back to the castle to present the prisoners to the Duke who was already awaiting the troop on the steps of the castle.

"We will need to bring them before the Prince," Gareth stated and then looked meaningfully at Guy. Guy nodded as Gareth asked, "Are you prepared to make a statement to the Prince?"

"Yes. Though I fear it may place this family in further danger to tackle the Order, I recognize something needs to be said to alert the Prince that not everything is being done in his name."

Gareth was uncharacteristically grim, "We must act cautiously. I recommend brevity."

"Agreed."

"We will need to ride out immediately." Guy winced, collected himself, and asked, "You are to accompany me?"

"Yes. I will bring the charges and you will back me up." Turning to his Master of Arms, Gareth commanded, "Taharqa, give me four of your strongest men to accompany us and then step up security here while we are away."

As Gareth started up the stairs to give his farewell to his wife, Guy took hold of his sleeve. "Gareth, where is Morgaine?" Though his voice was low, Gareth could hear the concern in Guy's voice.

He placed a hand on Guy's arm, his voice weighted with unease, "She is in bed, recovering. Go visit with her before we leave. Be quick though. We must away."

Guy could not climb the steps fast enough. He had felt her with him through most of the journey. But that would mean...she was not taking care of her body, as she was not in it. He held his ribs tighter, grimacing as he kept moving. Though he knocked on her door, he entered without waiting for a reply. Marian was at Morgaine's bedside along with Meggie.

Marian's face lit up and she jumped up to greet Guy. "Guy, you are here! She only woke a day ago and told us what was transpiring." As she saw him holding his ribs, she cried, "Oh, you are injured! Come. Sit." Marian steered him to where she had been sitting at Morgaine's side.

Morgaine held out her hand which he kissed as he came to sit by her side.

"My love, what have you done?" Guy's voice was full of concern.

"I wanted to be sure you were mending."

His tone was only slightly scolding, "But to your own detriment."

Morgaine ignored his tone, saying lightheartedly, "I shall recover. My body is just weak from lack of water and food. And it was important for us to gain the upper hand. So, are they incapacitated?"

"Yes. Your people brought the two down. Your father and I, and a small company of men, now ride for Wallingford."

"But how can you? You are still mending."

Guy gave a weak smile, mimicking her words, "I shall recover."

Meggie had just clambered off the bed and motioned to Marian; the two withdrew to give the lovers privacy with what precious little time they had.

"Oh my, Dragon's Breath." Morgaine reached both hands to Guy and he drew them up and kissed them, and held her hands to his heart.

"I could swear you've called me that before. What does is it mean?"

"I suppose I should not be surprised that you do not know, but I am. There was a band of soldiers long, long ago, in the time of King Uther, the Pendragon. These men wore black, a force that struck at night, in the shadows. They were called the Dragon's Breath. They were protectors of the High King and the realm."

Guy was perplexed, as he had never heard this account. Then wondered, "Are not your guardians then the Dragon's Breath?"

"No. They are priests and protectors of the High Priestess of Avalon. I am not sure they would consider themselves soldiers or knights, though some of the training would be similar between these two secret groups. I suppose the title would be apt for them too. Dragon's Breath."

"So you have your guardians and now you have your Dragon's Breath." Though Guy's smile continued to be weak, he felt proud by the title.

Morgaine nodded, "Yes. There is a sense that some cycle has come full circle for a Black Knight to return to protect the realm."

Guy thought about her statement about the Black Knights and then about the embroidery he owned, his attraction to the dragon stitched into the cloth. He would have to show it to Morgaine. He was about to say as much when the pain in his ribs crested like a wave as he shifted his weight.

"Guy!" Morgaine exclaimed. He doubled over in pain and that only made it hurt more. Morgaine called out, "Meggie, get Mother!"

Meggie, having only withdrawn as far as the door, ran down the hallway to Evelyn's room. Tana received her and drew her in. "Where's the Mistress?"

"With her Lord."

Meggie nodded and left to go to the Duke and Duchess's bedroom, knocking on the door rapidly. Sophie opened it. Upon seeing it was Meggie and that she was white as a sheep on the moor, she let her in. The couple was in an embrace but broke it as Meggie came in.

Evelyn looked intently, "What is it, Meggie?"

Meggie barely caught her breath, "It's Guy. Morgaine bid I come get you."

The Duke and Duchess embraced again and then, hand in hand, followed Meggie swiftly to Morgaine's chamber.

As they came in, Evelyn commanded Morgaine, "No! Do not!" She could see that her daughter was preparing herself to do a healing. "You are too weak, Child. Allow me."

Morgaine relented and Evelyn came toward Guy who was now doing his best to prop himself up against the bedpost at the foot of the bed. "Meggie, find the Bugle, mash it into a poultice and bring it to me. Meanwhile, make a strong tea of Betony and Birch and Yellow Ghost." Evelyn knew that Morgaine had been schooling Meggie in herbs, so she gave it no more thought as the woman scampered off into the herb room adjoining Morgaine's. Evelyn looked from her daughter to her soon-to-be son-in-law shaking her head in concern.

Gareth was also concerned; he did not know if the two scoundrels in their keep had some system for contacting their superiors and he wanted to be sure to get to the Prince before they did. Before he could speak, he watched he wife slip into trance, her hands on Guy's shoulders as she stood over him.

As practiced as Morgaine was, she never failed to be amazed by her mother's skills in healing. Evelyn had mastered the ability to draw up the energies from the Earth and create a circuit without taxing herself. Morgaine always put so much of herself into the healing, whereas Evelyn brought the energy up from the Earth and acted more as a channel for facilitating the healing than the substance itself.

Guy felt a warming sensation moving through his body as Evelyn worked on him. His breathing grew less labored and his ribs hurt less. There was no comparison to explain what the sensation actually felt like. But if he had to describe it, he might have said it was like being dipped in warm honey and having all his bones coated with a substance that felt warm and soothing. He relaxed and slowly tried a deep breath. He touched the ribs that had been broken that Morgaine had been healing over the last few days. Now they just felt bruised. He was healing. He gently touched his face. Still bruised, but it didn't hurt so much either, and he could now see out of his blackened eye. He welcomed all the energy that Evelyn channeled into him. And he knew, like mother like daughter, Morgaine would reach this ability in time as well. Sensing Morgaine had heard her name in his thoughts, he slowly opened his eyes to slits to see that yes, Morgaine was watching him. He smiled and she returned in kind, the concern easing away from her face as if a cloud passed over the noonday sun.

While Taharqa's men watched the prisoners, Mouse came down the steps to see if Guy had brought any belongings with him. He found Midnight just standing about, looking in the direction of his human charge. "Worried about the Master?" asked Mouse to the horse.

Midnight nickered softly. He hadn't moved. And since no one had taken him to the stable, he just stood there waiting for Guy's return.

Mouse continued to talk to the horse, "Few animals are so devoted to their humans. Though, few humans are so devoted to their beasts. You must think yourself pretty special to Lord Guy to justify such behavior."

Midnight turned his head slightly to eye Mouse before turning his head back toward the castle.

"Unbelievable! I could swear you understood what I said," Mouse said shaking his head slightly.

Midnight merely looked at the frail-looking human.

"I am not sure how much longer it is going to be, but I see that Lord Guy has several packs on your back. I am going to take them to his room. And I swear to you that I will only take them to his bed and will do nothing else. Are we clear?" Mouse started to lift the heavy packs off Midnight.

Midnight continued to look Mouse in the eye, giving Mouse the unsettling impression that he was being assessed for his honesty. "I promise," assured Mouse.

Midnight blew air out of his nostrils as if in tired recognition, his only available statement of understanding and acceptance of what Mouse was doing.

Mouse felt quite burdened by the packs, huffing to Midnight, "How did you manage?"

Midnight again blew air from his nostrils as he eyed the human, unsure what the human could mean; after all, he was thin and small, while Midnight was large and muscular. Midnight then turned his focus back on the castle, waiting for his human to emerge.

"Uuff! I think I will have to make two trips. Watch the other satchels, will you?" Mouse winked at Midnight as he walked up the steps with half the load.

Midnight watched the small man depart with his human's belongs. There wasn't much he could do. He released a deep breath and started mouthing his bit, a gesture of acceptance.

Mouse walked to Guy's room and heaved the bags onto the bed. He thought he heard a chink and a jingle. No matter. He had promised the horse that he would only drop off the loads and not peek. So he simply walked out, shutting the door behind him to retrieve the other bags. Upon his return, he saw that Midnight was still standing in the same spot watching the castle. "Goodness. I am impressed. You could wander off in search of apples but here you stand."

At the mention of the word "apple" Midnight's ears pricked forward.

"Oh, you like apples, do you? I will take the rest of the lord's belongings and fetch an apple for you. How's that?"

Midnight nickered.

Mouse heaved the remaining satchels and slogged up the stairs. He dropped off the rest of Guy's belongings and headed for the kitchen whereupon he met up with Brighid. "Well hello there, Brighid."

"Hello, Mouse. What can I git ye?"

"I need an apple for Lord Guy's horse. Patient fellow. Still standing at the castle steps, waiting for his master's return. I don't dare move him."

"I think we can spare an apple for such a devoted creature." Brighid tossed Mouse an apple.

"Thanks!" Mouse said, catching the apple and heading out the door. As Mouse walked down the steps he waved the apple at the horse. Midnight was still focused on where he thought Guy might be in the castle, though he really wasn't entirely sure. But the waving motion of the small human sent apple molecules wafting through the air, and Midnight could not help but turn his head in the direction of the heady scent. "Oh, I see that caught your attention. Here you go. As promised." Mouse held the apple open-handed to the horse and Midnight took it, munching it down. "What a good horse you are," said Mouse, patting the horse's neck.

A short while later, Guy and Gareth came down the stairs. Guy came to Midnight and patted his trusty steed. "You waited for me," he murmured. Midnight leaned his large head into Guy's and nuzzled his human. Guy noticed all his belongings were missing except his smallest satchel containing his immediate clothing needs and his sword. He looked around. Ah, Mouse.

Mouse was standing meekly to the side but brightened as he noticed Guy looking at him. "I took your belongings to your room, My Lord. And then brought your horse an apple for being so good, patiently awaiting your return."

Guy tilted his head and nodded once in acknowledgement. "Thank you, Mouse." He turned to Midnight, whispering, petting him as he spoke, "We are to travel by carriage, my friend, so that you and I both get a rest. Let Mouse take you to the stable and get you settled in. I'll be back as soon as I can."

Midnight raised his muzzle to Guy's cheek and blew softly. More mutual nuzzling between human and horse heads. There was such a strong, loving bond between these two creatures that there was no way to discern who was more loyal to whom.

CHAPTER 22

How Traitors Are Dealt With

THE CARRIAGES ARRIVED and the prisoners were thrown unceremoniously into the second coach, still groggy from the drugs. Four Glastonbury guards surrounded their charges. Then, before Wyvern or Matthew could come to, they were knocked out again, each receiving a needle, coated in the same herbal sedative, pricked into their necks. Gareth and Guy had climbed into the first coach and settled in for their ride to Wallingford.

There was little sleep for the company as they made haste for Wallingford. Upon arriving at the castle, Gareth and Guy were ushered in to see Prince John. The Prince was quite perplexed to see two of his Black Knights brought before him trussed up and surrounded by guards. He gestured to Duke Avalon to speak.

Pointing at Wyvern and Matthew, Gareth pronounced the men's treasonous intentions against the royal Avalon family. There was a stunned pause upon hearing Gareth's charges. John's face puckered in distaste. He eyed Guy, then narrowed his brow upon the Black Knights before him. "No one punishes my pets without my permission. And no one orders the deaths of nobles without my leave," he thought to himself. John motioned with his hand for Guy to elaborate.

Guy, still holding his ribs, explained. He was not sure why he was reluctant to divulge that William was behind this plot, so he focused on the plot itself.

"You said four. Who were the other two?" questioned Prince John.

"Lane and Payton, Your Excellency."

The Prince drummed the arm of his throne with his fingers. He eyed Wyvern and Matthew in turn. "Well, what do you have to say for yourselves? And this had better be good," Prince John hissed loudly.

The men were silent. Even if Guy would not adhere to their code, they would do so unto death.

John shouted, "Who ordered the beating of Guy and the death of the Avalons?"

The men were stony-faced. Prince John looked Wyvern and Matthew up and down. Wyvern had just been here and John was annoyed that Wyvern had left without having been given leave. Neither of the men was overly pleasant and they certainly weren't pretty to look at. He had better things to think about. A lesson in loyalty was in order. "Right. Lord Guy, run them through." Without hesitation, Guy pulled out his sword and ran each man through, satisfied to kill them and watch them die.

Guy whispered in Wyvern's ear as the sword when in, "To think I was afraid of you. You have no power over me."

Wyvern's face was furious but the curse he wished to speak died with him.

Gareth observed Guy's actions in contemplation while Chancellor Roderick grimly watched from the shadows.

Meanwhile, stories about Guy's demise ran amok. Robin decided to let the folks of Nottingham think what they would. Several tales circulated; some more believable than others. Did the Sheriff truly run Guy, his right hand, out of town? Another story was that the Sheriff slit Guy's throat in the castle during one of his tantrums. Yet another was that a love-struck Guy ran off with a mysterious lady back to her home in a lake. In a lake? Yes, she was a water spirit and witch, and made her home in a lake near the shores of the Isle of Apples. It had been witnessed that four Black Knights turned on their own and beat Guy to death, dragging his body out of town to be dumped in an unmarked grave. The one story that topped all the tales was of Nottingham's cherished hero, Robin Hood, dueling the villainous Guy on the King's Road, and Robin running the rogue through with a sword. One even heard tell that the good Robin of the Hood beheaded the cruel traitor, Sir Guy of Gisbourne, and threw him into a shallow grave. A ballad about the duel was even created and sung around the fireside.

It is incredible what a pronounced hero can get away with and what can be accredited to him.

There were no inconvenient questions asked of Robin because everyone preferred to believe that heroes defeat villains and that there were distinguishable traits that could easily tell the two apart.

CHAPTER 23

Wedding Invitations

THERE WAS NOT much time. The wedding was a scant month away. As the family was not well connected outside of Glastonbury, there were few friends and family to invite from the outside. The Prince, of course, must be invited. Guy listened to the conversation with a brooding ear. He had no interest in inviting anyone he knew. He suddenly came to the painful realization he really had no friends.

"What do you mean 'no friends?'" asked Morgaine with surprise and concern. She had waited until they were alone, but she heard his grief loud and clear.

Guy just shook his head. "I have no one." He paused and then smirked, "If you weren't already coming, I would invite you though."

Morgaine's whole face smiled. "And I you, my love."

They let the moment sit between them like a warm fire, comforting, soothing. They were friends, too, and soon to become family. It felt so easy to be together.

The next morning Morgaine gently brought up the subject of Guy's sister, Delphine. He had not communicated with her in years.

He was not sure if it would be a good idea to invite her to the wedding. "How could she forgive me? I could not save her from her marriage. She was just a child."

"She may not, my love. She may choose to blame the brother who did not save her. But you can let her decide. If it is your heart to invite your sister, then do so."

He sat in thought with a heavy heart, but eventually decided it was the right thing to do. She was family after all.

The four of them continued to review the list and Evelyn and Morgaine wrote the invitations.

Guy pondered, "We could invite Mary and her family...and Caron and her husband."

Morgaine nodded in agreement, "I think that is a lovely idea, Guy. I am sure they would appreciate the gesture. And I would like you to invite your teacher."

"My teacher?" He looked at Morgaine as she smiled mischievously. "Oh. You mean Ann."

Morgaine nodded.

"Hmmm. If you want."

"Yes. Don't you?"

"I don't know. I suppose it could feel good to see her after all these years and show I am doing well for myself."

"I think that is a most excellent idea. And I can tell her thank you."

"Oh dear."

They both started laughing. Evelyn and Gareth looked to the couple and then each other. Gentle, bemused smiles passed between them as they recognized they were overhearing some inside joke.

CHAPTER 24

Getting Back on the Path

It wasn't that Guy wanted to be secretive, though by nature he could be. It was just that he was used to having his own room. He had never had to share space with a spouse, and as much as he loved Morgaine, he wanted something private, just for himself. He put it to Morgaine, "Love, is there a room in this castle that I might occupy as my study?"

She didn't even bat an eye at the request. He was thankful she wasn't offended. Not that he was entirely sure what could actually offend his betrothed.

With a hint of mirth in her eyes she responded, "Surely, you can have any unoccupied room that suits your fancy and your needs."

He looked at her questioningly, "What are you playing at?"

"I am just curious to see which room you shall choose."

That afternoon Guy allowed himself to just wander the castle halls with a clear intention for finding his study. This led him to a door at a corner wall that was part of a turret. He was drawn to the door. But when he tried it, the door was locked. Small matter. He took a slim, thin-pounded piece of metal from the pouch laced through his belt. He held up the piece of metal. It was rare that he needed this little tool that he had acquired while in London, but he was thankful he had asked the blacksmith to make it for his shady dealings in that city. Click; the lock gave and he unhooked it from the handle. Now when he tried the door it opened. His eyes danced in merriment. The room was perfect! First, it was, according to Morgaine's stipulation, unoccupied. Second, it was clearly a study. There was a table. Chair. There were shelves for books. And upon closer examination Guy could see outlines in the dust where books had been. There was a window that looked out onto

233

the courtyard. Whose study had this been? Instinct directed him to treat the room as the spy he had been, to uncover any secrets within. Guy carefully brushed his hands along the walls, feeling for a change in tactile sensation. And ah, his fingers felt it; there was a secret panel. He pulled the stone and it moved easily enough to show an empty space for hiding something. Again, Guy wondered whose room this had been. In his exploration of the room, he found several more secret hideaways which made him full of glee. This room was a dream come true. He closed the door and went in search of Morgaine.

His proud demeanor was almost explosive as he sauntered into a sitting room where he found Morgaine, Meggie, and Marian. All three women looked up.

Marian was the first to state, "You look like a cat who licked all the cream."

Guy was not about to be deflated by Marian's reference and dig at him.

Morgaine looked between the two of them and decided to leave the comment, instead agreeing with Marian. But with a gentler air, "Yes, Love, you do look like you have found something quite satisfying."

Guy nodded. "I have my study."

"Oh? So quickly?"

Guy nodded again. He held his hand for Morgaine. She got up and took his warm hand, looking back at Marian and Meggie with a sly smile and giving them a wave with her fingers at her side as she followed her beloved out the door, into the hallway.

He led her through the halls until they were on the floor above their bedroom and down the hall to the end. He stopped at the door.

"This room?" Morgaine sounded mystified while at the same time proud.

"Yes."

"The door was locked."

"No door remains locked for me."

She chuckled. "Quite cocky, aren't you?"

"Yes," Guy responded with mischief in his eyes as he brought her hand down to his groin.

Her smile widened as she felt the growing outline beneath his trousers. They both laughed as he pushed the door open for her and walked in.

She looked around. How fitting. Now, to tell Guy. "Sweetheart, what drew you to this room?"

"Well, it wasn't just that it was the only one I found with a lock on it." He paused in thought. "I am not sure why. I just knew I had to get in here."

Morgaine nodded, still smiling. "This was Merlin's room. I think my mother had hopes that it would stay locked until the next one appeared."

"Does this mean I may have to give this room up at some point?"

"No, I don't think so. I think Mother will find this appropriate. You may be too old to begin such a process, but by opening the door, you may very well be the spur for the next."

Guy nodded, then added in mock protest, "I'm not old."

Morgaine giggled, patting his chest. "No, you are not, Love. But The Merlin is trained to be such from boyhood."

Guy cocked his head in consideration. "Is 'Merlin' a name or a title?"

"Both. As far as we know, the first Merlin was his name. When he died, subsequent magicians connected to the Lady of the Lake called themselves Merlin and were referred as The Merlin."

"Why is there no Merlin here now?"

Morgaine's eyes grew sad. "The Merlin disappeared several years ago without naming a successor."

Guy touched his beloved's shoulder, seeing the memory brought her pain, and asked her no more questions.

When Morgaine walked into Guy's study two days later she was struck by what she saw — the Pendragon embroidery on the wall. She exclaimed, "Where did you come by this?"

Guy strode to the cloth, stoking it. "This? Ah, it is a terrible story. But the old man said it was meant for me."

Morgaine drew closer to study the cloth embroidery. She recognized the cloth. This embroidery had belonged to The Merlin. It was very old and had been in the keeping of The Merlins for centuries. It went missing ten years ago when Merlin left on his mission. There was mixture of emotion and thought swirling in Morgaine's head. After all this time, the Pendragon embroidery found its way home. And with Guy. Fingering the cloth, Morgaine asked, "Old man? Tell me."

Guy recounted the tale, "Wyvern, one of the men I have just killed, and who was plotting against this family, was riding with me. It was what, ten years ago? He cut down an old man walking along the road. I called out in shock. I couldn't understand why he would just slay a stranger. But that just is...or was, Wyvern."

The punishment that came was most severe and Guy was knocked off his horse, Crown, with the blow.

"Fool!"

Guy, lying on the ground winded and wincing, nodded subserviently at the Black Knight who was still on his horse glaring down at him.

"Check him. See if he has any papers or coin."

Guy scrambled over to the dying man. The man moved his head, his eyes searching. He had a most complex look on his face as he fell away from all knowing. Guy felt horrible, as if losing this old man was some tremendous loss. Still, he did as Wyvern said and felt around in the garments. He threw the small money pouch up to Wyvern and opened the paper which turned out to be a map.

"What's that?"

"A map."

"A map of what, you fool?"

Guy scowled but said nothing to displease his companion further. "A map of England."

"Push him off to the side and then come along. Bring the map." Wyvern left him to complete the task.

Guy heaved a staggered sigh, mentally telling himself, "You will survive this." He didn't understand why Wyvern was so malicious. He didn't know how he allowed himself to be so tangled up with this man.

Guy rolled the old man off the road and into the shrubbery. He then checked the man again for any more incidentals.

Suddenly, the old man grabbed at Guy's arm with such fierceness and eyed him intently. "It's you!" There was a straggled pause, then the old man labored the words from his lips, "You must get on the right path, boy!"

Guy jumped, but the dying man held him fast, gazing deeply into Guy's eyes. And then, as if plucking out a thought that would have personal meaning, whispered, "It's the one that is left; what remains after all else falls away." The old man paused again, wincing in pain as he spoke, "Take it. Under my shirt. It is yours and yours alone. Let it guide you back onto your path, back to your true destiny...to..." With that, the man said no more.

Guy wrinkled his nose and clenched his jaw. He would not shed a tear. No, not with Wyvern so close. He closed his eyes and forced calm, trying not to think too much on what the dead man had said. Still, Guy tugged at the dead man's clothes and reached around his waist. There, he found a cloth scroll. He stuffed it in his own shirt to look at later in privacy. He grabbed the map as well. He noted that were notes scribbled on the side and a circle around the region of Nottingham. He hoped to study this potentially valuable piece of work but he knew not to tarry further. Quickly, he pulled the satchel from around the old man's body to go through later.

"When I was away from my companion, I secretly unraveled the scroll and was immediately drawn to it. It's one of my few cherished possessions." He didn't mention that Crown's hide, his beloved horse who had died, was the other.

Morgaine turned from the embroidery to face Guy. A look of surprise and grief was written on her face. "Wyvern killed Merlin?"

Guy nodded as they were piecing the story together. "And now I have killed Wyvern, your Merlin's killer."

Morgaine didn't realize she had been holding her breath until she released it in a harsh sigh. "Merlin left us a note about ten years ago. He was searching for the one he thought to be my mate." Morgaine reached back into her memory to recall the letter. "I remember Merlin wrote,"

"Dear Ones, I have read the signs and, though you may not wish to hear it, Lorrac will not fulfill his calling. There is another. But quickness is an imperative. Morgaine's potential mate draws near a precipice. He has lost much and evil surrounds him, drawing him away from the Faie who guide him. I must find him."

"It was the last thing Merlin wrote that we could find. His last journal, possibly on his person, was nowhere to be found. There was no identity. Nothing to go on. Nowhere to start. And all the spells we did showed nothing. It was as if, when The Merlin disappeared, all trace of you did too. Your identity was veiled. It was you all this time." Guy drew closer and she reached out her hand to touch his face. "All this time…"

In his haste and his hope to locate the lad who he would never know was Guy of Gisbourne, The Merlin walked out into the night, stuffing his journal into his satchel, and met evil on the road to Nottingham. "Wyvern, why…" was the last thing he heard.

It was, of course, not The Merlin's fault that even he could not find Guy until he was right on top of him, or as the case was, the other way around. For Guy, upon becoming a Black Knight, became cloaked in a manner of sorts. The current manifestation of the Black Knights knew little of what they were saying despite still speaking an English language. Though weaker with misuse, the incantations were infused with a cloaking magic to make them dangerous adversaries. It was actually the original Merlin who had created the chant and taught it to the men who would be the High King's most trusted allies and protectors. The chant protected them from other magicians searching for them, should the enemy employ such magic. The consequences became apparent in this new age when The Merlin and the Black Knights no longer served on the same side. And Merlin, the original, had not committed the spell to writing, or if he did, it was not in any of the manuscripts that had been found.

Morgaine turned back to the embroidery, tracing the Pendragon with her finger. "This was Uther's and then Arthur's before Guinevere had him take up the cross." She turned back again to Guy. "And now it is yours. You are a man of Avalon. The Dragon's Breath has come home."

Guy staggered from the weight of what he was hearing. His emotions were jumbled in a knot of frustration. All these years. The Merlin had come to look for him. For him. And Wyvern had cut him down. He could have been here all this time. He could have been with Morgaine all this time. But to be cloaked from this family and not even know it. What made the difference now was that Guy wanted to be found. His sheer will to be with Morgaine had broken the spell; the cloak had begun to lift when he opened himself to her. But Wyvern stole his time. It was little consolation that the thief of his time here was dead.

Wyvern, though a brute, had some understanding of magic and considered the map again, like a thought unbidden. "Let me see the map," he demanded of Guy.

Guy fumbled for it in the old man's satchel where he had put it. He handed it to Wyvern.

Wyvern studied the map. Without looking up, he harshly added, "Did you find a journal or a ring or something else of value in that satchel?"

"No," Guy lied. He wasn't sure why he lied, but something told him not to give up anything else to Wyvern.

Wyvern then looked up at Guy, piercing him with a deadly look. "Are you lying?"

"No," Guy stated as flatly as he could.

"Give me the satchel." Wyvern held out his hand and Guy handed it over.

The dead man's satchel did not contain the journal or scroll; those were on Guy's person for safekeeping. Wyvern rummaged around the satchel. There was some clothing. Some bundles of herbs. A bit of bread and cheese. Wyvern sniffed the herb bundles, in turn, but nothing looked suspicious. Wyvern drummed his fingers on the satchel in contemplation as he eyed the map again. "This is a locator spell."

"You killed a wizard?" That was not the best wording or timing Guy could have chosen and he realized that as he fell back and sideways away from Wyvern's cruel punch to his jaw. But his feet stayed planted in his stirrups and his hands on the reins as Crown did his best to shift his weight to keep his human on his back. Guy slowly rearranged himself back in his saddle, rubbing his injured jaw and pride.

Wyvern continued as if nothing happened, "He was looking for someone, someone in Nottingham or Derby. Hmmm. Well, now no one will ever know, including the poor sap he was attempting to locate." Wyvern chuckled slightly at screwing up someone else's plan. Well, if it was that important, he should have been in the know. His back prickled suddenly. He looked at Guy again, cocking his head, his eyes going to slits as he assessed the young man with uncanny blue eyes.

That night, as the two camped under the stars in the forest, Wyvern, still holding onto the stranger's satchel, decided to cast an evil spell on whoever the stranger was looking for, just out of pure spite. Guy watched on as Wyvern spun the satchel over the fire. He listened to what the mean-spirited man was banefully proclaiming.

"Tua vera voluntas celatur omnibus donec veri amoris basium."

Being Catholic, or at least being born to Catholics, and of noble birth, however distantly, Guy had been schooled in Latin. He shuddered at Wyvern's words. "Your true purpose is hidden from all until true love's kiss."

Wyvern laughed wickedly as he threw the satchel into the fire. He looked over to Guy, "Now that poor bastard is completely fucked. True love is for some skyrta's bedtime story."

Guy just looked at the man, dumbfounded. He wanted to ask, "Why would you mess with someone else's destiny?" But he knew better and thought that Wyvern would only answer, after hitting him again, "Because I can." So Guy just lay there in silence, praying that curse wasn't for him, praying a curse couldn't possibly be real, hoping for sleep, and to be back in Derby with his benefactor, Lord William de Wendenal.

Guy was lost in memory, realizing it was he who had been the "poor sap." He shook with rage. Wyvern hadn't even cared. Without thinking, Guy questioned aloud, "How did I ever allow myself to be so transfixed by that man? I let him and the others take me so far away from myself, so far away from my path. Why did I believe him? Why did some part of me think he was cursing me?" His thoughts continued unravelling and then bunching and knotting up again. "Why did I stay with them?"

Morgaine watched Guy in sympathy. She could tell he was haunted by his memories and his choices. To bring him out of this memory, she laid her hand on his arm and rubbed it gently. His eyes looked haunted as he returned her gaze.

Morgaine returned to the fact that it was Guy who was last with Merlin. She asked him, "Guy, did you find The Merlin's journal?"

Guy licked his lips, nodding, then gave her one of his endearing lopsided smirks. The journal was one of the few books on the bookshelf. He went to the shelf, picked out the journal, and handed it to her.

"Did you read it?"

Guy admitted as much. "To be honest, at the time, it made little sense. Much of it appeared coded and it was a newer journal, so only a wedge of the pages were filled. I am not sure what possessed me to hold onto it or even to hide it from Wyvern, but I did. I hope it brings your family peace."

Morgaine clutched Merlin's journal to her breast. There was a long pause between them. Then Morgaine cried, "How could you have been so clouded from me? We met over four years ago. How could I have not recognized the pull?"

Guy searched his memory too. "I ignored the pull as well. I did not understand it and I dismissed it."

She was shaking, "Forgive me."

He pulled her in. "Love, there is nothing to forgive between us. This is the time we have been given." He had to believe that, else he would rage against a man who was but a ghost now. He stroked her hair, adding, "Love, it was you who broke the miserable spell, one I didn't even know was cast upon me by some malicious man with rudimentary skills in wizardry. At least now my destiny can no longer be hidden from me, now that true love's kiss has awoken me."

Morgaine tilted her head. Her eyes welled up. She smiled sweetly at the most beautiful thing to be said of her. She placed her hand on Guy's cheek and leaned in and up to kiss him full on the mouth.

CHAPTER 25

History Revealed

LATER THAT DAY, Morgaine went to her mother and told Evelyn of Guy's Pendragon wall hanging. "He is the Dragon's Breath."

Evelyn was firm-lipped. He was more than the Dragon's Breath. This confirmed the face of the Stag superimposed on Guy's face. He was Uther returned. Her heart ached for her daughter. She wondered silently, "How much time will you have with your love before he fulfills his destiny again?"

When Guy first came through Glastonbury, before he left with his new horse Midnight, he rode up to the Tor. It had always been surrounded in mystery and romanticism. The Tor itself made him ponder. It was so old. It was apparently built before the Romans came through. Then there was the monastery. Though it was still under reconstruction after experiencing a devastating fire in 1184, there were monks who yet dwelled there, claiming that the abbey had been founded by Joseph of Arimathea and must therefore be preserved and rebuilt. He wandered a bit through the ruins and the remade structures, including the Lady Chapel, which had only been completed a year before. He thought he would feel something; he didn't know what, but something. Nothing here stirred him though, not even the magnificent Tor. As he walked out and around the hillside, he looked out at the Lake. He cocked his head as if listening for something. Something replied; it was so faint, he hardly noticed and with the monk walking up behind him, he turned to face the little man, distracted from whatever it was he hoped to hear.

Guy knocked on the door. Sophie opened it and showed him into Evelyn's receiving room where Evelyn and Morgaine were talking.

Evelyn looked up upon his approach. "You were hidden from us and from yourself." She picked out his memory, "What did you hear those four years ago at the Tor?"

Guy hadn't been quite sure how he had found himself in Evelyn's room. He had just been drawn here. He closed his eyes to search his memory to answer Evelyn's question. "I was not sure. Perhaps just the wind, though it sounded like a voice calling to me. I made myself dismiss it. I didn't want to believe in magic at the time because of what Wyvern had done. I equated magical intent with malevolence."

"And now?" questioned Morgaine.

"Now I know the difference. I wished I could have stopped to listen then."

Evelyn could feel the anger rising in Guy. She gazed upon him with tenderness, saying gently, "Hate is too great a burden for you to bear, my son. You must put it down."

Evelyn rose and went to her bookshelves. She looked among the treasured books and drew a large tome from the shelf. She carried it back and handed the book to Guy. As they each held the book, one giving, one receiving, Evelyn stated to Guy with utmost seriousness, "If you are going to be part of this family, it is important to know who and what we are. I am entrusting you with The Merlin Manuscripts. Please read them."

Guy accepted this very generous gift of trust. Though his exterior read as calm gratitude, his interior self was almost giddy. He experienced a rush of potential in the reading of these manuscripts.

For days after, he cloistered himself in his study reading the history of Morgaine's dynasty in the manuscripts. Generation after generation of Merlins wrote about the wedding of Faie to human, creating a strong bloodline that was deeply connected to the Land, and more specifically to Avalon, which was now part of Glastonbury. Guy read how the first Morgaine created a spell on her descendants so that each daughter would recognize Faie blood in a potential mate to strengthen the bloodline. Though this bloodline created strong resilient humans who were slightly longer-lived than most humans, there were consequences. Offspring did not come into sexual maturity until they were well into human adulthood which meant the window of fertility was slightly before the woman became too old to bear any more children. Given what was known of the Faie, that they had small broods and the span between siblings tended to be decades; the Avalons, as a result, had had only one girl child every generation thus far.

Guy paused his reading in consideration. What if a child had died before she could find a mate? How would the line continue? The Merlins asked the same question over and over again, but in each case, the mother always lived to see her daughter grow to breeding age. Now he also understood why, upon finding him, they were rushing the marriage, in hope of assuring offspring between the two. But why me? He set aside that uncomfortable question and continued reading.

The Manuscripts were set up in an interesting way. Instead of each titled Merlin keeping his own account of all that transpired in his life, there were different types of manuscripts. Those Guy had been given were an account of the Avalons, but he could see other manuscripts on the shelf in Evelyn's receiving room. He suspected that all the books had once been in The Merlin's study but that, at some point when Merlin hadn't returned, Evelyn must have moved them to her room.

When Guy had been in Evelyn's receiving room those days ago, she had responded to Guy's unspoken question, "Those are spell-books of The Merlins and the Lady of the Lake."

He considered asking to see those as well but thought it a bit premature.

She caught the question on his face and answered vaguely, "Perhaps."

Perhaps he could read them or perhaps the request would be premature; he wasn't sure.

Guy tried to remind himself that he had his whole life to read these manuscripts but he couldn't put them down. He was thirsty to understand this family into which he was marrying. He started taking notes, trying to understand how the men came into play. Some were commoners, some were royalty; all were English. Guy, born of French parents, couldn't fathom how he fit in. This made him skip over chapter after chapter, in search of when this generation's Merlin picked up the story. Guy also could not figure out how each Merlin came into being. He read how each one had been trained since boyhood, but where were they found? It seemed that some had come from the Guardians' line but that was also a mystery still needing explanation. He had no idea where and how the Guardians lived. He made a note to question Rainer. Merlins appeared to also have Faie blood in them, but there was no instance where a Merlin and the Lady of the Lake wed.

This Merlin, though, had hopes for Lorrac, Morgaine's first love, to be the next Merlin, given that he had the blood and was drawn to Morgaine. But Merlin wrote down more than a decade ago that Lorrac did not have the discipline for magic studies and instead was starry-eyed about the far off Holy Land. Guy cross-referenced with the journal that Morgaine had lent back to him. Now it made sense. Though Lorrac had not left by the time that The Merlin went in search of Guy, it was only a short time afterward that he did.

Guy meditated on who to ask to shed some light on the issue of Lorrac and the bloodline. He decided on Gareth. He got up and stalked the halls to find his soon-to-be father-in-law. He found Gareth in his receiving room rough-housing with his hound, Prometheus. It was a smaller room than Evelyn's but Gareth seemed to appreciate it. "It's easier to keep warm," Gareth had said once. It was not overly ornate, decorated mainly in browns and reds and greens. There was a tapestry of Bacchus on the wall that Evelyn had had made for him; she occasionally teased him that he reminded her of this Roman God of Revelry.

Gareth's servant, Reeve, a slight, thin-limbed graying man with a careful smile, brought Guy over to Gareth. Guy stood there amused at the Duke as he played with a very happy and large hound. Gareth had to keep on his toes and alert with this exuberant animal friend. Reeve coughed a few times, a weak "ahem" in hopes of getting the Duke's attention. Even the dog was distracted by his human's attention; but eventually both dog and human suddenly noticed there was company. Prometheus was a very large and intimidating-looking mastiff. But as long as he knew a person, he was really quite tame. Guy held his palm open as Prometheus trotted over to greet him.

Gareth got up, with a bit of unwanted help from Reeve, brushed off his trousers, and then captured Guy in a big bear hug. "Guy! What can I do you for?" He patted Guy on the back and steered him to a sitting area.

Prometheus followed close behind his human and sat down next to him, waiting to be pet.

"I have been reading The Merlin Manuscripts," started Guy.

"Ah," stated Gareth as he absentmindedly pet his pooch.

Guy continued, "And I have some questions for you, if you wouldn't mind answering."

Gareth continued to pet Prometheus as he offered, "Well, I will do my best. I would think Evelyn might be the better person to ask. But, obviously, you chose to come to me for a reason."

Guy nodded and then launched into his questions. "Was Morgaine in love with Lorrac?"

Gareth wondered at the question but responded honestly, for there was really no other way he could be. He was very much like his wife in the way — direct. "Yes, she and Lorrac were in love."

Guy was perplexed, "Why would he leave her if they had performed the same…blood ritual she performed with me?" He paused, then continued earnestly. "After that experience, I couldn't imagine being without Morgaine. I have never felt anything like it. There is such clarity in my own need to be by her side."

Gareth looked at Guy with tenderness, as he knew well that sensation with his own wife. Then he looked out the window in thoughtful contemplation. "Lorrac…we had hopes for him. They were childhood sweethearts. His father was…wary of Morgaine and this family's history. And when Lorrac's older brothers came home from their adventure in the Holy Land, they implored him to return with them. He was swept away by the lure of adventure. He told Morgaine he would return, but she broke it off with him. She even performed a spell to break the bond."

"That can be done?"

Gareth shrugged, "It was." Gareth then put a hand on Guy's shoulder, "You have nothing to fear; she has no feelings remaining for him." Gareth patted Guy's shoulder, then, went back to petting his dog.

Guy didn't feel the conversation was complete though. "But he has the blood."

"Yes."

"And he was from Glastonbury?"

"Yes. He was one of Gwenhwyfar's older brothers. When Lorrac left with his two other brothers, the father married off Gwenhwyfar, Morgaine's dear friend, and sent her away. It was all so very heart-wrenching to Morgaine."

"Is any of the family here now?"

"No. Much grief befell that family. The father disappeared sometime soon after Gwenhwyfar left, and the wife killed herself. The three brothers never returned."

"How could Lorrac have been compelled to leave?"

"It happens. Sometimes people run away from their calling. No matter. Morgaine found you and that is what is important. The bloodline will strengthen with you."

Guy considered the bloodline. He must have Faie blood; that is what Morgaine meant when she said the blood would recognize itself. "Gareth, my parents are French. How could it even be me?"

Gareth became guarded, surmising the truth of the matter but responding cautiously, "You must have Faie somewhere in your bloodline."

"I only have one English ancestor that I know of: my father's mother."

Gareth shook his head and shrugged. He didn't want to delve into a subject he thought Guy might not want to be enlightened about...not yet anyway.

Guy assessed the response pensively, wondering how much he really wanted an answer to this particular question.

CHAPTER 26

Guy's Motivating Factors

GUY AND EVELYN were sitting across from each other in Evelyn's receiving room. Guy agreed to allow Evelyn to facilitate a walk through Guy's history and motivations to help better prepare him for his future with the Avalons. He recognized he was willing to do anything to be fully accepted and fully claimed by this family, even if it meant showing his vulnerability to the Duchess.

Evelyn started, "I want you to quiet your mind; though now that I have said that, you probably have many thoughts flooding into your head. Let them pass. Breathe deeply and slowly." Evelyn paused, watching Guy's closed eyes and the forced gentleness of slow, deep breathing. She could hear other questions lurking in him. She echoed softly in his mind, "Another time."

His brow furrowed, but just for a moment.

She could tell he was someone used to biding time, to having to be patient. She waited until he was at his edge of tolerance for this quiet breathing bit. She started slowly, but to the point, "Guy, what motivates you? What pushes or pulls at you?"

Guy replied easily enough, "Well, Morgaine motivates me. Her love for me inspires me, makes me want to be her champion."

Though Evelyn smiled slightly at this, she continued her pressing, "And before Morgaine?"

Guy's face turned dark as if what was in his mind made his whole body step into the shadows. "Power."

"There is usually another feeling behind the seeking of power."

Guy took a big breath, "Jealousy."

"Jealous of whom?"

Another big breath, sounding faintly strangled with hesitancy. He had told himself he could trust Evelyn and he had promised himself to be subject to her lessons, regardless of how odd or self-revealing they might be. With that will of trust, his heart overtook his brain and what came was a flood of words and anguish. "Robin had everything. He was the Baron's son and could do no wrong. I was always the scapegoat even though I am older. Robert sent my father on some campaign. He took everything from me. He took Mother, bedded her while my father was gone and when my father came back a broken man three years later, he sent him away, proclaiming him dead to us all. I couldn't even hug my father goodbye because he had leprosy. I was only thirteen! Robert took everything. And Robin had everything, even the girls. They all mourned his going to the Holy Land with King Richard, even Marian. He was always the hero."

Evelyn felt compassion for her son-to-be; he was so tragically broken. But to be broken, could also mean there was an opening. She grabbed hold of that crack, his defiant will to survive. "And so what did you decide?"

"To gain power, to gain respect. To be feared."

Evelyn spoke softly, "To be the villain to Robin's hero."

Guy nodded. He finally felt the force of the shame as he revealed his traitorous act against his own sister. He said with clenched jaw to keep his emotions from overwhelming him, "I even agreed with Lord Locksley to have my little sister married off. She was only thirteen at the time. It was just after her courses started. I told myself I was helping her have a better life. But she was so young and with Mother dead just months after losing our father, we were at the mercy of Lord Locksley for years. I just couldn't take care of her. And she had so many needs. I could never do enough for her; it was never enough and I couldn't bring back our dead parents. We had nothing after Mother died, not even a real home. So I let her go. And then the Baron let me go. He sent me away to Derby. William seemed to appreciate me. I felt valued by him. Perhaps it was just that I was related to the crown and Delphine and I were sold to the highest bidders for safekeeping. I don't know. William introduced me to the Black Knights. Their power was very alluring. With the backing of the Order, I made a name for myself and with Robin gone off on the Crusades and his father dead, I was able to claim Locksley Manor with Prince John in power."

Evelyn's voice was firm yet compassionate, "Guy, though you may not be able to wash away your sins, your jealousy has outlived its purpose. All that you have done in your life has brought you to this point and you have the ability to choose to live differently. Do you wish to release your jealousy?"

"Yes."

"Are you sure? Could you survive without your jealousy?"

"What do you mean?"

"Who would you be without your self-imposed title of the villainous Sir Guy of Gisbourne?"

"I'd…." Guy had to really think about that. Was he really a villain? Of course other people thought of him as a villain, but that was their opinion. That didn't make it real, did it? That didn't make him just a villain, did it? He recognized that was too simple. True, there were many things he did that weren't considered good; that were considered bad, cruel even. But there were other actions he took that would be construed as good. He admitted they didn't necessarily cancel one another out.

Evelyn could see that Guy was working through her question and waited for his response.

He finally said, "I would still be me. I might make other choices. I might even see other choices. In fact, I do."

She could tell Guy was honestly appraising himself and his actions. She wanted to know if he could let go of the past so that it would not continue to define him. Evelyn asked, "If you had no opinion about Robin or anyone else who you thought had it better, who would you be?"

Guy's brow continued its descent into his eyelids. "I would still be me. Me without the labels."

"But those titles also gave you power."

Guy's nod admitted as much. "My Lady, I think I understand where you are going with this and I want you to understand. By the very fact that I am in this room, preparing myself as a worthy consort to your daughter, I am ready to shed attachment to my past and to my titles."

Evelyn's quiet smile pounced on Guy. "Do you think you are unworthy of Morgaine without preparation?"

Guy smirked. "Evelyn, you are playing with my words but I understand you." He took a big breath, continuing, "I have never given much thought to being worthy...until now. I want to be the man to whom Morgaine looks with love and devotion. And I know she does. I am not sure whether I deserve such devotion, but she gives it freely."

Evelyn was quiet as she waited for Guy to consider if he had more to say.

He watched her and picked up that she was expecting more. Thoughts bumped around in his head, organizing and reorganizing themselves. "I have done horrible things; yes, it is hard for me to think I deserve Morgaine. It is difficult to state this as you are not only acting as a mentor but you are also her mother."

Evelyn merely nodded and allowed him to continue.

"My Lady, I think you know my heart. As a warrior, I am not sure I can lay down my anger. It is something that stirs me to action."

Again, Evelyn nodded once.

"But my jealousy of Robin is something of which I can let go. I see that it has led me nowhere good, and now the issue is moot because, truly, I have everything I ever wanted."

Evelyn maintained her quiet smile on Guy. She was quite satisfied with his responses and his honesty. The better he knew himself, the more he would understand and accept his place in the realm. Evelyn spoke with compassion, "Guy, I appreciate your honesty and willingness to look deeper within yourself. The deeper you look, the more you will understand your purpose in this life. I shall be proud to call you son; this I know."

Guy blinked in awe at her statement. He then smiled back at her, saying, "Thank you, My Lady."

Evelyn smiled and then got up and walked around to stand behind Guy. "Guy, I want you to close your eyes and think of the most serene place you can." She placed her hands on his head.

Guy closed his eyes and thought of the Lake and then the woods. Places in Nature were where he felt most at peace. He continued to allow the images to pass by his inner eyes when suddenly he heard a whisper in his ear, "Walk to Me." Compelled, Guy found himself walking through the woods out to the Apple Orchard. The Lake was in the background. But in the foreground, seated upon an ornate living tree-like throne, was a lady in blue. She was like the sunshine itself and it was hard to see her features. He wasn't even sure why he thought she was wearing blue. She felt so familiar. "It's you," Guy stated in awe, as if he were remembering Her from a childhood dream.

The Lady in Blue smiled, "It is I. Come."

The closer he got, the larger she and the throne appeared. As if a child, Guy found himself on the lap of the Goddess, the Lady of Light. She rubbed his temples.

She crooned in his ear, "Welcome home, my sweet, wild son."

Waves of elation washed over him. All his feelings of inadequacy, of his grief for the loss of his father, the anger of his mother's decision to become Lord Locksley's lover, Robin's taunts, his sister crying as she boarded the carriage that bore her away — they all ebbed away. Suddenly he was facing the Goddess, the Mother of All. She had Her hands on his shoulders. She smiled at him and kissed each cheek. He swooned. "I remember you."

She whispered, "I never left you. I have been here all the while, waiting for your return." Then with Her forefinger She tapped his forehead twice and he woke up.

Guy was still sitting and Evelyn had shifted to face him, standing over him smiling. She patted his shoulder then took her seat. She picked up a cup and sipped at her tea. Then she said, "Guy, the Goddess welcomes you."

Guy had a slightly bewildered look upon his face as he nodded in awe.

Evelyn continued, "You said something in your trance. You said you remember Her. When did you meet the Lady of the Lake, whom you call, the Lady in Blue?"

Guy swallowed. He tried to remember. It was so long ago. "I was with fever. Very young. I overheard I might not make it through the night. She came, this Lady in Blue, a lady made of light. She brushed the sweat from my brow and bade me "stay" and sometime later my fever broke. My mother said her prayers to Mary were answered. I did not know if it was Mother Mary who visited me. I did not dare tell anyone and I made myself believe I was hallucinating. But She is real, is She not?"

Evelyn smiled. "Yes, Guy, She is real and alive. She is the Lady of this Land. And it is obvious She has chosen you as She has chosen us. It is a blessing you came here."

Guy took a big breath, his whole chest expanding before slowly contracting again. He felt the honor and weight of Evelyn's statement and recognized a huge responsibility was now secured upon his brow.

CHAPTER 27

Tana's Story

AFTER HIS LATEST session on the history of Avalon, Guy lingered. He watched Tana as she stood completely still, as if she were a statue. Her eyes moved slowly and rested on his as surely she felt this man's observational gaze. They looked into each other's eyes for a few moments before Guy decided to ask the questions he had been holding onto for the past month.

Guy spoke to Tana, "Tana, would you mind sharing your story with me? I want to know how it was that you came to live here in England in the company of the Avalons."

Tana tilted her long neck ever so slightly. She carried herself with a proud, regal air. Her full lips slid into a slight smile as she told her Lady's son-to-be her story. "I am Tana, daughter of Yeturow and Merymaat. My mother, Yeturow was a Priestess of Nekhbet, the Goddess of our land. She fell in love with a man. The temple priests and priestesses agreed to the marriage so long as they gave back their firstborn daughter. I was promised to the temple the day I was born. There I stayed doing the work of the Goddess. One day many years ago our temple was raided. I seemed to be passed along like so much cargo. It was a hard life. On a ship, I met Nasrane. There was much…heat between us." Tana paused as she thought back to the only man she ever gave herself to willingly. "But he was taken away and I was sold to a Crusader who was on his way home. He did not touch me. I did not understand why he took me. But he brought me here before a young woman on a throne and presented me to her. He said, 'Forgive me, Lady. You were right.' And she said, 'It is good you came home. Who is this?' 'Lady, I present to you, Tana. I gather she was a priestess to the Goddess in her own land. I brought her here so she would not be so ill-used again. I give her to you freely.' Then the Duchess turned to me to said, 'Tana, do you want stay and give birth to your baby here or do you wish to return home?' I did not know English very well then but I understood I was being given a choice. I saw what I now know to be a dragon in the tapestry behind the Duke and Duchess. I thought, whether I serve the Goddess there or here is no matter. I saw kindness in this woman, and strength. I decided to stay. I am glad. The Lady and I gave birth around the same time. We helped each other. Taharqa and the Lady Morgaine became playmates. They are good friends. Life is good here. My son and I have a good life here. My son is well respected. He showed great aptitude with weaponry and was trained by the Master of Arms Sir Hammond. My son took over as Master of Arms when Sir Hammond retired after a bad injury." Tana paused in thought, adding, "Taharqa is living into his name."

Guy asked, "What does Taharqa mean?"

"Taharqa was a Nubian Pharaoh who ruled long, long ago. He was a great leader and knew the ways of weaponry and strategy. My son is a great man too."

Guy mirrored her smile, "I can see that, Tana."

Tana lifted her head and nodded with pride.

CHAPTER 28

―――― ❈ ――――

It's About Power

THE PREMISE OF the ride was to show Guy more of Glastonbury's lands which were mostly up, down, and wet. It was a hilly terrain with lowland marshes and upland grasslands that surrounded the town, with the Tor on the highest summit. But Gareth had an additional motive. As they crested a hill, Gareth slowed his horse so that he and Guy could walk side by side. Midnight complied and fell in step with the other horse as the two men talked.

Gareth started, "Guy, though Glastonbury is not vast in and of itself, it does encompass Avalon, which Morgaine has been showing you."

Guy nodded absentmindedly as he listened.

Gareth continued, "And just as the Guardians live to protect the Ladies of the Lake, so I — as Duke — protect the Land She inhabits. I am consort to the Lady incarnate."

Guy tilted his head in contemplation as he took in the information.

They rode quietly for a bit, enjoying the sunny day and taking in the beauty of the landscape.

Gareth interrupted the peace by stating, quite suddenly, "A true ruler is a servant of the people. Are you ready to serve, Guy?"

Guy reflected on the statement and the question. He hadn't considered that a ruler was a servant. He did not see that in the men in power who ruled. Gareth was the first to give him pause that there was another way. He responded, "I am beginning to see there is another way to rule. I hope I prove worthy of the challenge."

They were quiet as their horses walked alongside each other. Guy thought about what it meant to be in power. He said, "While serving the Earl of Derby, the Sheriff, I saw him as the route to power and position in the world. In

Nottingham, I was no one before I aligned myself with the Sheriff. But with the Sheriff I was someone, someone with power."

"Power over," Gareth specified.

"Pardon?"

Gareth clarified, "You had power over others. Your ruling derived from fear."

Guy suddenly felt ashamed. "Yes," he said softly.

Gareth was philosophical, "Well, it is the way we are taught, the way we know. We are not usually taught that there is any other way other than power over. It is in our nature to compete."

Guy thought about what was in his nature to do and to be. He thought about how Gareth and Evelyn ruled together and how he would be expected to rule in partnership with Morgaine.

Gareth continued, "It's not always easy, ruling in partnership. Taking someone else into consideration when making decisions. Sometimes, just to get something done you want to make a decision and put it into action. But your spouse is still mulling it over, or worse, disagrees with you."

Guy was silently considering what it would be like to rule with Morgaine, or to disagree with her. During their ordeal of getting her parents released from prison, they did work well together. It certainly took a lot of trust on both their parts. And they came through it a stronger couple. Standing as a unified force made them more powerful. Guy said out loud, "Power with."

Gareth smiled, "Yes. Yes. Power with. Power in partnership."

Guy considered his love and trust of Morgaine and said with mirth in his voice, "I think we can manage it."

Gareth nodded, "No doubt. If there had been doubt, well, I just don't think it would be you I would be having this conversation with."

"Then who?"

"Gods, I hope not just myself." Gareth chuckled at himself. "No. No. There is a reason it is you, Guy. I can trust that. Can you?"

Guy looked slightly baffled but persevered good-naturedly, "God, I hope so."

Guy watched Evelyn and Gareth more intently after his conversation with Gareth. He watched them as they presided over court and listened to the few woes of their people and as they came to joint decisions on matters of state. He observed them at meals and in casual conversation. They seemed so content together. When they discussed a matter, they appeared to listen attentively and respectfully. Guy could only hope the same for himself and Morgaine.

"Morgaine, do your parents ever argue?" Guy inquired aloud rather suddenly.

Morgaine had been watching Guy study her parents and wondered what prompted such a question. She responded, "Do you remember when I told you that my father asked me to dance for the Prince?"

"Yes."

"Well, there is quite a bit more to that story. When Prince John came to visit my parents we could tell he was gathering information. We all knew that Richard would be the brother made king, so why was John asking questions? At the time, we had no quarrel with King Henry and did not expect to with Richard. But John asked us questions relating to religious matters and my parents stated that those questions were best left up to God and each person's conscience and that they would not dictate that the people in their care follow a specific religion. That, in and of itself, was a dangerous thing to say. But I am sure my parents must have felt it was the right thing to say. In the end, when Richard slaughtered his own people on his way to the Holy Land — just because they were Jewish — I think John knew we would be displeased, and that he would have our support. But back to your question. It is rare; but yes, my parents have had disagreements. That night at dinner, John asked if I danced and if I did he would very much like to see. My father said that I did, and then asked me to dance for the Prince. Which I did. And I was content to do so. I saw no harm, though I did notice the lust in his eyes. I trusted my parents could keep me safe; and they did. Later that night after the Prince had retired, my parents talked about the evening. I lingered, as it felt to me to be a family matter and they did not tell me to leave. My mother was visibly upset. It is rare to see her lose her composure."

Evelyn started, "Why did you ask your daughter to dance for the Prince?"

"Evelyn, remember it was the Prince who asked if she danced, and said that he wanted to see her. What was I to do? Lie?"

"But you see the lust in his eyes. He wants to bed her."

"I know. And we must not let that happen if we can avoid it. But we are getting pulled into politics whether we want to or not. John came here sniffing for our support and though we stated neutrality, we gave him a bone should he ever have need of it. In the meantime, it is not his castle so he will not invite Morgaine to court as a courtier."

"How can you be sure?"

"I cannot. But we must tread carefully. When Richard is King, how long do you think it will be before he turns his attention on us? You have seen how grave he is in his religious beliefs. We may need John."

"John will not go against his brother for us, or for anyone. No, we cannot trust him. And we certainly cannot trust him with our daughter."

"Love, we may be forced into picking a side; you have already foreseen that."

"I fear that by choosing a side it will hurt us in the end."

"It may. And though we need to safeguard the future, we must protect our people and this land now."

"I know. But using Morgaine…"

"Wife, that is unfair. I did not mean to use her. But if he likes her, he can protect her."

"Unlikely."

"Forgive me for not discussing this with you so that we could have reached consensus. There was no opportunity that I saw for that. I did what I thought would appease him."

"I know. I am just upset and I am sorry I am turning my anger on you when I am really angry at the situation and its implications."

Morgaine came back out of the memory. "It was painful to watch my parents in such heated talk. But even in anger, they made it through and recognized that they needed to continue to trust each other and do their best to keep one step ahead of the brothers. When Richard ordered the Jews slaughtered in London at his coronation, it was just too much on us. We have Jews under our care here. In fact, we lost two of our own. Sarah, out at the horse farm, where you bought Midnight, had two brothers. They had gone to London to study with a Rabbi. They never returned after the coronation. We could not abide by Richard's cruelty. Then John invited us to his annual party, and my parents went while I remained at home. The next year they claimed I was ill so he came to visit, thankfully with his wife. There has been much energy put into making sure I am not requested to go to London as a courtier. Still, I play my part and enjoy his company when I am in it. And the only reason I was in attendance at this last year's party was because John included me specifically in the invitation." Morgaine thought back on that conversation.

"I don't want you attending." Evelyn was in visible distress. She had a vision of John and Morgaine together in a bed, John on top of her daughter with lecherous hands.

Gareth cautiously interjected his reasoning into Evelyn's troubled thoughts. "Evelyn, you know that we cannot keep avoiding this. And our daughter needs to find a mate. This may be the Gods lending a hand. Morgaine's mate may be out in the world. We must keep ourselves open to opportunity."

Evelyn knew she had been cloistering her adult daughter away from the world, away from danger. She was willful. "It puts us all at risk every time we leave. Others may question our validity to continue to claim Glastonbury."

Gareth said gently, "I, too, am concerned, my love. And we are careful. And Morgaine's mate has not stumbled his way into Glastonbury." Gareth turned to Morgaine who had been listening to them discuss her future as if she hadn't been there. "Daughter, what is your wish?"

Morgaine looked from one parent to another. Then she closed her eyes and tried to see the party, if her mate would be there. But the image was clouded. She opened her eyes. "Though I feel fearful, I cannot say for sure if it is any of my own fear, or if it belongs to you, Mother."

Evelyn sighed. She quieted herself and centered, breathing slow and deep and not projecting herself onto her family.

For several moments the family was quiet, all eyes closed, thoughts turned inward. Both Morgaine and Evelyn continued to see an odd cloud upon the party in their minds.

Morgaine whispered, "Do you see that, Mother?"

Evelyn figured her daughter was seeing the cloud too. "Yes."

"There is a cloud."

"Yes. Someone is clouded."

Morgaine brightened slightly, "Well, that has my curiosity."

Evelyn was not sure whether she should be more fearful or less. It could be a cloaking spell by a very dangerous cunning person. There would be no way to know without attending.

Guy's eyes opened wide as he exclaimed, "I was the cloaked person."

Morgaine responded, "Given your story about Wyvern that makes the most sense."

"But you saw me," Guy smiled.

Morgaine returned Guy's smile warmly, "Yes, I did. Thank the Gods I saw you." She leaned into Guy and he held her tight.

Guy then turned his thoughts back to his original question about how Evelyn and Gareth communicated. He took in all that Morgaine had said. It was more than he asked for. But he was glad to know the whole story, and that his soon-to-be parents-in-law were so levelheaded and respectful of each other that they could have disagreements without causing damage to their trust. He appreciated that they talked an issue through to its conclusion. Also, they did not cajole Morgaine into picking a side but simply asked for her input. If Morgaine grew up with this as her model then she would expect the same from her mate which meant he could expect the same from her. He breathed a sigh of relief.

Morgaine looked at him quizzically, "What was that sigh for?"

"I am relieved that, given how your parents relate, you would expect the same. This means I can, too, which means our relationship will not be volatile. We can get through a disagreement without lasting damage."

"Of course we can, Love. It is a matter of trust. We need to trust each other that even if we disagree, we each have our reasons; we shall continue loving each other through our disagreement. It is also a matter of communication. We must always be open and honest with each other."

Guy nodded in agreement.

Morgaine put her hand to his cheek, "Is it so foreign to you to be able to trust and rely on someone else?"

Again, Guy nodded. He searched her eyes and received her compassion. "Lady, I pray this elation I am feeling is longstanding."

"Guy, I can see you are grappling with your trust. It appears that too many times you have been hurt by those you trust. So with every word, every action, may I demonstrate to you that you have not misplaced your trust in me. Know that I love you and that I see your love for me."

Guy grabbed hold of Morgaine and held her close, shaking with emotion, repeating loudly in his mind, "I am yours, Lady. I am yours. I am yours."

Morgaine returned the fierceness of the embrace and whispered in his ear, "And I am yours."

And then Guy picked up on a silent thought, "Trust that no matter what, I am yours."

Guy suddenly wondered, "What would have happened if I had said I was Catholic, that I could not take such a vow to the Lady?"

They were seated in Evelyn's receiving room, finishing up another session in discussion of the Avalons' faith. Evelyn was confident, "It would not have happened. If you were not up to the challenge, if you could not wrap your mind around our beliefs, you would have foresworn your love for Morgaine and left."

"Like Lorrac?"

"Yes, like Lorrac." Evelyn then shook her head to get that boy out of her head. He was the past, and useless to her. Thinking he could run away to another land to find himself — the fool! But she cleared her thoughts of the man-child who did not know how to be a man but to fall prey to the voices outside of himself. He could not take that inner journey, only the outer one. She focused on the man before her, "But you remember Her. You remember Her call, Her touch."

Guy nodded. "Yes."

"And with that, you did not turn your back on Her but went to Her. Accepted Her. Accepted Her claim on you."

His brow furrowed slightly at the thought of being claimed, as he wasn't sure he understood what that implied. Still he responded, "Yes."

Evelyn paused in contemplation, then added, "Guy, I am curious why you so readily accepted the Goddess and willingly moved away from your God."

Guy looked down, averting his eyes as he thought of how to respond. This family seemed so accepting, but to try his hand on this one point.

Evelyn waited with a compassionate gaze upon him.

He knew, if she really wanted to, she could invade his thoughts, his memories and pluck out the reason behind his aversion to the Church. Did other faiths have such specific prejudices? Would it be the same? Would there always be a piece of him that he had to hide? Guy then took a breath and returned Evelyn's steady gaze.

Her face did not give her away completely, though she did allow for a slight smile. She gave him a nod, maintaining her gentle smile.

He returned her nod. His response, though not entirely complete, was honest, "The Scriptures are interpreted prejudicially against so many. I have struggled with how God could have created everything and yet, though He created everything according to His plan, there are things of His creation that are somehow not right, but wrong." Guy opened each arm in turn as he continued, "I wonder why there is only the right path, why the left is not simply another choice or way to be but, rather, is portrayed as wrong."

Evelyn nodded. She had wondered the same thing with that faith. It did not make sense to her that they could not coexist, that the Divine did not allow for multiple paths that led to a deeper sense of connection. Evelyn assessed Guy anew; this man was more contemplative that she originally thought. "Guy, for someone who has been called a villain and one who has instilled fear in others in hopes of gaining power, you are quite an open man, accepting more than anyone would credit you."

"You sound impressed, My Lady."

"I am."

Guy smiled; he did not think it was possible to impress the Duchess and he was relieved to be mistaken on this account.

Evelyn took hold of her daughter's hand as they walked the garden that morning, just the two of them. "Daughter, there is another reason we allowed the Handfasting to take place and for you to consummate your love. Do you know why?"

Morgaine gave her mother a sidelong glance, "You could sense we may not be able to wait a whole month?"

Evelyn grew serious and Morgaine realized this was not the time for play. "Mother, what is it?"

Evelyn stopped walking and got in front of her daughter, gazing at her with a mixture of love and dread. "You know that Prince John will be in attendance at the wedding."

"Yes."

"And you know how he has lusted after you."

"I have sensed that, yes. And I have allowed his affections and even encouraged him."

"All too well."

Morgaine was about to protest.

"Nay, Daughter, I did not mean you did more than you should, only that… I need you to be prepared that he may demand Lord's Right."

Morgaine shook her head, "No! He wouldn't. That is what lords do upon their peasants. Surely, he would not commit this upon other royalty."

There was grave concern on Evelyn's face. "He may. And you will have to go through with it. We must stay in his good graces."

Morgaine was disgusted at the thought. "Oh Mother, no."

Evelyn spoke compassionately, "Morgaine, I wanted your first time to be magical for you and it sounds like it was. It is good that Guy is an attentive lover. John may not be so. But either way, I think it is possible; I need you to continue to be kind to him. Can you do that?" Evelyn had tears in her eyes, knowing what she asked of her daughter.

Morgaine took a deep breath, "Yes."

"If he does take you, treat it as work of the Goddess. She will guide you as if performing a ritual. He has no power over you if you do not let him."

Morgaine furrowed her brow and wrinkled her nose. "What do I tell Guy?"

Evelyn shook her head slightly, "He will fret about it and it may drive him mad and then perhaps it will not happen. Your Father and Taharqa will be at his side to help him through if it does."

"So I tell him nothing?"

"There is nothing to tell at this point. I am telling you because I am counting on you to maintain your composure as difficult as it may be. But no baby from John's seed. Understand?"

"Yes."

CHAPTER 29

Wedding Guests Arrive

MORGAINE PRACTICALLY RAN at Gwenhwyfar and wrapped her arms around the giantess. The women hugged. There was nothing small about her friend. Big swirling ringlets of red hair, ample bosom and hips, a wide, generous mouth, large emerald eyes, freckles aplenty.

Gwenhwyfar reacquainted her family to Morgaine, introducing her husband, Rufus, and her sons, Rodney, Julius and baby Neirin. With Rodney, and even with Neirin, their Roman parentage through Rufus was clear. Julius on the other hand, looked much like his mother, only he had the most curious eyes for a redhead: brilliant kingfisher blue.

Guy came up to stand at Morgaine's side as she introduced everyone.

Julius, in particular, appeared captivated by Guy. "Lord Guy?" he shyly asked.

Morgaine laughed good-naturedly, telling the boy, "Your mother and I are like sisters. Call us Auntie Morgaine and Uncle Guy."

This appeared to overwhelm the young lad with gladness. "Uncle Guy."

Guy, never having been overly fond of children, was surprised that he was enjoying having this little redheaded boy wrap himself around him.

Meanwhile, Julius felt flooded with a deep sense that he had come home, that he had found the "Dragon's Breath," that his dream had kept whispering to him for months.

Julius' father, Rufus, on the other hand, was scrutinizing the eye color between his son and the man called Lord Guy.

Delphine and Bartholomew arrived. Guy came down to greet his sister with as much love as he was able; they had been estranged far too long. "I am happy you came."

Delphine steeled herself against any affection, instead commenting, "Well, well, Guy, you have done quite well for yourself. You remember Bartholomew, my husband."

"Yes of course."

The men shook hands. Bartholomew then placed his large hand on his small wife's back. It was a gesture of kindness but also of control. Bartholomew was a rather rotund older man, a man who really should have no business with such a young thing as Delphine.

Guy tried to ignore his assessments of his sister's husband, making what he thought was small talk. "Any little ones?"

Already stony, Delphine replied simply, "Dead."

"I am sorry," was all Guy could say. What did one say? There was no consolation for a parent losing a child. He could only be sad for her loss, sad to see her in pain.

"Yes, well…" Delphine maintained her composure though there was a tiny part of her that still wanted to be held by her older brother, to be told it was alright — that she was alright. Instead she changed the subject, "Well, when do we get to be introduced to your bride?"

"Right now." Guy took his sister's stiff arm and led them up the stairs.

Morgaine caught sight of them coming up the stairs out of the corner of her eye and broke away from Gwenhwyfar, turning to meet them as they came to the landing.

"Morgaine, I would like you to meet my sister, the Lady Delphine, and her husband, the Lord Bartholomew. Delphine and Bartholomew, meet the Lady Morgaine, future Duchess of Glastonbury and my bride."

Delphine and Bartholomew respectfully curtsied and bowed. Bartholomew, seeing a possible opportunity at more power and position, made a grand production while Delphine looked on rolling her eyes, though she did not attempt any further disrespect to her husband. She knew that Robert made Bartholomew promise to take care of his ward and keep her safe all those years ago. Still, there were so many ways he could keep her "safe" if she misbehaved. She bowed her head, feeling defeated.

Morgaine nodded politely as she listened to Bartholomew yammer on, but she was not interested in talks of houses aligning and this man's estates.

As soon as she heard a pause in Bartholomew's voice, she turned to Delphine, took her hands in hers, and said compassionately, "It is lovely to meet you, Delphine. I am glad you decided to come. I do hope that whatever past pains have crossed between you and your brother that you two can walk anew and we can share some happy times together."

Delphine was completely taken aback. This wasn't some polite wan hello. This was an honest gesture for healing and she wasn't sure how to take it. She just nodded.

More guests arrived, and Guy and Morgaine were pulled away to greet them. Delphine watched on, wringing her hands. Her husband noticed the gesture and quietly placed his large hand over hers and gave a squeeze; it was meant to be gentle, sympathetic. It did not feel that way to Delphine. She did not allow herself to love Bartholomew or even to make the best of it. She just kept repeating in her mind, "You will survive this." Though by now, after all these years, she wasn't sure she wanted to.

Guy and Morgaine were making their rounds during the dinner festivities in the grand dining hall when a large Venus of a woman caught Guy's eye. He laughed and shook his head and nodded toward the woman. "Okay Morgaine, you are the one who wanted to invite and meet my teacher." He steered Morgaine in Ann's direction. "Beloved, this is Ann…my teacher."

Ann cocked her head; she'd been called many names, but this was a first for introductions. She laughed heartily.

Guy continued, "Ann, I am delighted to introduce you to my betrothed, the Lady Morgaine, future duchess of Glastonbury."

Ann curtsied, but was thrown a bit off balance by Morgaine wrapping her arms around her in a hug.

"Thank you, Ann!"

Ann was puzzled at the gratitude but laughed just the same. "Whatever for, my dear Lady?"

"For everything you have taught My Lord and my love."

"Oh," Ann chuckled lustily, her ample bosom jiggling. "Well, I am glad my lessons were appreciated."

Guy looked sheepish. It wasn't often your lovers past and present were speaking with each other in such happy terms.

Ann pulled at their hands so that the couple was seated before her. "Well, I pray much happiness and great sex upon you."

Morgaine and Guy both blushed.

"Oh my, what a gorgeous couple you two make! I have had many a beautiful maid and lad and I would gladly take the pair of you to bed with me in a heartbeat!"

Morgaine and Guy blushed a deeper shade of red. "Oh, there will be others who hold similar thoughts; take my word for it. You are exquisite."

Guy laced his hands through Morgaine's. "Well, they can't have us."

Ann caught a saddened expression on Morgaine's face and intuitively she knew Morgaine was concerned. And there would be only one person who could have the power to give a bride concern about such matters. She patted Morgaine's hand. "There, there, dear. It will be alright."

Guy looked perplexed, "What do you mean? What are you talking about?"

Morgaine and Ann shared a glance. "My Lady, I would think it best if you have this concern to share it with your lord so that you can both cope with it."

Morgaine heaved a sigh. She really didn't want to have to think about this, and certainly not at her wedding. She looked at Guy and took his hand. "I am concerned that Prince John will claim Lord's Right."

"He could not...you're royalty...He would not...would he?"

"My mother thinks he may and warned me. I have been sitting with this for days, just basking in the reassurance of your love and not wanting to give it too much thought."

"Oh Morgaine, you look so sad. Do not worry. I love you. I am sad you felt you had to hold this alone. You do not."

Ann chimed in, "What a man you have grown into; what a champion you have become. Guy, I am proud of you. Trust that even if John does this, your lady loves you."

Guy nodded, though his insides were knotting up at the thought of any man having Morgaine.

Guy had already dispelled the illusion that he held chambers in any room other than Morgaine's, and so days ago the servants prepared what had been his bedroom in order to welcome Prince John. But Prince John had not arrived yet. More guests came the next day and Guy met Morgaine's other childhood friend, Nichole, and her husband, Will, and their children, Rowan and Godric. Rowan was a bouncy little hazel-eyed, brown-haired lass who could not seem to keep still; there was so much to see and do. Will joked of wishing for a tether, knowing full well this little wild one would gnaw right through it. Godric, though similar in looks to his sister, was more contemplative, and thankfully ever watchful of his little sister. The children were mirror images of their comely, well-endowed mother. Will, a handsome, full-bodied man with dark features and steady, kind smile, was a merchant and the family made their home in Weymouth, along the southern coast of England.

After another long day of meeting guests, Guy was thankful to have his soon-to-be-lawfully-wedded wife to himself in their bedchamber. He flopped down on the bed and then dramatically spread his arms out and fell backward.

Morgaine giggled. She came up between his legs and climbed on top of Guy, sitting down, their groins touching. They could both feel an invisible current between them. It was warm and pulsing and made them each feel very much alive…and lustful.

He opened his eyes and looked up her, saying slyly, "We're not going to sleep yet, are we?"

Morgaine shook her head slowly, her eyes aglow, her mouth in a wide mischievous smile.

CHAPTER 30

Summer Solstice 1192 Initiation

THOUGH NORMALLY A consort would not be initiated until after a lengthier training process and years of trust building, the coven was not at luxury to wait for Guy to catch up — and so he was initiated, by a trial of fire, so to speak. For the weeks leading up to the Summer Solstice, he was educated in the Goddess tradition. He was like a deep pool, willing and able to soak up everything that Evelyn and Gareth, Morgaine and Rainer poured into him.

It was at sword point that Guy met the rest of the members of the Avalons' tight circle. It was the eve of Summer Solstice. They gathered in the gloaming. Their robes looked like shadows.

As Morgaine led him to the circle she whispered, "We celebrate during the night so that we have more privacy and protection. You may have heard what happened to the Druids. We have no intention of being slain in our grove with the sun in our eyes."

Morgaine let go of Guy's hand and stepped into the circle. Guy would have simply followed her, but her father blocked his path into the circle. Guy looked at Gareth, not sure what to expect. He watched Gareth draw his sword, the metal glinting in the firelight, pointing at Guy. Though perplexed, Guy remained calm. He did not believe he had come all this way just for Gareth to change his mind about allowing him to marry his daughter and instead run him through. So he waited, breathing as slowly as he could, watching Gareth.

Gareth appeared to be summing up something from within. When he opened his eyes, he looked formidable. He was not the jolly Gareth Avalon that Guy was used to. In an intimidating voice Gareth called out to Guy, "It is better to fall upon this blade than to betray your kin."

Guy tilted his head assessing the challenge. He saw the similarities between his initiation into the Black Knights and this coven, but he doubted he would ever be forced to harm another as part of a ritual. In a heartbeat, he swore to protect the coven. "I would rather die than betray your trust. My life belongs to Morgaine. If she will have me, I will do whatever it takes to protect her and this family." He looked around the circle to let them know that if Morgaine considered them family, he was willing to as well.

Gareth smiled, "Well said. Welcome, Guy of Avalon."

Guy came to stand in the circle, walking around to be beside Morgaine. She reached out her hand as he came to her and they grasped hands to stand together. He looked at her and smiled, and she smiled back. Then both turned their heads to face into the circle as Evelyn began to speak.

"We gather on this night, on the dawning of the Longest Day, to celebrate the holy union of the Lady and Her Consort. Theirs is a fierce, bright love that burns away all facades, all pretenses. All is burned pure in the wake of Their love. We now have a young couple who embodies that love, that depth of commitment." Evelyn swept her arms toward Morgaine and Guy.

She then smiled and nodded at her husband, and in unison the Lady and the Master of the coven exclaimed, "To our new Summer Queen and Sun King! All hail!"

The coven members beamed back at Evelyn and Gareth, their leaders, then turned their heads to face Guy and Morgaine, clapping and cheering, "Come, Lady and Lord, wear your crowns."

Morgaine easily chose a crown of wild summer flowers. Her father put it on her head.

Guy saw that there were actually choices and was perplexed at which one to choose.

Evelyn, at his side, whispered, "Choose the one that calls to you."

He looked at the one on Morgaine's head. No, it was right that she wear that one. There was one that was brass and bejeweled and reminded him of fire and royalty and though he coveted it, he was not called to that one. There was one made of beautiful feathers but that one didn't stir him either, nor did the silver crown with blue stones — as much as the blue would match his eyes and made him think of The Faie. But the antlers drew him in. He picked them up. "I choose the hart."

Evelyn took the crown from him and placed the antlers on his head. She wrinkled her nose in an effort to hold back her emotions. It was how she had seen it.

The couple stood together and everyone formed a circle.

Evelyn began. She took up Guy's right hand in her left, stating, "Hand to hand..." then with their hands grasped she guided his hand to her heart and then to his heart, saying, "...and heart to heart, we create this circle in love and trust."

He looked at her, smiling at the sweet words. She nodded at him and he understood that he was supposed to say this as well. He turned to Morgaine, taking her hand, echoing, "Hand to hand and heart to heart, we create this circle in love and trust."

The words and actions were repeated all the way around the circle ending with Gareth to his wife, "Hand to hand and heart to heart, we create this circle in love and trust." The couple then kissed to seal the circle.

There was great joy around the circle this night. Friends reunited. A marriage to celebrate. The honoring of the union between Lady and Lord. And though it was in some respects considered a peasant tradition, Nichole brought out the broom and waved at it everyone, signifying that the Jumping of the Broom would now commence.

Nichole proclaimed, "The humble broom. It cleans the home, sweeping out all the dirt and cobwebs. It represents the hearth, what we come to each day to find solace and a good meal made by loving hands. Morgaine, Guy, jump the broom, and jump into your hearth together." She laid the broom down before them and they jumped over it, holding hands. A "hoorah" went up in unison from the circle.

Three other couples followed, recommitting to hearth and home together — Nichole and Will, Elizabeth and Wild Herb, the older couple from Beltaine, and

Evelyn and Gareth. Guy watched the other couples jump the broom and noticed that even though he had been introduced to Gwenhwyfar's husband, Rufus was not among the coven members. Meggie, Rainer, and Taharqa did not jump the broom either and he assumed they must be without mates or that if they did have sweethearts, they were not of the same faith.

Evelyn motioned with her finger so the two sweethearts would come forward. Guy and Morgaine came to stand before Evelyn who gently pulled at the braided cord draped around her daughter's neck. "The Handfasting Cord, woven together by two in love, by two committing to become one life lived together." She looked to each of them, continuing, "Guy and Morgaine, are you willing to be so bound?"

Both nodded in agreement.

Evelyn took the cord and wound it gently around their clasped hands. "As Lady of the Lake and Priestess of Avalon, I so bind you. May you live into your sacred vows to each other every day. May you look upon each other to see the Divine gazing back. May you grow in love and devotion for each other."

The pair blushed and beamed in bliss.

Evelyn then placed her hands on each of their chests, then lips, then foreheads, stating, "I bless this marriage, in the name of the Lady. Feel love, speak love, know love." She then steered them around and presented them to the coven, stating, "Guy and Morgaine, here is your family, bearing witness to and honoring this marriage. These are the people you can turn to, in love and trust, who commit to supporting this marriage." Evelyn then spoke to the coven, "Family, do you so swear to love and honor this couple and support them in their shared life together?"

"Yes!" exclaimed the coven in union, "We so swear."

Evelyn then asked, "Morgaine and Guy, do you promise that you shall turn to us in good times and in troubled times, that we may support you in your commitment together?"

Morgaine and Guy happily proclaimed in union, "Yes, we so swear."

The coven members embraced and kissed the happy couple.

Gwenhwyfar chuckled with glee as she then took Morgaine's and Guy's corded hands, pulling them toward the large flat stone. It was now covered in furs. Releasing their hands, she sauntered around the stone so that she was on the opposite side, facing the couple. "Your nuptial bed," she smiled widely, displaying the scene by the dramatic opening of her arms over the stone.

Guy was dumbfounded. "Do they really expect us to have sex here, in front of them?" he asked himself.

Morgaine squeezed his hand and he caught her wink out of the corner of his eye.

Gareth came up from behind, put his hands on each of their shoulders, and with mirth in his voice, he whispered in Guy's ear, "It is called the Great Rite."

He patted Guy on the back and Evelyn and Gareth came around the stone to be on opposite sides of it. They both stepped up onto the stone to meet in the middle. They raised and spread their arms wide. The entire coven followed suit.

Lady of the Lake, Evelyn of Avalon began, "I am the flower. I am the well. I am the Land. I am the Lake."

The Lady's Consort, Gareth of Avalon responded, "I am the reeds that grow. I am the fish that swim. I am the ones who live and die. I am the Antlered One coming to drink."

Evelyn brought her hands together and Gwenhwyfar was right there with a pitcher of water to fill the Lady's cupped hands.

Gwenhwyfar stepped back down as Evelyn said warmly, "Then drink. Drink of me and be filled."

Gareth lifted his Lady's cupped hands and drank the water and then kissed the palms of her hands.

The couple smiled to each other and then Evelyn continued, "I am the fire's spark. I am the breath. I am the love that lives in the world."

Gareth responded. "I am the passion. I am the inspiration. I am your Lord begging a kiss."

Evelyn's smile widened, "I am your Lady and surely I am inspired to kiss you."

There were much "ahs" and "oohs" as the couple passionately kissed each other.

Guy noticed how playful Gareth and Evelyn were being, more playful than he had seen before now. "They are still in love," he mused to himself with a joyful heart.

As the couple kissed, Elizabeth and Wild Herb stepped up on the stone stating in unison, "Oh Sweet Lady, Oh Gentle Lord, will you yield your place this night for the Summer Queen and Sun King?"

Evelyn and Gareth looked to one another, and in unison proclaimed, "We so yield."

Upon that, they reached their hands out to Morgaine and Guy and three generations stood upon the stone. The elders gently led the Lady and Lord down off the stone so that Morgaine and Guy were standing on the stone alone.

All cheered, "Hail the Summer Queen and Sun King! May their love shower the Land."

With that, a rhythmic clapping commenced and the couple was encouraged to kiss and embrace.

Guy whispered in Morgaine's ear, "What are we supposed to do?"

She responded by nibbling his ear, whispering back, "Our nature."

"But your parents are watching."

"They are also the Lady and Lord incarnate and blessing our union."

"So we are really going to have sex here?"

Morgaine giggled, "Yes."

"This is a bit embarrassing."

"No more than if we were in our bed, being presided over by a Catholic priest and all the lords of the land."

He looked around. His new coven mates were not really watching them and some of their eyes were even closed as they clapped and chanted. The fireflies were out, winking at them; stars were twinkling, and a warm breeze was blowing upon them. "Hmmm. No, this is better," he playfully growled in her ear.

With loving eyes dimly focused upon the air around them, Morgaine and Guy shed their clothing as best they could with bound hands. Their capes remained fastened at the neck. The couple helped each other down upon the fur-covered stone. Guy heard a song start up and of course did not recognize the tune or words for they were of a faith he was only now embracing. There was a part of Guy that found this all so bewildering and intimidating but he allowed himself to be bewitched by this magical moment and found himself kissing Morgaine all over her body, taking in her scent, her taste and reveling in her touch. The betrothed performed the Great Rite on the large stone listening to each other's moans, barely hearing the chanting and clapping around them.

Sweet, magnificent Lady. Gentle, wild Lord.
We hear you calling in the day and in the night.
You create the world with your delight.
Summer Queen, Sun King, Solstice be thy wedding bed.
Shower your love upon the land and we will all be fed.

The song slowly altered as Evelyn and Gareth started up the call and response. Both chants could be heard for a time before the whole coven switched to the female to male call and response chant.

Come to me. I come to you.
Sing to me. I sing to you.
Kiss my body. I kiss your body.
Touch my soul. I touch your soul.
Come into me. I come into you.
Two become one. Two become one.

The call and response was mesmerizing for all involved. And as the couple on the stone pulsed into climax, so did the song, becoming a simple chant sung over and over to call the Divine Couple forth.

Shower Your love and the Land be fed. Shower Your love and the Land be fed.

Though Guy wasn't really hearing the words with his ears, his subconscious was obeying a command. It felt as if he had two selves: his body and his spirit. And as his body curved around Morgaine's, intertwining limbs, his spirit and hers seemed to merge into one shining being. The two did become one. It was an incredible sensation that knew no words, just the bliss of being joined, of being home.

CHAPTER 31

Getting to the Church on Time

FATHER STEPHEN, THE High Priest of Glastonbury Abbey was instructed to watch for the Prince's carriage and bring him directly to the Lady Chapel. The formal wedding could not begin without the Prince; since he had said he would be coming, he would be presiding over the wedding. Father Stephen, doing his best to remain calm — as it wasn't everyday one was responsible for attending to the Royal Crown in these parts — was a trusted advisor of the Duke and Duchess. And part of his job was to ensure the family's privacy and secrets. In their gratitude, the Avalons offered their blessing and support so that Father Stephen and his monks could continue their good work at rebuilding the Abbey. The Father did have to contend with a most cantankerous man, The Bishop of Bath and now Glastonbury too: Savaric fitzGeldewin. The Bishop was not a kind fellow, and he was a strong advocate of King Richard which put him in opposition to the Duke and Duchess. Though he did not know that, and Father Stephen "protected" him from such information. Thankfully, that man was off making appeals and other mischief and rarely in Glastonbury.

Father Stephen anticipated that Prince John would come first to the castle. And he did. As the carriage door opened, Father Stephen peered in, "Good Morning, Your Excellency."

Prince John sniffed. He appeared annoyed that there was not a crowd to greet him. "Where is everyone?!" he demanded.

"Your Excellency, all are preparing for your arrival to preside over this most joyous wedding."

"Ah," was all Prince John allowed.

"Will you allow me the highest honor to bring you to the Lady Chapel? You could freshen up and take libations and from there you will have the best view of the procession."

Prince John sat up. A procession to him? He nodded, considering. "Yes, that would be acceptable."

The Prince motioned for the High Priest of Glastonbury Abbey to step up onto the carriage. The doorman then closed the door while Father Stephen clambered up onto the carriage to join the driver. Onward they went to the Abbey.

News spread fast that the Prince had arrived and was on his way toward the hill. Everyone made ready for the procession.

An open carriage arrived at the castle as Evelyn, Gareth, Morgaine, and Guy descended the stairs. The party climbed into the carriage, and they were off toward the hill.

Father Stephen, Prince John, Princess Isabella, and the monks watched from the hill, witnessing what appeared to be the whole town pouring from residences, coming to church to witness the marriage of their sweet Lady of the Lake to her consort. It looked like all six hundred souls of the town plus the few wedding guests from near and far turned out for this celebration.

Father Stephen ushered Prince John and the Princess Isabella into the chapel and to the front of the room. Prince John was seated on a throne at the head of the room. The Duke and Duchess had seats awaiting them to the right of him while Prince John's wife was seated to John's left. Guests funneled into the chapel. Most of the town's inhabitants were still outside just wanting to catch a glimpse of their sweet Lady, now finally getting married. Guy walked the length of the chapel by himself to stand beside the priest. Morgaine walked in with her parents, one on each arm. When they reached the front of the room, they bowed before the Prince, then each kissed Morgaine and placed her hands in Guy's.

When all parties had settled in, Gareth looked to Prince John, who nodded his approval to begin. As much as Evelyn was the lead in the prior night's ritual, Gareth took the lead for this ceremony. "As it has been the tradition for generations, when there is no son in the Land, the family adopts the daughter's consort. Guy, do you take the name "Avalon," forsaking all other lands and titles, to be our son, a son of Avalon, being bequeathed the realm in holding with our daughter, Morgaine, upon our death?"

Guy proclaimed loudly and with great joy, "Yes!"

Gareth and Evelyn each embraced and, in turn, kissed Guy's cheeks.

Prince John was surprised upon hearing this revelation but kept himself composed; it was more than Guy had originally let on back in Wallingford. Of course, it now made sense as to how this family had quietly kept rights to Glastonbury all these centuries and with the same surname. And, as this family was loyal to him, he would do his best to keep this little secret against his brother. He smiled conspiratorially as the ceremony continued.

Gareth and Evelyn then presented their children to Prince John.

Prince John majestically stood up and moved before the couple so brimming with love. He had lust in his eyes as he ogled the pair. He had not had the opportunity to marry many couples but he reveled in this moment with this beautiful match. So in love. He wished he understood this kind of love, that he could touch it. He reached out with both his hands and laid one on each of their outside shoulders. Guy and Morgaine watched the Prince expectantly. There was a long pause as he recalled the words. "Guy of Gisbourne, newly of Avalon, wilt thou have this woman to be thy wedded wife, wilt thou love her, and honor her, keep her and guard her, in health and in sickness, as a husband should a wife, and forsaking all others on account of her, keep thee only unto her, so long as ye both shall live?"

Guy nodded, turning to Morgaine, bringing her hand up to his lips, kissing it, stating fervently, "I will. I do."

Prince John's smile almost matched Morgaine's. Prince John then focused on Morgaine who turned to him, looking into his eyes with such happiness as he asked her the same question. "Morgaine of Avalon, wilt thou have this man to be thy wedded husband, wilt thou love him, and honor him, in health and in sickness, as a wife should a husband, and forsaking all others so long as ye both shall live?"

Morgaine looked from John to her parents to Guy. Tears moistened her eyes and she found herself in utter ecstasy as she exclaimed, "I will! I do!"

Prince John nodded happily, embracing Morgaine, then Guy. Standing back to admire the pair, Prince John stated in a jovial voice, "Well then, Priest, we need to get these two their rings."

Father Stephen approached with the rings that Guy had given him a week before. He held the rings up and then held them out to the Prince to bless.

The Prince inspected the rings momentarily, noticing they were a matching pair of silver braided rings. He nodded approvingly, clasped his hands over the rings and the priest's hand with a whispered prayer, and then looked up at the priest.

Father Stephen handed Morgaine's ring to Guy.

Guy accepted it, turned to Morgaine and clasped her left hand, stating, "I, Guy of Gisbourne…" He paused, restarted, "I, Guy of Avalon, take thee, Morgaine, to be my wedded wife, to have and to hold from this day forward, for better, for worse, for richer, for poorer, in sickness, and in health, till death do us part, and thereto I plight thee my troth."

Morgaine was in utter joy as she watched Guy place the ring on her finger. She admired the workmanship of the braided silver and then it dawned on her — she had seen this ring before. This is the ring she had coveted when she visited Nottingham. She looked up in astonishment at Guy. How did he know?

He smiled triumphantly at her as he could see he made the right choice in rings.

Now it was her turn. As she accepted the ring from Father Stephen she took a moment to study it. Amazing! Just like their braided Handfasting cord that she was now wearing around her waist. She breathed in quiet bliss, centered herself, and said the words, "I, Morgaine of Avalon, take thee, Guy, to be my wedded husband, to have and to hold from this day forward, for better, for worse, for richer, for poorer, in sickness, and in health, till death do us part, and thereto I plight thee my troth." She placed his ring on his finger. The look that passed between them was one of sheer jump-up-and-down joy.

It was obvious they could barely contain themselves even as they bowed their heads for the priest's blessing. With that over with, they turned and kissed and were locked in a marital embrace not even a lever could pry loose. The very ground could have shaken and they would not have shifted.

The newlyweds were finally ushered out, followed by the Prince and Princess and Duke and Duchess. The pairs entered their carriages as the throng spilled out of the chapel to cheer and wish the couple well. The carriages, followed by the droves, made their way along the main street to the castle. The couples waved to the happy populace that lined the hillside. The pairs walked up the castle steps and into the grand dining hall. Guy and Morgaine mingled among the crowd entering the great hall as John, Isabella, Gareth, and Evelyn took their seats. So many people to shake hands with and embrace. Guy and Morgaine felt exhausted but so full of joy. Mary had come with Caron and her husband, Robert, from Nottingham. And Guy and Morgaine greeted them with much enthusiasm and gratitude for witnessing their wedding. The couple moved among their friends and countrymen with a great sense of pride and affection.

After quite some time, they were encouraged to take their seats at the front of the room to the left of the Prince and Princess. There was much merriment as folks enjoyed their meal and the celebrational atmosphere.

When the couple finally retired to their bedroom, Guy stopped Morgaine at the bed. He looked from her to the bed and back at her. He then fondled their Handfasting cord that was belted at her waist: all those prayers for their marriage braided together and secured around his Beloved's belly. He closed his eyes briefly to recall the poem he had written for her and committed to memory. As he opened his eyes he gazed upon his new wife in adoration. He spoke slowly and with much fervor —

Come unto me, for you are my bride and my heart's desire.
Your life is a love song that I sing; I feel it singing through my very veins.
Take me into your temple and I shall cover you with my devotion.

Let me be your shield, your strength, whenever you have need.
Let me shelter your heart, for I love you with all of mine.
Let me make a home with you where I shall cherish you past the end of time.

Morgaine wept at Guy's words. A huge wave of bliss washed over her and her body tingled from the impact of Guy's commitment to her. She tightened her grip on Guy's hands. All she could utter was, "Thank you."

They both had tears in their eyes.

He whispered, "You know my heart, My Lady."

She nodded, "And you know mine." Then she giggled, "So are you going to cover me with your devotion now?"

Guy laughed lustily and gently pushed his wife backwards onto the bed. "Yes!"

They gleefully stripped each other of their clothing to feel the power of their blood pumping through their veins and their sweat beading up on their hot bodies.

CHAPTER 32

The Festivities Continue

ANN LINGERED THE next morning, hoping to catch sight of Guy before she returned to London. Though Prince John had done nothing last night except dance with Morgaine, she saw his lust and knew that he still might demand Morgaine share his bed. He appeared to have an appetite for conquering his own people in a variety of ways. She watched as the happy couple appeared, gliding down the stairs, so in love. They both saw her and approached. She curtsied then enfolded them in an embrace. "I must be off but I am deeply touched at being invited to witness your marriage. Thank you."

The couple beamed.

As they looked about to depart, Ann realized this was her last chance. She knew she could be overstepping bounds but she was always honest with Guy. "Guy, a word?"

Guy nodded, "Of course, what is it?"

Morgaine could tell this was something between the two of them. She gave one final hug to Ann, saying, "Ann, it was so very lovely to meet you. I hope we see you again."

"Thank you, My Lady. I wish that too."

Morgaine turned to Guy, "I will be in the main receiving room."

They kissed, and Ann and Guy watched Morgaine swish away in her beautiful pale silvery-blue gown. Her mother wore that color and similarly-cut gown often. It was the mark of an Avalon Priestess.

Then Ann turned to Guy to draw him to a bench in the hall. They sat down. She started, "Guy, I hope you know I am quite fond of you. So please know that this unsolicited advice comes from my heart and desire to see your continued happy marriage..." Guy nodded, so Ann could tell that he was curious as to what she had to say. She continued, "When you get that beauty with child, and you will, take care to not seek attention elsewhere while she is with child." She looked at him meaningfully.

Guy had an odd smirk on his face, one she knew well, one that stated, "What on earth are you saying?"

"Oh, Guy, for heavens' sake. Fine. A more plain explanation. When a woman becomes pregnant, at some point she won't want to have sex. She will be concerned more for the child growing in her belly..." She paused as Guy just continued to look at her.

He heard this was true.

Ann was forthright, "If you fuck some other woman while your lady is not fit for it, I fear you will break her trust. Some women really cannot handle a man looking elsewhere, no matter the circumstance."

Another man may have gotten angry at a woman giving him advice, but Guy was used to Ann's bluntness and her counsel, so he didn't bat an eye in offence. Ann could see this and relaxed a bit, knowing he was still that same Guy who never yelled at her for telling him what to do and how to do it.

Guy smiled at her and then turned enough so that he could put his hands on the outsides of her shoulders, saying, "Ann, you are a wise woman and I appreciate your concern for our happiness. You have never steered me wrong and I trust your counsel. When the time comes, I will..." he smirked, "...handle it myself."

They both chuckled.

Guy kissed each cheek and then brought Ann's hand to his lips and kissed her hand. Then he stood up and bowed to her. "Take care, Ann."

"You too, Guy. And I am really very proud of you."

He dipped his head in content acknowledgement.

With a proud smile, Ann watched Guy step into his future as he walked away.

The day was jovial with a great sense of joy about the castle. Folks sat in small and larger groups, talking and catching up. The Prince wasn't quite sure how to feel about the informality of the setup but, in spite of not being the center of attention, he found himself enjoying his time. Occasionally, he would slide his eyes onto Morgaine and Guy. Each of them, such great beauties. Each of them ripe and ready to be tasted.

Caron and Marian were on the other side of the room and away from much of the bustle. They caught themselves both looking at Guy in what appeared to be a strained conversation with his sister Delphine.

"I wonder if she will ever forgive him," Marian thought aloud fretfully.

Caron responded, "She may someday. I would hope by now she would realize that it really was out of her brother's hands. It was the Baron's decision after all."

Marian looked at Caron, a weak smile on her face. She sighed, "There is something about him that makes you want to forgive him. I have a hard time staying angry at him despite our disagreements."

Caron nodded. "Me, too. I suppose he will always be the boy who saved me from drowning in the river. I always felt safe around him. Even when he wasn't in the best of moods, I knew he would protect me. If that isn't the definition of a hero, I don't know what is."

Marian contemplated Caron's words. "And you love him."

Caron nodded, "And you do, too, in your own way."

Marian nodded. "More and more, I see the grown man who was that boy, our friend and our hero. This place does him good. He is a better man here."

Caron looked sad. "I miss him already. It was better when he was the Lord of the Manor."

"Really?"

"Yes."

"But Boxer is there."

"That doesn't matter. The Sheriff has Guy's replacement and though that man does live at the castle, he comes around and bothers the villagers. I think the Sheriff is angry with Guy for leaving, and is punishing us. Not that I am blaming Guy. It is good he got out from under that wicked man. And he looks like he mended well from his terrible beating."

Marian was just nodding, thinking, wondering where Robin was in all of this. Finally, she said, "Yes, Guy did mend well." She asked cautiously, "Is Robin Hood helping out the village?"

Caron replied, "Oh yes, of course. Though that just incenses the Sheriff and Sir Grigor more."

"Sir Grigor?"

Caron nodded.

Marian thought back on Grigor. Oh yes, if it wasn't Guy hounding Robin Hood's men, it was Grigor. Both Guy and Grigor could be quite ruthless but the difference between them was mountainous. For Guy was a man of Nottingham, so he often had his heartstrings tugged and did what he could to protect the villagers of Locksley Village. Grigor had no such loyalties having come from Derby with the Sheriff. The Sheriff had brought in so many of his own men who had no ties to Nottingham. She recognized it was easier to bring in a force from elsewhere, for when the people protested, it was not your daughters and sons and mothers and fathers you were keeping at bay behind a spear's point, or slashing with a sword's blade.

Princess Isabella was not a happy woman. She was glad to be out of her castle and allowed to join in the festivities, but she admittedly was not feeling very festive. John had little love for her and was not overly kind. Actually, the kindest he tended to be was in this family's presence, particularly Morgaine's. Morgaine was always complimenting the Princess and making attempts to draw the Prince's attention to his wife. Sometimes it worked. But right now Isabella was growing more annoyed with each passing moment. She couldn't help but look at her husband eyeing Morgaine. She shook her head slightly in disdain. She knew what he was going to do. She tried not to blame Morgaine. She tried to remember that Morgaine, like her, had little true power and could be shuffled around and toyed with like so much chattel. A part of her felt pity for this newlywed couple. Another part of her was humiliated as her husband sought the attention of another. She sat and fumed, unable to do anything about her situation or her life. In this crowd, Isabella felt very alone.

Prince John walked up to Morgaine, who was among her friends, Gwenhwyfar and Nichole. He plainly said, with his hand out, "Walk with me." Everyone curtsied.

Morgaine took the Prince's hand. She could feel a difference in him and she knew; she knew what he would demand of her. She felt rabbit-like, some part of her frozen in fear and another part of her forcing each foot forward.

Guy looked up from across the room, sensing his lady in distress and broke away from his sister, faintly apologizing.

Though Delphine fumed at such a disrespectful dismissal, her eyes carried her to follow Guy's trajectory and saw Morgaine leaving with the Prince. She then watched as a dark-skinned man-of-arms put his hand on Guy's chest. There was much heated talk. She smiled in quiet satisfaction at his anguish, pushing aside that small part of her who had loved her brother and only ever wanted his love. Now, eyes narrowed, she spit mockingly under her breath, "You will survive this, dear brother."

CHAPTER 33

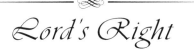

Lord's Right

TAHARQA COULD NOT console Guy. He had been keeping an eye on the room and when he saw the Prince approach Morgaine and take her hand, his first thought was, "Shit!" He saw Guy making his way toward Morgaine and shook his head, "This is not going to be good." He put down his cup and moved swiftly to cut Guy off. Gareth had warned Taharqa to watch for John attempting to separate Morgaine from the crowd. And knowing that one cannot reason with the Prince, Taharqa's job was to detain Guy and keep him from jeopardizing the realm over his jealousy.

Guy kept walking forward despite Taharqa's hand on his chest. He continued to force the larger muscled man to walk backwards. Both men knew they did not want to fight the other. But Guy, hearing Morgaine's silent pleas in his head, wanted to save her. Then her voice abruptly ceased. Guy stopped in his tracks, straining to hear her voice in his head; but it was no longer there.

Evelyn could hear her daughter's plea. In fact, the whole coven could. Each of them had their own considerations of how to stop John from taking her. Several wanted to believe there had to be a way to negotiate with John on Morgaine's behalf to get her out of this predicament. Could it be done with John saving face or would he be as a petulant brat, demanding his way? And when the crown Prince wanted his way, standing in his way could mean your head.

Twelve minds, in a concentrated effort, pressed upon John to change his mind, that a simple kiss was all he wanted from this newlywed. But John was single-minded and the rest of his brain was closed to receiving any new input. If he thought of anything else at all, it was to mentally wave away this hive of angry bees buzzing around him.

The coven sensed they were not being successful. Evelyn had seen the patterns. She had already scried and scried again but she couldn't see how Morgaine could get out of this situation without John punishing the family and possibly Glastonbury. There were no good scenarios. The coven accepted their high priestess' ruling so instead focused on lending Morgaine their strength and centeredness, gently telling her to be brave.

Guy continued to call out to her, "I'm right here, Love. I'm right here."

His anguish was overwhelming to Taharqa who was tasked with physically holding the grieving husband back from saving his wife. It was a job no one would want, including Morgaine's dear friend and Glastonbury's Master-of-Arms.

Gwenhwyfar's mind snapped back into her body as her husband jabbed her in the ribs. He saw her mind was elsewhere, that she was in some kind of a trance.

"Don't you play the witch around me," he growled in low hissing voice.

Gwenhwyfar glared at her husband.

Nichole split her attention as now both of her dear friends were in distress. "Rufus, you are a pebble in one's shoe," she spat and then walked away, pulling Gwenhwyfar with her.

But Rufus was not going to be so disrespected by a woman. He stomped up around the pair and slapped Nichole.

Both of the women were stunned.

Given the whole coven was linked though their trance work, they could each feel what the others were going through. And because of all the fractured emotions and dramas, they were losing focus. It was frustrating and painful to all. Morgaine, unfortunately, felt it the most, as she felt her covenmates' attentions split over the various ensuing dramas. She had to fortify her resolve to see this through.

Nichole's husband, Will, was now pulled out of the trance, too, as he felt his wife slapped by Gwenhwyfar's brute of a husband. He opened his eyes, scanned the crowd for his wife, and charged at Rufus, grabbing his hand, "How dare you strike my wife!"

Rufus snapped back, "She has no right to keep me from my wife."

Will looked at Nichole for explanation.

Nichole stated, "I did not like the tone he was taking with my friend so I moved her away from him."

Will turned back to Rufus, "And for this, you slap my wife?"

"She called me a pebble in her shoe."

Will chuckled to himself as he thought to himself, "Yes, you are. And now we must remove that pebble." To Rufus, he countered, "You slap a woman for some assumed mild insult? Shame on you!"

By this time, Gareth had made his way to the disturbance while Evelyn had made her way toward Guy and Taharqa.

As Evelyn walked purposefully across the room she called out to her daughter in her mind, "My sweet daughter, we are here for you, though we cannot save you from this and for that we are all sorry. I hope that you can forgive us. I love you. Be strong. Know that what you do, you do to protect the realm."

She heard Morgaine's voice; it was starting to steady and become like iron. "Yes, Mother, I will be strong."

And with that, she withdrew from the minds of everyone, quietly accepting and fortifying her resolve.

Evelyn reached Guy and put her hand firmly on his shoulder, whispering, "What she does this day, she does for all of us to keep the peace and protect Glastonbury. We must allow her the chance to make John happy and leave us all alone."

Guy wiped angry tears from his face and looked down.

Evelyn squeezed Guy's shoulder. "I know you want to dash in to rescue her. And, as her mother, I am very thankful for that. I know you would protect her in all things. With the Prince, we must tread delicately. There is so much more harm he can do to her and to all of us. I know you size up situations. Consider the options now."

Guy, head still bowed as he shook with frustration, tried to calm his mind but he could not. He was not going to be able to hold himself together.

Evelyn and Taharqa saw this and looked to each other and nodded. "Guy, please allow Taharqa to accompany you to your room and await Morgaine there. She will need you when it's over."

Meanwhile, on the other side of the room, Gareth was attempting to calm another situation. But Rufus was undone. He felt ganged up on and cornered.

He attempted to grab Gwenhwyfar's arm, hissing loudly, "We're leaving."

But she pulled away. It dawned on Gwenhwyfar that she was safe here. She had been told to return here long ago by her Faie lover and so here she would remain — somehow. This was where her sons needed to grow up. "No. I prefer to stay," she stated as plainly and as calmly as she could.

"Woman, I will beat you where you stand if you do not obey me."

To that Gareth countered, "Man, I will have you put out if you try."

Rufus looked at the Duke in a rage. Didn't being a husband trump the Duke in this matter? The Duke's guards were already converging on the scene. Rufus saw this and lost it. He again raised his hand at Gwenhwyfar and, with that, two guards seized him. Rufus screamed, "She is mine! I took her away from all you witches to make her a good Christian woman. That's right: 'you witches!'"

By now, of course, the room full of people who had been trying to ignore the rising voices, could not; all attention was now on the Duke.

But Gareth was not willing to have this scene continue. At Rufus' accusation, Gareth flung his hand away, making it clear to the guards to put Rufus out.

They marched the crazed man away and threw him down the castle steps. When Rufus got up and tried to come at them, they barred his way. After a few failed attempts and a much bruised body and pride, Rufus limped away.

Meanwhile, Gareth encouraged the partiers to resume their festive eating, drinking, and merry conversations. It was a mysterious gift of Gareth's: to lull a group back into a festive mood no matter what had transpired moments before. Evelyn had, on occasion, teased him for being like the incarnation of the Roman God of Wine and Revelry, Bacchus — for this uncanny ability to incite joy so easily, as if he could inebriate everyone with a smile and wave of the hand.

Prince John drew Morgaine down the hall and away from the growing commotion. He didn't appear to take notice of it. Morgaine, however, strained to hear what was going on in the other room. As she couldn't hear and she didn't want to intrude into the very minds of the people she now knew couldn't help her situation, she decided to leave it alone. They tried to force John off his course but John's mind was just too closed to any information other than that which he wanted to hear. She sighed resolutely and did her best to relax her body as they walked to the room they had made up for him and the Princess. Her mother had told her that sex could hurt more if her body was tense and at the moment she was a ball of knots.

The Prince's guards were behind them and he bade them to stay outside and guard the door. The two men complied. Prince John then drew Morgaine inside and to the bed.

He turned her to face him and began gently caressing her hair and face. "What a beautiful woman you are, Morgaine."

Morgaine made the best of it, smiling weakly, "Thank you, my Prince."

She continued to slow her breathing but he could tell she was nervous. John furrowed his brow then kissed her forehead, "Oh, my sweet. There is nothing to be nervous about."

She exhaled and let him think that was her concern and not that she was about to be forced into sex with him.

His hands roamed her and she continued to remain as calm as possible. She made the decision not to be a victim. John may have the right as crowned prince to take her body by force if he chose, but she could choose to allow her body to relax. She could choose that this was a duty to perform. She did not love John as she loved Guy. John was her ruler; Guy was her husband. Still, she blocked out Guy from her mind as she was humiliated by what she had to do and didn't want him to feel that humiliation.

John started kissing her on the mouth. She wondered to herself, "Can I just lie here and not be present? Can I just let him have my body without engaging with him on any level?"

Prince John pushed her lightly onto the bed and kissed her again and then looked at her, asking, "Morgaine, do you love me?"

"Oh Gods," she thought, and responded, "Of course, my Prince. You have my love as England's sovereign ruler."

He looked annoyed. "Show me you love me."

"Oh Gods," she thought again, "I am not going to be able to just lie here." She willed herself to look at John, really look at him, and see some part of him that she liked that she could hold on to. She took his face in both her hands and looked into his eyes. She smiled. She kissed each cheek and then his nose and then each eyelid and then looked at him again smiling.

John chuckled as he fondled her hair, smoothing it back behind her ear, her neck. He laid her down and kissed her neck.

His neck was now exposed to her. Instead of biting into it and tearing at it fiercely as one passing thought suggested, she merely kissed it. "I can do this," she thought silently, "I can do this." In her meditative state, she began drawing energy from wherever she could.

The coven members felt the pull.

"What is she up to?" Gwenhwyfar whispered to Nichole.

Nichole shook her head slightly. "She needs us. Let's just allow her to take what she needs to get through this."

Both women were sitting in Gwenhwyfar's room. After the uproar Rufus created, Gwenhwyfar wanted to retreat away from prying eyes so Nichole had gone with her to her room. Gwenhwyfar was nursing Neirin now and rocking him, more for her own comfort than his as he appeared content at his mother's breast. "What am I going to do?"

Nichole rubbed her friend's arm. "You are going to stay right here with your boys. With your family dead and gone, Gareth and Evelyn will not turn you out. They will protect you from Rufus."

"I am so sorry he hit you."

"I'm fine. It hurt but I am not damaged."

Gwenhwyfar touched her hand gently to Nichole's cheek. "Still, I am sorry."

The women sat quietly as they felt Morgaine's steady drawing of their energy.

Gwenhwyfar whispered again, "It's like she is pulling from the very walls as well. I pray she can get through this."

Nichole nodded, "She will." Nichole's eyes began to fill and she wept for her friend in the other room. Her voice was strained. "It's all so awful. What a horrible little man."

Although Gwenhwyfar's eyes too were moist with tears, she couldn't help but giggle, "Which one?"

They both laughed through their tears. They held hands and focused on Morgaine, whispering, "We are here. You can do this."

The reply was faint but audible, "I can do this."

Evelyn heard her daughter's words. She was still in the grand hall with Gareth and Will. They formed a tight circle, breathing together, while still maintaining the appearance of merely being in conversation. Rainer, Meggie, Elizabeth and Wild Herb, on the other hand, had left the hall to sit quietly together at one end of the courtyard. They felt the pull and just allowed Morgaine to take whatever energies she needed to see her through this ordeal. All eyes were moist with tears.

Guy was pacing in his and Morgaine's room with Taharqa watching him. Guy stopped as he felt an odd sensation. He looked at Taharqa whose eyes were now closed as he stood at the doorway. "Do you feel it? What is going on?"

Taharqa's eyes were moist and his fists were clenched. As much as Guy felt helpless in saving his wife, Taharqa felt helpless in protecting the Lady of the Lake and his dear friend. It was wrong that he was not right there at her defense and, instead, the very two who should charge in and rescue her were forbidden to do so. He hated the Prince for taking her like this. He hated a world that allowed this behavior and didn't behead the man, no matter his station, for raping a woman and someone else's wife. He hated himself for not saying to Guy, "Balls! Let's go rescue her!" Guy's question deserved an answer though, so Taharqa mustered what composure he could, saying, "What you are feeling is Morgaine pulling energy into her. As we are all connected to her, we feel that pull as well."

Guy's eyes were still red. "Why is her mind closed to me but yet she can pull at us?"

Taharqa shook his head slightly. "Guy, she doesn't want you, or any of us to feel her humiliation. I am sure of that. She doesn't want us to feel her body being violated or her having to respond to him in ways she would otherwise find repugnant. And believe me, there is nothing about this that she is enjoying."

Guy clenched his teeth and nodded. He knew this, and though it was little consolation coming from Taharqa, it was helpful to hear her friend and guardian tell him essentially that she only loved Guy in that way. Many newlyweds would probably feel similarly, having eyes for only each other. He thought what it meant to be a lord and the liberties such men could take. He couldn't imagine Gareth ever imposing himself on one of his subjects. He smirked silently; he couldn't imagine Evelyn ever tolerating such behavior. Guy had been a baron for such a short time. He wondered, shamefully, if he would have done such a thing to another man's bride. He would like to believe he wouldn't have; but it would have been expected of him by his former comrades. He didn't want to think any deeper on the subject, though he suddenly thought every man should have to. He realized with remorse, only now that it was happening to him, that he recognized it as disgraceful behavior to do such a thing; to condone such a thing; to allow such a thing.

As Guy's eyes looked down, he saw that Taharqa's fists were clenched. He looked into Taharqa's eyes. He heaved a sigh and nodded. He could now see how conflicted his brother-in-arms was. There was no way that this man, sworn to protect Morgaine, would be sitting idly by as his lady was being raped. No. They were all doing nothing because they all knew they were impotent in this matter. There was nothing they could do. Well, they could all sweep in and murder the Prince. It could be done. He would be vulnerable in this moment.

Taharqa could see his new friend and coven-mate calculating something and figured what it would be. "And you know why we are not all dashing into that room and stabbing him to death." It wasn't a question.

Guy nodded measuredly. "I am sure Evelyn must see John's death, certainly by our hand, as the immediate undoing of Glastonbury and all of our deaths."

It was Taharqa's turn to nod. "And even if the Duchess did not have the Sight, for us to kill a crowned prince would certainly mean all of our deaths."

"How will Morgaine get through this?"

Taharqa answered compassionately, "With your enduring love. With all of us loving her through it."

Guy gave a brief nod but his thoughts were turned toward his wife, "Beloved, don't shut me out."

But there was no reply, just the steady pull, as if she were diverting a stream to her shore or pulling an endless tapestry across the stone floor.

Drawing on all the energies from the castle, Morgaine summoned her powers as the Lady of the Lake. She found a calm at the center of this very strange storm. She felt her rage and humiliation and hurt swirling erratically around her but it did not control her. It did not take over her and so she did not gouge out John's eyes or jab her elbow into his windpipe. She did not rail against him or plea; she simply became a deep, dark pool of water. She returned John's kisses doing her best to taste the salt of the Earth on his tongue. She could not will herself to pretend she was kissing her beloved Guy but she could will herself to believe that she was acting in service to a greater power. The Goddess gave her no challenge that she could not meet. She breathed in the words of the Goddess, "All acts of love are Mine. Be as My reflection..." Morgaine loved past this bumbling, mean-spirited, misdirected human and found his connection to the Land. It was weak, but as with all humans, it was there. No one was disconnected from Mother Earth. So she tapped into that connection and loved through him to the Earth. He would be too stupid to know the difference. But at least she could feel some sense of cool composure as she spread her lips and her legs for this woebegone man.

John wrapped his body around Morgaine. He felt sated. "Ah Morgaine, you give me such peace."

The act of sex hadn't been overly long. There was grunting and thrusting and some pinching of the nipples, but John wasn't interested in pleasing the woman underneath him. She was just a pretty conquest.

And now it was his turn to be conquered. She felt the change, a brief moment of openness of which she could take advantage. Morgaine momentarily felt dirty somehow. Not working-the-land-fingers dirty but manipulate-another's-soul dirty.

She cooed softly in a hypnotic voice, "My Prince, I should get back to my husband now."

Prince John looked into Morgaine's eyes and was lulled, entranced. "Oh yes, of course. He would be waiting for you." John paused, then added slightly sleepily, "You two are such a lovely couple."

Morgaine continued to manipulate him with her lulling, enchanting voice, "Thank you my Prince. May we always be friends."

John smiled, speaking as though drugged with heather, "Yes, friends. Yes, we are friends, Morgaine. You have always been a lovely friend."

Morgaine continued to weave her spell, "Thank you, my Prince. My husband thanks you, too. We are your friends."

John nodded, feeling sleepy.

"Rest now, my Prince. Your princess will be with you shortly to attend to your needs."

John smiled, "Ah, my princess. My sweet Isabella. She is always so sad."

Morgaine lulled him further, "Oh, but my Prince, your princess will be so happy that you wanted to see her. And you do want to see her."

John nodded groggily, "Yes. Tell the guards to bring her to me."

"I will, my Prince. Sweet dreams, my Prince. And we will see you in the morning to watch you off to oversee all your lands." With that Morgaine kissed John on the lips and then the forehead.

She overheard John murmur, "Ah yes, I must be off in the morning to oversee my lands. It was good to stop here. It was good to marry such lovely pets."

Though her stomach turned at being called a pet, she breathed a silent sigh of relief as she dressed quickly and opened the door. The guards eyed her. Despite her disheveled appearance, she drew herself up and spoke authoritatively to the guards, "Prince John desires the presence of his wife now. Please bring the Princess to him and let her know that he wants to be with her."

The guards nodded and Morgaine walked away down the hall.

Morgaine scratched at the door to her and Guy's bedroom. Now that Guy could be trusted not to charge into the guest quarters and slay the Prince, Taharqa had decided to let the man be. He had left a short while ago to check on the state of affairs in the grand hall. Guy was alone in the room, sitting on the bed, leaning against the headboard, arms folded across his chest, legs extended with one foot over the other, waiting. What else could he do but wait? When Meggie had come to check in on him he sent her away. He then had to do the same to Mouse. He needed to be alone to wait for his wife.

Guy heard the noise and sensed it wasn't Meggie, Mouse, or Taharqa scratching at the door. He got up and went to the door. He opened it and there was his beloved, dress held up by her crossed arm, to cover her bosom.

"Will you carry me across the threshold?" she asked in a quivering voice.

Guy immediately complied, picking up his love in his arms and carrying her into their bedroom. He set her gently on their bed.

She cried, hands covering her face. "I need to wash." She felt fragile; her strength sapped away by all she had endured.

Guy nodded. Whatever she needed. "Of course. Do you want me to have a bath drawn?"

She shook her head no, with her head still in her hands. Now that she was out of the situation, her composure had left her. She was feeling ashamed and couldn't look at Guy.

Guy squatted in front her so that he was now below her and gently laid his hands on the outsides of her thighs. "Morgaine, Love, what do you need?"

She sobbed, "I need you to love me."

He started to tear up, "Oh, my Beloved, I do. I do love you. Nothing will change that."

She continued with her hands covering her face, "Even with what I have done?"

Guy got up and sat on the bed. He took Morgaine's hands and she let him. He looked at her and she at him. "Morgaine, you have done nothing wrong."

"But I..."

"You have done nothing wrong. Do you understand?"

She nodded, then opened her mouth about to say something, to which Guy placed a finger upon her lips, saying firmly, "Nothing. You have done nothing wrong. I felt the pull. We all did. You have done nothing wrong."

Morgaine bit her lower lip and nodded slowly.

Guy kissed her forehead and then each of her hands, saying, "I love you, Morgaine. You survived. You came back to me; that is what matters. That is the only thing that matters."

She leaned into him and sobbed.

He stroked her hair feeling such remorse, wishing he could have stopped this from happening. "I am so sorry. I should have stopped him. I should have killed him. I wanted to kill him. I wanted to save you. I was not there for you."

Morgaine squeezed her husband close. "I forgive you. I know that you could not save me. No one could." She squeezed him tighter, "But you are here now. I will get through this. We will get through this. Together."

He kissed her head, rocking her gently, "Yes, Love, we will get through this together." He continued to rock her gently trying to just be there for her, to not get any more caught up in his own guilt for not rescuing her. He knew she needed his strength now. It was not the time to make him feel better for his own failures. It was time to be there completely for her.

After a time, she felt she could move and she repeated, "I need to wash." Her voice was small and distant.

Guy responded, "Where?"

Her voice was so far away, "Downstairs."

He nodded. He knew where she meant. She had brought him down there before on a little adventure. The secret passageway had been an escape route out of the castle long ago. He picked her up and carried her across the room. He fumbled for the secret notch that would force the panel to move. He pushed at the door with his shoulder and set her down in the darkness. She slumped against the wall as he fumbled around for the lantern that he knew was there. He went back inside the room to the candles Meggie had lit the last time she was there. He vaguely remembered her mumbling that she didn't want Morgaine to come into a dark room. He lit the lantern wick with the candle and walked back to Morgaine who was still slumped in the passageway. He gently dragged her to her feet, holding her tight with one arm while holding the lantern up in the other hand to light their way. They cautiously navigated the stairs and twisting close corridors to the waterwheel below.

As they crept along, they passed a few rats, and Guy commented, "We should set Cream loose in here."

Morgaine made no comment, though some part of her agreed there should be cats patrolling these dank corridors.

Within moments they reached a low-ceilinged stone room that faced the waterwheel and the outside.

Guy undressed Morgaine and then rubbed her arms. "Are you ready? The water will be cold."

Morgaine nodded, as she stood naked in the dim, candlelit space.

Guy got the bucket that was against the wall and held it close under the wheel that slowly turned, bringing the water in small slots up near the wall against the kitchen. The water splashed into the bucket, filling it. He brought the full bucket over to Morgaine. First, he scooped out water with one hand and just gently dribbled it on her shoulders.

He heard her say, "I'm ready."

He picked up the bucket and dumped it over her head. She exclaimed at the cold water but asked for another bucket. Guy filled the bucket again and again, dumping it over her head.

"Gods," she exclaimed, this time sounding more like herself. She rubbed her skin vigorously then said, "Again."

Guy offered a fourth dowsing and she rubbed her pubic bone and thighs in a downward motion. Guy filled the bucket again and this time stood with it underneath her splashing the water onto her nether lips and rubbing her inner thighs with the cold water. He was not entirely sure why she wanted this, but it didn't matter. Whatever she wanted.

She then squatted over the bucket and continued to splash water up into her. She was crying, "I want his seed out of me. Get it out of me."

Guy murmured, "Yes, my love." He put his hand into the water to get it wet and then, as gently as he could, inserted his index finger into her and moved his finger around. He withdrew and did it again. Several times. He could feel her vaginal walls puckering up in the cold and he didn't want to hurt her any more than she already felt hurt. He had no idea if this was an effective method of getting John's seed out of her but if she wanted it done, he would do it. Then he gently rubbed her nether lips with the cold water. All the slickness was gone. He could sense her mood shifting again.

"I'm cold."

"I know, Love. Let's go back upstairs and get you into bed."

He was sure Morgaine was nodding in the darkness. He moved the bucket back against the wall, picked up her clothing, draping it over his arm, picked up the lantern, and then hoisted her up to standing. He brought her back, naked and shivering, to their room. He helped her into bed and brought the covers up around her.

"What now?" he asked quietly.

Her lips were quivering. "Get Meggie. I need her to make a tea."

He squeezed her shoulder gently and went to the door. He had no idea where Meggie might be. Upon opening the door, he almost tripped over her. She was sitting on the floor in her shawl with her back against the wall.

"Meggie?"

Meggie looked up with tears still in her eyes. "I couldn't leave, Guy."

Guy helped Meggie up. He took Meggie's head in his hands and kissed her forehead, saying, "And a good thing too. Come in. We need your help."

Meggie nodded and felt relieved that she stayed. She knew she would be needed at some point.

Meggie and Guy stood at the side of the bed. Morgaine was staring at the ceiling.

Meggie caressed her friend's hand, "Morgaine, what can I do?"

Morgaine shifted her body and turned on her side. Her left hand came out from under the covers and she placed it on Meggie's hand. She looked at Meggie. "Meggie, would you please make me a tea of Worm Fern root, the dried leaves of Rue and Thyme and the seeds of Lacy Carrot? I am going to need to take it several times so make up a large strong batch."

Meggie nodded.

"Also, get me the Mandrake root."

Meggie nodded again as she went through the other door into the herb room to collect what she needed to make the tea. She laid them out on the counter then picked up the pot that she would use to heat the water at the kitchen hearth. Before she left, she took out the mandrake, kissed it and said a prayer, then sliced off a piece. She brought the piece into the bedroom with the pot. She placed mandrake into Morgaine's hand, closing it over the root and then left with the pot in her hand.

Guy breathed slowly. "What is that for?"

Morgaine took the mandrake, her hand disappearing under the covers. He watched movement under the covers as she inserted the root as deep up inside her to her womb as she could get. She would take it out later. She then held her womb with her hand, whispering a prayer, "No baby."

Guy heard her and knew that she and Meggie were doing all they could to be sure that John's seed did not impregnate Morgaine. He watched as Morgaine oscillated between a strange cold, calculating calm and the edge of hysteria. He wished he knew what else he could do.

Meggie was back with the pot of tea and handed a mug to Morgaine to drink.

"Ugh! Oh, that is vile." She took another sip and felt like she would retch. She kept sipping slowly.

Guy looked on, concerned, but he knew he couldn't help her drink the tea. All he could do was be present with her. He sat at the opposite end of the bed while Meggie sat in a chair by the fireplace. After a while, she started slumping in the chair. It was getting late into the night. Guy and Morgaine looked to each other and then Guy got up and went over to Meggie, gently placing his hand on her shoulder. She startled herself awake.

Guy spoke gently, "Meggie, go to bed. Thank you for being here. I am not sure what else you can do."

Meggie looked over to the bed and Morgaine, "She may experience cramping. It could be intense, I hear. You can come get me though I wouldn't know what to do." Her grief was overwhelming her. She blinked back tears, her voice aquiver, "She hasn't told me what to do."

Guy soothed Meggie, "If that happens, we can get Evelyn."

Meggie nodded hesitantly. She was exhausted, yet she protested; she did not want to leave her friend. "I can sleep here."

"Meggie, that is very sweet of you. Go to bed." Meggie nodded, got up, and left.

Guy climbed into bed next to his wife, her back to his belly. They spooned and he held her all through the night. "I'm right here," he whispered, kissing the back of her head gently. As tragic as the experience felt to the two of them, they each felt reassured by the other's touch. It took over half the night, but they finally fell asleep.

All Acts of Love

THE NEXT MORNING Guy and Morgaine arose with purpose. They waved good-bye to Prince John as he was blessedly off on his new and important task of reassessing his lands. And then, with the Prince's carriage out of sight, Morgaine collapsed into Guy's arms.

Nichole whispered to him, "Head to the circle."

He nodded.

Guy brought Morgaine past the Lake to the circle in the forest. They sat facing each other, their legs crossing over each other on the flat stone, where only nights ago they made love as the Summer Queen and Sun King.

Marian watched the couple walk away and saw the sadness in them. Nichole slid up to Marian as she could see this new friend of Morgaine's was concerned for her and wondering what was going on.

"Prince John took Morgaine yesterday," Nichole whispered.

Marian turned, her face paling, "No," she exclaimed as quietly as she could.

"Can I trust you?"

Marian nodded. "What can I do?"

"Come with us. We want to circle around our friends and pray for them."

"I can do that." Nichole took Marian's hand in hers.

Gwenhwyfar came upon Nichole and gently nudged her, her face a question.

Nichole smiled and whispered up toward the tall woman walking next to her, "I think she can help too. I have a sense about this." Gwenhwyfar nodded, looking over her friend's head to Marian who was looking bewildered, but trustingly, at both of them.

Elizabeth and Wild Herb approached the circle from their home, deep in the Avalon Forest. They reached the stone only shortly after Guy and Morgaine and found them there, holding each other on the stone.

Guy was whispering gently but urgently to his distraught wife, "Open to me, Love. Don't close me out. Open. I am right here and I am not going anywhere without you."

The older couple stood at the flat stone in silence, compassionately witnessing the grieving pair, while awaiting the others. Rainer then appeared, also coming from the forest side. Approaching from the castle side was Gwenhwyfar, Marian, Nichole and Meggie, all holding one another as they walked. Will followed closely behind his wife. Gareth and Evelyn followed, holding hands. Taharqa brought up the rear, deep in thought. The remaining castle inhabitants and servants looked after one another and the visiting children and the lingering guests. They kept the peace and the privacy of the Avalon coven.

The coven, plus Marian, gathered silently around the stone, all respectfully witnessing the couple on the stone as they cried and rocked together. Marian had no idea what to expect. She also had no idea she was in the presence of a coven. She only knew these were the close friends and family of Morgaine and she was now being counted among them. She saw Guy's red face, eyes closed and looking so deeply sad. She couldn't help herself. She hadn't seen Guy with tears streaming down his eyes since he was a boy. The last time was when he lost his mother. In a moment of compassion she knelt on the stone and stroked his hair and then embraced the couple, her tears adding to theirs.

With her action, the rest of the attendants moved in and embraced the couple. Few, if any, had dry eyes. They allowed the grief to intensify. After a time, it ebbed and what replaced it was a strong desire to find healing, to feel whole. All who knew how were now connecting themselves to Earth and Sky.

There was an electricity in the air around them and, though Marian did not understand what was happening, she felt tingly and energized...and happy. She almost felt guilty for feeling so good, but she couldn't help it. She felt really happy, almost as if she had never known such happiness before. There was such love in this circle and she felt surrounded by it, part of — and built up by — it. It was like God had entered her and filled her up; that was the only thing that sounded right in her mind. But how could she feel this good in this tragedy? But as she looked around, she was not the only person now smiling. There was release, relief, washing over everyone, Guy and Morgaine included.

The day was warm and with everyone in such close proximity, the little company was starting to sweat. As the energy slowly dissipated, people moved back to give themselves some room.

Gwenhwyfar started fanning herself with her hands, humming a tune under her breath. Several others started to hum it as well. She looked around and smiled. Her eyes came to rest on Evelyn, who was looking back at her.

Evelyn started, "You know, my dear, you are like a daughter to us..." Evelyn took up Gareth's hand, their fingers interlaced.

Gareth finished, "...and we would be most joyous if you and your boys would stay with us and take up residence in the castle."

Gwenhwyfar's smile broadened, crested, and then fell. "What about..."

Gareth interrupted, "Never mind him. He will never hurt you again."

Meggie interjected, "I wish we could say the same for Morgaine with regard to..." her voice trailed off.

Evelyn spoke hopefully, "John will be distracted. Morgaine, we just need to find excuses not to go to court if he requests."

Morgaine nodded.

Guy kissed Morgaine's furrowed brow and then looked into her eyes. "Be here with me, Love."

Morgaine nodded again, saying, "I am so thankful for you." She looked to each person in turn, "All of you. Thank you for being here for me and for us."

Nichole leaned over and kissed Morgaine on the cheek, "I would be nowhere else, my sister."

"Nor I," stated Gwenhwyfar.

"Nor I," added Meggie.

Marian started to cry, exclaiming, "How can I feel such happiness, know such love? You all move me. Thank you."

Nichole chuckled, "Feeling an epiphany of sorts?"

Marian nodded. "I shouldn't feel such happiness. I feel filled up with God and we are all here mourning."

Morgaine took her hand from around Guy's waist and brought it up to Marian's face, saying, "We are all healing. It is wonderful that you feel so good, so filled up. Hold on to that feeling."

Marian nodded, looking from Morgaine to Guy, and with tears in her eyes and a quivering, emotion-filled voice, she cried, "I wish you both such happiness. I have seen such beauty and grace in the two of you. You love each other so much. It is so inspiring to witness your love."

Guy thought he was just getting his bearings on his emotional state and now Marian had to say this. His eyes filled up again. He uttered, "Thank you, Marian."

She brought her hand that had been on his shoulder to his cheek. He shifted his head and kissed her palm and a wave of forgiveness washed over both of them. Marian realized she couldn't hold back anything, the words just tumbled out. "I forgive you everything, Guy. You really are a hero. Caron and I were talking about that yesterday. How you saved her from the river. How you have protected me so many times from the Sheriff. How you've become the man who was that boy. I am so grateful to see it."

Guy wasn't feeling like a hero in this moment, Gareth could tell; so he spoke up. "Guy, you did what you had to in that moment, and not because you wanted to. But you are here now. You didn't run away, not even emotionally, like so many can and do in this situation. None of us ran away despite our shame for feeling helpless. We are all here to bear the burden. You are loved, Son."

Guy looked around at each of them. Wave after wave of love battered him so that he could not refuse it. He had to accept that he was loveable, that everyone here loved him.

Morgaine sat and basked in all this love. And in spite of her queasy stomach from taking the abortifacient herbal concoction, she was actually feeling good. Her rage and grief were still there swimming around in her mind, but she wasn't in their grip. She was allowing this love to permeate and saturate her. She was not running away into pity or vengeance. And thankfully, neither was anyone else, especially Guy. She smiled, "Thank you, everyone."

Gwenhwyfar stroked Morgaine's head, speaking softly the Goddess' adage into her ear, "All acts of love are Mine. Be as My reflection in a deep pool."

Everyone envisioned a deep serene pool, even Marian. A sense of calm immersed the group in deep love and compassion.

The coven sat there a few more moments but everyone could feel the energy shifting, that it was time to leave. They took turns hugging Morgaine and Guy and then paired or tripled off so that everyone had someone to hold onto as they stood up.

Meggie giggled as she mentally counted, "Did anyone count? We number thirteen." Marian didn't get the joke but she laughed with everyone else anyway.

CHAPTER 35

Departures

THE GUARDS HAD been warned that, should Rufus show up, he was under no condition to be allowed in the castle or to take his sons. And it just so happened that Rufus did show up and after a failed attempt at arguing with the guards, he was sitting dejectedly on the castle steps. He had already run after the Prince's carriage screaming "Wait," only to have an arrow shot toward him as a warning shot by one of the Prince's guards. This meant either walking the distance and somehow catching up with the Prince in hopes of being granted an audience or going back and demanding one from the Duke. He had stood in the road debating, but the shorter distance won out.

Rufus was no strategist. The fact that he had won the hand of Gwenhwyfar was due only to his own father's wealth as a merchant in Plymouth and the fact that Gwenhwyfar's father wanted Gwenhwyfar away from Morgaine's family. So much of the transaction was through letters between the fathers.

There was no real reason for the animosity. Gwenhwyfar's father just didn't trust the Avalons; he thought of them as heathens. He had heard too many stories as his children grew up around the castle. So when the deal was done, Gwenhwyfar was carted away at the age of sixteen to a man she didn't know, away from her friends and family.

Morgaine and Gwenhwyfar corresponded over the years, Morgaine sending Gwenhwyfar gifts of parchment and ink and quills to be sure she had everything she needed to respond without asking Rufus for money or supplies. And Morgaine would have traveled to Plymouth more often but Rufus made it a challenge. He had always been so unpleasant. So mainly, when Gwenhwyfar could find Rufus in a rare good mood, she would succeed in securing a trip either to Glastonbury Castle or to Weymouth, where Nichole resided, and it was in this way the friends had stayed in touch.

Rufus sat on the steps fuming. He heard his wife's voice and looked up. There she was, surrounded by the Avalons, walking together up the road to the castle steps. The guards were already eyeing him and as soon as Rufus got up, they made their way to cut him off and block direct access to the family. This, of course, did not go over well with Rufus.

With Nichole safe behind the guards, she quipped to Gwenhwyfar, "Is he always in this state?"

Rufus glared at the woman, but he knew not to attempt to lay a hand on her again. He turned his attention to the Duke. "Your Grace, I would appreciate an audience with you."

Gareth stated plainly, "You have it."

Rufus floundered, "Here? With everyone?"

Gareth simply nodded.

The Guards parted just enough so that Gareth was still behind them, but Rufus could look directly at him instead of at their crossed spears. Still, Rufus could not help but notice that the spears were there and at the ready. Somewhere in his brain he had to have realized the futility of his further botched attempt at taking Gwenhwyfar and his sons away with him. But that part of his brain must have slipped on a stone one too many times and his mouth ran the show. "I demand that Gwenhwyfar and my sons be returned to me."

Gareth merely folded his arms with a look on his face clearly stating, "Go on, you bumbling arse."

Rufus again fumbled, "Well, that's it. I want them back. They are mine. On what grounds could you stop me?"

Gareth had the slightest hint of a mischievous grin on his face. He turned to Gwenhwyfar, "My good lady, Gwenhwyfar, I would ask that you and your sons stay for a visit. Morgaine is sure to be with child soon and I am sure it would give my daughter much peace for you to stay on. We would, of course, provide you with compensation for being separated from your husband, who must get back to run his business. And, of course, we would provide rooms for you and your boys."

Rufus looked from Gareth to Gwenhwyfar in silent hostility.

Gwenhwyfar's smile broadened as she looked triumphantly at Rufus and then at Gareth, saying sweetly, "Your Grace, I would be overjoyed to look after my dear friend, the Lady Morgaine. How could I refuse such a generous offer?"

Gareth turned to Rufus, "It is settled then. Go home, Rufus, and perhaps in time, we will see if you have greater need of her than we do."

Rufus stood shaking with rage. He clipped his words, "What will you tell my sons?"

"If you are willing to be generous in your disposition, you can tell them yourself that you need to get back and that they have been invited to remain here for a time with their mother."

Rufus, realizing he would not be able to drag his children away, wasn't sure what the purpose would be in saying goodbye. He was not overly fond of children. His own father was distant and so he was distant with his children. They were more like livestock; messy, expensive. But they had their uses. Some part of him must have loved them, but it was hard to know.

The situation was decided for Rufus when Rodney, Julius, and Godric ran down the steps after Rowan who had caught sight of her mother and was running to greet her with arms open wide. Mouse was following a few steps behind the herd, realizing he had failed in corralling the children. But they were only running to their parents and not up a tree, or into the Lake, or somewhere else more difficult to follow and fetch them out. Anwen stayed at the top of the steps at the door with Neirin in her arms. The two young people made excellent nurse maids and they appeared to enjoy the work.

"Mommy!" exclaimed Rowan. She leapt at Nichole who made an audible "ouff" sound as her wee one ran into her.

Nichole grunted a bit as she picked up her growing daughter. "It is good to see you my little wiut."

Rowan giggled, wrinkling her nose, "Wiut? Who's wiut?"

"You, my little wild one."

Will drew closer and Rowan felt bliss as she was sandwiched between her parents.

That felt like a cue and Nichole said, "Come children, tell your parents what adventures you have been up to this morning." With that she winked at Morgaine as she and Will herded their two children back up the stairs. She nodded at Mouse as if to say, "your work is done," to which he turned and followed them up the stairs.

At that, Taharqa turned to Gareth, formally asking, "Do you have any further need of my services, Your Grace?"

Gareth stated formally back, "No. That will be all, Master of Arms. Thank you."

Taharqa bowed and departed with a nod from Gareth, which then left Marian, Morgaine, Meggie, Guy, and Evelyn as witnesses to the drama between Gareth, Rufus, and Gwenhwyfar.

Julius had, like Rowan, ignored the scene with the guards standing before his father, and came from the side, down the stairs to his mother. He was now standing in front of her with her arms wrapped around him.

Nichole, upon reaching the door, told Anwen to go inside and wait for Gwenhwyfar in her room. This way the baby was taken out of the equation.

Rodney, conflicted, still stood on the stairs with his hands on his hips. He could tell something was wrong and he wasn't sure which parent to go to. Neither of the boys knew what had happened yesterday, only that their parents had fought and Rufus did not come to bed. Since that wasn't out of the ordinary, they did not expect what was to come.

Rufus wasn't sure how to start. He didn't think the guards would kill him in front of his children but he also realized that if they did not go willingly with him, he could not force them with so many witnesses. And what would he do with them on his own anyway? They were both old enough to help out and certainly Rodney was more successful as the eldest in doing his share, but...

Rufus' thoughts were broken as the Duke spoke, "Boys, come to me." He eyed both of the boys, and shyly, as they did not know the Duke well, only that his station in life afforded him respect and the ability to command others, they came to stand before him. Gareth squatted slightly so that he would be at eye level. Putting a hand on the boys' shoulders, he stated, "The Duchess and I have asked your mother to stay on and be a companion to our daughter, the Lady of the Lake. Your mother and our daughter are dear friends, as you know, and Morgaine has missed her terribly."

The boys just nodded.

"Your father needs to get back home. But you and your mother will stay here for now."

The sons nodded, each in his own thoughts. Julius was mainly elated as he had been dreaming about this place and Uncle Guy for years and now that he was here all his happy dreams were coming true. Rodney, the young explorer, was also happy to have new territory to roam. But he loved his father and wanted to be with him, too. It was hard for him. He saw how much his parents fought and how unkind his father could be. And he was angry at his father for that. At the same time, he just wanted to feel his father's love and continue to help him in the shop. He also thought this whole thing might be a cover for his parents splitting up. He heard of such things happening where one parent just disappears.

Rodney looked the Duke hard in eye, trying to tell if the Duke was telling the truth or lying. But he was disarmed when the Duke then asked, "How do you boys feel about this?"

Feel? The brothers turned their heads and glanced at each other, as if to mentally ask each other, "Did this man just ask us how we felt about staying here with our mother and without our father?"

Julius spoke cautiously, not looking at his father but only at the Duke, "Are you giving us a choice?" Julius searched the Duke's eyes but the Duke simply continued to look on the boys with compassion. As there was no immediate response from the Duke, Julius continued, remembering hearing that they were asked how they felt, not if they wanted to stay or not, "I would like to stay with Mother and learn from Uncle Guy."

Guy was not prepared for being inserted into the equation and had a slight look of surprise. But when he looked at Julius, who was looking back at him, he smiled and nodded approvingly.

Julius beamed.

Rodney looked at his younger brother, emotions knotting up. Then he looked at the Duke, and then to his mother, and then his father, and back again at the Duke, asking, "Father will be all right, right?"

The Duke responded diplomatically, "Well, young Rodney, that is up to your father. But, yes, he will be able to manage his business with you here for the time being."

Rodney looked to his father in question, as if to ask, is that true?

Rufus motioned to Rodney while eyeing the Duke.

The Duke gave a slight nod that stated "proceed cautiously."

Gareth released his hands on the boys and stood up. Internally, he winced as his back cracked and popped with heaving age. He was not so young anymore, he realized.

Rodney turned and went to Rufus whereas Julius merely turned and looked at his father. He and his father were not close, and he remembered too well the argument some years ago when his parents thought the boys were sleeping, when his father accused his mother of being a whore.

"That boy looks nothing like me," Rufus hissed at Gwenhwyfar. "He's got strange eyes."

Gwenhwyfar scolded back, "How can you accuse me, saying that of your son? And besides, when would I have time? It is enough just to keep after them. And you!"

"Enough, woman!"

Julius remembered hearing the smack and his mother's resulting tears.

Rufus again motioned to Julius, and this time Julius went to his father. Rufus hugged his boys. In that moment, Rufus felt something; he was suddenly feeling loss for something he had taken for granted. He held on tighter and then turned stony as he straightened up. He looked menacingly at Gwenhwyfar, mouthing, "This isn't over." Then he patted his boys on the back, stating stoically, "Be good, my sons. I will see you again soon."

The sons nodded and then Rodney reached up and wrapped his hands around his father's neck, saying with deep emotion, "I will miss you."

Rufus dispassionately untangled himself from his eldest, saying simply, "There, there. You be a good young man, and take care of your mother."

Rodney stepped back, hearing the formality and finality in his father's voice. "Yes, Father."

Guy took that as a cue to separate the boys from the parents while Gareth navigated the rest of the one-sided negotiations. "Julius, Rodney, come with me down to the Lake. I was hearing the frogs in the reeds."

Julius practically exploded, "Really, Uncle Guy? You will take us to the Lake to catch frogs? Mother, can we?"

Gwenhwyfar nodded and mouthed to Guy, "Thank you."

Julius turned to his father, giving him a quick hug as this was all so awkward and he just wanted it to be over, "Good-bye, Father."

Rufus merely felt the hug, patted his son on the back, "Good-bye, Julius."

The boys happily ran off toward the Lake, though Rodney turned around and waved at Rufus who did at least wave back.

Guy kissed Morgaine, "I will be back shortly. I just thought…"

She squeezed his hand, "It is fine. It was kind of you. And I have the ladies with me."

Marian reached for Morgaine's hand and took her by the arm, saying to Guy, "Off into the reeds with you." She led Morgaine away with Meggie taking up Morgaine's other arm.

Evelyn took Gwenhwyfar's arm, "Come, my dear; let's get you settled in."

Gwenhwyfar started to turn away when Rufus said, "So that's it?"

She turned back. "What would you have me say, Rufus? There is little love between us. You accuse me of whoring, of witchery, of laziness, of being too tall, of having eyes too green. I am happy to remain here where people accept and love me."

"What about my things?"

She turned to the guards and asked, "Would you please accompany my husband to our rooms and see that he obtains his belongings…just his belongings?"

Rufus scowled at Gwenhwyfar but she had already turned and was walking away with Evelyn to meet Morgaine, Marian and Meggie, who were waiting for her on the stairs. The women embraced and continued to hold one another as they climbed the remaining steps.

The family was still housing several guests. Though spirits were a bit higher than earlier, there was still a sadness in the air. Caron and Mary had approached Marian discreetly to inquire about yesterday's upheavals.

Marian responded quietly, "Prince John claimed Lord's Right."

"He did not!"

"That scoundrel!"

The pair were in shock.

Caron asked with concern in her voice, "How are they?"

Marian bit her bottom lip. What to say? She could not say what took place this morning at the stone. Instead, she stated, "They are coping. It is a blessing they are so devoted. They will get through this."

Mary pressed on, "What about that woman who was slapped? What happened?"

Marian answered as best she could, "That was Nichole. She was coming to the defense of her friend, Gwenhwyfar. It was Gwenhwyfar's husband who slapped her. He seems like a nasty man. He's just been banished by Gareth. Gwenhwyfar and her sons will remain here with the Avalons. She and Morgaine are childhood friends so she will be well received here."

Mary thought about the names. So curious, Morgaine and Gwenhwyfar. The ancient legend continued to work its magic. A part of her wished she had reason to be here too, but her home was in Nottingham with her husband. Mary looked around the crowd for Guy. "Where is Lord Guy?"

Marian chuckled, "Mary, you will never believe this, but he is off playing in the reeds with Gwenhwyfar's sons."

Mary looked aghast. Playing? Guy was playing? "No," was all she could manage.

Marian nodded.

Mary shook her head, thinking, "Will wonders never cease?"

Caron smiled quietly as she listened to the exchange. This place did Guy good. Her hero was reemerging.

Delphine was not sure how to act around her brother. A part of her wanted him to hurt, to have his heart torn to pieces by what she could only guess was Prince John taking the Lady Morgaine to bed. But another part of her felt some compassion for her older brother. Some part of her was waking up to the fact that he really had been just a boy when she was married off. What could he have done? Her old friend, Caron, had approached her this morning and said as much. She openly hoped for reconciliation.

"He is a good man, Delphine. And he adores Morgaine. Pray for his happiness. He never wished you ill will…" She paused and then decided to add, as she laid a hand tentatively on Delphine's arm, "He thought of you."

"Did he now?"

"Yes. Did you know that shortly after you were sent away, he was too?"

"No."

"The Baron sent Guy up to Derby. We didn't see him for years. He came back a changed man…and not for the good. But when he took up residence at the Manor, he told me he wondered after you. He regretted not having been able to protect you."

Delphine was astonished. "Truly?"

Caron spoke gently, "Yes. He hoped you had a good life. I asked why he didn't call on you, have you visit. But he just shook his head. I think he thought you hated him."

Delphine's eyes watered as she whispered, "I did."

Caron pressed, "Can you forgive him? Can you forgive that boy, your brother, who did not save you from a marriage you were not ready for?"

Delphine bit her lower lip. She had been angry at him so long, hated and blamed him for so long. The only real reason she was down here was because Bartholomew insisted they attend. He wanted Guy and the Avalons as allies. He was always making new "friends." But they weren't really friends. She wasn't sure she understood the purpose of gathering people to him and squirreling them away like documents of allegiance. But her husband seemed to do little harm and she led a quiet, though unhappy life. She found joy in so few things. She watched Morgaine and Guy as they and their remaining guests ate supper. They appeared very much in love. They could be happy. She did not want to watch anymore.

Within days, the lingering guests made their way out of Glastonbury. Mary and Caron hugged Guy and Morgaine tight and wished them well. Caron's husband, Robert, even shook Guy's hand. Bartholomew again made a production of keeping in correspondence.

Guy took Delphine aside, holding her stiff body in a one-sided embrace, whispering in her ear, "If you need me, please send word. Come to me. Seeing you reminds me of the past and of how much I love you. I didn't ever stop loving you, Little Sister. And if you want me in your life, know that I want you in mine."

She drew back and saw her brother's bright blue eyes moist. She was speechless. In the background she heard Gareth keeping Bartholomew engaged in goodbyes.

Morgaine suddenly appeared at Guy's side. She put her arms around both of them, whispering, "Delphine, if you need us, we are here for you."

Delphine looked from her brother to his new wife. She wanted to scream at them, to yell; it was too late. But she swallowed that rage. Clenched her teeth and closed her eyes. Guy enfolded her again and gently rocked her. Tears fell unbidden and she allowed herself to stay wrapped in the cocoon of her brother's arms. It felt familiar; her body remembered the warm, soothing embrace. He had always been there…until he was not. She pushed that thought away just to soak up this last little bit of brotherly affection.

But then a familiar voice boomed behind her, "Delphine, my sweet, it is time to depart."

Guy felt his sister's frame go rigid once more.

She pulled herself back, reached up and kissed her brother's cheeks. Then she turned and kissed each of Morgaine's cheeks. Her voice quivering, she said, "Thank you both. It was good of you to invite us...and...and...I am glad we came."

Guy and Morgaine looked at her, questioning if she was all right.

She squeezed both their arms and composed herself before she turned to her husband to let him know she was ready to leave.

CHAPTER 36

Of Strawberries and Cream

THERE WAS LITTLE emotion for Morgaine to attach to her experience with John at this point. Though he was her ruler, she decided the experience should not hold power over her. And though some part of her felt enraged at John's actions, she recognized it was a duty she had performed to protect the realm. She could only pray he did not attempt to rule over her again in that way. She and Guy made a pact not to blame each other for something that was out of their control. This was something they survived together and they would go on — together. John's actions were ultimately not what was important here but, rather, how they continued to love each other through John's violation upon Morgaine. Surrounded by friends and family, she felt cleansed. Remorse, pity, self-doubt, depression — these were not feelings Morgaine was familiar with and so within a short time she had moved on from her ordeal with John. Recognizing there was nothing she could do about it and nothing that was harming her relationship with Guy, she simply finished her treatment of the abortifacient herbal concoction and went about her happy business of being a new wife. And her dear lady friends kept her more than occupied with fond memories and amusing advice.

One fine and warm afternoon found the ladies Morgaine, Nichole, Gwenhwyfar, Marian and Meggie, all under the larger of the two Ash trees past the gardens. They were chatting away while consuming large amounts of fresh strawberries. As they ate and licked at the strawberry juice running down their hands, they all began to giggle, and the conversation took a distinctive turn toward sexual acts. Had husbands been within earshot, they would have been sure to blush at the intimate details their ladies gleefully shared together.

Nichole turned to Morgaine, "So, what was it like with him the first time? Did he pluck your maidenhood most deliciously?" Nichole was closing her mouth around a strawberry in a graphic display of sexual allusion.

The ladies all shook heads and laughed uproariously.

Morgaine's eyes glinted as if she was in the company of co-conspirators. She recounted the first time, "He told me it would feel like a flash of lightning and rumble of thunder."

"Oh my," said Gwenhwyfar, fanning herself as if the atmosphere suddenly warmed dramatically.

Marian blinked, eyes widening, as she asked, "He said that?" Marian suddenly became quite a bit more curious about sex and wondering how much longer before she would wed Robin and if he could claim such epic sensations.

Nichole pressed on lustily, "And did it?"

"Oh yes! It was the most magical few days."

"Days?!" squealed Nichole and Gwenhwyfar in union.

Meggie giggled, adding, "Yes, I made sure to bring food out to them in case they came up for air."

Everyone laughed harder.

Nichole smiled approvingly. "What a romantic!"

Gwenhwyfar added, "The Gods chose well for you, Morgaine."

Morgaine finally blushed, nodding vigorously, "Yes!"

There was a brief pause as the ladies fell back into their own thoughts.

Morgaine then decided that if they were going there, then they should go all the way. She posed the questioned out loud, "How do you deal with the…?"

Before she even got the words out Nichole knew the question and immediately responded wickedly, "You mean the outflow?"

The women all laughed harder.

After much holding of bellies, they managed to vaguely compose themselves, with Nichole wiping tears from her eyes, adding in breathy fits of giggling, "I keep a small cloth on me. Will can be quite amorous when we are out and about. The birds and bees and trees and the seas just seem to really bring it out in him."

The friends all collapsed again into uproarious laughter.

It was only a short time later that Will came bravely upon the gaggle of women, asking for his wife's hand. He mentioned he wanted to show her a spot he had found in the woods. She rose, taking his hand and turned to her friends with a quick uplift of the eyebrows in a conspiratory act. There was much muffled laughter behind the pair as Nichole sashayed away with her husband.

The couple did not return until the evening meal and Nichole's hair was looking wild and unkempt. Both were flushed and rosy.

Gwenhwyfar could not resist. When the intimate guests were gathered around the table, she leaned across the table looking teasingly at Nichole, and with her index finger just giving the hint of a touch across her lips, she asked, "So, did you happen to have some cream with your strawberries today, Nichole?"

Nichole blushed, her cheeks turning crimson. As she took a dramatic sip of her wine, she replied wickedly, "Why yes, I did."

It took several minutes for the troop to stop laughing and settle into dinner. Gareth and Evelyn were quietly holding hands under the table and smiling knowingly at one another as they ate and pretended not to notice the jovial uproar. Will, on the other hand was scarlet, as he knew perfectly well that the brunt of the joke involved him. But he took it in good stride, dabbing his mouth with a napkin with equal drama. That action was not missed by Gwenhwyfar who shook her head as she leaned in, her mouth forming an O as she "ooooooooed" enthusiastically at the pair.

Guy looked slyly at Morgaine, whispering loudly for the party to hear, "I think I missed something. But if you still have strawberries to share, I'll whip up the cream."

The double meaning was not lost on anyone and the entire group erupted in laughter. Except the children, of course. Four pairs of eyes looked bewilderedly at the merry crowd of adults. Neirin ignored the matter completely as he continued to suck on his mother's finger and she bounced him gently while she laughed.

The friends thoroughly enjoyed a fortnight together but Nichole and Will realized that they needed to get back to their home in Weymouth, a coastal merchant town facing neighboring France. It would be a solid two days' ride home. Nichole and Will promised to return more frequently. There were hugs all around, as the coven, plus Marian, said their goodbyes to Will and Nichole.

As the four childhood friends formed a tight circle, holding one another, Nichole caught sight of Marian on the periphery and grabbed her, pulling her into the circle; Morgaine immediately shifted so her newer friend could join the circle. Marian had never known such close friendship as this small troop had, and she wept at being included.

Evelyn looked on the merry women in quiet satisfaction, thinking to herself, "There now; this is exactly what you needed to blossom, Marian."

CHAPTER 37

One Steamy July

BRIGHID APPROACHED THE Duchess in her receiving room. As she curtsied to the Duchess, she turned her head slightly and a secret smile passed between her and Sophie.

When she faced the Duchess, Evelyn noticed "that look" was on Brighid face. "Yes, Brighid, speak."

"That creepy little man approached me again. He wants to know if Morgaine is pregnant. What do you want me to tell him?"

"Easily enough, my dear, the truth. Morgaine got her courses about a week ago."

"Isn't that early?"

Evelyn pushed the comment away, "No one needs to know that. That would be unimportant information, would it not?"

Brighid nodded, agreeing that the creepy little man who paid her to inform him, so he could inform the Prince, didn't need that level of detail. It would only serve to make him question further and she certainly didn't want that. She very much enjoyed this intrigue and was grateful to be in the services of the Duchess, who also appeared to occasionally enjoy stirring up a pot of trouble. But in this situation it was best that there be no confusion over whose child Morgaine would bear. No one wanted the sweet Lady of the Lake to fall into the Prince's hands. Brighid curtsied again. "I will inform him when he comes creeping up to me again. I do wish we could be rid of him."

Evelyn nodded. "Agreed. But then they would just send another creepy man, right? At least he is not creeping about in the castle. Then we would have to do something about that. We have one calling on occasion already and he is one too many."

All three of the servants, Brighid, Sophie and Tana, nodded in agreement.

Brighid added, "Well then, I suppose I am off to market…to catch a fat pig."

Sophie giggled, her hand covering her mouth.

John was still visiting Nottingham Castle when the note came by bird a few days later. He was taking his afternoon libations in the garden with William when the messenger approached. John read the spy's note —

The Lady is not pregnant.

John knew exactly which lady that was, as he had only inquired recently about one. Ah, well. The stallion was sure to impregnate the little mare soon. And if not, he would see them again in the fall.

"You look disappointed, Your Highness?" William inquired.

Prince John looked at the Sheriff assessing what to say to this man, whom he knew to be responsible for having his beautiful stallion beaten as well as for planning the Avalons' murder. Still, the rat did have his uses. It was the only reason he didn't put this one down. Besides, William was one of his only friends. He was just misguided…and ambitious, that's all. "Oh William, it's nothing. Either way it works out in my favor."

"Ah," was all William could say.

"And William," added the Prince,

"Hmmm?"

"Leave my pets alone."

"What pets are those, Your Highness?"

"The young Avalon couple."

"Ah. Of course, Sire."

They both went back to drinking their wine.

Morgaine had been planning her little surprise for Guy for the past few days. Now that her courses were over, she was ready. She told Anwen to find Col and prepare.

The day was long, given it was summer. And Morgaine had made herself unavailable to Guy. He sensed a plot but he knew not what, so he had busied the day with continuing to read The Merlin Manuscripts. Generation after generation of magicians, all keeping record of the Avalons and of spells and intrigues. They were dangerous volumes if any were to fall into the wrong hands.

Dinner came and went but Morgaine playfully pushed off his advances.
"Woman, I want you!" He was fingering their Handfasting cord that was tied around her belly and tugging on it. He loved that she wore it daily, but right now, he wanted everything off her…Well, she could leave the cord on.
Her eyes brightened and eyebrows rose. "And you shall have me…soon."
He bit his lip and threw his head skyward but she only laughed.
"Come to bed after the skies have darkened."
"But that is not soon enough!"
Her fingers played with the fabric covering his cock, whispering mischievously, "I'll make sure the wait is worth your while."
Guy grunted and then pushed himself into her, backing her against the wall and kissing her most hungrily. When he pulled away they were both breathless. "Have it your way," he clipped lustfully before sauntering away.
Her breasts heaved as she watched him walk away. "Oh my," was all she could manage and then quickly went to their room to be sure everything was in place.

Though it was their room, Guy knocked before entering. The sight before him, as he entered, was magical. There were candles lit and, of all things, fireflies dancing and blinking throughout the room. And there in the center was the love of his life — Morgaine. She was wearing a skein of gossamer fabric dyed in a multitude of bright shades of red and pink. Guy's eyebrows rose and his heart started thumping faster. He had never seen his lady dressed so. She motioned to him to take his seat on the bed. He readily complied. From the corner of the room nearest the door to the herb room, and hidden by the dressing panels, came the sound of a drum beating, first like a heartbeat then slowly picking up in tempo. He looked at the panels momentarily but Morgaine drew him in and he was entranced by his wife as she danced for him. Only for him. And he heard the words of her dance in his heart —

He was her champion
her Black Knight who protected her in the shadows.
She danced for him
her desire reverberating against the walls
like a sweet sound from the deep
candlelight quivering in anticipation.
Lustful pupils dilated black
he longed to enter her with reverence
kiss her tenderly
and lay his head upon her breast to hear her heart beating for him.
And yet some primal animal part of him,
like a midnight creature never startled by the sun
wanted to take her
thrust himself so deep inside
until he could feel her heartbeat with his loins.
They made love wildly that night
her enchanting sighs and exclamations of "O" feeding his passion and delight.
He brought her to heights and depths of ecstasy she never knew before.
And as they lay entangled together
utterly spent
he kissed her forehead with a promise of undying love;
its embers are still smoldering to this day.

Morgaine danced her way toward Guy. She smiled playfully, seeing his eyes wild with lust. She swirled close enough to be within reach of her husband and he reached out and grabbed at the sheer fabric. As he pulled at the fabric, she unwound and spun out of his grasp, but also out of her clothing. She was left naked, with nothing on but their Handfasting cord, standing poised before him as the drumbeat came to a climax, before ending on a series of slow heartbeats. Though Guy had not been dancing, he was breathing as heavy and fast as Morgaine. He reached one hand toward her, palm up, waiting for her palm to fasten to his. She practically glided toward him and placed her hand in his. He pulled her to him and put his arms around her back, one hand reaching up toward her head, the other kneading her buttock.

She murmured breathily in his ear, "Are you not hot?"

He responded, equally breathy, "Yes."

"Then let's get you out of these clothes."

"Yes, let's do that."

They peeled off Guy's clothing so that they were now both naked on this warm summer night. Perspiration glistened on the pair of them as they roamed each other's bodies.

Guy purred in Morgaine's ear, "You may be slight of stature but the way you dance fills up the entire room."

As the married couple was otherwise engaged, Anwen helped Col, the drummer, out of the room through the herb room door. She turned to close the door and was entranced by Guy and Morgaine's horizontal movements. This was a whole new dance entirely. Though blind, Col could feel that this plump lass beside him was still lingering at the door, watching the couple in the room. He thought how she smelled rich, like cream. It excited him.

Col whispered to Anwen, "Are you watching them fuck?"

She jabbed him in the stomach with her elbow. Not hard, just hard enough to let him know he was being crude...and correct. He stayed close to her as she slowly led him from the couple's room, through the apothecary and out into the hallway. She paused at the door and felt Col against her. An odd and delicious sensation swept up her back and she leaned briefly into Col before leading him through the hallway and down the stairs to his room.

The next morning, after they were sure Morgaine and Guy had risen, Anwen and Meggie walked through the couple's room in search of fireflies. Best to return them whence they came so that they, too, could mate, making more fireflies. They were certainly trickier to find during the day; nobody was blinking and so the little bioluminescent insects were camouflaged in the tapestries and furniture of the room.

After Anwen finished cleaning up the bedroom, she approached Morgaine who was reading in the shade of the castle in the back, facing the Lake. Anwen remembered to frame her request by addressing Morgaine as a priestess and the Lady of the Lake. She knew that dancing was sacred to Morgaine. And she knew that Morgaine practiced to Col's drumming. Morgaine smiled at the request and agreed. It would be fun to work with someone. And she could tell that Anwen had a budding romantic reason for wanting to learn this art.

The next day Morgaine led Guy on a little adventure through the castle. Though he had been exploring the layout and had a sense of where he was, she surprised him by touching a wall and suddenly turning a corner where there did not appear to be one. He turned the corner with her and then pulled at her hand as he looked back. He studied the wall, up and down, but could not see how he was turning a corner.

Morgaine pulled at him gently. "Come."

They walked down a short corridor that opened up into a round room with a very large, wooden, round table taking up the majority of the room. Guy stopped short taking in what his eyes were seeing, but that his brain was telling him he could not be seeing. He whistled, recognizing he had found himself in the middle of a legend. Morgaine let go of his hand and sauntered to the table. Caressing the wood, she eyed him with a glint of mischief in her eyes.

"This is…," Guy wrapped his brain around what he was actually seeing. He walked to the table, touching and caressing it. "This is King Arthur's round table." His mind reeled, "Then this is Camelot!"

Morgaine smiled conspiratorially and nodded affirmatively.

"How could this be kept a secret for so long?" He paused, considering the spell book he was reading, "The wall. That wall is enchanted."

Morgaine nodded, her smile still planted firmly across her face, as she said, "Yes, by my namesake."

Guy stroked the table and then moved to a chair. "This one was Arthur's."

"How can you tell?" Guy wasn't entirely sure. It just felt like it. He examined and compared the chairs. "This one is slightly more ornate."

"But that is not what drew you to know. You felt it, didn't you?"

"Yes; it's like the chair…" Guy realized he was about to sound ridiculous, "…told me it was King Arthur's." There, he said it, and noticed that Morgaine only smiled approvingly back it him. "This is Camelot!" Guy exclaimed again, slapping the table. "Why is this not, then, the seat of power? Your family could claim title." Morgaine shook her head and Guy understood. "Because your line is his half-sister's and she went down in history as a sorceress and Arthur never had any children except Mordred. Did Mordred have children?"

"It is quite possible, but even we are not entirely sure. It's Morgaine's line through the Faie that we claim." Guy looked unsure and Morgaine continued, "Morgaine left the Faie pregnant, returned here, and took up residence with the chief who lived here. He took her as wife but the only child she had was a girl. He apparently died shortly after the girl-child was born and Morgaine ruled and so has her line, our line, ever since. We keep Camelot a secret for it would only bring war down upon this realm. We have no army behind us. Besides, we can let people claim Cadbury as Camelot. For, surely, Arthur had Cadbury built as the Saxons were rumored to be gathering strength before they invaded. This place, Uther had built for Igraine so that she could be closer to Avalon and her sister Viviane. After Uther was killed, Arthur ruled from here. As far as we can tell, he left this smaller home for a grander one with a more strategic view. It made sense. It was rumored that Arthur gave this castle to Morgaine, my ancestor, as her place, as it had been originally given to their mother, Igraine. Given that women couldn't and still can't own property, it was in holding with one of Arthur's cousins, Morgause, and Lot's eldest surviving son."

Guy pondered, "Even if Morgaine had claim to this castle and she managed to marry the warlord or duke who laid claim to it, how did your ancestors manage to keep it? Some king's relative could have been granted this property long ago."

Morgaine nodded grimly as she watched Guy. She replied, "They haven't...yet. We have seen to it the best we can."

He looked at her a bit perplexed but realized that more spell work would most certainly be the reason behind this family maintaining their holdings. He continued, "If an army descended, you would not be able to protect yourself without an army of your own."

Morgaine nodded sadly, "A few of the Guardians you have met, but they are small in number. They are what remains of the Brownies who hold fast to the traditions of the Land. We do train any resident who wants to be trained in self-defense, but we do not alarm our people by demanding it. No, Avalon's time is passing. The Lake breached long ago and is slowly filling in. What remains is a small apple grove on what was once a magnificent island." She paused, then added slowly, "It's all the spell work we have done over the centuries that keeps us here. But for how long?"

Guy's calculating brain couldn't help but consider lineages and allegiances. But those died out in the war centuries ago when the Saxons overtook the land. There were too many chiefs, too many kings, too many families in between. He could understand why the Avalons ruled quietly and preserved what they could of their line. And now he was part of it. He was adopted into the family and their daughter would continue the line. He knew at that moment that Morgaine and he would have a daughter and that is where his legacy would be preserved. He could feel Morgaine's eyes on him and could tell she was entering his thoughts. His mood shifted as he envisioned their daughter and he felt lustful toward his wife. He leaned on the table smiling wickedly, "I will take you on this table now, Wife, and get a baby in your belly!"

"Oh, will you now," Morgaine responded flirtatiously. "You'll have to catch me first," she laughed as she jumped up onto the table and ran across it. She jumped down and was now on the other side. He gave chase and they both laughed at their romp. She jumped back up on the table, prancing across, teasing him. But then she misjudged a dodge and ended up grabbed by the legs. He managed to catch her back to lighten her fall onto the table and then he had her. He pulled at the lacings on his trousers, pulled off her undergarments, and thrust himself inside her against the table; her silk dress glided them back and forth until they were completely spent.

Trousers still down around his legs, he heaved off her and onto Arthur's chair.

She propped herself up on her elbows to look at him and they started laughing again. She then became entirely serious. "We are like cats, feral, surefooted, navigating the narrow spaces in between. We keep this place because of our quiet tenacity and willingness to traverse the gray areas. I knew you were the right one because you are like us."

Guy tilted his head in consideration. He had never thought that he was like anyone else, that he had kin who knew him and understood him and accepted him for who he was. He suddenly saw Morgaine not only as his lover and his wife, but also as a sister, a companion, a mirror. She knew him and she loved him. And she too walked the gray landscape of morality — all to protect herself and her people and the Old Ways. Now they were his people and his ways too. And he knew he would protect them all with his very life.

He smirked at the memory of someone else referring to him as a cat.

"What is that smirk for?" asked Morgaine.

"Hmmm? Oh. It's just a curious juxtaposition; you are not the first to call me a cat, though the comparison was not a compliment from that person."

"Who?"

"Marian actually. It was when I was...courting her."

"What did she say?" Morgaine looked merely curious, not jealous.

Still, Guy was pained to bring it up further. He sighed and said, "Marian put my advances off several times, and yet she seemed conflicted; so I continued to pursue. Then she told me one day, 'Guy, you are like a cat, kind one moment then a cold-hearted killer then next. I just cannot accept this. I cannot return your love.' I was, of course, hurt by her words. I asked, 'you cannot love me for who I am?' 'No,' she replied. So I find it ironic that you not only claim I am a cat, but that your family are... that I am in the company of people like me. But you don't seem like me. Not with the things I have done."

"Ah, Love, but you are wrong. This family's history is wrought with certain unsavory acts to protect ourselves, the Land, and its people. I am sure as you continue reading The Merlin Manuscripts you will come across how we have manipulated events to our favor. My namesake especially."

Guy nodded, agreeing. Then his thoughts turned back to the table before him. "How did this place stay intact? When the Saxons came through centuries ago I would have thought this all might have burned to the ground."

Morgaine was thoughtful, "You are right at that. It might have. From The Merlin Manuscripts, it appears that Morgaine enlisted the help of her mother Igraine who was living, of all places, at the Abbey, and together they brought down the mists to include the castle or parts of it. It's unclear. But this room and this table survived."

Guy was perplexed, "How do you shroud a castle? Wouldn't folks bump into it?"

Morgaine giggled. "Perhaps. Yes, this type of spell would be quite tricky and Morgaine did not bother to write it down. We know that when she returned, she was pleased to see it still standing and that she managed to take up residence in it. I am not sure what happened to the prior occupant after he married her, but I have imagined his demise at my namesake's hands. And somehow, within a generation, this was titled land to the Duke and Duchess Avalon of Glastonbury and it has been that way ever since. And since this family has been able to manage keeping out of politics, we have been quietly ruling here and little bothered by the King or the Church."

Guy was solemn, "Until now."

Morgaine sighed, "Yes, until now. There's been intrigue before; there is always intrigue at court, but Prince John may be our undoing. So frets my mother."

"Why now?"

Morgaine frowns, "All things come to an end, else how could there ever be a new beginning? It may just be that the magic is running out of this Land."

"Do you really believe that?"

Morgaine was pensive and unsure. She responded after a long pause, "Not entirely. I just see how Christianized England is becoming. And if their young god Jesus was really the head of the pantheon, we might not be in such trouble. He sounds like a very caring and gentle Lord. But the Father, He sounds very stern, very hard, and very jealous. And Mary appears to have no power."

Guy was also frowning, "Unfortunately, you are right, Morgaine. But it is not all their fault. It is really the Church who interprets for the masses. My own mother loved Mary and prayed to Her daily. I see many similarities between Mary and your Goddess. Perhaps that was intentional on the Church's part; to bring people who missed the Goddess into the fold."

Morgaine agreed, "I am sure you are right."

Both were deep in thought when Guy slapped his hands on his thighs, stating loudly, "Enough of this wasteful brooding!"

He stood up, only to realize he couldn't move because his pants were down at his ankles. And though a tad embarrassed, he shrugged it off smirking, sat down, quickly removing his boots and pants, stood up again, and maneuvered between Morgaine's open legs. Morgaine had watched him in quiet pleasure as she anticipated what would come next. And as he stood over her, her feet dangling from the table, her legs open and her dress hiked up high, she looked up at her lover in complete adoration. Her arms coming up around his neck, she pulled him down on top of her, her legs coming up and wrapping around his lower back to pull him in, deeper and deeper inside her.

A few nights later, Guy woke up in the middle of the night with his hands tied to the bedpost.

Morgaine purred wickedly, "You will stay at attention for me, won't you." It was a command not a question.

Guy tried the knots. He might be able to free himself. His voice in mock anger, "Morgaine, what is the meaning of this? What if someone came in?"

"Darling, your sword is by the bed where you always leave it and here is your dagger…" She waved it in front of his face.

His eyes crossed as he watched the dagger move and hover above his head. If she accidently dropped it, it would hurt, and possibly poke out his eye. He held his breath and reminded himself that he trusted her with his life. He then asked gruffly, though with a touch of amusement in his voice, "What are you up to?"

Morgaine's eyes sparkled in the candlelight by the bed. "I am just playing. You seem to have me at the disadvantage of strength and speed, so I am making up for it in strategy. How am I doing?"

Guy tried the knots again. "Quite well. You caught me completely off guard. I had no idea my wife would want to tie me up and seduce me at dagger point."

She laughed. "Well, now you know."

She kissed him and nibbled his bottom lip as she began to ride him. And loving her as he did, he could not resist her unbridled passion. He allowed himself to be taken by her as he had taken her on the table. And he thoroughly enjoyed himself…even as the knots came loose. He really was going to have to teach her how to tie better knots.

CHAPTER 38

A Request and a Promise

CHARLTON, MARIAN'S FATHER, continued to seclude himself in his room. It wasn't that he didn't trust the family; the Avalons were certainly kind enough, they were just…odd. And he had never quite recovered from his ordeal in Nottingham's dungeon. His health was failing but, proud man that he was, he hid the extent of his illness even from his daughter. Evelyn observed Charlton with perplexity. Though polite, she could tell Charlton was uncomfortable with his new surroundings and that he was hiding his ill health. The cough he had picked up while in the dungeon had never left him and his breathing often times sounded labored. But he brushed away any help offered, so the family and Marian simply continued to make Charlton as comfortable as possible. He took more and more of his meals in his room, when he was even up for eating. Sometimes Marian would call upon Guy to help her prop up her father in bed. She ignored her father's grumblings. It was obvious that Charlton still carried misgivings toward Guy. To his credit, Guy was patient with Marian's father but one could see the strain Guy bore when dealing with Charlton as he had a tendency to mutter unkindness under his breath.

It was not long after Morgaine and Guy's wedding that Robin came for Marian. Robin knew better than to attempt sneaking into the castle. It was one thing to do it during a large party; it was entirely different to attempt it when it was just the family about. So he did what any civilized man would do — he walked up the stairs and requested an audience. He knew he was well known and had a price on his head, but he also sensed that the Duke would not throw him into prison and send him off in chains back to Nottingham. It was after-noon when he approached and requested an audience with the Duke. To the guards, he announced himself as Lord Robin of Locksley; the name did not appear to give them pause or concern. They took him to the entryway and the next set of guards escorted him to the Duke's receiving him. They had Robin wait while Reeve, Gareth's servant, went to find the Duke. He returned some time later to escort Robin to the gardens where the Duke and Duchess were. The guards followed behind.

Robin came upon the whole family, plus Marian, in the garden. His in-stinct was to reach for his weapons as soon as he saw Guy. But his weapons, of course, had been confiscated and were with the first set of castle guards. Guy looked up and caught Robin's movement. He smirked, seeing his ad-versary at a disadvantage and knowing he had no need to capitalize on that disadvantage. He gave Robin a slight nod. Robin heaved a sigh and realized Guy not only saw his involuntary movement reaching for his weapon, but that he did not feel in the least bit threatened by it. Robin smiled good-naturedly and gave a nod of acknowledgement back. It was a new moment for these two enemies, each realizing that the territorial lines had shifted and neither had to be on the defensive. With this tentative truce in play, Robin approached. Marian had her back to Robin, as she was busy playing with Neirin, Gwenhwyfar's youngest.

It should be noted that the game of peek-a-boo is never out of fashion for a baby, even though it endangers the participating adult to be looked upon as a complete ninny. But to Robin, Marian could never look like a fool. It only endeared her more to him seeing her playing with a baby. A wave of want-ing a family with her crested and fell upon him, soaking him in a sensation not unlike drowning; but instead of air he mentally gulped for, it was love he swallowed.

When Robin was announced by Reeve, "Lord Robin of Locksley requests an audience…" Marian lost her whereabouts and it was all Neirin could do to wave his hands in an up and down motion to let her know that her attention was supposed to be with him, not the oncoming stranger. Her eyes aglow, her heart aflame, she scooped herself up and ran at Robin, exclaiming, "Robin!"

Though Neirin was displeased at the sudden disappearance of his playmate, Gwenhwyfar quickly took over and all was well again in his little world.

Robin had hoped his approach would be more dignified, but he happily took Marian's enthusiasm over his plan. She kissed his face excitedly and he returned her eagerness with equal vigor.

Gareth looked on and chuckled. "Well, Robin, are you here to claim your bride?"

Robin approached and bowed the best he could with Marian latched onto him. He had never experienced her expressing such utter passion. It was like she was a ripe strawberry, her very scent screaming to be devoured. His heartbeat quickened. That was exactly why he was here, wasn't he? Passion caught him like a moth to a flame, and he responded fervently, "Yes!"

Gareth continued to chuckle, "Well, man, come join the party."

"Thank you, Your Grace."

Gareth eyed Robin meaningfully, "You are not actually here, though."

"Of course, Your Grace."

"We didn't actually invite the infamous Robin Hood to sit with us."

"No, Your Grace."

"Ah. Sit down then."

Robin bowed again and Marian led him back to her spot on the blanket and swooned against him. The happy party resumed their talk of summer teasing and Robin merely listened in, recognizing that this is what he missed, this leisurely pastime of just passing the time. He watched Guy out of the corner of his eye. He had never seen Guy so at ease, so comfortable with his surroundings, so at peace. And he wasn't wearing his usual black. He had on something more fitting for summer: light brown pants and a white shirt with a red vest. The vest had a golden dragon on it. Robin thought that was odd, but he couldn't remember the Gisbourne family crest. He thought back to family crests and realized with surprise that Guy was wearing the Pendragon crest. It was the same as Gareth's. This family had claimed Guy and these Avalons had laid claim to the Pendragon. Robin suddenly felt he had walked into a fairytale. His silent musings were interrupted as supper was announced.

A picnic supper was brought out to the family and all dined on the simple pleasures of good food and good company. Marian fed Robin with teasing gestures as she had observed Morgaine and Nichole do with their husbands. And Robin, for his part, reveled in this new side to Marian. His eyes twinkled at her as she had him sample foods from her fingers. Internally, Marian thought she was going to pop. She had heard enough sex talk from the ladies to know she that was feeling excited sexually. She wondered if Gareth and Evelyn would handfast them like Morgaine and Guy had been. They could have a Christian wedding later. She wondered if Robin would approve of such a ceremony.

Morgaine approached her from the other side and leaned into her friend, whispering, "You are aflame, my friend. I could hear your lust from where I was sitting."

Marian blushed, "Oh you are wicked, Morgaine."

Morgaine laughed lustily, "Yes, I am." To Robin she teased, "You had better marry this woman soon. She is on fire for you."

It was Robin's turn to blush.

Guy slapped his thigh, laughing as he demanded, "Come here you wicked woman."

"Oh yes, My Lord," responded Morgaine as she sauntered to her husband and sat down on his lap.

Everyone laughed and the embarrassed couple, Marian and Robin, were left to rub against each other without too much more friendly harassment.

Robin was shown unofficially to a guest room. He was, after all, not actually visiting — according to the Duke. It was agreed that he would be allowed to take Marian on the morrow as long as her father gave his blessing.

Early the next morning, while Robin went to Charlton to ask for Marian's hand, Marian approached Evelyn and Gareth. "I know that my father must give me away, but I would love your blessing."

"Of course, my dear," crooned Evelyn, "you have become very precious to us."

Gareth nodded, "You have our blessing."

Marian had tears in her eyes. Part of her did not want to leave. She enjoyed her easy life here. But she missed Robin terribly and there was some part of her that felt duty bound to the people of Nottingham.

Evelyn could see the younger woman's internal deliberations. She gazed into Marian's eyes and looked deep within her. She again saw pages that told of a love story, of a woman fighter, and knew that Marian would need to leave this cocoon. Still, she offered Marian a choice, "Marian, you know we are fond of you and appreciate the sweet friendship between you and our daughter. You are welcome to stay here if you so choose."

Marian reached out to Evelyn and Evelyn reached out her hands for Marian to clasp. "Thank you, Your Grace. And I would so very much love to stay here. This place is so magical and gives me such peace as I have never known." She paused just to enjoy the weight of those words. Then she continued, directing her question to Evelyn, "My Lady, you somehow can see more than what is apparent. Tell me, should I stay?"

Evelyn squeezed Marian's hands. "I do not know the when of the leaving, but leave you will, and with Robin. You are meant to be together. I daresay, you will become a well-known love story."

Marian's eyes widened. She exhaled, suddenly aware that she had been holding her breath when she asked Evelyn that question.

Robin returned to Marian, and the family, crestfallen. Gareth looked perplexed as he asked the younger man what transpired. Robin came to Marian's side and took her hands as he said gravely, "Marian, your father would agree to the marriage..." Marian looked elated and suddenly wondered at Robin's sober mood, thinking it in jest. But he continued, "... upon King Richard's return and my title and lands reinstated to me."

Marian's eyes flew wide in fear as she realized she might never marry. "But, the King could die over there. You could remain an outlaw forever." For guidance she looked to Evelyn, who held her with a compassionate gaze. Marian realized she should not leave her father in his ill health; she did not want for him to worry about her. She knew he was only trying to protect her, even though on so many levels he could not. Tears fell as she realized she could not go with Robin yet.

Gareth walked over to her, picked up her hand, and patted it. "There, there. Do not fret, Marian." He winked at the couple, adding, "You wait and see. Love conquers all."

There was no plan in formulation, just recognition of having to wait. Robin made himself discreetly scarce for the next few days. He wasn't ready to leave without Marian, though he knew at this point he would have to. Meanwhile, he did not want rumors to start that the Avalons were harboring a known outlaw; so he camped out in the woods. Though he disagreed with their politics, he understood that their motivation to side with Prince John was purely to protect their town. Everyone knew how the Prince could be. Other towns suffered at Prince John's hands, but Glastonbury thrived.

Marian came to visit each day. Their time was ever so precious. They spoke of everything and nothing. Each knew that Robin felt duty bound to return to help the people of Nottingham survive the Sheriff's rule. Robin promised he would visit again within the next several months, hoping perhaps, that with some time, Charlton would soften his stance on the matter. It was not said, "Or die." Despite her father's refusal for care and adamancy that he was fine, Marian knew her father might not make it through another winter with that cough and rattling sound in his lungs. She could only hope that he would, in the end, give her his blessing.

It had been several days since Robin departed when Gareth came to look in on Sir Charlton.

Charlton attempted to prop himself up better in his bed and to be cordial, "Ah, Your Grace. What brings you visiting?"

Gareth pulled up a chair so that the men could look at each other eye to eye. "A matter of the heart."

Charlton coughed, "Truly?"

"Yes."

Charlton looked perplexed, "Pray tell, whose heart, Your Grace?"

"Your daughter's."

"Ah."

Gareth continued, "You want to see her happy, do you not?"

Charlton's demeanor had the distinct impression of a petulant child: face in a frown, arms folded over each other, head slightly bowed. Gareth realized this was not going to be an easy win.

Still, he persisted, "Marian is an adult and should be married."

Charlton interrupted, "I think I would rather see her in a convent than married to an outlaw."

"Do you have such misgivings toward Robin?"

"Misgivings? No. I had wanted to see them married. But he has nothing to offer her. No title, no lands. No home, no security…"

Gareth shook his head, admonishing, "He offers her his heart. They love each other. Home, title, lands, as you know, can all be taken away. But love remains. It is a short life, my friend; allow your daughter the only thing she truly wants in this life."

Charlton continued looking down. He did not appreciate this talk. He felt scolded. He thought to speak up but he was unclear in what capacity the Duke was visiting with him. Was he being told what to do?

Gareth patted the sick man's hand as he got up to leave. "Think about it. Your blessing is important to her."

CHAPTER 39

The Torc

MORGAINE WAS SITTING under an apple tree in the Apple Orchard when the Guardian came to her.

"I think I hear a request," Rainer said, sliding up behind her with the tree in between. In his gray-green attire he was suited to camouflage amongst the trees.

Morgaine smiled. "I wasn't sure. I didn't officially call for you but now that you are here I could use your counsel."

"I am always at the beck and call of the Lady of the Lake."

Morgaine held her smile and continued, "Guy is very drawn to the Pendragon. He has the banner in his room."

"Ah."

"I have been having an image of him wearing the Torc, but I also recognize that by aligning him even more with the mythology of the sacrificial king that he could become such."

"He will have the Torc by Lammas."

"Then you agree? But it is the High King's Torc and we do not have the power we used to. I fear that if we brought it out it would only serve to confuse."

"My Lady, if you have had this vision then it is right and good that Lord Guy should wear the Pendragon Torc. Though it may never be accepted again as the mark of the High King, it will be noticed that the Lady of Lake claims her consort to be the Pendragon. Do you think it is in his heritage, or is he the Pendragon returned to us?"

"I am not entirely sure, though I had a dream that Uther and Igraine returned. I suppose I am having a hard time accepting what wearing the Torc will mean for my husband."

Rainer put his hand on Morgaine's shoulder, looking deeply into her eyes, "It means he is aligned to Avalon and he pledges his life to the Land."

"Yes, and we both know how that goes. It just seems only fair that one of the royal brothers should lie down for the Land and serve as the sacrificial King."

Rainer closed his eyes and breathed in long and slow as he sought for an answer in the ethers. He responded, "Though they will each die in turn, you know neither will sacrifice himself for the people or the Land."

After Morgaine left the Orchard, she headed to her mother's room for confirmation. "Mother, I…"

Evelyn held up her hand, stopping her daughter from saying more. "I know. Come." She beckoned her daughter forth to the scrying bowl. Mother and daughter went to the basin and looked into the water. Evelyn scried, seeing the lineage again, seeing the face of Uther. "Yes, it is again confirmed."

"Again? What do you see, Mother?"

Instead of answering Morgaine's spoken question, Evelyn responded to an unspoken one, a question Morgaine hadn't wanted to think about in her elation marrying Guy. "My daughter, why do you think your father and I allowed the wedding to move at such a rapid pace? You know the Handfasting tradition of a year and a day."

"Yes."

"Well then, why would you think we would ignore it?"

"Because we all feel the energies aligning against our way of life. And because Guy is connected to this lineage."

Evelyn came back to Morgaine's initial question, stating authoritatively, "The scrying bowl showed me Uther's face. Guy is the Pendragon returned."

Morgaine seemed dumbfounded, "But that would make me…Igraine… wouldn't it? I had a dream shortly after I met Guy. A voice called out to Igraine telling me to call forth the Pendragon." She looked at her mother. "Oh, how tangled this family is. And to return again to this Land. We must all be quite anchored here."

Evelyn nodded, then put her hand on her daughter's shoulder, "Your love is a deep love. It is a love that persists through the lifetimes. As does mine. I find it ironic that in this lifetime our roles are reversed. For you see, I am not only your mother but also our ancestor, and in fact, Morgaine, the great lady we named you after. Your father was Accolon. Only in this lifetime have we had more peace. But you see, the spirit of your father is not a fighter. He is a quiet, loving man, a man on whom I can always depend and who gives me strength to do what I must. The spirit of your man is a fighter, a champion. And we need the Pendragon back to serve the purpose he served before."

Morgaine shook her head, "But how can he unite England?"

"He cannot. Not in this lifetime. The purpose he will serve is to give you strong seed and to lay down his life for the Realm."

"So the Torc…"

"It is the proper gift to give the Pendragon."

"Oh Mother…" Morgaine fell into Evelyn's arms sobbing.

Evelyn petted her daughter's hair. She remembered Guy choosing the antlered crown at Summer Solstice. She whispered to her daughter, "Guy is the Hart, after all." She paused. Then continued gently, "Your deep, unwavering love for him gives him courage to be the man he must be to fulfill his destiny. And Guy loving you will give you the strength to endure."

It was Lammas. During the ritual, the Guardians of the Lady of the Lake appeared and came to bow before Guy. Rainer presented the Torc to Guy. There were looks of surprise, pride, and fear in the group for they all knew the true reason behind Uther's death. "Lord Guy of Avalon, Keeper of the Pendragon banner, you are being honored to wear the Pendragon Torc. We, the Guardians of Lady of the Lake, removed this torc from Uther's dead body and have held onto it through the centuries until now."

When he was given the Torc to place around his neck, Guy could feel some familiarity with the object. And when the metal with dragon head points was settled around his neck, it felt as if it had always belonged there.

Gwenhwyfar's Sons

GWENHWYFAR WAS LYING in bed with Guy at her shoulders and Taharqa at her feet. Morgaine was sitting on the bed beside her as the men gently but firmly pulled Gwenhwyfar in opposite directions.

"Ieee! Oh, it hurts!" exclaimed Gwenhwyfar.

Morgaine stroked her friend's forehead as she said, "You don't want to be hunched over so, do you, my sweet?"

"No."

"You are a tall woman. You must learn to stand straight."

The men continued to stretch Gwenhwyfar. They had been at this for weeks, all the while coaxing Gwenhwyfar to sit up and stand up straight. As the men stretched her, Morgaine cooed encouragement in her ears. Meanwhile, Taharqa started to massage Gwenhwyfar's ankles as he pulled at them. He then worked his way up her calves. Kneading and pulling. Kneading and pulling. It was meditative…almost. Somewhere in the back of his mind he became distracted with feelings of arousal. He didn't dare inch up beyond her strong, shapely calves.

Gwenhwyfar started to relax as the men stretched her again. Then another sensation slipped in, a sensation she had not felt in a long, long time. Through slit eyes she assessed Taharqa. "Strong hands," she pondered; "a handsome, muscular frame, tall like me…and, oh really strong hands."

The young brothers had been acclimating themselves to Glastonbury castle and their new life here for the past two months. Though their explorations had tended to be closer to the castle, as each grew more confident and their mother Gwenhwyfar grew more comfortable, the boys started to roam. And as brothers, one might expect them to be both fiercely loyal to each other while at the same time getting on one another's nerves. So the brothers would walk and sometimes rassle. When arguments ensued, they each voluntarily separated and took time alone. And it was actually during these times, while the brothers were off alone, that the explorations took on greater meaning for each of them.

"I am Rod of the Green! I am Green Rod!" Rodney proclaimed loudly as he stood on a mound he had found. He was farther afield than he ever had been before, deep in the Avalon woods.

Unbeknownst to Rodney, an old man watched the boy with keen interest.

Julius, on the other hand, found himself indoors more, not because he was drawn inside but because he was really taken with Guy and he had an aptitude for reading and an interest in magic. The two of them would sit in Guy's study and pore over The Merlin Manuscripts.

One morning, Gwenhwyfar heard voices at the end of the hall. She could tell the voices belonged to her son, Julius, and Guy but she did not hear what they were saying. It was still early but Julius must have left the room. She got up and threw on a dressing gown, padding down the hall quietly. She could see Morgaine at the door. Morgaine turned, winked, and put her finger to her lips. Gwenhwyfar came up silently. The door was open and Morgaine was sure that Guy knew she was there, but he allowed himself just to focus on Julius' questions. The two women peered in to see Julius on Guy's lap as they poured over a manuscript and Julius struggled with the words. The women looked to each other and smiled, then slowly backed away to leave the pair be.

"Guy is wonderful with Julius," Gwenhwyfar said, a content smile crossing her lips. She knew Julius was in the right place. Morgaine nodded in agreement. The women were now back in Gwenhwyfar's room so she could check in on Neirin. As she fed the baby, she thought about her sons. Rodney was already up and out but she was content with that. She knew they were all safe here. Rodney would be out in the woods and he was sure-footed, so even with a mother's fretfulness, she gave him his space.

Rodney was out in the woods. He felt Julius get up and though he lingered in bed, once his mom left the room, he got up and dressed, went to the kitchen to get a bit to eat and out the door and down the stairs to the street below and from there, out into the field. He walked through the marsh and grabbed an apple as he passed the Apple Orchard. He wandered through the woods. Deep into the woods he went. He heard a sound he had not heard in the woods before and followed the sound. It was a flute and he was entranced.

Wild Herb set the trap well, for it was not too long before he heard the young lad crashing through brush. He had been watching Rodney for a while now, learning his patterns. He knew he would be out today and he had decided today was the day to meet Gwenhwyfar's eldest.

So it was on a sweet-smelling sunny morning when Rodney met Wild Herb. Rodney just stood there and watched and listened as the old man of the forest played his flute. Wild Herb continued to play, momentarily ignoring the boy.

But after a time he looked up and pretended to just notice the lad. "Well, hello. Where did you come from?"

Rodney cocked his head and smiled. "From the castle."

"From the castle? You don't say? Hmmm. You remind me of someone. You must be Gwenhwyfar's."

"How did you know?"

"You look like her."

Rodney shrugged, then redirected the conversation, "Do you live here?"

"Yes, my wife, Elizabeth, and I live in these woods."

"Why?" asked Rodney, cocking his head to the side like a playful pup.

Wild Herb matched the boy's playful air with his own, as he mirrored the boy, cocking his head too. "Why not? It is a beautiful place to build a happy old life."

Rodney smiled at the old man's smile.

After that, Rodney was hooked. He came out every day he could. He would meet Wild Herb at his and Elizabeth's home in the glade and from there the pair walked together and talked together and built a steady friendship.

Wild Herb took Rodney to check his traps. Slowly, he came to teach Rodney animal tracking and how to make a fine snare to catch a rabbit or a squirrel.

Rodney wrinkled his nose at the dead animal in the snare. It was sad to see this dead thing.

Wild Herb looked at the boy with compassion as he said, "You want to eat?"

Rodney nodded, knowing it was this animal they were about to skin. Still, it was hard to stomach pulling the skin up over the eyes, seeing the rabbit so exposed, the eyes so haunted.

"Death is part of life, my son. Honor this creature and know that he feeds our bellies this day," said Wild Herb gently as he handed Rodney the knife to make the incision as he had shown him.

Elizabeth welcomed Rodney into her home and into her life. She was glad that her husband took an interest in the boy and mentored him. She watched the lad in contemplation. She noticed how he bottled up his anger and she was keenly aware of his need for a father figure. Then there was his curiosity, his inquisitive nature. She recognized her husband was probably the best thing for him and was content to spend more days alone busying herself, in hopes of keeping all of Gwenhwyfar's sons in the fold.

CHAPTER 41

Budding Romances

COL WAS DRUMMING as Morgaine taught Anwen belly dancing. He could feel their footsteps on the floor as he played. He dreamed of touching Anwen's face and seeing her with his hands. No waif was she. She would not blow away in a breeze. People would think I am rich, indeed, with such a bonny lass as she, he thought to himself.

After the lesson Col asked Anwen for help. Morgaine secretly smiled, as she knew damn well that Col didn't really need help. He managed to walk about the castle just fine. Once, she asked him how. She remembered the conversation well.

Col responded to Morgaine's question, "I count."

"Count?"

"Yes. For example, I have learned how many steps from your room to the kitchen to my room. I just have to remember my starting place and where I am going."

"That is a lot of numbers to keep in your head."

Col smiled, "Yes it is."

Anwen looked to Morgaine to be sure that Morgaine didn't have need of her before she responded to Col. Morgaine nodded once as if to say, "go on" as glee came over Anwen's face. She curtsied and then went over to assist Col, even though she, too, knew perfectly well he made his way around the castle without much assistance. Still, she feigned ignorance just so she could be close to Col. He made her heart beat faster, especially when they "accidently" brushed up against each other.

Together Anwen and Col left the room. Morgaine followed them to the door and then peered around the corner to watch their hands tentatively reach for each other. She could almost see the energy between them as lightning connects earth and sky. She nodded approvingly knowing that there would be a marriage sometime in the future between these two. Morgaine then smiled slyly as she turned her thoughts to her friends Gwenhwyfar and Taharqa. She observed sparks between them too. But they moved even more cautiously than this young pair. She wondered if they would allow themselves to fall for each other. Gwenhwyfar had known so much grief. And then there was her nasty husband to consider...or not. Gwenhwyfar was young enough yet. Love did not have to pass her by.

CHAPTER 42

September 1192 Saving the Line

MORGAINE WAS SURE of it. Her courses had not come in over three weeks. She was pregnant! She slipped into her mother's receiving room, always appreciating its exquisiteness. It had an elegant ambience, decorated in blues and browns, imbuing the room with a soft serenity. She found her mother reading on a pile of cushions near the window.

Evelyn finished the sentence and then looked up at her daughter. "You appear to be bursting forth in excitement. Pray, what is your news?"

Morgaine glided in to her mother's side, looking at her with merry eyes, and stating most exuberantly, "Mother, I believe I am with child. I have not had my courses in three weeks."

Evelyn embraced her daughter elatedly. "Oh, that would be splendid! We must be sure."

Guy heard the news shortly after as Morgaine came up behind him, giving him a tight hug from behind. He shifted to face her, seeing her face lit up with excitement. He touched her nose with his forefinger and brought it down her lips to her chin, then grasped her chin and brought her lips up to his. Kissing Morgaine made Guy hot with desire and he felt his cock stiffen in anticipation. They rubbed noses.

In a husky voice, Guy inquired, "What has you so excited?"

Morgaine beamed, "You...and...I...am with child."

Guy's eyes widened in joy as his whole face smiled. "Truly?"

Morgaine nodded vigorously, still beaming.

He picked her up and spun her, shouting, "We are going to have a baby!"

They laughed and held each other tight.

The happy news spread quickly through the castle.

The day was quiet with Gwenhwyfar's boys exploring Avalon Forest. Gwenhwyfar sat under the Ash enjoying the gentle rustling of the leaves and the sunrays playing peek-a-boo with her eyes. Neirin had fallen asleep at her breast and she gently removed him, settling him on the blanket. She hiked up her dress over her exposed breast and lay back against the tree trunk. She sighed. Life finally felt good again. She was home and with loved ones and Rufus hadn't returned to bother her. She felt peaceful.

"Uncle Guy, do it again. Do it again." That would be Julius. He must have found Guy. She continued to lean against the tree as she opened her eyes and looked around. And there they were, the pair walking up through the field. Guy was showing Julius some slight-of-hand trick involving a coin and the boy's ear. She chuckled softly, "That man is so good for him. One would never know he wasn't already a father."

Julius noticed his mom and yelled to her, waving. He ran toward her with Guy following. "Mother, you have to see this. Uncle Guy, please show Mother your magic trick."

Guy came up and squatted before the trio, his well-known lopsided smile planted securely on his face. It was a lucky thing that Neirin was not so fussy and merely looked up wide-eyed at being woken up by his older brother's excited voice. Guy showed them the coin, snaking it between the fingers of his left hand. Then he dropped the coin into his right hand but when he opened it, the coin wasn't there.

Gwenhwyfar shook her head wonderingly, "But where did it go?"

Guy reached up behind Julius' right ear, "Right here." He held the coin between his thumb and forefinger. Then he started snaking the coin between his fingers again.

"That is quite a trick. Where did you learn it?" inquired Gwenhwyfar.

Guy recalled a bittersweet memory. "My father taught it to me. I was probably about your age, Julius."

Julius' eyes widened and he beamed, "Will you teach me?"

Guy was enjoying the deepening connection with the lad. "You want to learn?"

"Yes!"

"Well then, the first thing I want you to practice is moving the coin between your fingers. Like this." Guy showed Julius how the coin snaked through his fingers. He gave Julius the coin. Julius tried. It was hard and the coin kept dropping. But before Julius could get disappointed Guy tousled the lad's red mop of hair, "Keep at it. It took me a while to get too. Once you get that part down, I will teach you the next."

Julius nodded, now completely absorbed with his task.

His mother, however, interrupted him, "Julius, would you please go get me some water."

The boy looked at his mother and then nodded.

When he tried to give back the coin to Guy, Guy held up his hand, "Hold onto that coin and keep practicing."

Julius was overjoyed as he got up and went in search of water for his mother. The two adults watched him walk off.

"You will save this line. And our line will continue," Gwenhwyfar stated plainly and out of the blue.

Guy turned his head from watching Julius to look at Gwenhwyfar. He changed his position from squatting to sitting on his knees. Then asked, "Our line?"

Gwenhwyfar replied, "The Faie-human bloodline. You didn't think you were the only one to feel the pull?"

"I heard from Gareth that Lorrac was your brother."

"Yes, and so even though I cannot give Morgaine a daughter, I feel the pull of her. Sometimes it is so strong; it hurts to be so close and know I can never give her what you can. Fate brought me back to Glastonbury with a son who could strengthen the line even more."

Guy's eyes widen. "How?"

"Guy, only Morgaine knows this. Well, knowing Evelyn, Evelyn probably knows of her own accord as well. Several years ago, a man — a strange and wondrous man — came to me when Rufus was away. I was a dutiful wife but I felt compelled to go with this tall, willowy man of the Faie. He had red hair and bright blue eyes…like yours," she noticed. She wondered about Guy's heritage. She had never come across the same blueness in human eyes. Gwenhwyfar could see Guy was a jumble of thoughts as he considered a woman's infidelity. She waited, just looking at him. She continued her story when Guy looked at her, apparently deciding to set his confused thoughts aside. She continued, "I knew later that the baby in my belly was from him. He never returned, only whispered before he left, 'Get back to Avalon. Your place is there; this child's place is there.' And then he just seemed to vanish." Gwenhwyfar looked dreamy as she thought back onto the single most perfect afternoon she ever had with a man. He was so tender and so passionate and attentive. She swooned at the memory and her cheeks flamed.

Guy's expression softened. He heard Morgaine speak of Rufus and she had little good to say of him. So this Faie male had given his friend a sweet memory and wonderful child. He breathed through his judgments to a place of compassion. And a new thought emerged. Guy took Gwenhwyfar's hands. He understood now that his daughter would be blood-oathed to one of Gwenhwyfar's sons. "Which son?"

"Don't you know?"

Guy responded quietly, "Julius."

"Yes. Who else could it have been? He has my bearing and none of Rufus'."

"What was the Faie father's name?"

Gwenhwyfar held a delicate smile as she remembered her Faie lover's face. She whispered, "Cynewelew."

Guy was silent for a time, thinking back to The Merlin Manuscripts. Only Merrek's name was listed; the others were not named. He wondered if that mattered.

Julius still hadn't returned, but he was sure to soon. Guy continued his questions while the two of them were still alone. "Gwenhwyfar, I read in The

Merlin Manuscripts that half-breeds are..." He was searching for the words for "less procreative." "...That is to say, they produce fewer offspring."

Gwenhwyfar nodded, "That is true. If I were half and of the Avalon line, I would not be so fertile. There is Faie somewhere in my family line but none of us are half. I am mostly human and perhaps that, in part, is why I have had three sons. The Avalons were willing to accept my brother, even though a baby by him would have weakened the line; but in the end, he rejected the calling. Honestly, now that I am getting to know you, I think you are the better choice. And your bond is obviously so much stronger."

Guy nodded thoughtfully. He had other questions but just then Julius showed up with a wooden goblet and a pitcher of water.

"I thought I would bring enough for all of us," stated Julius happily.

Gwenhwyfar smiled adoringly at her son, "Julius, how thoughtful."

Julius sat down and looked at Guy who was smiling at him too. He beamed at the two of them, proud of himself and their approval. He poured the water and offered it to his mother. She drank her fill and passed the goblet back. Julius filled it again and offered the goblet to Guy, who gladly accepted it.

As Guy drank he watched the boy who was still gazing at him and considered all the ways this boy was entangling himself into his life. It was a good feeling even as it unsettled him when he continued to recognize how much and how quickly he was changing. Who was that notorious Guy of Gisbourne? That man really must have died on the road as the bards were singing.

Guy had put it aside long enough. He hadn't touched the question bumping around in his head since that day months ago when he questioned Gareth about the bloodline. He decided to approach Evelyn with the question he had spinning around in his head, particularly about the blue eyes. Both his parents had brown eyes. It was always remarked that he must have the eyes of some past relative. But now he wondered. Because how else could there be Faie blood in him unless one of his female ancestors laid with a male Faie? And then there was the passage in one of The Merlins' books about Merrek, a several times great grandfather of this family line. His physical description was uncannily similar to Guy's.

He knocked on the door of Evelyn's receiving room and then entered, whereby he saw that she was already talking with Morgaine. He could see Tana standing behind and to the right of her throne. Just patiently present, ever ready for her mistress. On the other hand, Sophie was nowhere to be seen. He had not expected to be confronting both Evelyn and Morgaine; but whatever he had to ask Evelyn, Morgaine should know.

He approached Evelyn, first catching his wife in an embrace and kissing her on the cheek, and then bent at the knee to kiss Evelyn's extended hand. "My Lady. My Lady," he stated to them each in turn.

Morgaine giggled. "Guy, my love, why so formal?"

He stayed so. "I have questions."

Evelyn cocked her head, "About?"

"Apparently I have Faie blood in me and that is how Morgaine and I recognized and were drawn to each other."

Evelyn nodded, "You have read the text."

"Do I remind you of anyone?"

"What an odd question," Morgaine proclaimed.

But Evelyn was silent.

Morgaine turned to her mother, "Mother?"

"The eyes are a giveaway for those who know. In the Faie, eye coloration is much more vibrant and your blue eyes show the family resemblance to a Faie ancestor."

Morgaine could see the hurt in Guy's eyes. She knew he bore the pain of his mother loving another — Robin's father. But then to consider that Marguerite may have had yet another lover and that the child — Guy — was not Auguste's but of the Faie. Oh, that would be much for Guy to bear. She then looked at her mother, her eyes narrowing in contemplation of how her mother was going to handle this delicate situation.

Evelyn sighed. There was no way to skirt his question. She must be direct. "My children..." She looked from one to the other and then focused on

Guy, "I have scried on this very question when you came to us. I saw the faces of Merrek's children, and you were among them. So, though one of your ancestors may too have bred with another Faie, it is clear that Merrek is your father."

It would be an understatement to say that Guy was in shock. As he moved through shock, he found anger. He grew angry with his mother. She was dead but still he had anger to feel toward her.

Evelyn waved her hand in an arch in front of him. "Nay, stop that line of thinking. Your mother was no whore. She was chosen by Merrek for a reason. And though it would have helped, had we known, so that we could have brought you here, there were other complications at the time. Merrek, our old goat of an ancestor, makes sure that there are Faie kin to mate with to keep the line strong."

Guy's voice was still charged with anger and grief, "So Auguste is not my father."

"Of course he is your father. He raised you. He loved you as his own for he knew nothing else."

"Well, where is this Merrek?"

Evelyn shook her head. "I do not know. He stays in the mists, holding his reasoning to himself."

"So that means I am actually related to you both."

"Yes, by several generations. And Merrek may have chosen your mother due to her sharing a bloodline with the Crown so that a match between my daughter and you could seem appropriate to some."

"You mean the Prince."

"Yes."

"So Merrek can see the future?"

"He possibly lives straddling time. He is attached to this family; that much is certain. And so he must have abilities to craft outcomes." She sighed as she added quietly, "And he has his comrades who believe in a melded Faie-human line to keep the Faie in this world."

Morgaine added, barely above a whisper, "You mean Julius' father."

Evelyn nodded.

Guy felt more hurt. "So I was crafted to serve some purpose?"

"Oh Guy, do not cause such anguish for yourself. We all serve some purpose. Be at peace that you are here with your Beloved."

He turned to Morgaine. "I accepted the magic that drew us together. But I feel like a marionette. Who pulls my strings?"

Morgaine got up and held her husband. She whispered, "You may have felt the pull, but it was you who decided. We all have free will. The Goddess does not demand. And Merrek is but another creature of Hers. Perhaps he is a craftsman..." She widened the space between them, outstretching their arms, "And if he is, just look at the man he created who stands before me."

Guy heaved a sigh, resigned. Being so in love with Morgaine brought consolation.

It was only days later when Guy approached the topic of the Faie-human bloodline with Gareth. Gareth was heading out with Prometheus as he often did in the afternoons when he was up for the challenge. The dog was so big and gave quite a pull at the leash. It did give the pair some exercise and Gareth enjoyed the connection with his animal. Normally wanting this time to himself, Gareth appeared a bit reserved in his response to Guy but agreed nonetheless. The three of them walked through the field toward the Lake. Each was quiet.

Guy then asked rather abruptly, "Gareth, did you know your father?"

Though Gareth knew who Guy meant, he instead said, "Of course. He raised me."

Guy blinked. "You were raised by the Faie?"

Gareth chuckled then shook his head. "No. My parents raised me. The Faie male just gave his seed." Gareth paused then chuckled again. "A cuckoo I suppose."

Guy did not understood, "Pardon?"

Gareth clarified, "A cuckoo. The bird who lays her eggs in other birds' nests."

It was Guy's turn to laugh. He repeated with a hint of mirth in his voice, "A cuckoo." That explained it. "Did you ever meet the Faie who sired you?"

Gareth replied plainly, "No. No, he never came to me. Never introduced himself. Truly, these men are like the cuckoos who leave their broods in the care of another specie" Gareth paused in deeper consideration. "I have dreamed of him on occasion. It seemed very real, more like a conversation than a dream; though a dream nonetheless, for when I awoke he was not there."

"Do you know his name?"

"Dewlynd. The Faie who sired me is Dewlynd." Gareth looked at Guy with empathy; it was too much to take in and he was sure Guy must be feeling angry at Merrek and his mother just as Gareth had felt angry at Dewlynd and his own mother. But he had made peace with his parentage just as he knew Guy would. Gareth reached his hand up to squeeze Guy's shoulder as they walked, "I know this is not easy to take. Remember that both your mother and father loved you and raised you. And know that the Faie do not mean to harm us with their actions. They merely want some part of themselves to survive in the world." Gareth let go of Guy's shoulder as Prometheus tugged harder at him; they all picked up their pace. Gareth, now sounding a bit winded as he spoke, continued, "Morgaine, the first Morgaine, came back into this world having made a pact with the Faie that she would help carry on their line. And we are all the result of that pact. And I am honored to be a part of this lineage."

Guy reflected on all Gareth said. He had not yet been able to quell his anger toward Merrek at seducing his mother. But for all he knew, Merrek could have appeared to her as Auguste in glamour; perhaps she never knew it was other than her husband with whom she made love. A part of him wanted to believe this is how it happened, but there was no way to know.

CHAPTER 43

A Lesson in Love

GUY WALKED THE castle's halls, wandering really. He was still trying to familiarize himself with this place's twists and turns. He wanted to get back to the room with the round table, but thus far he couldn't find it on his own. It was such an old castle, and in places the wood beams looked trussed up one too many times. But the castle was certainly glorious to behold on the outside. And most of what he had seen looked like a fine work of art. But these underused hallways definitely showed the centuries.

Just before he came around a corner, he heard giggling. He stopped short and looked around; but the sound was coming from ahead of him. He peeked around the corner. Though he knew he was a lord of this castle, he had the distinct sensation that he was intruding on something.

And there were Brighid and Sophie, together in a very intimate stance. Brighid was leaning into Sophie with Sophie's back against the wall. Brighid was fingering Sophie's necklace. Guy's eyes just about popped when they kissed. Some part of him found the whole scene distasteful. They were servants, and two women, and not working. Another part of his brain thankfully kicked in and told him to just walk away. And that is what he did, continuing to hear the giggling as he removed himself.

He reassessed what he was doing and found himself on a balcony overlooking the landscape that reached out to the Lake and beyond to the Apple Orchard. So preoccupied was he that he hardly noticed Evelyn until she was standing at his side. He tried to control his internal jump and not appear so startled. Too many people here were able to sneak up on him. It was most disconcerting. He had been known for his keen sense of awareness and here he felt a bit out of his depths.

"Why, Guy, you look alarmed? Whatever could be the matter?" Evelyn was being playful.

It was rare for him to experience this tone in her voice and he wasn't sure how to respond. He continued to look out at the Lake. "I have never been snuck up on so many times in my life."

Evelyn mockingly scolded, "I did not sneak. I never sneak."

He again heard the playfulness in her voice and recognized that really, she was just trying to reach out to him. "I am sorry, My Lady. I am just out of sorts."

"Why?"

"I am not even sure why I should be."

"Well then, perhaps you shouldn't be."

"I saw something that I wasn't supposed to see and I am not sure what to do about it."

"To do about it? Guy, what did you see? A spy?" Suddenly Evelyn was concerned. Guy was a serious fellow so she realized it was no longer time to jest.

"No, Lady, not a spy…" He hesitated. He felt childish, tattling. It wasn't any of his business.

"Guy?"

"I saw two servants kissing."

"Oh."

"Two women servants."

"Oh." Evelyn's "ohs" were very noncommittal. Then she inquired, "And what did you think needed to be done?"

"I am not sure. It seemed…inappropriate."

"Why? Were they not attending to their duties?"

"Well, certainly not at that moment. Their affections were unbeseeming."

"Why?"

"Well, they are servants and two women and…"

"Guy, dear, you need to stop right there."

He looked at Evelyn, perplexed. "As long as our servants do their work, I have no issue with them taking a break to become friends or become friendly."

"But shouldn't Sophie be at your side?"

"Ah, Sophie. So you caught the budding romance between Brighid and my Sophie."

Guy nodded, then asked, "Budding romance?"

"Those two are like wildflowers blooming and enamored by the other's blossoming. They each came here from different lands. One by choice, one by command. But they do well in this castle that they have made their home. And obviously something sparked between them."

"But they are two women. It is not natural. I have heard that girls or boys may play with each other, but they grow up and get married."

"Oh dear. Guy, sometimes things just work out differently than we think they will. Did you ever imagine yourself here?"

"Not before it was happening."

"Brighid and Sophie might have felt the same. There are few marriageable men here for young women with no dowries. This may have certainly taken the pressure off them and allowed them to simply feel a sense of lightness and play to explore each other."

Guy nodded, his brow furrowed.

"Come, my sweet son. Do not be so judgmental of them. They found love. And as the Goddess says, 'All acts of love are Mine. Be as My reflection in a deep pool and love deeply.'"

Guy considered this. He brought his eyes to hers as he noticed she was weaving her head to get him to look at her in the eyes.

She looked at him expectantly, asking, "Does their play threaten you or our safety?"

If he was to be honest, "No. I can't say that a kiss between two lovers threatens anything."

Evelyn reached up to pat his shoulder. She smiled. "I am proud of you."

He looked surprised. "Why?"

"Some people would stay prejudiced forever, no matter the facts before them. You recognize that no harm is done. Only love."

He nodded again, holding on to the words, 'only love.'

CHAPTER 44

October: Death and Taxes

"You have tears in your eyes." Guy felt ashamed and turned his face from Morgaine. The large white furry body of what had been Cream lay in Morgaine's lap as she petted her dead cat.

> Morgaine entered her room and heard odd sounds coming from the corner behind the dressing panel. She cautiously stepped up to it, peering around. And there was her cat, Cream, convulsing. Morgaine exclaimed in shock and grief and went down on the floor to try to scoop up her beloved friend. The convulsing persisted and then abruptly ended; Cream was lying limp. Morgaine cried out, "No!" She did not pay attention to the feet running louder in the hall; didn't hear movement in the room until Meggie was upon her, wrapping her arms around her companion, rocking her, doing her best to comfort her sobbing friend.

Morgaine continued, "Love, it was a statement, not a judgment. Or perhaps it was. I am so touched by your tears," Morgaine sniffed through her own. "Look at me." She weaved her head slightly in an attempt to get his attention. It was the same action he noticed Evelyn do when she was trying to get him to look at her.

Guy looked at Morgaine, tears still streaming down his face, noticing that tears were streaming down hers as well. Biting back as much emotion as he could, Guy said, "I will miss her. I have grown very fond of her, even with her jumping up on the bed while we are making love."

They both laughed through their tears and then Morgaine collapsed sideways into his arms so that he was holding her as she held Cream.

Morgaine sobbed, "She has been such a good friend to me. My constant companion for so long. My sweet Cream. Oh Guy, it hurts!"

Guy rocked Morgaine on the bed for quite a while, just holding her and rocking her as she cried. His eyes remained moist. Losing Cream made him remember losing his steed Crown. He kissed the top of Morgaine's head and recounted the tale. "I lost an animal I loved well too. It was almost five years ago. Crown was a magnificent stallion and my pride and joy. I lost him during a joust at King Henry's Tournament. I was weeping in my tent when Prince Richard came in to congratulate me for my high marks in the jousts."

Prince Richard swept majestically into Guy's tent. Guy's face was in his hands, so distraught was he over losing his best friend. He looked up and saw Richard. He came to his senses, stood up, and bowed.

Richard eyed Guy, sneering, "Your face is red. You look like you have been weeping like a woman. Why?"

Guy responded, trying not to clench his jaw too tightly while at the same time trying to hold back his emotions that were getting the better of him, "I lost Crown."

"Who?"

"My steed, Your Excellency."

"You cry for a beast? You pitiful man! You are not worthy of my honors." Prince Richard turned and left, stripping Guy of his winnings.

"He humiliated me for loving another. I felt so alone that day. Richard was cruel when he didn't need to be. Why so many young men flock to him I am not sure I will ever understand. So there it is. I am prone to weeping like a woman."

Morgaine pulled away from Guy's embrace so she could look him the eye. "No, Guy. You weep like a man with compassion in his heart. Truly, you are a most incredible man, to have the strength and courage to weep when you are taught — and harried — not to. I am a most blessed woman to have such a man as you by my side! I am sorry you felt so alone in your grief. Thank you for being here for me in mine."

As the hours ticked by, Morgaine realized it was time to bury her beloved cat. Meggie brought some cloth and Morgaine wrapped Cream in it. Then the three of them walked to the Apple Orchard, Morgaine weeping all the way, cradling Cream, leaning into Guy. When the trio reached the Orchard, Meggie put down the shovel and bent close to the earth. Guy helped Morgaine to a similar pose.

Morgaine prayed aloud, "Oh, sweet Earth, please gladly accept this little body back into You. May the body of Cream feed You as You have fed her, her whole life. Please open for us so that we may return her to You."

She nodded to Guy who then picked up the shovel and began to dig.

Meggie held the woman who had saved her from the streets and became her dearest friend over a decade ago, wishing she could console her. She watched Guy dig into the dirt. He eyed the cloth-covered body and gauged the size and depth he needed to dig so that other creatures wouldn't disturb the body.

Morgaine laid Cream into the hole. Meggie handed her herbs from a bag she brought and Morgaine sprinkled them on Cream before she pushed the dirt into the hole. She cried, "I am burying my little love. Oh Goddess, I grieve. It hurts to lose her."

Meggie helped Morgaine add the dirt. Guy came to his knees and joined them to fill in the hole. Meggie handed more herbs to Morgaine who then sprinkled them on the fresh grave. The three of them rocked together. Guy realized he wept not just for Cream but for Crown as well. It finally all came out; it didn't have to be stifled any more. He was past the point of caring if Meggie saw him weep too. He was just being present with his emotions, something that felt like a luxury he had rarely allowed himself to have in the presence of others until meeting this family. It felt cleansing somehow. After a time, the three of them slowly regained a sense of calm and picked one another up, heading back to the castle.

Cream was not the only death in the family. Only a fortnight later, Marian came into her father's room to find him stone cold. He must have died during the night. She quietly cried at his bed in grief…and in relief. She wished for Robin to console her but instead it would be the Avalons who cradled her in her grief. It was at least some consolation that just nights before Charlton's death, while she had been sitting with him, bored with her needlepoint, he had given her his blessing.

"Marian?"

Yes, Father?"

"Come, sit by me. I have something I want to say."

Marian got up from the chair she was in to sit on the bed. She sat across from him. He reached out his hand and she picked it up in both of hers and bent down to kiss it.

He smiled weakly. "You are such a good child, Marian, all a father could want."

She leaned her cheek against his hand, saying gently, "I am no child, Father."

He put both hands on her shoulders, gently pushing her so that she would lean back and he could see her face. Marian sat up as he said, "I know that. But as a father, you will always be my little girl." Before she could say anything, he swallowed and continued. "Marian, I know I am not long for this world. I know I have made you wait. Know that all I ever wanted was your happiness and to see you secured in marriage. I know I may not ever see that day. Perhaps you won't either. But if it is my blessing you need, you have it. Marry the rogue. Be happy. Perhaps that means more to you than a pretty title and a grand home." He coughed.

She squeezed his hand. "Thank you, Father."

Marian got up and went to the door calling out for help.

Anwen came scurrying up to her. "Was is it, Miss?"

"Would you please ask the family to come? My father has passed on. I do not know…" Marian tried to stay composed, "…what to do."

Anwen nodded. "I will go fetch them."

Marian went back into the room and sat on the bed next to her dead father, stroking his hand as the tears began to flow.

Robin had just been there for a visit and they agreed he would return in the
spring. Marian knew she would spend the winter with the Avalons. It was not
so bad. Though she longed for Robin, Morgaine, Gwenhwyfar, and Meggie
kept her company and in good spirits. The four friends read to one another,
took long walks, and went for rides. And on full moons she stole out with them
to sing and dance in the woods. It was magical. She felt a bit sheepish before
her father, knowing full well that she was participating in pagan rites and not
being a good Christian woman. Oh, but to have the wind upon her breasts,
to feel so wild and free. Truly, this could not be sinful. Occasionally, Marian
would even practice dancing with Morgaine and Anwen, but this highly erotic
form of dance made her uncomfortable before an audience. Gwenhwyfar had
said she tried it long ago but felt awkward and clunky in the movements. Still,
she too, would sometimes join in the lesson by singing and clapping, adding
to Col's drum beat.

Marian arose one morning, considering how much she was changing. She
was not just her father's daughter. She was coming into her own living in
Glastonbury. And now that her father was dead and could no longer judge her
actions as unbeseeming in a woman, Marian had another activity in mind;
something she was secretly itching to learn. She had been pondering her decision long enough. She approached Guy after breakfast.

"Guy, may we speak?"

"Of course, Marian."

"I have been thinking…"

He teased, "A dangerous pastime for a woman I hear."

She shoved his shoulder playfully, then said seriously as she searched his eyes, "I want to learn how to use a sword."

Guy raised his eyebrows. "Truly? Why?"

"Because in the spring, Robin will come for me and I will leave with him. I will return to Nottingham. I know it will not be an easy life. I do not want to be a burden on Robin. I want to be able to defend myself. And to see if I cannot do some good for the people we left."

Guy nodded. "I understand."

"Will you help me?"

Guy smiled. "I would be glad to and I think that you would learn best with someone whose life is dedicated to teaching weaponry."

Marian looked perplexed, knowing full well that Guy was a master of the sword.

At that moment Morgaine walked back into the hall. Guy caught his wife's movement and waved her to him. She approached.

He gave her a sideways hug, saying, "I think our friend would like to join you in your studies."

She looked at Guy, trying to read which studies he may be referring to. Then she looked at Marian in anticipation of insight.

Marian beheld her friend. She remembered back to the time with the carriage, when Morgaine had held a sword up to defend the carriage from Robin's men. She realized that Morgaine must know how to use a sword too. She started, "Morgaine, I want to learn how to use a sword."

Morgaine's eyes alit. "Truly?"

Guy bumped his wife playfully with his hip, "That's what I said."

Morgaine bumped him back and looked up at him, "Did you tell her of my father's edict?"

"Not yet. Why don't you tell her?"

Marian watched both of them with interest, "Tell me what?"

Morgaine happily proclaimed the good news to Marian, "Years ago, my father decreed that any person — man, woman or child — wishing to learn defense, could approach the Master of Arms and request lessons at no charge. Taharqa devotes some of his time, almost every day, to teaching those who wish to learn basic skills in the sword. He helps you choose one to work with that is right for your body."

Marian was mesmerized by her good fortune but still had to ask, "Why would the Duke allow this?"

Morgaine cocked her head in slight confusion. "Why not? The edict has been in place for generations, with each new duke proclaiming it. That way, we have a populace that can defend itself against invaders."

Marian looked bewildered, "Who would invade?"

Morgaine shrugged, "You never know. But this way, we empower our people that they may protect themselves and their homes. They would, of course, be no match against soldiers; but even a little practice may give one enough time to defend and retreat."

Marian nodded. It was a generous gesture. She was uncertain as to whether it would do more harm than good if Glastonbury actually had to fight to defend itself, but then, some defense is better than no defense. And London was several days' journey away if there was internal or external conflict.

Morgaine continued, "Besides, as a woman on the road, with thieves about, I would want to know how to protect myself."

"And you do."

"Yes. I have been training since I was a child. Taharqa and I trained together with the old Master of Arms, Sir Hammond. And now Taharqa is Master of Arms. He can train you." Morgaine's smile grew more mischievous as she said, "We could even spar together."

Guy laughed, "That sounds dangerous. Start with sticks. Marian's nasty with a poker."

Marian shook her head in denial and then remembered what he was referring to. She laughed, "Now, Guy that is not fair. It's all I had to defend myself."

He retorted, "And you did well." Guy then explained to Morgaine, "Marian was in a foul mood."

Marian interjected, "I was not. It was Matthew who put me in that mood."

Guy's smirk remained firmly planted on his face as he continued, "We were children. Matthew was trying to boss Marian."

"He was a prick."

"Yes he was. Anyway he's dead now. Marian finally had it. She went into her house and came back out with a poker. Matthew tried to take it from her but she managed to hold her own and severely jab him in the buttocks and then hit him on the head. He went home crying that day."

Marian was willful, "And I am not the least bit sorry. He was mean."

Morgaine quipped, "Well, Marian, it certainly sounds like you made your point."

The three laughed, Guy adding, "Well, I suppose we should not poke fun at the dead man for being the butt of this joke."

The three continued to laugh.

"This isn't enough."

The four Avalons sat around the collected monies and realized that no matter the good graces they experienced with Prince John, he would not accept less than what he had demanded in taxes. And then there was the matter of the taxes that his brother, King Richard, demanded. But they couldn't give what they didn't have. And their priority was to protect the people in their care, which meant that whatever they had must go to the ruler on the throne here in England, not one in some foreign country.

Guy moved his chair back, "I'll be right back." Guy climbed the stairs to his study, moved a brick, and grabbed a small sack. He returned, "Will this be enough?"

Gareth looked surprised and pleased. He pulled the drawstrings and whistled at the gold and silver.

He eyed Guy who responded, "My wealth is Glastonbury's wealth. I amassed this wealth through unscrupulous means. I know that. I cannot undo what I have done in the past. I cannot make up for it. But right here, right now, I can make a positive difference. In this short time that I have been here, I have quickly learned that a ruler's job is to sacrifice his needs for his people. Though truly, I have all I ever need: a devoted wife, a family, good food and good company, a place to call home. So surrendering this coin is of little sacrifice to me."

Morgaine beamed at her husband in adoration. He was truly a champion, she thought. He could rise to any occasion and meet the need. Her elation diminished suddenly as she considered what other needs he might be called to meet. But not now. Now, was the time to rejoice in his gift to the family, to the town?

CHAPTER 45

Falling into Winter

"OH LADY, I am not sure you are going to like it. It came out odd." Sarah, Morgaine's seamstress, was distressed over her latest creation.

"Let's see it."

Sarah brought the gown out and held it up so that Morgaine could see the full effect.

Morgaine smiled. "No, I like it. In fact, I love it. It looks like a winter forest. How did you manage it?"

"To be completely honest, My Lady, I am not sure. The creases in the folds seemed to have picked up extra dye and look dark gray whereas the rest of the dress is, as you see, silvery."

"It's perfect. Let's be sure of the fit as I will want to wear it to Prince John's annual party." Morgaine put the gown on and stood admiring her reflection in the polished metal mirror. It really did appear that she was dressed as a winter forest with bare branches against a moonlit forest. "Do you think you could repeat this with Guy's shirt?"

Sarah pondered, "Given it was unintentional, I will do my best."

Morgaine and Guy showed up to Prince John's annual party looking like a magical winter wonderland. There had been no way to get out of the invitation that read more like a command. Guy's silk shirt matched Morgaine's gown almost exactly. In addition, Sarah had decided to embroider silver branches on Guy's black wool overcoat. And if one was paying attention to the detail in the embroidery, one could make out the silhouette of a stag looking out from the winter forest landscape.

But that was not what Lord William de Wendenal was paying attention to; he was scrutinizing the face of a traitor, one who must be dealt with, and in a very painful way.

There was much animosity in the room and Guy would have liked nothing better than to leave. Several Black Knights pressed in upon Guy in an act of intimidation. Guy held his ground. He could feel William gloating behind him as he pressed into him, hissing in his ear, "Traitor."

Guy turned in the tight press to face William. "You had me beaten and threatened my new family when the Prince gave me leave. You have no right…"

"I have every right. You betrayed the brotherhood."

"I never would have, had you not threatened…"

"Your skyrta! The brotherhood should come first before any woman!"

Guy's eyes narrowed, he was done showing William any kindness. He stood tall and leaned in toward William, "Just remember, I could have told him it was you who gave the order. You may have lost two of your own…"

"Four! He rounded up Lane and Payton and had them executed as well."

"You still have your life," Guy shot back.

The venom in William's eyes should have been enough to make his former protégé back down, but it was not. Guy glared back at him. Swords might have been drawn if it were not for Prince John. He had been secretly watching the exchange. He knew William had been behind the plot. But William had his uses and he figured by executing the four Black Knights who had misguidedly been more loyal to the brotherhood than to the Prince would prove a good warning to William to stay in line.

The Prince entered the room with a majestic air, "Gentlemen, my comrades, speak with me."

Everyone watched as Prince John swept through and spun to sit dramatically upon his receiving room throne. All bowed. That brought the boil to a simmer. There were several plays for attention and much bantering.

It was hours later. Guy had wanted to go to bed but no one had been dismissed. Finally, Prince John feigned a yawn and rose to his feet. As he walked, it was clear he was searching the crowd. He found his quarry. "Lord Guy, walk with me."

Guy rose from his bow and followed the Prince out. Had Guy known what was in store for him he might not have been so relieved to leave that room. He might have thought the wolves' den was a safer place to be than in the company of the lion's brother. But then, even if he had thought to consider his options, he would have had to then conclude, when it came to the Prince, there were no options but to obey His Majesty's command.

CHAPTER 46

In the Prince's Bedchamber

THE PRINCE ADMIRED Guy's form; his muscles, his naked skin warmed by the firelight, his midnight hair, his brilliant blue eyes. "Surely, he is the most magnificent of my Black Knights," he mused to himself.

Guy bristled at John's touch. He was not sure he could handle this. He drank more wine, tasting the heather-laced alcohol and doing his best to lose himself.

Guy excused himself to go relieve himself. While he was away, John snuggled closer to Morgaine who had been brought into the room to await them and had been lounging next to the fire and her husband. She was also concerned about what was going to transpire this evening. She had been watching Guy drink, never seeing him lose himself in alcohol.

John whined in her ear, "He should love his Prince. Why does he resist me?"

Morgaine patted John's hand, "He does love you. Consider his loyalty to you. You just have an expanded sexuality. You take pleasure with both sexes."

John grinned wickedly, "Morgaine, my dear, you have a unique perspective."

Tenuously Morgaine added, "I am not sure Guy can love you the way you are wanting, My Prince."

Prince John was scolding, "Morgaine, he should love me in all ways. I am his ruler. Everyone should love me in the ways I desire. It is my birthright."

They looked at each other; Prince John's demeanor was very commanding. Morgaine knew there was nothing more she could say and there would be no redirection of the conversation, so she slowly lowered her eyes and looked down at the floor. Studying the stone had its merits. She recognized that John was not necessarily attracted to both sexes. This had everything to do with exerting power over others. That's not sex; that's control. What he had done to her, even though she didn't want it. Anger climbed to the surface as she remembered John commanding her to "love" him as he wished. She feared for her husband now. She could not see him taking this well.

Guy returned to see Morgaine and John cuddling. He was displeased, but knew there was not much they could do about their situation.

Morgaine, feeling his displeasure, called out to him in her mind, "Love, please do not abandon me to him. I am trying so desperately to make the best of this but I want to be alone with you. We cannot risk displeasing him but I…I can only be so charitable."

"I am sorry, Love. I did need to pee. I am here." Guy came over behind Morgaine to spoon her.

She was now in between both men. She was tired and wished to go to bed. Hoping that by feigning exhaustion they would be released, she yawned loudly. Guy followed suit. John could not help himself, by hearing and seeing their yawns, he yawned too.

"I suppose we are more tired than we thought. Tomorrow night perhaps." He brushed his hand at them in dismissal as he got up.

Upon exiting through the Prince's secret door to their bedroom, where John had strategically placed them, he added, "And my dears," Morgaine and Guy paused at the doorway, turning to him, "we shall dine together for supper."

Guy bowed and Morgaine curtsied with tired smiles upon their faces. Though they left the room, they both felt trapped. They sensed that John wanted something from them, something neither of them wanted to give.

The next morning they dined quietly with Evelyn and Gareth. The parents could tell their children were stressed. Evelyn laid her hand on Morgaine's. Morgaine shook her head, looking down.

"So we cannot dismiss ourselves this day, can we?" Evelyn questioned.

Morgaine shook her head again.

The evening came on too quickly. Morgaine and Guy made their best attempt to occupy their minds with more pleasant thoughts, but they had been left rattled knowing that the Prince wanted their affections.

They were summoned to the Prince's chambers where he had a wonderful spread of food for them. They ate cautiously.

The Prince sounded annoyed, "Come now, you two. I give you delectable treats for you to savor, not pick at."

"And we thank you most kindly, My Prince," Morgaine responded sweetly, adding, "It is just that I have been feeling a bit ill of late. I believe the child in my belly intends some changes to my diet."

John chuckled as Morgaine patted her abdomen. "Well, what would you have, my pet?" asks John in a jovial, accommodating voice.

"Oh, My Prince, the food is delicious. I am just eating slowly so that it doesn't make a repeat performance."

At that, the three of them broke out in laughter. Though if John had been paying attention, he would have heard the strain in Guy and Morgaine's voices.

After dinner they retired onto the furs and cushions the Prince had laid out closer to the fire. He had the fire burning hot. "Warm, is it not?" The Prince asked as he assessed when he could coerce them out of their clothing. He could see that Morgaine was already perspiring. He didn't want to spook his pretty pets, but he could see that he might have to exert some delicate force.

"Morgaine, are you showing yet under all that clothing?"

Morgaine groaned internally then answered the Prince playfully, "My Prince, I showed you last night and you remarked that you could hardly tell there was a small mound rising."

"Ah yes," John replied absentmindedly. There was a pause, then John slyly said, "If I stated I could hardly tell, then I must not have gotten a good look." John bit his bottom lip as he ogled Morgaine.

Guy meanwhile seethed. He felt powerless. He thought about the dagger hidden on his left ankle and how quickly he could reach for it and stab John in the gut with it.

The Prince redirected, "You two are so in love with one another. I want to see that love. I want to understand it. I want to touch it. Kiss each other."

They looked at John and then at each other. They touched each other's shoulders; putting their foreheads together, they breathed together and then kissed.

"Pretend he is not here," Morgaine called to Guy in her mind.

They tried to lose themselves in each other. They were feeling somewhat successful when John gathered himself close to them, tugging at their clothing.

"Disrobe," he crooned earnestly.

Guy could hear Morgaine as she uttered a prayer to herself. "I can do this. Be as a deep pool. He cannot harm my spirit; I shall prevail."

Guy looked into Morgaine's eyes. He swallowed nervously. He kissed the top of her forehead as he repeated the words to himself.

John caressed their skin as they kissed and caressed each other. They knelt on the furs, continuing to hold one another in each other's minds as they did with their bodies, when Guy's eyes went wild in rage and fear. John pulled Guy's hair back and forced him onto all fours with one knee pushing into the back of Guy's knee. The force of John's action pushed Guy down into Morgaine and Morgaine fell back, her back into her heels. It was most uncomfortable and it was only a blessing that she was flexible enough and could bend backwards that far.

Guy braced himself with his hands, as John crooned in his ear, "My stallion, my gorgeous pet, it is high time I took you for a ride." John thrust himself into Guy's backside and Guy felt his anus split in searing pain. As hard as Guy was a second ago while he touched his adoring wife, his penis went flaccid from the shock of being taken from behind. Guy bucked in an attempt to shake John off of him but that seemed only to make John all the more titillated. He held Guy fast by his hair and one arm, making it quite challenging to roll out of the hold without harming Morgaine and the baby. And as much as Guy should have been in self-preservation mode, his immediate instinct was to protect Morgaine over himself. He strained against John's weight on his back, but without crushing and rolling over Morgaine he was stuck. And she was in no position to move out of the way as pinned as she was between his arms and legs. He considered tilting his body to the side; that might throw John off balance and off of him, but it could also just enrage John into punishing Morgaine and Guy for Guy's disobedience. Still, the movement of his head toward his clothing and the hidden dagger he had secretly removed from his ankle gave him away.

John followed Guy's line of sight, considering what Guy might have hidden within his garments, and murmured in his ear, "Et, et, et. No, my pet. That would be unwise. You are mine. You cannot defy me. I will have you."

So, to protect Morgaine and his own life, he took John's vigorous thrusts, hating every second of it. In his disassociation from the moment, Guy's rage took over. He imagined placing all his weight on his hands while relieving the pressure from his leg so that he was able to free his leg enough to wrap behind John's leg, and in a twisting motion, unbalance John to fall backwards. With satisfaction, Guy heard John's knee twisting and crunching backwards as he shattered his knee. And as John fell, in midair Guy reached around with his hands to John's throat, and with all his weight he slammed John's head to the floor, crushing his throat. As John's head hit the stone floor there was a skull-shattering crack. Guy watched in gratification as the blood leaked out of John's skull.

Unfortunately, Guy was snapped back into reality: John smacked him on the thigh as if he were a horse being ridden. He bucked in instinctual response.

Meanwhile, Morgaine, unable to maneuver out from beneath the two men, and seeing what Guy was considering doing to John, called out into Guy's mind, "Guy! Beloved! Look at me!"

His eyes looked at her but they were out of focus. Pained and humiliated at being dominated by another man, he focused internally on surviving the experience. He wanted to scream at John, GET OFF OF ME, but he held his tongue. He desperately wanted to overtake John and break his neck, but some part of him knew that would surely bring about his death and Morgaine's. There was no commanding the Prince; the Prince was the one who commanded. Guy ground his teeth in hatred as John ground his body into Guy's backside.

Morgaine called out to him in his mind; her voice like a waterfall plunging him into a deep, serene pool, "Beloved, feel no shame. This is not your choice. Breathe. Focus only on me. Look only at me. Breathe. I love you. I love you. I love you." She continued to repeat her thoughts to him. "Come into me," she beckoned him and he felt his spirit lift and move into her body. He sensed her spirit wrapping around his like the flutter of so many wings upon the water. He hardly felt what was happening to his body now.

John was overstimulated by the complete ecstasy of having his way with his pretty stallion and the act was over in minutes. John crooned to Guy, "There now, my pet: my strong and steady steed." He tousled Guy's hair and then got up. Yawning and scratching himself, he poured himself some wine and drank. He looked at the couple on the floor, a most disconcerting grin on his face.

Guy was still on all fours, breathing heavy, doing his best to hold himself in check and not spring up to pummel John. He had to keep reminding himself that physically fighting John would only bring about his death, and possibly Morgaine's. He looked at Morgaine. She could see the pain and anguish on his face. She nodded her head once as a question about if he could move his hands. Guy gingerly started shifting his weight back to his knees, slowly removing his hands from the floor and onto his thighs. Oh, but his anus hurt. And his back had seized up. And his thighs burned. He couldn't lean back anymore. He hung in position, gritting his teeth, whispering something to himself. As Morgaine propped herself on elbows and cautiously swung her numb and tingly legs out from underneath her, she could barely hear, "You will survive this." Over and over, he said this to himself. His eyes were now closed and he had gone completely inside himself. She could tell he was forcing himself into some sort of trance that kept him still. She remembered that force of will. She felt it now as she wished she could kill John with her thoughts. Stab him with her eyes. She slid herself out from underneath Guy, doing her best not to touch or disturb him as she could tell he was at the edge of some mental cliff.

Morgaine slowly stood up and split her attention away from Guy, seeing an opportunity as the Prince downed another cup of wine. She couldn't kill

John but...Her voice lulled, "My Prince, may we retire to our chamber? My body is aching and I do not want to distress the baby."

The Prince looked at them as she smiled tiredly pushing her will upon him as best she could. "Yes, of course, we must consider the baby. You may retire." He dismissed them with a few flicks of the wrist.

"Thank you, my Prince." She added, again in her lulling voice, "We should be leaving on the morrow..."

John looked at her, shaking his head in a sad, entranced voice, "Oh, no, not on the morrow. Stay another night. I insist."

Morgaine was more than annoyed that John was refusing to accept the push but she could do no more. She must attend to her husband. Morgaine nodded then prodded Guy, saying to him internally, "Look at him. Do not let him think you are beaten."

Guy breathed deeply and pushed himself up and off the floor. He turned to face John, showing himself in his full naked glory to the Prince. He stood there looking at John for a moment. John noticed Guy stand up, and turned his head to face his stallion, his nostrils flaring in excitement at Guy's beauty.

But Guy's eyes narrowed and John was suddenly aware that Guy was not happy. "Oh, my beautiful stallion, was that too much?"

Guy just looked at him and continued to breathe slowly.

Morgaine, seeing that the situation had the potential to deteriorate rapidly, patted Guy's stomach gently to center him, "Come, Love, take me to bed."

They bowed to the Prince, donned their robes, and left through the door to their adjoining room.

As John retired to bed and a happy, triumphant sleep, Guy called out to a servant to fill his bath. The servant did not protest at the lateness of the hour, but simply complied. Guy leaned over the bed while the water was poured. Morgaine rubbed his back gently.

The servant bowed as he finished filling the tub by the fire. Morgaine dismissed him and guided Guy to the bath. Once the door was closed for the last time, Guy finally let the enraged tears fall. Morgaine climbed into the bath with him, water spilling over the edge as she gently hovered over him.

Behind a clenched, despairing voice, Guy cried out, "I feel so violated!"
Morgaine's eyes welled up. "I know."

"I hate him."

"I know."

Guy looked at her, "Morgaine, how did you bear it?"

Her tears fell, "I am not sure. I just knew I had to. I trusted in your love
for me. And, I knew you were waiting for me."

"You were right there for me as you are now, loving me. I see no judgment
in your eyes and I felt none while we shared your body. How did you do that?
You gave me respite from my pain. Thank you, Beloved. May I always do the
same."

She kissed his forehead and then fully on the mouth, whispering, "I love
you."

The water was cool by the time Guy felt he could move again. He was sick and
frozen with a wretched mixture of humiliation, grief, and anger. Morgaine
just sat there in the tub with him. A memory came back to him unbidden. It
was a different woman lying next to him. He had been rough with her but still
she stayed by him. He wanted Marian but she would not have him, but Caron
would. But he did not want Caron in that way, until she let him know she
would take whatever he was willing to give her. He knew now that her hope
was to be enough of a distraction that he would grow to love her. But he did
not love her in the way she wanted; she was a childhood friend. He thought of
how he was with her and felt remorse. And then a flood of remorse and anguish saturated his thoughts, all the things he thought he had done wrong that
he must have deserved what had just happened to him. "Forgive me," he wept.

Morgaine heard him, felt the flood in his mind, and roused herself, "Hush.
All is well between you two. Remember? She forgave you. And I forgive you
for taking another woman to bed when you desired someone else. And I forgive you for your unkindness to others. And I forgive for not rescuing me
from John because you could not without jeopardizing our very lives. And I

forgive you for being taken by the Prince. Again, you had no choice without risking our lives. Now please, sweetheart, forgive yourself. You do not deserve pain. You did not deserve to be violated or dominated. This is just one of those terrible, impossible situations that we have to manage to get through. And we can, together."

They looked at one another and kissed each other tenderly. Gratitude registered momentarily in his eyes.

After a long pause, Morgaine added, "Though I must say, I cannot stand one more moment in this tub so we must get out of it…together."

He smiled wanly at her attempt to lighten the mood. They helped each other out of the bath and clambered into bed, intertwined around each other for comfort and security.

CHAPTER 47

Devising How to Be
Dearly-Departed Guests

"WE NEED TO get out of here!" Guy longed for home and as he did a haze formed in front of his eyes.

Morgaine looked on in astonishment, as it appeared her husband was starting to vanish from her eyes. She pulled at him, "No, my love. No!"

He shook his head to clear the vision of the Apple Orchard before him, saying bewilderedly, "I had no idea I could do that on my own."

Morgaine was perplexed. She asked, "Did Rainer feed you an enchanted apple?"

"Not that I know of."

"Maybe when you held the one meant for Midnight?"

Guy thought back to that time. It felt so long ago. "Perhaps….Oh, I actually had that apple in my mouth before I gave it to Midnight."

Morgaine looked at him questioningly.

Guy shrugged. "It's a thing I do with Midnight, a little tease."

Morgaine went on, "Well, we can't simply disappear; it would bring John down on Glastonbury." She didn't mean to sound callous but she could tell by the expression on her husband's face that he was teetering over some horrible abyss. She realized he might not be able to endure being raped again. And really, who could? His mind was ready to snap.

His eyes, still haunted as he whispered hoarsely, his voice edgy and nearing panic, "Well, what can we do Morgaine? I don't think I can take that again."

Morgaine gently touched her husband's hand. "I tried pushing him last night. He's budged before. But not last night. Darling, he wanted you something fierce. You were like a…"

"Conquest," Guy said flatly.

"Yes," responded Morgaine with remorse. She paused, then, "We need to enlist the others to help us push our will."

"We can do that?" She nodded. "Well, why didn't we do it before last night?" She looked hurt. Guy added, "I am not blaming you, Love. I just want to go home."

Morgaine and Guy breakfasted in Evelyn and Gareth's room. Voices were low and barely audible as Morgaine delicately explained the situation that they were stuck there at least one more night. Guy didn't want anyone knowing what had happened and Morgaine did all she could to avoid giving details to her parents who continued to press on them in concern.

"Should I approach him?" asked Gareth.

"I am not sure, Father. I fear he may dismiss the two of you but keep Guy and me here at court."

Guy's eyes were showing the strain and Evelyn was piecing together John's infatuation, not just with her daughter, but now with her son-in-law too. While observing Guy, Evelyn asked, "And Morgaine, you say the enchantment did not work?"

Morgaine shook her head. "I need more…involvement. He let us leave to go to bed, but he refused me when I said that we would be leaving today."

Evelyn nodded, "Prepare yourself this day and make yourself…interesting to John. Then draw upon all the energies you can. As soon as I feel what you are doing, I will assist."

Morgaine nodded.

Evelyn hated to add this as she could see their distress, "As a family, we have gone on so long because we have gone on unnoticed. We can't afford too many questions about our rights to Glastonbury. We must get out of here."

Three heads nodded in agreement.

Morgaine and Guy retired back to their room to talk more about their strategy, while Gareth and Evelyn decided it was best to keep themselves scarce so as not to engage with the Prince or anyone else.

Morgaine looked disgusted as she said, "I have an idea."

Guy looked at her, saying glumly, "I can see by the look on your face that I am not going to like it."

"Neither of us are going to like it but it is the most likely thing to work."

"What?"

"I have to…see the Prince."

Guy looked suspicious but Morgaine continued, "The only time I met with success in pushing him was after he fucked me. He was happy and sleepy."

"What about last night?"

"Well, we were allowed to leave the room, weren't we?"

"Yes, but…"

"I was pushing, Love. At the time, all I wanted was for us to get out of that room." There was hurt in her voice. She felt blamed for not doing enough.

Guy looked at her, hearing her hurt. "I am sorry, Morgaine. I am not blaming you. I just don't understand this gift of yours or how it works."

"It's not a talent I exercise. Remember when you first asked me if I could force another and I said I wasn't sure? Well, that was true. John was the first. I was mad but had found my center. I drew in all the energy I could to have my way. It worked…once he was sated."

"But that would mean…oh no Morgaine…"

"Maybe I can sate him another way. I don't want his seed sloshing around our child."

Guy shuddered, looking repulsed.

"Please know I would much rather do it your way and just disappear back to the Orchard. But we have to be given leave now."

Guy closed his eyes, his face clenched.

She pressed on, "Think, Love. You are so good at weighing the variables."

He tried not to shout, "You are not a variable!"

She nodded, tears in her eyes.

Guy went on, "I don't want to be strategic if it means he takes either one of us again. How is it strong to allow ourselves to be taken?"

Lips quivering with emotion, she said, "Because we get to live another day together."

Guy took a big breath and exhaled forcibly. Morgaine waited as she watched her husband go through scenarios in his mind. Finally he said, "I hate this. There is no good alternative."

Morgaine spoke gently, "If it gets us all out of here alive…Please, my love. I need you to be strong for me. I can't do this without your strength."

"It is not strong to allow you to be taken."

"And in so many cases I would agree with you, but if this gets us home?"

"But he could just decide to keep us around as pets. It could backfire."

She nodded, "This is why I need to prepare. You bore the pain last night to protect me. But we both were in such shock and I didn't have the ability to draw on all that I needed to…but I will. I promise. I can do this."

"I hate this."

"I know. I do too. I just want to go home. I hate it here at court. It… frightens me."

Guy looked surprised. "Frightens you? That is not a word I imagined you would use to describe court. You seemed in your element, though I could tell you were not your usual self. You appeared more guarded yesterday."

Morgaine nodded. "I don't like all the scheming voices. It is alarming how many frightened, angry people there are here. Last year I was falling in love and by focusing on you, the other voices diminished."

Guy found his smile at her last statement. Then he thought back to the day when she introduced him to Brighid in the kitchen and how life seemed so gentle and sweet in Glastonbury castle, where he swore that he would not want her to have to live under such conditions as he had at Nottingham with all the fear and hate. He relented, "Very well, Morgaine, let's prepare."

Guy stayed in their room while Morgaine went to find John. She found him in the company of several guests. His eyes perked up when he saw Morgaine and he motioned to her to come attend him. Morgaine curtsied low. John looked around searching. "Where is the Lord Guy?"

"My husband is feeling unwell."

"Ah. Too bad. Perhaps he will feel better by this evening."

"Perhaps." She then started gathering in, pulling in the energies within the castle; even the tapestries lifted slightly off the walls, as if a breeze came in from behind them. She looked at John, stating in her mind to him, "Walk with me."

He eyed her slyly as if a delicious idea was coming to him. He stood up. Everyone else stood up bowing. His eyes on Morgaine, "I think I need some fresh air. Lady Morgaine, will you accompany me?"

"It would be my pleasure, Your Highness."

He offered her his hand and she placed her hand on his, and he escorted her out of the room. There was much whispering behind them, but neither seemed to care.

Though it was chilly, they did a brisk walk around one of the smaller gardens. There was an easy silence between them. Morgaine continued to pull in the strength she would need. Evelyn, Gareth and Guy all felt it. Evelyn knew this might draw some attention from anyone sensitive to magic but that couldn't be helped. Given it was the first time here, Morgaine might not be found out. Evelyn split her attention to draw a protection spell around the family and to cloak their identity.

John broke the silence, "How is Guy?"

Morgaine had not expected this question but it did not matter, she was ready. She teased, "My vigorous Prince..." she began.

John's mouth formed an impish smile at that. He whispered excitedly, "I didn't break him, did I?"

In a conspiring tone she responded, "No. He is just... recovering."

"Ah."

She began again, "I am enjoying our walk." She thought to say more but then thought better, not wanting to lead him down a memory path and consider her staying on to take more walks.

The Prince simply nodded.

She tried hard not to be revolted as she pushed a thought into his mind, "Suck me."

John's eyes narrowed in mischief. He drew her in between the shrubbery. "Morgaine dear, be a love and suck on me."

She looked at him in mock shock, "How crude."

He laughed, "Do as I command; don't be rude."

She feigned a giggle, her voice then altered, again lulling, an enchantment at work, "Yes, my Prince." She knelt down, unfastening his trousers. As she did, she kissed the fabric that held his hardening cock. "It's just his manhood," she thought, "It can't hurt me if I don't let it. Relax." She took hold of his cock and kissed it.

"Oh Morgaine, my dear, that feels delicious. Yesssssss." John closed his eyes and braced his legs, slightly propping himself up against the evergreen.

Morgaine started licking and sucking him, as she knew it would give him pleasure. While one hand was helping the process, her other hand dipped into her cleavage and drew out a handkerchief, holding it at the ready. Longer strokes made him moan. She pushed thoughts into his mind, "They can go after this. I just need this."

"Mmmm," was all she heard from him. She drew more energy from her surroundings. It was almost as if the trees' branches leaned in toward her. "This is all I wanted from them. They need to leave."

A moaning "yes," was all he said.

Morgaine was a bit exasperated by this point but she followed this task through to its completion, continuing to press into his mind.

"Oh yes," John exclaimed as he climaxed.

"Blech," she thought, doing her best not to gag as that would be unseemly. She held the kerchief to her mouth and spit the contents into it. Though soggy, she placed it back in her bosom to deal with later. She slowly got up and faced him eye to eye. She smiled. He smiled. She lulled, "I am so glad I got to say goodbye in this way."

His eyes glazed over and he droned, "Yes, I am glad you said goodbye this way."

She purred, "My family and I have so enjoyed your hospitality. We appreciate your trust in us."

He nodded, "Yes, I trust you."

She continued her lulling voice, "We will be leaving on the morrow."

He nodded, "Yes of course. You need to get back. Pity though. I am so fond of you."

"You can continue to be fond of us from afar. And of course we are fond of you." She added, "My baby must be born in Glastonbury."

John continued to nod his head, "Of course. Babies should be born at home."

"Goodbye, My Prince."

"Goodbye, My Lady."

Morgaine kissed John on the cheek, asking, "Walk me in? It's chilly out here."

John smiled, coming back into himself, and out of the enchantment, "It would be my pleasure."

Upon reaching the castle, Morgaine reiterated her goodbye. "My family shall be taking our leave back to Glastonbury on the morrow. We thank you so much for having us."

Prince John patted Morgaine's hand, "My Lady, it has been a pleasure." He kissed her hand and she curtsied. She was hardly up from the pose before the throngs cloistered in around him, drawing him away.

Morgaine fled swiftly back to her room. She walked in and found Guy stretched out on the bed where she left him. "Do you trust me?" she asked.

"With my body and my soul," he replied.

"I did a vile thing."

"It is no vile thing to help get us the hell out of here."

"Oh, but you don't know what else I did."

"What did you do?" She pulled out her kerchief.

He eyed it dubiously.

"This is soaked with his seed."

"What do you plan on doing with it?"

"I haven't decided. But I thought it might come in handy."

Guy wrinkled his nose and looked at the object distastefully, but got up and came to her side, saying in a wicked colluding voice, "I am sure we can think up something to do with it."

It was on the ride back home when the four of them left the road and secreted into the woods not far from the boundaries of Glastonbury. Rainer was there to meet them while the other Guardians kept watch. The five of them lit a fire. Rainer had a bundle of dried herbs with him. He brought out the Rue, Nettle, Vervain and Agrimony. He looked in four pairs of eyes, asking plainly, "Do you accept the consequences of your actions?"

They all nodded grimly. Their thoughts were in alignment. Though protection of the realm was paramount, neither could they afford to lose a family member to the clutches of Prince John. Nor could they have John's continued interest in the family. One transgression and all could be lost. They could not possibly appease his appetite forever. They must protect themselves. He must be banished.

Though Guy had never cast a spell, he guessed he was about to, and he was willing to do whatever it took to protect himself and his family from John. He considered that the spell could include John's prick falling off but recognized that the power to conquer others could come in so many other forms. So despite his hatred for being raped by John, Guy did not add this specification to the spell.

Rainer asked, "Do you have something of his?"

Morgaine nodded. She pulled the dried cloth from her bosom. "It is soaked with his seed."

Gareth's and Evelyn's eyebrows rose but they said nothing. All they knew was that Morgaine had done something to get them all out of there alive. Still,

Evelyn's stomach became queasy as she thought about what her daughter must have had to do.

"That prick!" she spat silently. Would that it fall off. She looked at Guy, sensing he had the same thought.

Rainer took a pinch of each herb — the Agrimony, Nettle, Rue, and Vervain — and placed it into the open cloth in Morgaine's hands. As he placed each pinch of herb into the cloth, he stated quietly the name of the herb, followed by "protect us and banish Prince John from our bodies and our lands."

With all the herbs in the cloth, Morgaine folded it up. In that moment Evelyn got up, scanning the woods. They all waited as she went to an Ash tree, asked its permission, took out a small knife from the side of her gown, and flaked off some bark. Guy was surprised to see that Evelyn had a knife hidden on her person. He had not expected that of her. It seemed to have come from the folds of her gown. He studied her gown and saw part of a discreet pouch tied to a cord around her waist. It reminded him that he, too, wore a hidden weapon.

She returned with the Ash bark. She held it in her hand and nodded to Morgaine and Rainer to continue.

Rainer touched Morgaine's back, saying, "Cast the bundle into the fire."

She did. They all watched the cloth and herbs burn. Evelyn added the Ash bark then held out her hands to each side. They all touched hands palm to palm around the fire creating a circle. Evelyn started up a chant, "Come no farther." While the four chanted, Rainer added his voice and a command on top of the chant —

"Spirits protect us from harm. Send Prince John's affections back on himself. Quell his lust and let him linger no longer. No thought of the Avalons or of Glastonbury. Do not cross into the realm. You are not welcome, John. We banish you, John. Come no farther."

Morgaine added, with an edge of anger in her voice, "Spirits protect me. I banish you, John from my body. You cannot hurt me."

Guy looked at Morgaine then repeated her words forcefully as he gazed back at the fire. "Spirits protect me. I banish you, John from my body. You cannot hurt me."

As he spoke the words, Evelyn was now sure that John had taken Guy too. Her heart wept that her new son had been violated so. She grieved for both Morgaine and Guy.

They watched the fire burn the cloth into ashes. As the fire had been made intentionally small, it did not take too long for the wood to burn to charcoal and then ash. Rainer poured water on the burning coals, which spit and sizzled. He stirred the coals. He then brought out his plate from his pack. He shoveled as much of the ash and coal as he could onto it then walked back out to the road. He did a banishing sign in the direction they had come from and then sprinkled the ash and coals across the road. He came back to the circle and scooped up another load, repeating what he did. He did this three times as the family looked on. Then the five of them came back out onto the road, stretching across it. Guy looked to Rainer and then to Evelyn to see what would come next. Evelyn took in a deep breath as she held her hands together in front of her face. When she exhaled she did so forcefully and threw her arms out in front of her, palms out, signaling "stop". They all repeated her gesture three times. Then they turned around to let the energy lie across the road as a barrier; the spell was cast. The Avalons climbed back into their carriage and continued onward toward home.

CHAPTER 48

Warm Bodies

SNOW COVERED THE land and the blanket of white seemed to clear the Avalons' hearts of woe. It was like a new passage could be written, a blank page to fill with happy moments, preparations for the Winter Solstice, and much singing and dancing.

Guy came home in quite a bit of pain. His back was aching badly after a fall he had taken while hunting. It was a stupid accident. He slipped on a patch of ice and fell backwards, his back hitting a small boulder behind him. He was bruised but would mend. His ego was more bruised, his fellow hunters having seen it. They had helped him back home. Anwen brought several hot kettles of water for his bath and then left the couple alone. He soaked and listened to Morgaine as she read to him.

When he got out of the bath, she lovingly dried him and took his hands to bring him to the bed. "Lie down, Love. Let me work the soreness out of your back."

Guy sprawled across their bed as Morgaine gently rubbed oil infused with herbs into his back. She then left his back alone and worked more deeply on the knots in his neck and shoulders. Morgaine hummed as she worked and he could feel himself drifting into a feeling of peace. How did I ever deserve this, he wondered? I fought for money and power and it brought me no happiness, only some empty satisfaction I was doing better than Robin. How stupid. Now I am able to just be myself and I have everything I ever wanted. I didn't have to be mean or bullying to obtain any of this. Love brought me

398

home. Love gave me success. He sighed and Morgaine smiled as she stroked her husband's muscular frame.

Elsewhere in the castle…

Anwen tiptoed up behind Col as he sat by the fire gently thrumming on his thighs, listening to a beat inside his head. He stopped and turned. "Anwen?"

"Aw, how did you know? I was real quiet. Did you hear me?"

"No, I smelled you."

"Smelled me?" Anwen had a mixture of shock and mock disgust in her voice.

"My sweet, I can pick out your scent from across a room. You smell of the sweet cream you like to drink. Yummy."

Anwen giggled and her whole fleshy body jiggled in delight. She came to him, kneeling beside him to give him a hug. At the invitation, he wrapped his arms around her and held her tight. He then ran his hands up and down her torso. "You are so beautiful."

"How would you know? You can't see me."

"Oh, but I can. I can see you by touching you. You feel beautiful, luxurious, rich."

Anwen giggled again.

Brighid and Sophie did not hear Anwen's giggles from where they were, which was in Brighid's room near the kitchen. The premise, of course, was all about keeping warm. But under the covers, sweet friction created quite a lot of heat. The young women came up for air from beneath the covers. Giggling and kissing, they held each other's faces delicately by fingertips.

"I think the salt from the venison is coming out your pores," teased Brighid.

"Oh yes? How can you tell?"

"You taste salty…here," Brighid teased as she drew her fingers down under the covers and swirled them around in the folds of Sophie's nether region.

"Ohhh," was all Sophie could answer at that point as her body arched in pleasure.

Meanwhile, a certain guard was about to be seduced at the other end of the castle. Aelred, a tall, muscular brunette was ending his evening patrol and walking toward the guards' quarters. As he walked, he imagined his masked friend sauntering toward him. Though rarely slinking about in the castle, this particular Guardian was known to drop in for unannounced visits. And when he did, it seemed he would simply appear. One could be walking around a corner and there he was...and there he was.

Rainer approached Aelred from the opposite direction, sauntering like a wild cat. The two closed the gap between them and Rainer took Aelred by the shoulders and pulled him in to kiss him. Aelred's loins burned with a passion that was easily fanned by his mysterious friend. As Rainer bit his lip, Aelred pulled Rainer's head back by the hair exposing his throat. He kissed his lover's chin and down his neck. Rainer then pulled his head forward and his shadow loomed over Aelred. The antlers of the mask flickered in the torchlight.

"Come," said Rainer huskily as he drew Aelred down the hall and around a corner that did not seem to be there but a moment before.

And still elsewhere in the castle, Gwenhwyfar had snuck out of her room after her boys fell asleep, praying Neirin would sleep through this night. He had gotten much better over the last several months so she felt she could finally trust the chance. She scooted down the cold halls quickly and quietly, then rapped on a door.

Taharqa opened it and smiled widely. "You came."

She giggled mischievously, "Not yet." And then fell into his arms.

"Do you hear that?" Gareth questioned.

Evelyn strained her ears. They were cuddling in bed, keeping each other warm. "What I am listening for, Love?"

"It's the sound of sex. There are many people having sex in this castle."

"Really?" Evelyn questioned in mock astonishment. "Sex? On a cold December night?"

"Yes."

"Well, as Lord and Lady of this castle, what should we do about it?"

Gareth, leaned over and nibbled on his wife's ear, chuckling, "We should join them."

"Oh, my sweet Bacchus," moaned Evelyn.

Gareth exclaimed as she placed her chilled hands on his growing member, "Iieee!" Gareth winced, then regrouped. "Come! The night is younger than we. Join me in some revelry."

The older couple kissed and slid their hands along one other's frame, crooning. Aging aches fled as the Lord and Lady began to dine on each other in extreme bliss.

CHAPTER 49

1193 January Spies on February

INTRIGUE HAS ITS way of developing out of sheer boredom.

"Quelles nouvelles, ma douce?" ("What news, my sweet?")

Why Monsieur Rochefort continued to snoop around here was beyond her. She never gave him anything juicy enough to know what to do with. And Sophie was annoyed at being called "my sweet" by this lecherous man. She wondered: did she really owe the French anything? They put her here in this wild land of England. At first she complied, but she wasn't given access to know anything that might be of value. Then, as she quickly grew to love her mistress, the Duchess, she had reservations about giving this man any information regardless of its possible value. "Je n'ai rien à vous announcer," ("I have nothing to report") she stated demurely.

"Menteuse. Dis-moi ce que tu sais!" ("Liar. Tell me what you know!")

She really wasn't sure what to say to get the man to leave her be. "Il n'y a rien à dire. La famille n'a pas encore décidé." ("There is nothing to tell. The family hasn't decided yet.") This was untrue and she knew it. Then she added, as if this was supposed to be important information, "On parle tout simplement de vouloir la paix dans la région." ("They talk of wishing there was peace in the land.") This was true.

However, the Monsieur was bored. "Quel ennui." ("How dull.")

Sophie wondered if she could just end this uncomfortable conversation now. "Puis-je me retirer?" ("May I go?")

The scheming Monsieur Rochefort placed a coin in her hand, stating, "Quand tu auras de vraies nouvelles à m'annoncer, tu en recevras plus." ("Have some real news to report and you shall have more.") He thought that money would be motivation to keep her in his services. He was unknowingly mistaken. And it didn't help his case any as he gave her a kiss full on the mouth, patted her bottom, and sent her on her way.

As she walked away, she muttered under her breath, "Dégueulasse!" (Disgusting!)

Guy listened in secret and he, too, was disgusted. He hadn't meant to come upon them. It just seemed that he and Sophie happened to be creeping around the same underused passages of the castle. At least Sophie gave nothing away. He let the Frenchman disappear down the corridor still considering what was to be done about him. Meanwhile, something had to be done about Sophie. He stayed hidden behind the corner and waited for her. There was no other option but to go the way of the Frenchman or come back to where Guy had planted himself.

As Sophie came around the corner, she was surprised to come across Guy leaning against the wall, arms folded across his chest. She had almost bumped into him, but managed to stop short. She curtsied, "My Lord."

She was about to continue walking when he stopped her with his words, "Que faites-vous là, Sophie?" ("What is your reason for being here, Sophie?")

Sophie was shaken, not only that Guy had just grabbed hold of her wrist with lightning flash speed, but also that he spoke French to her. She fretted that he had overheard her with the nasty little Frenchman. She pretended not to understand. "What do you mean, My Lord," she asked in English?

He responded in French, "Vous le savez bien." ("You know what.")

Sophie heaved a sigh.

Guy could tell from her conquered sigh that she would not bolt, and let go of her wrist.

She rubbed at the soreness, saying, "Monsieur Rochefort brought me here from the French court. He presented me as a gift to the Duchess. As you may have overheard, I am supposed to be a spy. But you could hear for yourself that I am not."

Guy nodded but was unconvinced.

"Please, My Lord. If you heard, then you know I gave no secrets away."

Guy's eyes narrowed, "What do you think you know about this family, that you think you are hiding from the man to whom you were speaking?" Guy had seen the Monsieur before. He vaguely remembered he had been at the wedding and engaged in a small banter with Prince John. But Guy had not seen him skulking in the corridors unattended before.

Sophie searched Guy's eyes wondering what to say. He could be so hard to read. He generally appeared to be a kind man and Brighid spoke well of him, how adoring he was with Morgaine, which she, too, had noticed. She responded to Guy's question, only slightly looking up at him from a bowed head, "I know the family is not Christian," she paused. "But still you are good people. I do not know how that can be. But I love my mistress. She is good to me. That is all that matters."

Guy nodded again, assessing Sophie. "And what would you do for more coin?"

Sophie shook her head. "Please, I..."

In another time Guy might have simply killed her and not bothered to give her any more chances. Instead, he took her by the arm, commanding, "Let's have a visit with the Duchess, shall we?" as he led her to Evelyn's receiving room.

Guy knocked on the door and then entered Evelyn's receiving room. Guy still held Sophie's arm as he led her in to stand before the Duchess.

Evelyn looked perplexed. "Guy? Sophie?"

Sophie curtsied as low as she could with Guy still holding her arm.

Guy bowed and then started, "Evelyn, I caught Sophie in secret conversation with Monsieur Rochefort, the French dignitary who is visiting. She is a spy."

"Indeed?"

Sophie looked like a rabbit frozen with fear.

Evelyn sounded slightly exasperated, "Oh, for Goddess sake, Guy. Let the poor woman go."

Guy released his grip on Sophie and Sophie curtsied again, rubbing her sore arm.

Evelyn sighed. "Sophie, what did you tell Monsieur Rochefort?"

Sophie shook her head, "Nothing, Mistress. I keep your secrets. I promise."

Evelyn looked to Guy, "What did you hear?"

"Monsieur Rochefort offered her more coin if she came to him with more information on the family. It is obvious he wants to know our political leanings. To Sophie's credit she stated that we have not chosen a side. What concerned me was the bribe."

Evelyn turned back to Sophie, "Did you take his coin?"

Sophie nodded.

"If he offered you more, would you betray me?"

Sophie shook her head.

"Can I still trust you?"

Sophie nodded her head vigorously, adding, "Please do not send me back, Your Grace. I would rather die. I am happy here. I know you are good people. I do not understand your ways but I see that you are good…" Sophie realized she was running at the mouth and fell silent, bowing her head.

Evelyn commanded, "Come here, Sophie." Evelyn's arms were outstretched and Sophie allowed herself to fall into them, kissing Evelyn's hands.

Guy looked on incredulously. "That's it?"

Evelyn nodded.

"But she was sent here as a spy."

"And my dear son, you were once a villain in league with a devil of a different sort. Observe how much you have changed. I know both of your hearts. I know Sophie was sent to me as a spy. A gift? From the French court? Please. I know they wanted information, I just did not know what information. As Sophie and I began to trust one another, she has been sharing with me what Monsieur Rochefort wants. She does not tell him anything I do not want her to say, for she knows my justice would be swift and unyielding. Is that not correct, Sophie?"

Sophie's head, still in Evelyn's lap, nodded. Evelyn patted Sophie's head and then brought her hand under Sophie's chin, gently forcing Sophie to look up at her. Evelyn looked intently into Sophie's eyes. Sophie felt a sense of awe. If she didn't know any better, she would have thought she was looking into the face of God. But that was blasphemous. But then so much that went on here was blasphemous. And yet the family was kind to her and life was good here. And they accepted her, sinner that she was. But looking at Evelyn was like looking at the Mother Mary and she felt forgiven. As she gazed at the Duchess she thought, "I swear, I swear on my life that I shall always be true to you, My Lady." She did not need to speak this. Evelyn heard her. She did not know that Evelyn heard, but she did feel understood by this greater woman than she. Evelyn bent over and kissed the top of Sophie's forehead and then raised her head looking triumphantly at Guy. Guy nodded. He witnessed the sincere devotion Sophie displayed toward Evelyn and that had to be good enough for him. He approached and laid a hand on Sophie.

Guy could feel Sophie recoil slightly in fear but she stayed in place as he said, "My apologies, Miss. I can see your devotion is most earnest. I will trust My Lady in this matter."

Sophie turned to face Guy and then bowed her head, "Thank you," was all she said. She was still wary of him.

Turning to a new insight, Evelyn inquired while Sophie was still at her lap, "Guy, how did you learn French?" Though not surprised, Evelyn wondered.

Guy shrugged in response, "How else? My mother. But she taught my sister and me in secret, when Father wasn't around. He wanted us to grow up English. I think my mother always had hopes that we would return to France and serve there. But I really had no interest in that."

"Why not?"

Guy glanced at Sophie, considering the length and breadth of conversations that servants overheard, but then responded to Evelyn, realizing it didn't matter. "To be honest, I am not sure. I had never been to France. There was no allure. I agreed with my father that we were as English as we could be. But I learned French to make my mother happy. And then William capitalized on my ability to speak French. He thought it would make me a better spy." He eyed Sophie who quickly turned her head back to study the folds of Evelyn's gown. Guy continued, "Many royal families who habituate London and seek proximity to the throne speak the language."

Evelyn shrugged. She couldn't be bothered. This was England and she refused to speak anything but the native tongues, English — obviously, and Fegan, the language of the Faie — not so obviously. Fegan, in English, meant, "To join," and that is exactly what Evelyn's mission continued to be: to join this Land's inhabitants, those who clung close to this Land, to make them stronger.

CHAPTER 50

—— ✖ ——

Gwenhwyfar's Boys Are Introduced to a Family Tradition

It was a frigid winter night as Morgaine crept into Gwenhwyfar's bedroom. She knelt beside her friend and gently rubbed her cheek.

Gwenhwyfar's eyes fluttered in the dark. She asked sleepily, "Is it time?"

Morgaine whispered back, "Yes."

"Let us wake the boys," Gwenhwyfar responded gleefully, even as she yawned.

Neirin was easy as he was asleep in bed with Gwenhwyfar and she slowly wrapped him up and swaddled him to her chest. He made little fuss, particularly as now he was closer to his mother's heartbeat; the sound soothed him. Morgaine went over to the boys' bed and gently rubbed each of their cheeks. Rodney was a tad startled, but both woke without a fuss.

Julius asked dreamily, "Auntie Morgaine, what is it? Is it time for your surprise?"

Morgaine chuckled softly, "What surprise is that?"

Julius rubbed his eyes and yawned as he replied, "You came to me saying you had something special to show me."

Morgaine smiled at the lad's clairvoyant abilities, "I do. I want you all to get up and get dressed, as warm as you can. We are going on a little adventure."

"Will Uncle Guy come too?"

"Yes. He is waiting for us outside the door."

That got Julius moving. He threw off the covers, much to the annoyance of Rodney who was not so motivated, though he did like the sound of an adventure; he just wished it would take place at a more reasonable hour. Only slightly grumpy, Rodney got dressed with no further prompting.

When the boys and their mother were ready, they accompanied Morgaine outside the room and stole down the stairs into the main hall. Guy, Evelyn, Gareth, and Meggie were waiting for them. Everyone was bundled up. The boys had no idea what to expect as their mother had never dragged them out in the middle of a winter night for any adventure. But it was clear she knew what was happening.

"Mother, what are we doing?" asked Rodney.

"Shhh, you will see."

The family quietly walked down the main street until they got to the stables. From there, they turned the corner and walked to the end where there was another stable and a large enclosed area. They walked into this next stable and there was a bustle of activity. Several more townspeople were in attendance helping out. There was a little girl in one of the pens with a mother sheep and her newborn lambs, only a day old. Julius had been holding Guy's hand but then unclasped his hand as he felt drawn in. Rodney too drew closer. The girl looked up and motioned both of the boys to slowly come nearer. The boys looked at one another and then crept in closer.

"Are these yours?" asked Rodney.

The girl smiled proudly, "Well, not exactly mine," as she nodded her head toward the large ewe, "but yes, I take care of these animals."

Gwenhwyfar came up to stand behind her sons, hugging them close as she said, "This is a very magical event. In the darkest hour before dawn, new life is born and we give thanks to the mothers and the babies."

The boys turned their heads to look at Gwenhwyfar. She smiled at each of them as she continued, gently bouncing Neirin who seemed like he was getting bigger and heavier every day. "Morgaine, Nichole and I came here year after year when we were children to help the mother sheep give birth when they needed it. And I have so been wanting to bring you here and introduce you to our tradition." Gwenhwyfar's eyes were moist.

Rodney touched his mother's cheek and wiped at her tear, "Mother, why are you crying?"

She smiled tenderly, "Because I have missed this and I have been wanting to share this experience with you."

It was not that the boys had never before seen sheep or even baby lambs. But they had never been woken up in the middle of the night to watch lambs being born. It was a bit bloody — which was, of course, disgusting and thrilling at the same time for them. And they got right in there. Neither was squeamish about handling the afterbirth or the babies as they worked with the other town folk. They both listened to instructions respectfully and did as they were told.

As Gwenhwyfar worked with her sons, she thought back on how they played, on how most boys played together. Boys seemed to have an innate gravitational pull toward playing soldier not shepherd. But Gwenhwyfar wanted to nurture the shepherd in her sons and she could now that Rufus wasn't around to tell her she couldn't. There had to be balance, she believed. A boy who could see life being born would be more compassionate when, as a man, he had to take it away.

Guy petted a lamb, feeling the rough, lumpy fleece as he watched Morgaine delight in cuddling with two lambs across from him. She sat amid the hay and chaos that was new life being born all around them, and was completely at home. He smiled, watching as the lambs nibbled at her hair and suckled on her fingers. Guy's upbringing in a small village was nonetheless fairly hierarchical. So as children of a knight and of distant relation to the crown of England, Guy and Delphine were not encouraged to participate in farming or animal husbandry activities. As a Catholic, he knew this time to be Candlemas, or as his mother pronounced it in French, la Chandeleur. It was a holiday that took place forty days after Christmas. Guy remembered his mother telling them as they lit the candles, "We light candles in the darkness to drive evil away. For evil cannot abide by the splendor of God, for He is so bright." He didn't remember her saying anything about ewes or how other religions might practice this holiday. Morgaine looked up at him and smiled as she felt his eyes upon her. He asked, "What do you call this night?"

She tilted her head as if in question. She watched her parents as they gave their blessings upon the ewes and lambs. She responded, "I know in Ireland they call it Imbolc which means 'in the belly.' It is when ewes give birth and when their Goddess, Brigit, comes to bless them. Catholics call it Candlemas, yes?"

Guy nodded.

Morgaine added, "I grew up knowing it as 'that freezing cold night when Mother and Father took me from bed and brought me to the stables to help bless the ewes and newborns'."

Guy chuckled, "That's a long name for a holiday."

Morgaine shrugged and laughed as she snuggled with the lambs. "I think we shortened it to 'Ewe's Night' or perhaps it was called that already. We also call it 'Bright Ewe,' for these moms and babies are a symbol of hope in the dead of winter."

CHAPTER 51

Progression

As Guy continued to devour The Merlin Manuscripts, he was piecing together the family's genealogy. The Merlins made their attempts to figure
out how many of the Faie were connected to this family. And though Gareth
had regal parentage, there was an "FF" next to the father's name. He found
that in instances all the way back on the father's side. He guessed "FF" stood
for "Faie Father" but no actual names were given. The only Faie listed in
the Manuscripts by name was Merrek. The other male Faie had kept their
anonymity. Merrek certainly did appear quite keen on maintaining a strong
hybrid Avalon line. There was no way to be sure of the numbers, but it was
surmised that there were several male Faie siring male offspring with other
English women to mate with Avalon women. The last entry was Morgaine's
with a dash and a blank space. Did he dare take up the quill and write in his
name next to Morgaine's? He was not a Merlin. But then who would add his
name? He debated about it and then took up the quill, dabbed it in ink, and
penned his information, copying it as he saw it done above.

Evelyn of Avalon – Gareth of Avalon
of Alice and Charles of Bromdon / F.F

Morgaine of Avalon – Guy of Avalon
of Marguerite and Auguste of Gisbourne / Merrek

The angle of his writing looked different from those who penned before him.
But then, he was left-handed. He had learned to write right-handed. But when
he was alone, he wrote with his dominant hand, as the penmanship looked

better on the page than when he wrote right-handed. All this time Guy had kept it a secret, for the one time he was caught, his hand hurt for days after.

Guy was just a young boy. He was at the table practicing his letters. He thought he was doing rather well. His father came up behind him, initially just looking over his shoulder to assess the letters. But then he noticed what hand Guy was using.

His father slapped his left hand most severely, saying with fear and anger in his voice, "What if the priest sees you? You must learn to write with your right hand, Guy."

Guy looked up at his father with tears welling up in his eyes. His father rarely showed such anger at him, so the shock of his words hurt just about as much as the slap to his hand. Guy sniffed, "But Father, I just can't do it. The letters don't look right when I try with my other hand."

"You must try harder then, Son. You cannot use your left hand. It is of the Devil."

"But it's just my hand. How can my hand be bad?"

Auguste did not have an answer for his son, but his disobedience could not be tolerated. Auguste stated forcefully, "You will learn to write properly!" And with that he took hold of Guy's left hand, picked up a book from which Guy was copying letters and beat his left hand several times with it. It hurt as much, if not more, than the wooden spoon to his left hand years ago when Guy was learning to eat with a utensil.

Guy sobbed, begging his father to stop, which, for some reason just brought out more anger. "Stop those tears! This is for your own good, Guy."

Guy's hand throbbed but still his father wasn't through with him.

"Now pick up the quill with your right hand and write."

Guy did as he was told.

Still, Guy was willful in one respect. Though he did as his father demanded, he also continued to write with his left hand. He would take his paper, quill, ink and a book out into the field to sit under the apple tree where no one else was around and he would practice writing with his left hand. Then he would come into the house and practice with his right hand in front of his father. As Guy grew, though he ate only with his right hand, he intentionally learned the sword with both hands as well as the bow. He did not see how a hand could be of the Devil. It made no sense. Why would God create left-handed people if they were not equal in all ways to right-handed people?

Guy laughed at the paper in front of him. The angle of the writing might be slightly different, but that did not make it wrong. And in all these years no god struck him down for using his left hand. And he doubted there would be anyone on the other side of death waiting to mete out punishment for something he was born with. Guy felt freer in this moment. He felt more and more that he was coming into his own, shrugging off all the ways in which he was told how to be, how to do, how to live. He felt more and more in alignment with his own being, his own knowing. It might have been a small thing, this act of writing with his left hand in a book that was not his and that others might see, and yet it shifted everything. He was fully claiming his right to be who he was.

It was only a few days later when Morgaine put all the pieces together about Guy being left-handed. Guy was writing a letter to his sister, painstakingly choosing words that wouldn't further upset his childless sister as he wrote of Morgaine's pregnancy and his contentment with his new life in Glastonbury. The door to Guy's study was open and Morgaine came to the doorway to watch her handsome husband. She noticed that he was writing. It took several moments for it to register that he was using his left hand as he wrote.

"Now it makes sense," she mused.

"Pardon?" Guy looked up from his writing.

She gestured to his hand. He looked at it too, quill poised to finish the letter. He realized he hadn't shut the door. It was the first time that he didn't take care of his privacy while writing. He looked a bit sheepish, then decidedly confident.

Morgaine continued, "The dagger. You hide the dagger at your left ankle, not because it would be unexpected but because it's more natural for you to reach for it with your left hand."

"Yes," Guy agreed.

"Mmm," was all Morgaine replied as she nodded thoughtfully. Then she asked what she came in to ask, "I wanted to take a walk to the Apple Orchard and would love for you to accompany me if you are not too busy."

Guy smiled as he put down the quill, leaving the finishing of the letter for another time. "I would be most honored, My Lady." He got up and went to her side.

She gave him a hug and leaned her head against his chest. "Thank you."

In that moment, Guy realized it didn't matter to Morgaine; she was merely remarking on a fact. There was no value judgment attached to it. He kissed the top of her head, feeling a deeper sense that this is where he belonged.

"I am proud of you, my son."

Guy's dream self was writing at his desk. He looked up, startled by the unfamiliar voice at the door to his study. Guy gazed inquisitively at the man who looked so much like him. Uncanny. He realized he must be dreaming. The man was thinner, more willowy, the black hair was longer and sweeping around his shoulders. But the brilliant blue eyes were the same. Guy wanted to be angry at this man the family called Merrek, this Faie who impregnated his mother. But he as looked at him, he couldn't summon up his anger. It just wasn't in him. He was frustrated though. "You come to me now, after all this time? Why? Why now? And why did you choose my mother?"

Merrek was calm and proud as he answered his son. "I chose you so that the bloodline would strengthen. I knew that if you survived your trials you would become a great protector of the realm."

"But why did you mate with a married woman?"

"So that her mate would protect you the best he could, raising you as his own."

"That did not work out so well."

Merrek smiled softly, "Well enough. I needed you in the world. I needed you to see the world from the fallacy of being human. You are exceedingly adept at taking in all sides to formulate your own decision."

"I have not always been a good man."

Merrek was thoughtful, "Men rarely are. What matters is what you decide to do now."

"I will be her champion."

"I know you will. I am counting on that."

When Guy awoke he told Morgaine his dream. "Was it just my mind making all that up or can the Faie visit us in our dreams?"

"What do you think, my love?"

"I am not sure. It felt real. But if it was real, I would have thought I would have felt anger."

"Why?"

"Because he impregnated my mother and then abandoned us."

"But he didn't. You had a father, whom you loved and who loved you."

"And who was taken from me too young. It seems like all my life I have looked for a father, put my trust in father figures, only to be abandoned by each and every one." Guy took gentle hold of Morgaine's abdomen considering the growing life within. "How will I show up as a father with such poor examples?"

Morgaine could not be swayed by Guy's doubt. "You will be fiercely loyal. You will be everything you judge your fathers not to be."

Guy nodded. That felt true. And yet — "What if I fail?"

"We all fail at some point in another's eyes. Redemption is a cyclical process."

"I don't want to fail in your eyes," Guy stated earnestly.

Morgaine smiled tenderly at him, tilting her head as she gazed into his beautiful eyes, "Love, you cannot. Wherever, whenever, you failed, it is in the past. Those eyes in which you fail will not be mine."

"But how can you be sure?"

"I just am. As sure as the Lake, as sure as the sky, as sure as the sun that rises — you are my Beloved and I trust that you will always do the best you can, and that is all I can ask of you."

"That doesn't sound perfect."

"Life is not perfect. Best is not perfect; it is what you are able to do."

Guy took that in, adoring this sweet, wild lady all the more. If he had ever been lost, he knew he was found in her eyes and would never be lost again.

Julius knocked and came in to stand next to Guy, who was seated at his desk in his study. He peered over Guy's arm studying the words upon which Guy was focused. "What are you reading about now?"

Guy brought his arm up and around the young lad, bringing him in closer. "About this family. There are several Faie connected this family. Merrek is at the center."

"Your father."

Guy still had a hard time thinking of this absent person as his father, and he was unnerved by Julius' bold statement, as if Julius could see into his dreams. But he nodded just the same, "Yes."

Julius continued to look at the words on the page. "What is my father's name?"

"Rufus," Guy said with slight annoyance. Rufus, as disagreeable as he was, had been raising Julius. The male Faie had simply implanted his seed and vanished. Julius then looked at Guy with eyes that spoke of the hurt that statement caused. Guy hugged Julius closer as he said, "Rufus is your father. He is the only father you know, for good or for bad, just as Auguste is my father because he is the man who raised me."

Julius shook his head, "But Uncle Guy, we both know that Rufus suspects I am not his. Perhaps you have two fathers but I only have one who I know only in my dreams.

Guy sighed, "These Faie, they meddle in the lives of humans."

Again Julius shook his head, "Uncle Guy, but doesn't it feel comforting to know we are being guided? So many people don't know their purpose in life. We do. We are here by design to protect the Land and the line." Guy looked quizzically at this youngster, amazed at his precocious insight.

Contrary to what Guy had been told, Morgaine's sexual appetite had not diminished with the progression of her pregnancy. He had expressed concern about jostling the baby with their lovemaking but Morgaine assured him that the baby would be fine. "How do you know?"

"I just do. And I want the baby bathed in your strong seed."

He smirked, unsure how else to respond.

Morgaine was reassuring, "I have been making inquiries."

"Oh?"

She beamed. "Yes. It appears that wives who have good relations with their husbands continue to have sex almost until the baby is due. They just find other positions to accommodate the growing belly."

Guy was fascinated with this new information, "Is that so?"

Morgaine nodded vigorously. "And wives who do not have good relations with their husbands...Well, they just tell their husbands that sex would not be good for the baby."

"Interesting."

"Yes, isn't it? Sad, too. I had been hearing conflicting messages so that is why I started asking more women."

The most important question came to the front of Guy's mind, "So, we can still continue having sex?"

Morgaine's smile widened and her eyes alit with mischief, "Yes!"

"Well that is wonderful news! Let's get started."

The couple did not emerge from their bedroom until much later that morning.

CHAPTER 52

Spring Robin

ROBIN HEADED INTO Glastonbury, toward the castle. There were new shoots coming up, reminding him how long it had been since he had seen his love, Marian. Autumn leaves covered the forest the last time he had come this way. Charlton was quite ill but there was no way to tell how long he would go on. Though Robin chided himself for wishing Charlton's end so that Marian did not feel tethered to this place, he secretly wished that this was the last time he would have to come here in hopes of taking Marian away with him.

Upon handing over his weapons to the guards, the archer was brought to the Duke's receiving room and announced.

"Ah, Robin. Come in," Gareth stated in a friendly tone. To the guards, Gareth said, "Thank you. Please fetch Marian."

When Marian entered, she was overjoyed to see Robin. It had been a long winter without him. Marian looked to Gareth who nodded slightly. She pulled Robin by the hands. "Come, let us go for a walk."

Gareth nodded to the guards who had been eyeing him, wondering what their next set of instructions would be. That silent upward nod told them to keep a covert eye on Marian. They kept their distance but followed Marian and Robin.

The couple ambled through the town holding hands as Marian guided Robin down to the Lake. Robin told her of his most recent exploits with the Sheriff. Marian nodded as she looked out on the water. She then squeezed his hand as she said, "My father has passed."

"Oh Marian, I am sorry." There was a strange mix of elation and sorrow in his voice. "When?"

"Would you believe shortly after you left last fall? I think he hung on just to give me another winter here."

"Why?"

Marian said with slight exasperation, "Oh Robin! Because as fond as my father had been of you, you are currently an outlaw and what father would wish that life upon his daughter?"

Robin was crestfallen. "So you will be staying on with the Avalons then?"

Marian felt like she had been slapped. Her voice was hurt and cross, "What would give you that idea?"

Robin was confused, "But you just said..."

"What?"

Robin thought back on her words. She hadn't actually stated that her father's dying wish was for her to remain here or that she could not go with him. Nor had she stated that she didn't want to go with him. He took a deep breath and a leap of faith. He bent down on one knee as he faced her and took both her hands, "Marian, my darling, will you marry me?"

Her annoyance with Robin was stopped dead in its tracks as she heard Robin's earnest request. She looked at him in bewilderment. Robin looked at her cautiously expectant. He had caught her off guard. She felt as if she had tipped over; but no, both feet were still on the ground.

Robin squeezed her hands, "Marian..."

She recovered from her momentary shock, "Yes! The answer is yes!"

He jumped up to embrace her.

"Oh Robin! When? When will we marry?"

Robin whispered in her ear. "Soon, my love. Soon. A monk has joined our merry little band. He will marry us when we return to Nottingham."

Though she had heard enough snippets of Morgaine's Handfasting stories to wish Robin and she could have that same magical ritual, Marian was too happy to be disappointed that he did not suggest they marry here.

The couple was to leave promptly, though they did share a final meal with the family. There was an unspoken truce between Robin and Guy, though Robin found it hard to get used to. Guy continued to be at ease around Robin throughout the evening and that actually put Robin more on edge. He had never remembered Guy appearing so at peace with himself and his world. It was disorienting not to be dealing with the black-clad villain any more. Guy was a family man and appeared to be well-loved and well-respected. "He's found home, his clan," Robin thought to himself.

The next morning, Marian was packed with her few belongings, which included her new sword, Taharqa's parting gift for her. She was, as he put it, "a most dedicated student." He had the smith craft the sword especially for her smaller stature so that she could use it nimbly.

After Marian hugged and kissed each of Gwenhwyfar's boys in turn, Guy came up to her, enfolding her in a tight embrace and whispering, "Marian, I release you to your destiny and a beautiful love story."

Though she could see that Robin was edgy with their affection, Marian kissed Guy's cheek, whispering back, "And, Guy, I release you to your destiny and a beautiful love story."

Gareth then gave Marian a big bear hug, stating, misty-eyed, "You will be missed, Marian."

It was the ladies' turn now and Evelyn, Gwenhwyfar, Meggie, and Morgaine encircled Marian, holding her while chanting barely above a whisper. "We encircle you as the Lady holds Her own. You are never gone from us as you are never gone from Her."

The women's eyes were wet with tears. Marian swooned with emotion. It would be painful to leave this strong circle of women. And yet she also knew she must honor the pull to return to Nottingham. But for one more moment she allowed herself to bask in this blessed feeling of kinship.

As the couple walked down the road hand in hand, Marian allowed herself to open to a new life, a new adventure. And she secretly looked forward to showing Robin that she could defend herself with a sword.

CHAPTER 53

—— ❦ ——

Rod of the Green

ELIZABETH WATCHED YOUNG Rodney with her husband. Rodney had been learning quite a bit from Wild Herb. Making fire, traps. He even made an impressive burned out bowl and spoon. He was still young enough that he could go into training as an Avalon Guardian. She mentioned as much to Rainer who always had a habit of appearing when she put a pie out to cool. It didn't matter if it was inside or outside; Rainer seemed to know.

"Rainer, how do you always know when I am baking a pie?" Elizabeth teased him when she opened to the knock on the door.

"Well, hello to you too, Elizabeth. I thought it was our signal."

With hands on her hips, the elder retorted playfully, "Signal for what?"

"For me to come and eat."

They both chuckled.

"Actually, you sprang the trap I set for you. I did have another reason for luring you here."

"Another reason beyond my good company?"

The pair had an easy bantering friendship, having grown fond of each other over the years. Elizabeth looked on Rainer as the son she no longer had. Though the Avalon Guardians had their own discreet village deep in the Avalon Forest, Rainer was more deeply connected to the Avalon family on a personal level. He had been raised on the fringes of both worlds and so, though he preferred the woods, Elizabeth's and Wild Herb's house seemed to be an extension of his home.

Elizabeth cut him a slice of pie and sat down with him at the small table.

Rainer put his nose near the treat. "Hmmm. Savory!" Between bites, he inquired, "This is a mighty fine trap! What did you catch me for?"

Elizabeth was contemplative. "I know that it is not for me to say, but I have been watching the young Rodney."

Rainer interjected, "Gwenhwyfar's eldest?"

Elizabeth nodded and continued, "Yes. Rod of the Green, as he calls himself… or Green Rod. He switches back and forth daily." She noticed Rainer's sly smile. "He has been spending quite a bit of time here and I think he may still be young enough to go into training."

Rainer's mind was assessing. "Have you spoken with Gwenhwyfar about this?"

"Not yet. But he appears to have the temperament and capabilities for the life."

"That would be two sons dedicated to Avalon."

"What do you mean?"

"Did you know that Julius, the middle child, is studying with Guy at the castle?"

"Studying what — the sword?"

Rainer chuckled. "Actually, no. Evelyn has given them access to The Merlin Manuscripts."

Elizabeth was a bit surprised; she had not heard this. "You are the Master Cunning Man, Rainer. You are the…" Elizabeth's voice uncharacteristically trailed off before she added "Merlin," in respect of Rainer's reluctance to take up that mantle.

Rainer shrugged. "I love the Ladies but I cannot live at the castle. I am always there when they need me."

"But perhaps you could train Guy and Julius."

Rainer waved the thought away. "I was not formally trained by Merlin either. Guy is really too old to have designs upon the title and I am not convinced he has the aptitude. Like his horse, he may be magical in nature but not in vocation. Julius, though, is certainly young enough. But I am not sure what I could offer either of them."

"For the Lady's sake: your time. Your talents."

Rainer mused, "I think we need to bring Gwenhwyfar into this conversation."

"Well, yes of course. My question, though, had more to do with, would the Guardians take on another young one?"

"Our numbers dwindle, so yes. Besides, I have some reservations about the foundling."

"Jack? Bring him round here. He just needs the comfort of a mother's arms."

"We do have Grace."

"Grace is no mother. She is a hunter. And don't give her dish duty too often or you will end up with dishes cleaved in half."

Rainer snorted, "You are right about that."

There was a pause in the conversation as Rainer happily munched on the treat before him. He had the distinct sensation Elizabeth was still watching him intently. "What?"

"What, what?"

"I hear your brain grinding. What else is on your mind, Elizabeth?"

She was thoughtful. "Why didn't Merlin name you his successor?"

"Elizabeth, we have been over this before."

"I know. It just doesn't make sense. And why don't you just claim the title?"

Rainer shrugged. He wasn't sure why.

"You could train the boy."

"Which one?"

"Julius."

Rainer nodded, "I will."

There was a silence between them suddenly, almost palpable. They knew what wearing the Torc would mean for Guy. And they knew that it would be Rainer, not Guy, completing Julius' training in the years to come. They just hoped it would be a long time before Guy fulfilled his destiny. He was growing on both of them and they found themselves quite fond of this newest member of the coven. Guy was kind and strong and so completely in love with Morgaine. It was heartwarming to watch those two.

It seemed too sad for words to see the brothers arguing more. As close as they had been, they continued to grow apart. Rodney's anger over the loss of his father continued to put a wedge between them. It had never been fully explained to him and he was mad that Julius didn't appear as angry as he was at the loss. Rodney started imagining himself as one of Robin Hood's men, fighting against the tyrant Prince John. This did not go overly well with others in the castle. And Julius came to Guy's defense when Rodney egged on Julius with a nasty comment about Guy being one of the Prince's men. "He is his own man and he does what he does to protect the realm!"

It was only days later when Rodney came to Wild Herb with a black eye. "Well, you should see my younger brother," he retorted as Wild Herb looked at the eye.

Wild Herb responded with harshness in his voice that Rodney had not heard before, "Shame on you! Fighting with your little brother. You two should stand together. We have enough brothers warring in this country."

Rodney looked up at Wild Herb, "You mean Prince John and King Richard?"

"Well, those two, yes, but they are not the only brothers to fight against one another for righteousness or power."

"But I was only telling Julius the story I heard. Wasn't Guy of Avalon, Guy of Gisbourne?"

"Yes, he was."

"But I heard Guy of Gisbourne was a wicked man in league with the villainous Sheriff of Nottingham."

"Well, you know Guy. Is that what you think?" Wild Herb's voice was firm and Rodney hung his head in shame.

He shook his head, "No. Lord Guy is nothing but kind to us." He hesitated then asked, "How could he be the same person?"

Wild Herb was thoughtful, "Men can have a change of heart. And, the stories you hear are not usually the whole story or the whole truth."

Rodney became indignant, "But what Lord Guy did was wrong. He was bad."

Wild Herb continued to look upon the boy with patience and compassion, "Wrongdoing is not the same as being a bad person. Sometimes you can think you are doing what you have to do, for all the right reasons. But that doesn't necessarily mean you are doing good. Right and good are not the same, young Rod."

Rodney looked confused, "I don't understand."

Wild Herb patted the boy's head, "I don't expect you to fully understand in this moment. As you continue to make decisions in your life, it will become clearer. All I ask is that you will always search yourself for your true intention." Wild Herb could see the frustration in Rodney's face and he placed his hand on the child's shoulder, giving it a squeeze. "Life doesn't need to be such a struggle. Be a model for what you want to see in the world. Yes, there is conflict and suffering, but you do not need to let that define who you are or how you show up in the world. You do not need to allow your prior decisions to define you. Our Lord Guy sees that and you can too." Wild Herb let that sink in, adding, "So, Rod of the Green, what new decision will you make when you see your brother again at the end of the day?"

Rodney sighed. Besides being his brother, Julius was his best friend. Julius wasn't bad by association or wrong because he loved Guy and found comfort in Guy as a father figure. Both boys so desperately wanted their father's love. And without their father around, they just wanted to be seen — really seen — and cherished even, by some caring man. As if hearing Rodney's silent plea, Wild Herb brought the boy in close and gave him a hug. Rodney's tense body relaxed and his eyes began to tear. He didn't want to be, or feel, bad or wrong. And somewhere within him he realized that Julius wasn't bad or wrong either.

CHAPTER 54

The Definition of Friendship

"I PROBABLY SHOULDN'T have taken him," lamented Julius.

Guy squatted down near the child as he eyed the baby bird. "Where did you find the crow?" Guy simply asked.

Julius showed a sigh of relief that his hero was not starting out by scolding him. "I was in the Orchard."

Guy smiled knowingly; where else would this little wizard-in-training be, but where the converging magic was?

Julius offered, "I looked everywhere for a nest. I did. I swear. But he started following me so I brought him home."

"How do you know he is a he?"

"Oh. I suppose I don't." Moving on, off a topic that was out of his reach, he pressed, "Can I keep him?"

Guy smirked and tousled the lad's head. "I am not sure you can keep a crow. The crow may decide to keep you, though."

That was not a no, Julius was sure of it. Julius threw his hands up, exclaiming, "Hoorah!"

Guy met the little redheaded mop with temperance, "Whoa. You have to ask your mother. But as long as she is okay with it, you can raise the crow until the bird can fly. Then you must let it go back into the Orchard. And if you are lucky, it will return to you." Guy looked at the little black bird, adding, "And you are going to need to protect this little carrion bird from the cats, without hurting the cats. You will not be in my wife's good graces if you hurt her pets."

Julius nodded vigorously, full of glee, "Of course."

"Nn-k. Nn-k," said Ink the Crow.

"Look, Uncle Guy; Ink knows his name," exclaimed Julius, triumphantly.

Guy smiled at the easy camaraderie between human and crow. As he looked fondly at the pair, he considered the concept of friendship. He thought about how easy it was to find companionship with creatures other than humans. His horses. This crow. He did have friends growing up. Marian. Caron. Much. Even Robin…sort of. And then there was Matthew. A friend, a bully, someone to test his limits for good or for bad…It all intermingled in a bizarre, tragic way. When it was he, his sister, Marian, Caron, and Much there was a greater sense of gentleness. Marian always wanted to be sure everyone felt heard…including her doll. There was a lot of talking of feelings if there was a disagreement. Sometimes it went on too long and he got tired of following along, making sure everyone was heard and felt good and no one had hurt feelings. Once Robin or Matthew joined in, though, there was more competition to assess who was one-up and who was one-down. Some were up by birth: that was Robin as his father was lord of the manor. Some were one-up by sheer brutishness; that was Matthew. Some just said 'to hell with it all' once there was too much teasing or harsh words; that was Marian who would walk away. And some were always one-down, putting up with it all; that was Much, the miller's son. Poor Caron, too, she being the youngest of the group and the daughter of a herdsman. And Guy was always somewhere in the middle, being the son of a knight but not of a lord, being related to royalty but always reminded — distantly.

Julius interrupted Guy's brooding, "Uncle Guy? Who are your friends?" The lad had an uncanny knack for picking up on people's thoughts and then questioning them based on those silent ponderings.

Guy looked at Julius, at first a bit sad; who were his friends? Then a smile formed. "Morgaine is my friend."

"Your wife is your friend?"

Guy nodded, "Yes. She is. Your mother is my friend too."

Julius had a more pressing question, "And me?"

Guy's smile broadened, "And you." He leaned over and tousled the boy's hair.

Julius persisted, "Do you have any more friends?" Guy thought about it. He certainly had other people with whom he was friendly. There were his fellow hunters. His coven-mates. He certainly had more friends than he ever had before. But close friends? A confidante? He realized Morgaine was his best friend. She was everything.

Julius was quietly observing Guy.

Guy gazed back. "The number of friends you have isn't what is important," he told Julius. He continued after a pause, "It's the quality of the friendship. A true friend is someone you can trust and someone you love. Someone with whom you can share your secrets."

Julius scratched his crow friend's head, just behind the base of the skull, as Ink hopped up to him. Ink seemed to enjoy being petted there, dipping her head down, and standing still.

Guy watched the show of affection and continued, "And friends don't have to be human."

"They don't?"

"No. In fact, Midnight is one of my dearest friends. I trust him with my life."

Julius' eyes widened at this interesting admission. It was a revelation. Julius looked at Ink as the crow tilted her head up to study the human child. Somewhere in the crow's brain she recognized that this creature was not her parent. Still, she trusted this pale being who made curious sounds and scratched her head with his very dull yet attentive claws.

CHAPTER 55

June 1193 A Child Is Born

MORGAINE LAY IN bed, her feet heavy with pain. She had been on her feet too long at Col and Anwen's wedding. She moaned.

Guy was quick to her side, inquiring with concern in his voice, "What is it, Love?"

"Oh, how I ache," Morgaine replied.

Guy kissed his way down Morgaine's body to her feet and lovingly laid his warm hands upon them. He massaged them and willed the pain to subside. He moved up her calves and legs. He felt his wife's body relax into his hands, into their bed. He loved having this kind of power; this was true power: the ability to make his woman feel at ease. He felt useful and appreciated. Truly, what man didn't want the power to make his wife happy?

The morning was hot when Morgaine went into labor, her shift already soaked with sweat. Guy insisted on staying with her and though the women were surprised, they decided as long as he didn't get in the way there was no harm in it. Morgaine leaned against her husband and he cooled her head and breasts with water, fanning her. Evelyn told her daughter to push, and Gwenhwyfar and Meggie assisted as each of them had received some training from Evelyn in how to deliver a baby. Words of encouragement and gentle instructions were heard throughout the morning; but Guy just held his wife, for that was all he could do. Morgaine pushed and groaned and kept her eyes on her mother, breathing and bearing down as she was instructed. Guy's presence was reassuring to her as were Meggie's and Gwenhwyfar's. The women cooed at her, stroked her, and told her she was doing beautifully. And she was.

Guy watched his daughter being born; he saw her slip out from between Morgaine's thighs into the coaxing hands of Gwenhwyfar. Evelyn told Morgaine to push again and the placenta fell out into the bowl Meggie was holding.

"There, now. Rest." Evelyn said with satisfaction.

Morgaine's slight weight fell deeper into her husband's chest.

Meggie looked at the contents of the bowl, "I will take this out to the Orchard and bury it among the trees."

"Thank you, Meggie," said Evelyn.

Morgaine leaned into her husband and felt a wave of love wash over her as her husband wrapped his strong arms around her.

Gwenhwyfar presented a small bundle to the couple, "Here's your baby girl."

Both parents gazed adoringly at their child.

"Rhiannon," stated Morgaine, turning her head to make sure Guy still approved.

"Rhiannon Faie," he smiled back. They had already chosen her name. Rhiannon meant "Great Queen," a Welsh Goddess who, through her trials, persevered and overcame all obstacles. And Guy was pleased to hear that this goddess was associated with horses. For him, she was "The Great Queen Who Rides" and he felt that was becoming for this little bundle in their arms.

Guy touched his daughter's tiny fingers and wondered why he never heard of men participating at their child's birth. What father wouldn't want to be present? Guy felt so alive, so present, so happy. He was exactly where he wanted to be.

Morgaine insisted on breastfeeding Rhiannon herself and not handing her off to a wet nurse as was practice of the nobility. But that was the way of the Avalons

— forsaking current customs that made no logical sense to them. She cherished the intimacy with her daughter, knowing that it was her life force that was continuing to feed her. Guy loved watching the two of them. Sometimes when he caught them at the right moment, just before Morgaine was to start feeding Rhiannon, he sat on the bed, patted his chest, and Morgaine happily sat down and leaned against him. "I am the luckiest man alive," he whispered in her ear. She smiled as she nursed Rhiannon and felt completely cherished as Guy gently rocked the two of them.

"What is that?" Morgaine was surprised to see what appeared to be an animal pelt in Rhiannon's cradle.

Rhiannon was happily caressing it with her hands on either side of her. Guy was standing at the cradle admiring his daughter and seeing that she was enjoying the pelt he had given her. He had thought that it would be a perfect way to honor his horse, Crown, to lie down with this "Great Queen Who Rides." Morgaine put her arm around Guy and wriggled under his arm and into his side.

He bent and kissed the top of his wife's head, uttering, "Our Great Queen has her first steed. That pelt belonged to Crown, my first horse. It had been so traumatic to lose him and I didn't want to leave him, so I did the only thing I could think of at the time."

"You took the skin."

Guy nodded, confirming, "Yes. I know it may seem gruesome but somehow it was comforting to have a piece of him with me."

"I do not judge you, Love. You are right; it does seem a fitting blanket for Rhiannon."

CHAPTER 56

If You Knew it Was Dangerous Would You Still Go?

MORGAINE HAD FELT cloistered for long enough in the castle. It was a lovely warm autumn day and she decided it was time for an outing. She missed the sea. She hadn't visited in many moons and she had promised Nichole that when the baby was up for travel, that she and Guy would come for a visit. Morgaine swaddled and strapped Rhiannon to her chest and clambered atop her horse, Merryweather. She didn't want to bother with a carriage. With Guy beside her, she figured they could sleep under the stars or find an inn. Guy was impressed with Morgaine's bravery and sense of adventure. They knew there could be risks. Nothing had been settled with regard to Guy unofficially leaving the Black Knights. But there had be no mishaps, no treachery, no threats carried out. With provisions and clothing in their saddlebags they headed out. Guy felt so free. It was like the layers of him that had shielded him all these years fell away and he was unbridled. He was a different man. He laughed more easily and was not ashamed of his tears. His friendships with his coven-mates deepened and he felt the love of kinship. He thought back on the conversation he had had with Julius those many months ago. He did have friends, true friends whom he loved and trusted and who loved and trusted him.

Their arrived at Will and Nichole's home in Weymouth in good time, even sleeping out under the stars one night on the way, which thrilled the pair as they made love and let the falling leaves tangle in their hair.

The friends took to swimming everyday they could in the ocean with Godric babysitting Rhiannon on the shore. He still had a cautious temperament and was not partial to being in the waves that could knock him over. He happily watched over Rhiannon as he had, and still did, his little sister. But long after the others retreated to the shore, Morgaine stayed, swimming, and reveling in the sensations of the salty water lapping at her form. Will jokingly commented on Morgaine's stamina at being able to stay in the cold water so long. He likened her to a seal or Irish Silkie undulating through the waves. Guy gave an inner chuckle at the comment as he imagined his wife undulating upon him as she turned from seal to woman upon the sheets.

When Morgaine finally came up onto shore and sat down where the rest of the troop was sitting, she snuggled up close to her husband and whispered, "Undulating, huh?"

Guy slyly glanced sideways at his wife, nodding slightly. They laced their fingers together and knew what their evening activity would be.

The two couples enjoyed their time together with fresh fish and long walks on the beach. And Godric and Rowan enjoyed playing nursemaid to the baby, Rhiannon. It was one of those perfect moments with friends, one of those "remember when" times, a memory that could sustain someone even through the most woeful of times.

A fortnight later, Morgaine and Guy sensed it was time to return home. As much as they enjoyed the sea, they missed their Lake and the Avalon Forest.

It was a good thing Guy had kept up his sword play and sparred with Taharqa for it wouldn't have done him any good to go soft. And as it turned out, this day he might just need those skills. There was a small company of men on the road to Glastonbury awaiting the trio upon having heard that Guy had left the safety of Glastonbury; and really, anything could happen on the road.

They were clearly Black Knights but Guy did not recognize the men before him. He had Morgaine pull up short upon seeing the men come from the side of the road to block their travel.

She looked over to Guy with some trepidation, "Are they bandits?"

Guy shook his head, "No, they are Black Knights." He sensed it in his bones. These men in black were not mere ruffians. They had the look of retribution on them. There were three men ahead of them. Instinct told him to turn around. Yes, two more behind them.

Morgaine was now becoming frightened, "How did we not sense them?"

Guy clenched his teeth, "It must be the same cloaking spell, why you and your mother were not able to sense me." To the thin air he addressed, "Oh Merlin, if you ever had known this is what could happen, would you ever have taught this spell?"

"Guy, what do we do?"

The men just stood there enjoying the fear they were causing. They wanted to unhinge Guy. They were told to be sure Guy knew who ordered his death for betraying the Order. Looking at the pretty skirt next to him, they figured on a bit of sport.

Midnight sensed that his human was very nervous. Which made him nervous. He knew very few things that made Guy anxious. But with both his human and his human's mate feeling so fearful, Midnight did the only thing he could think of: envision someplace peaceful, someplace where these men would not be... Someplace familiar.

Guy saw the haze before his eyes almost too late. "Grab my hand, Morgaine!"

Without thinking, she reached over and took hold of Guy's hand. She saw the haze and understood what Midnight was focusing on. She whispered to Merryweather, "Apples."

Merryweather's ears pricked up despite sensing her human's fear and in her mind she saw the Apple Orchard. And together horses and humans disappeared before the eyes of the men.

One Black Knight yelled, "Where the fuck did they go?"

The men looked to one another in amazement and anger and then to the place where their quarry was not. Now it was their turn to be unhinged. They argued amongst one another on the road.

"What the hell do we tell him?" shouted one.

"Nothing. We saw nothing," seethed another.

"This is witchcraft," spat a third.

"I don't give a blast. I am not saying I saw them disappear before my eyes. They'll lock us up. Think we're crazy," said the second.

"We've got to tell him. With power like that — we could use that," said a fourth.

The fifth man said nothing, but charged at the thin air with sword swinging. All he cut through was the air. Guy was no longer there.

Guy and Morgaine were still gripping each other's hands as they looked around the Apple Orchard.

With Guy's free hand, he patted Midnight, "Good horse!"

Morgaine was nodding bewilderedly, "Yes, good horse."

Midnight nodded, neighing deeply, quite pleased with himself.

CHAPTER 57

※

1194 A New Year, New Troubles Brew

IT WAS THE same dream. He felt the sword go into him. He saw himself dying in his wife's arms underneath the apple tree. Guy woke up with a start.

"What is it, Beloved?" Morgaine's sleepy voice rose to him.

Guy's chest was heaving under her cool hand. He focused on his breathing and gradually it slowed. "Morgaine, I have seen my death by sword."

Morgaine nodded, thinking back to her talk with Rainer, though instead she sighed, "Well, you are a swordsman."

Guy gave her a sidelong glance and weakly smiled, hearing how Morgaine was trying to play this dark conversation light. "I would have very much enjoyed growing old with you, my sweet, and being happy as a plump old duke."

Morgaine chuckled, "I can see it."

He continued, "I am so happy. I do not want to die. I want to be with you forever."

Morgaine responded, "If it were possible, I would live and love with you until the end too, my love."

There was a long pensive pause between the couple and then Guy whispered, "Promise me, Morgaine, that when I fall my body is given as an offering to the Land. It is ultimately the only gift I have to give to the remnants of Avalon."

Morgaine's eyes welled up knowing that she was right. The vision was accurate. He was the true king to sacrifice himself to the Land. She could only say, "I promise."

Evelyn too was experiencing troubling dreams. She saw a future of war, of a people and a land torn apart, of the very ground exploding and casting soil and limbs into the air. She saw the shadows of a cross, a crescent moon, and a six-pointed star upon the land, their points locked as if crossing swords. Evelyn got up and went to her scrying bowl. She poured fresh water into the bowl, cleared her mind, and concentrated on the water just below the surface. She scried and saw strange, horrifying images. So many bodies burning. Forests burning. Men in round helmets marching. And again images of the cross, the crescent moon, and the six-pointed star interlocked with swords. She agonized, but continued to look and slowly it emerged — a five-pointed star with the antlers of the Stag King. She gazed and witnessed all the work they had done in service to the Goddess, though it might seem all for naught in the centuries to come. There was a dim shine from this five-pointed star in the distant future, when all elements would work together in harmony. The star moved to the side of a large hoop standing on the ground with many symbols surrounding it. The circle unified all. "And in this unification, what then?" Evelyn pondered silently. The water in the scrying bowl rippled. A new image emerged. A water bearer was pouring out water upon a parched land, watering an apple tree and the people and animals rejoiced and prayed to the Goddess in this guise. Evelyn clung to this image of the water bearer with her beloved apple tree. She knew she may never see this day; but it lightened her mind that this moment might yet dawn.

Guy's dreams came more vividly now, as if preparing him. He was watching Morgaine wave goodbye to someone and then turn to reach out for his hand.

"Why?" he asked.

"He is good and principled and is willing to die for a cause. He is a soldier. But I do not need a soldier; I need a champion. I need someone who will see past a cause and live and die for me."

This did not make sense to Guy. "I do not understand."

"Yes you do. That is why you have returned."

They were no longer on the balcony but in the Apple Orchard. He looked around. "Why?"

"Because you needed a love you could see and feel and touch. You would not lay down your life for a cause, but to fulfill a need." Morgaine was no longer herself. She was larger than life, The Lady of the Lake, shimmering in blue; she was waiting for him. "Guy, like all men who represent the Antlered One, the Stag King, your blood feeds Me. You die into Me and we become One. And the cycle continues."

"But why me? I am no one. I am no hero, no king."

"Oh, but you are wrong, my love. You did not abandon Me on some boy's adventure of glory. You did not ride off to fight some demons somewhere out there. A true king clings to the Land from which he is born. You stayed, yet journeyed many inner roads, battling your demons and Mine, becoming the Champion I knew you could be."

"Then why ask me to die? I do not wish to die."

"All men die. I would have your death have meaning to Me. Be in the service of protecting Me and Mine."

Guy woke up with tears in his eyes. "Very well, My Lady. I am yours."

Guy was brooding and withdrawn all day after waking from his dream. And though the Land was cold with winter, he walked the Land and imagined his hands brushing the summer barley. His palms tickled from the sensation. The breeze he felt was not iced with snow crystals but felt as if he was being swayed back and forth, as if he was now that barley daring the scythe in the wind.

Morgaine gave her husband his space and just made herself available should he have need of her.

Guy went to Evelyn with his dream. She listened intently. Upon finishing recounting the dream, he noticed her eyes were moist. "So it's true? This was not just a dream?"

Evelyn shook her head slightly, saying, "You are the Stag King, Guy. You took up the antlers as your crown without provocation."

Guy brought his hand up to his eyes. He placed his thumb and forefinger each to the inner corners of his eyes as if he were trying to hold something back, something more than just physical droplets of salty water threatening to fall.

They sat quietly, each in their thoughts. Then Guy broke the silence, "What will happen?"

Evelyn spread her arms slightly, palms up, shaking her head, then saying, "You will protect our people; that much is clear. But I don't see the fruits of our labor coming to fruition until a most distant future."

"But where is the hope then?"

Evelyn sighed, "You may not like it…Robin will be known as the hero of the people. I have seen it. Robin and Marian will have a love story that will be remembered and told by the people to give them hope in hard times."

Guy's lips grew thin with tension as he considered Robin being remembered as the hero; no matter what Guy did, history would cast him as the villain to Robin's hero. Because there always had to be a villain in the stories; that's what made a good story, right?

Evelyn heard his thoughts and interjected, "So many boys take the outer journey, thinking that is the hero's journey, thinking that the adventure out in the world makes them a man. Guy, you took the inner journey. Your adventure took you deep within the caverns of yourself. I know it has been wrought with pain and anguish, learning how to live into your true self, but you have succeeded. Let those who love you be the judge. Forget the rest."

Guy heaved a sigh. He recognized it should not be important. Still, he felt compelled to ask, "Will we be remembered? Will any of the stories tell our side?"

Evelyn's eyes lowered for a moment, then she looked directly at him, saying, "If we are remembered at all, it will be as villains. It will be a long time before our legacy is discovered again. Though we love the Land with a passion, England's people are becoming more Christianized. We pagans are seen as being of their devil, for all the Church sees are opposites. Right and wrong. Not right and left."

Guy smiled that Evelyn remembered what he had said about the right hand versus the left hand; that conversation felt so long ago.

Evelyn continued, "I fear you will be Avalon's last champion for some time to come."

"Me?"

"Yes, you, Guy." She placed her hand on his shoulder and suddenly he was not just seeing Evelyn, but who she represented, the Lady of the Lake, the Shimmering One. He bowed his head in acceptance of his fate.

It wasn't until Guy and Morgaine returned to bed that evening that she could hear his voice caught in his throat. She waited, knowing he would speak when he was ready. She busied herself getting Rhiannon ready for bed and laying her down in her cradle beside their bed. Morgaine realized the cradle was now too small for Rhiannon's growing form. She was already over seven moons old. Rhiannon made little fuss as she had recently been fed and was tuckered out from a day of peek-a-boo with Mouse. Morgaine then laid her body alongside Guy's, setting her head and her hand upon his heart.

Finally the words found themselves, though they were not the words either of them expected. "Morgaine, what did you love about Lorrac?"

Though surprised by this particular question, she responded, "That he was good and kind and loved me."

"And what do you love about me?"

"That you are good and kind and love me."

"What is the difference between us then?"

"Because he was a boy. He had to go off on some grand adventure to find himself. He needed confirmation from the outside. I don't know if he ever got it. You are a man. You found yourself right here. You found yourself in relationship, whereas — apparently — he could only find himself outside of relationship."

Guy chuckled as he thought about how daughter, mother, and Goddess were all in agreement.

Morgaine cocked her head, "What is amusing you?"

"That you, your mother, and the Goddess from my dream all said basically the same thing." Guy held his wife and felt a sense of relief, realizing, "I did stay. I battled my demons from without and from within and I found myself right here at home. I am not good. I am not bad. I am just what She needs." He paused, adding as he tilted her head gently so that they were looking into each other's eyes, "Morgaine, I adore you. You are a door, some magical portal, through which I see the world. I found myself in your eyes and I am forever grateful."

She squeezed her husband tight. She felt the same. She looked up at him as he gazed down at her. They kissed tenderly, knowing there were no more words.

CHAPTER 58

King Richard's Return

IT WAS MARCH 1194 when King Richard landed back in England, returning from the Third Crusade. His brother Prince John had immediately fled London and was basically cowering in Nottingham Castle.

Gareth addressed his people with Evelyn standing beside him on the balcony, her hand on his, "We have received word that King Richard has landed and Prince John has fled. As you all know, we put our hand in with the Prince. Prince John stayed to lead while King Richard left us to battle in a foreign land. While King Richard was away he still demanded taxes to pay for his war and men to fight. We sent him only those men who wanted to go and no monies, as we realized this town did not have enough to pay both rulers. We watched as some towns suffered trying to please both brothers. Richard will not easily forgive this family. If Richard's soldiers come for us, we want the castle emptied. We do not want any of you harmed. Stay in your homes or in the countryside and do not come to our aid, for you would be dealing with men of war who have come home but may still be seeking a winning fight. These men may have forgotten they are the sons and husbands and fathers of England, that they should not make war on their own people."

Only some scant few months later, the King took notice of a town called Glastonbury, a town that appeared to be thriving. He did not recognize the family name well. What he did notice, when the Lord Chancellor brought it to his attention, was that the Avalons had not paid their dues to him while he was away. It was not long before the Duke and Duchess received an official summons to court.

Gareth and Evelyn braced themselves as they were brought before the King. They bowed deeply.

"Do not think we have forgotten that you did not pay us tribute while we were away," boomed King Richard authoritatively.

They hesitated, waiting for an actual question from the King. It would be unwise to speak up otherwise.

In the end, Gareth and Evelyn were given leave to return home, but their hearts were heavy. Though banishment from court came as a blessing, the judgment against them was harsh; their lands and titles would die with them, pending an investigation. They did not ask what merited an investigation or what it concerned. The wicked look on the Lord Chancellor's face told the tale of retribution. And it mattered not to King Richard that Guy was connected to the Crown. They knew enough of past dealings to know Richard did not like Guy. In his ruling, Richard deemed Guy to be a knight at best; the title of Baron was revoked as there was already a true lord of Locksley. Thus, Morgaine lost titles and land by having married him. Then there was the matter of unpaid taxes. A huge sum was levied against the Avalons. Evelyn could sense the whole coven protecting them and knew that was the only reason they escaped with their lives.

"Remind me why we let them go, Lord Chancellor?" The King was drumming his fingers on his throne. It had been several months since the Avalons had been summoned and released. The taxes levied against them had been slowly trickling in.

"You are speaking of the Avalons, yes, Your Highness?" Roderick posed.

"Well, of course I am speaking of the Avalons," shouted Richard, forming his hand into a fist and pounding the throne with it. King Richard had

Roderick send out spies after them to gather information on the Avalons and the goings on in Glastonbury.

"We thought it would solicit more evidence against them, with them thinking they were released on your good graces, Your Highness."

Richard sighed with exasperation. That was not what was happening. With every report, he was repeatedly met with deflection from Father Stephen and Father Hale. Their letters were vague and offered little real evidence that the Avalons were traitors or heretics. Though something was amiss. His spies returned ill and unable to remember anything they saw. The King was becoming more irate with each new obstacle presented before him in gaining any pertinent information.

Meanwhile, Prince John kept his distance from the Avalons as he heard via his spies that his brother was gathering information against this family. "What news?" he asked his servant who came in and bowed.

"Nothing new, Your Excellency. There is no word from Glastonbury. But your brother does appear vexed at not gaining any evidence against the Avalons."

John nodded and flicked his fingers at the servant in dismissal. He felt so alone and wished for companionship. His old friend William was now dead. When the populace of Nottingham had heard of the King's return, there was a riot. After the angry townsfolk swept through the castle, the Sheriff and several of his men were overtaken and killed. By the time Prince John got there, they were a bit more cowed. It was one thing to rise up against a sheriff; it was another matter entirely to come up against the crowned Prince.

CHAPTER 59

※

What Is in a Name

THE FAMILIES GATHERED together for supper in the dining hall as they normally did. There was much sweet and easy talk though there was an undercurrent of sadness, something that no one was ready to address, a knowing that these easy times in the castle would be ending. Though it was time for a strategy, there was no talk of it.

Julius sensed the adults' preoccupation with troubled thoughts even amidst their light tone. He wondered and listened with his heart. There was a feeling of unspoken concern; he felt the weight of it in the room. It had been this way since the Duke and Duchess got back from London. But he felt what he had to say was important, too, and if the adults were not going to talk about their concerns about the future, they could at least hear what he had to say about his future. He stood up and looked around. Only slightly slow on the uptake, the adults all turned to face the lad. When he saw he had their attention, Julius took a deep breath and stated, "I now wish to be known as Juwelin."

Gwenhwyfar looked at Guy in a mock accusing way before turning back to her son, asking, "Any particular reason?"

Juwelin nodded affirmatively, "Mother, I know Father is of Roman descent and he wanted us to bear Roman names. Julius does not fit with this Land but Juwelin does. I want to fit with this Land, keep part of my heritage while discovering my own way. I have had dreams that I shine a light from a jeweled scepter I carry. In The Merlin Manuscripts, it states that there comes a time on The Merlin's path where one consciously chooses a new name for oneself. This sacred act symbolizes coming into what one is meant to be."

Gwenhwyfar nodded, "I understand and I shall do my best to remember to call you Juwelin."

Juwelin looked around. All heads nodded in agreement. He sat back down, relaxed, and centered in his new being.

It was autumn again and young Green Rod was reveling in his life in Glastonbury. Though some of part of him missed his father, he was becoming more of a distant memory as Wild Herb took the lad under his wing. Green Rod emulated Wild Herb, taking on a meaningful descriptor before his name. He wanted to blend in with the landscape and feel that ticklish freedom of the grass on the edge of the woods and fields. He felt Green Rod suited him. He didn't make any big production of it at the dinner table like his younger brother; but out here, in Avalon Forest, he was Green Rod. And as Green Rod, he was spending more time at Wild Herb and Elizabeth's cottage, sometimes not going home at all. That did not go over well with Gwenhwyfar his first time away. She was sick with fear all night, with Guy doing his best to convince her that he was probably fine and with Wild Herb and Elizabeth, that it had just gotten too late to head home.

When Rod did eventually show up the next day, he realized immediately by the look on his mother's face that she was not amused by his disappearance. He came to her sheepishly. "I am sorry Mother. I did not mean to give you cause for concern. I stayed over at Wild Herb's last night."

Arms folded, Gwenhwyfar fumed silently as she did her best to calm herself. She knew her boys were growing up, as young as they were, and she knew they were safe as could be here in Glastonbury. Still, a mother's fears are hard to quell. She took in the apology. She nodded slightly as she considered her words, "I am glad you had the sense to stay there instead of attempting to walk alone in the dark. Can I trust that is where you will be if you do not come home some evenings?"

Green Rod nodded gravely, not wanting to upset his good fortune. His mother was accepting his actions. He gulped. Some part of him was ecstatic that she accepted he was growing up. Some part of him, though, suddenly wanted to cling to her skirts, protected by her arms, and to dwell in the innocence of childhood.

As another testament to Green Rod growing up, Wild Herb decided it was time to have the lad accompany the hunting party. He and Gwenhwyfar discussed it while Green Rod stood rigid waiting to hear his mother's response. He wasn't actually sure he wanted to go but he knew he did want to make his mentor happy. Mainly his mother nodded with pursed lips. In the end, she agreed to Wild Herb's continued training. She had been approached by Rainer and Elizabeth last year about the possibility of him becoming a Guardian. But it was actually Rodney who did not take to that. After four moons passing, Rodney was still resistant. He missed Wild Herb. He would not admit, even to himself, how much he needed a father figure around. But it was clear to Rainer, during the boy's trials, that Rodney did not have the aptitude for accepting that Mother and Father were within him and that he could self-soothe his angry heart. And so Rodney was released and sent back to Wild Herb and to his family. Rainer and Elizabeth were disappointed, but Wild Herb was secretly glad to have the boy around. His own son had died long ago and far too young; so to have this second chance swelled his heart.

Guy was in the lead of the hunting party as Gareth participated less and less now that his adopted son was there to give the hunt legitimacy in the eyes of the law. Guy was not overly excited to accept Rodney as a member of the group. He could see Rodney was keenly aware of his surroundings and did well minding Wild Herb, but the boy did not work well as part of a team. Still, it was obvious he wanted to prove his worth to this company of men.

The troop silently approached the herd. Guy nodded to Wild Herb who prepared Green Rod for the shot.

Green Rod had been practicing for a year and had proven to be a good marksman. Now was the time for his real life test with a large animal and he knew, not only was the hunting party counting on him, but the townspeople as well. It was a huge responsibility and he was nervous. He wanted to succeed in their eyes and to make Wild Herb proud.

Remarkably, Green Rod's aim was true and he hit the deer. But though the deer was shot, the deer did not drop; he bolted instead. Green Rod looked to Wild Herb in dismay, "Now what?"

Wild Herb replied, "Now we track the deer."

Guy nodded and let the two go so that the other hunters could continue deeper into the woods in search of more food. Another hunter accompanied Wild Herb and Green Rod as they tracked the blood.

Wild Herb explained to Rod, "Look at the blood."

Green Rod got down close and tried to figure out what he was supposed to be seeing other than red liquid splattered on the earth.

Wild Herb continued, "There are bubbles in the blood. It's a lung shot."

Green Rod was upset. "I shot the deer in the lungs? Gods, what a horrible way to die."

Wild Herb patted Green Rod on the shoulder and looked at the lad fondly as he showed compassion for his prey. Eventually, the three found the deer. The young buck, by this point, was not struggling much. Still, they approached him with caution.

Wild Herb was grave, "We need to help him die."

Green Rod looked on with a pained expression on his face which both hunters saw.

The other man spoke softly, "It is good you show remorse. Never forget you take this life to survive and to feed the people in your care."

Back in the woods at their homestead, Wild Herb returned with Green Rod. They started a fire to smoke the portion of deer meat they came home with. As they were finishing up working on their project, Elizabeth came out and flashed her ankle at her husband. Wild Herb smiled and nodded. Green Rod saw the movement but had no idea what silent conversation had passed between the couple.

"Green Rod, I want you to finish this up and then head home."

"Why?"

"When you are older, you will understand that when your wife gives you signs of interest, it is time to put all else aside and attend to her."

"Why?"

"Because it is the good and right thing to do and leads to sex."

"But you are too old to have kids. Why would you want to have sex?"

"Again, when you are older and ready to have sex, it is a grand and sweet way to spend time with your lover. Sex is not just about making babies. It is about deepening a bond with your beloved."

"Oh."

"There's my bonnie sweet lass," Wild Herb called to Elizabeth as he came in the door to find her lounging on their bed.

"You coming to bed?" she asked with mischief in her voice.

"Yes," Wild Herb stated slyly as he removed his shirt.

She giggled.

His eyes danced upon her. "After all these years, Woman, the flash of your ankle still awakens my manhood like there is no tomorrow."

Elizabeth giggled again, raising her eyebrows as she brought her hand down to her skirts and drew them up past the ankles and past the knees. Wild Herb bit his bottom lip and then practically pounced on his beloved. Their laughter and moans carried outside to Green Rod's ears. He found himself curious but not enough to approach and spy on the pair. He made quick work of his task and then quietly departed, leaving the older couple to their private delights.

CHAPTER 60

⸘

1195 Coping with the Known and the Unknown

OVER A YEAR had passed since Gareth and Evelyn had been brought before the King. Life went on in Glastonbury. Ever the darlings of the palace and town, Morgaine and Guy could be seen together much of the time holding hands in intimate conversation or sneaking off for a little afternoon delight. A more-than-budding romance was in evidence between Gwenhwyfar and Taharqa as they held hands and stole kisses from each other. There was no talk of the husband who had never written or returned to claim his family. It was like he simply vanished. The children all grew and thrived. Rhiannon would be turning two years old soon and she was learning words rapidly. And Neirin was no baby. He was a rascal of almost four years old and quite a handful for Gwenhwyfar. Luckily, her eldest two sons were old enough to occupy themselves. Juwelin was quite the astute student with Rainer and he and Guy spent much time in the Apple Orchard or up in Guy's study. And Green Rod tended to find himself in Avalon Forest with Wild Herb. Gwenhwyfar was glad her boys were finding themselves and seemed content with their life here. And Anwen was pregnant with her own child who was due soon, but she was still able to keep up with most of her duties. Thankfully, Mouse was a natural babysitter and if he wasn't helping out with Rhiannon, he was chasing Neirin around.

The Avalons continued to send King Richard money, trickling it in, in an effort, both to demonstrate their commitment to make amends, and to not alert the King that they actually had the funds. It was, of course, the riches Guy had amassed while at Nottingham.

"Well, you can't take it with you," he smirked when Evelyn and Gareth had told everyone what had happened. "I hate the idea of giving it up to Richard, but what does it matter if it will help keep him away?"

The four agreed to dole it out to the King over a period of time. And they were still doling a year later. The coins were running low but they had enough. Yet, the stress was wearing on all of them. Strangers came to town asking questions. Evelyn turned to the cunning arts more and more to encourage forgetfulness in these spies. At first she had some remorse in forcing her will onto these strangers. But as they kept coming, she reminded herself that everyone had a choice and they had made theirs; so she would make hers to protect her family and this town. And it was paramount to protect their way of life. Evelyn could see that the gentle peace of Glastonbury was showing strain as spies trickled in and out of town. People began to feel more guarded and wary as these strangers asked questions about the Avalons, even about the priests. They asked neighbors about neighbors and about churchgoing habits. They asked the townsfolk about people on the outskirts and then asked the people on the outskirts about the townspeople. There was an undercurrent of fear about what the future would hold.

And then Father Stephen disappeared. The Bishop had summoned him over three months before, and he had not returned from Bath. Gareth and Evelyn conferred with Father Hale.

Father Hale wrung his hands. "Should we make an inquiry?"

Evelyn closed her eyes and centered herself. He had been veiled from her and she still could not see where Father Stephen was. To make matters worse, she was not sure if making an inquiry would be making things worse for them. Could Father Hale safely make an inquiry?

"The monks have received no word?" Evelyn asked.

Father Hale shook his head.

Gareth pursed his lips, "Why would anyone inquire that he has not seen fit to communicate with the monks or whether the Bishop has sent a replacement? I think we may have to leave this one."

Evelyn liked Father Stephen. He served his purpose and he was a kind fellow. She continued to watch Father Hale. "Father Hale, do you have any suggestions?"

The priest continued to wring his hands. He liked it here in Glastonbury. He liked the Duke and Duchess. They were fair, kind sovereigns. And though he was sure they were not Christian, they certainly were not bad. Long ago he had come to appreciate how they ruled their realm regardless of their unorthodox beliefs. He did not want to see this thriving town come to harm, nor did he want to lose this ruling family. He shook his head. "Your Grace, I am at a loss. I do not know how we should proceed." He paused, weighing what he would be willing to do. "I could travel to Bath and appeal to the Bishop." He almost regretted his offer for fear of leaving his flock, but the look on their faces let him know they were not willing to risk him as well.

Gareth looked at Evelyn and then put his hand on Father Hale's shoulder, "No, my friend. We do not know what has befallen Father Stephen. If the Bishop has not seen fit to inform his own monks or you, then there is nothing to be done."

CHAPTER 61

Invoking the King Stag

RAINER'S DREAMS CONTINUED to grow with intensity and he grew fearful for the Avalons.

"No Guy. You must ride in." Rainer was pulling at Guy's arm, as they watched Morgaine, Evelyn and Gareth being hauled away by the royal guards. Guy fought Rainer fiercely, trying to get to his beloved, but Rainer willed himself to hold fast like an oak. In fact, his arms and legs looked like tree limbs and roots.

Guy sagged in defeat and screamed, "How could you?"

"You must ride in and save them. You must give your life for them, for Avalon."

The scene changed and he saw Guy on Midnight riding up the castle steps. But Guy was not himself; he looked monstrous. For he was not only clad in black, animal hide showed where skin should be, and a huge rack of antlers was upon his brow. Flames appeared all around him. It was as if every beast wished to claim him and clothed his body with theirs as he galloped through the castle hallways toward his beloved. Guy and Midnight entered the great hall and placed themselves between the Avalons and the King. Guy raised his sword and uttered a great scream that was comparable only to the sounds of the dragons of old. It was ground-shattering, and the stones of the palace shook with fear. Guy fought off the guards with ease, even as he jumped down off Midnight. His sword sliced and the blood of the guards splattered the guests of the great hall. Guy really was the Dragon's Breath fighting off the invaders. But then a sly creature came upon Guy from behind. It was a fox. And the fox slew the beast that was Guy. And Guy fell, his blood pouring out, drenching the stone. But where his blood soaked in, a mist rose and covered the Avalons so that no one could see them. They were safe. That was what mattered most.

Rainer awoke with a jolt and bolted for the castle. Through the forest he ran, branches making way for him. He was The Merlin, whether he accepted it or not. Though even that did not matter in the end, for he was too late as he reached the edge of the Lake and looked out at Camelot. He watched the family dragged away in chains. He could only pray that Guy played his part well. He did not call for his comrades. He merely watched… and prayed.

His first prayer was to the Stag King, invoking His being in an effort to quell his anger, and trust there was a reason for this path —

> *Oh sweet, gentle Lord of the Forest*
> *Come; be here now.*
> *I have followed Your trail and found Your tracks in the woods;*
> *You leave hearts wherever you step*
> *and I want to walk the path of compassion too.*
> *Let me walk by Your side, caress Your strong back, Your soft fur.*
> *Let me breathe in Your wildness, nose to muzzle,*
> *and feel Your breath upon me.*
> *Let me listen to Your heart, Your blood,*
> *Your vitality, pumping through Your veins.*
> *Let me gaze into those soulful eyes and join with Your spirit.*
> *Oh sweet, wild Lord, let me touch You and know the world.*
> *Come; be here now.*

Then Rainer saw Her. So close. Shimmering. Regal. He bowed his head in prayer to Her. She, too, was watching the family being carried away.

She was ancient yet timeless, known to many as the Lady of the Lake. If a man could see Her, he might think Her a spirit, a being made of light with a hue of blue. If a man could see Her move through the forest, he wouldn't say She was walking. More like a slow, steady glide. When the Guardians caught glimpses of Her, they bowed their heads slightly, bringing one hand to the mouth, kissing their fingertips, then bringing those fingertips to their forehead, then extending their hand out toward Her. It was a gesture of reverence.

These woods held such sacredness to Her, for Her people dwelled here, clinging close to Her bosom. And these woods held Her beautiful Apple Grove. She breathed in the scent. And if one could smell Her, She would smell of those same fragrant apples. She went to the shore and looked out onto the Lake, Her Lake. Her eyes scanned the landscape. "Ah, there He is; My Consort, the Stag King comes to Me." She sang and sang, calling to Him sweetly.

Rainer listened with his heart and he heard the Lady singing. It reverberated through his whole being. But the song was not for him. It was for the Stag King, his proxy in bodily form, who was being drawn away. Rainer knew it would not be long now. He called out in his mind to Juwelin, "Come. Let us prepare."

CHAPTER 62

Old Adversaries

IT WAS LAMMAS in the year 1195 when the Avalons were brought before King Richard again. Their people were out in the fields cutting the ripe grains, taking care with the scythe so as not to cut themselves. Drops of blood always spilled on the land this time of year. A good omen of sorts, this was all the Gods were requiring of a person in sacrifice to them.

It had been over a year since the Duke and Duchess stood before him. Now the four of them stood in King Richard's receiving room. Of all the people who stood flanking the King, they were surprised to see two couples: Marian and Robin and Thomas and Edwena. Upon seeing Glastonbury's High Priest, Father Stephen, sullied and in chains, they knew something had transpired that meant not just their doom but Glastonbury's as well. The biggest surprise was actually seeing the sniveling Rufus sneering at the family in triumph as he stood next to Father Stephen.

"Where did he come from?" whispered Gareth.

Evelyn shook her head not knowing how or why; and at this point it didn't even matter.

Morgaine's eyes caught and held Marian's. Marian had a pained expression on her face. She searched Morgaine's eyes, and Morgaine heard, "I wish there was some way I could help you." Morgaine gave an ever-so-slight nod in recognition and then forced herself to calmness so she could center herself for what was to come.

Little did the Avalons know that Rufus, shortly after leaving their home those few years ago, had approached Prince John about reclaiming his wife and children. The Prince wasn't overly fond of the Church but Rufus did have strong accusations. Still, he was annoying and did not bow low enough. And it did not sound like he truly loved his sons.

Prince John pressed, "And do you love your sons?"

Rufus was indifferent, "They are mine."

John considered having the rat-like man run through. It was only strategic to keep him around. So instead of being cut down, Rufus was thrown into the London Tower to sit and wait and rot until someone decided he might be of use. But it wasn't John who used Rufus; it was King Richard.

Rufus had heard the King's guards talking after locking up Father Stephen. His hoarse, vindictive voice carried and the guards overheard him say, "I will help. I will collaborate with what the Father is saying. The Avalons, they are witches and they have my sons."

Rufus was brought before the King. Enough time in prison had taught him to abject himself more properly. He abased himself against the stone when he was brought before King Richard.

The King hardly looked at the grimy simpleton lying at his feet. He merely asked, "You have evidence against the Avalons?"

Rufus meekly looked up as he replied, "Yes, Your Majesty. Those women, they are serpents. They are enchantresses."

"Of whom do you speak?"

"The Duchess of course. And her daughter, Morgaine. She hisses evil things into my wife's and children's ears as we speak."

"What evil things?"

"That there is a goddess. That a goddess reigns supreme. And that she is the Lady of the Lake of old."

King Richard's eyebrows rose at that last statement. Words went through his mind — "Lady of the Lake," "Excalibur," "Round Table," "Camelot," "King Arthur."

Rufus realized he had the King's ear, so he went further. "Your brother was at the Lady Morgaine's wedding. She bewitched him and slept with him even though she was married to another that same day."

"Silence! Do not speak so of my brother..." King Richard shouted. Then he paused, considering the prisoner's words. This could actually be fodder against his brother, to have it suggested that Prince John was in league with an enchantress. King Richard allowed the statement that the dirty prisoner made to hang in the air. The King wouldn't want to believe such a thing could be true. But by not having this man hanged immediately, the question would lurk, instead — rank — in the air. To one of the guards King Richard commanded, "Have this man cleaned up, fed, and waiting for when I have need of his testimony."

King Richard was condescending in his tone to the Avalons, droning on about how this family was traitorous to the crown and Christendom. He sneered about how they openly practiced pagan rites and converted good Christians to their wicked ways. "I have witnesses," the King proclaimed, nodding first to Father Stephen who stood hunched and with a cowed head, and then to Rufus who bowed to the King and looked upon the Avalons with an evil heart.

Ignoring the charges, Gareth spoke up, "They are our people, and they deserve our care and protection. You abandoned your own people."

"They are heretics. You are all heretics," spat King Richard with venom in his voice.

"Only according to you," retorted the defiant Duke. Did he dare add that the word heretic came from the Greek word hairetikos 'able to choose?' Did it matter in the end? The King would not listen.

Meanwhile, Guy maneuvered himself around Gareth to stand before the whole family, putting his body in the way of the oncoming guard. He bore the Pendragon emblem embroidered on a tabard that Morgaine had made for him. He figured if they were doomed anyway, it was time to make a statement about the family's heritage. Let the world know the Dragon still prevailed and protected Avalon.

Standing to the right and slightly behind the throne, Chancellor Roderick balked. He recognized the symbol. Somewhere in the Order of the Black Knights' history, so long ago, they had stood with the Pendragon. So few knew of this legend but Roderick made it his business to have studied the Order's past. The Black Knights were protectors in the night, shadows watching over the people, the Dragon's Breath against the enemy. For when stealth and secrecy were needed, it was the men of the Dragon's Breath who were summoned. But to belong in the shadows made this Order shadier in nature. To them, the hero on the white steed was merely a decoy. The real job at hand was done in the shadows, unseen, unsung, unappreciated. And so the Dragon's Breath in time became known as the Order of the Black Knights. These knights turned away from their true purpose for there was no one left to remind them of their true purpose. No Merlin to temper their strength with wisdom. They turned and twisted. They came such a long, tangled way from their original mission. And here was Lord Guy Avalon, a Black Knight himself, bringing the Order of the Black Knights full circle.

Though Guy had been relieved of his own sword, he deftly outmaneuvered the soldier nearest him and took his. This prompted more of the King's guard to come at him.

"I will not let you harm my family!" warned Guy.

Richard spat back, "You cannot protect them. You are a rogue and a heretic. I have God on my side."

Guy shook his head in defiance, "It doesn't matter what you call me — villain or hero; it is not that simple. I am here to fulfill what I am meant to do. I am here to do the thing that is left. Not the good, not the bad, not even the right. Just my purpose."

Richard sneered, "Then your purpose is to die."

Guy closed his eyes and whispered, "I embrace my path. Lady, lead me where you need me to go."

The King's guards descended upon Guy. Though he was outnumbered by several, he fought gallantly. But he knew he could not win this physical battle. Surely the Goddess had something else in mind. Then the King yelled for a halt. The guards broke away from the fight and Guy caught his breath.

"Lord of Locksley," King Richard called out, "I would have you slay this beast. Come, fight for your King and Christendom."

Robin drew a breath and looked grim but determined.

Marian grabbed hold of Robin's arm. "Robin, no," she whispered loudly.

He looked back at her in angered bewilderment, also whispering loudly, "What would you have me do, Woman? I am under the King's command." He drew his sword and walked purposefully toward Guy.

"So it comes to this anyway," stated Guy flatly.

Robin nodded slightly as if not fully wanting to commit. Though he knew he had to. But before the men could raise their swords a bloody hide was thrown at their feet.

"For Sir Guy," Richard mocked.

Guy looked at this king with despise. He must have found out what Guy had done all those years ago. And now, out of sheer malice, he had had some horse killed and skinned just to poke fun at Guy. Well, Guy would not be so jarred by this attempt to shake him. Instead, he picked up the bloody horse-hide and put it on, the horse's head atop his. Though the hide was very heavy and sticky with blood, Guy's bow was mocking the King who, in turn, only fumed at not having shaken Guy's confidence. Guy turned back to Robin who had the look of disgust on his face. But disgust turned to fear as Guy raised his sword and screamed a blood-curdling scream, "May the Dragon's Breath forever protect Avalon!" With that, metal clashed on metal and the old adversaries fought with deadly intent. They grunted and strained. Guy pushed Robin's advance off with his sword.

"Why do you fight for him? He kills his own people," Guy hissed.

Robin eyed the King and then retorted, "He is our King."

"You fought for freedom while he was away. You fought for justice and the common man. And now?"

Robin did not know how to answer. And to think of an answer while fighting this brute was proving challenging. "Aag-ha," he grunted instead as he lunged at Guy. Robin didn't want to think that Guy could be right. Guy was the villain, not he. He didn't want to think how Guy had stood in front of the guards protecting the Avalons; that family meant more than politics.

Guy, still in chains, could not gain the upper hand. There was no way he could beat Robin like this. Robin, smaller, quicker, and having all limbs free, fought like a fox hounding a wounded stag, jumping deftly away from danger after he slashed at Guy's body. They fought on, each maneuvering around the other. It was well matched with Guy's hands in chains, for though he was the better swordsman, he could not block or strike as nimbly as this younger bowman. With face slashed and right arm bleeding and with an aching weariness in his body, he switched the sword to his left hand and raised it once again to block Robin's advances.

Robin thought he had the advantage now, not knowing that Guy was equally, if not more, adept with his left arm. They fought on. And Robin was sorely mistaken for thinking that, by switching arms, Guy was at a disadvantage. And the gash in his right forearm was shocking proof of how quick Guy was with the sword. It was only now dawning on Robin that during swordplay when they were little would Guy switch in midstream to his left hand and more brutally attack. Clashing swords and the grunts and strains of two men locked in battle echoed in the hall.

But after fighting off the other guards and now fighting Robin with more wounds than he cared to notice, Guy's strength was waning. He slipped on the now bloody floor and fell with his back hitting the cold stone. Robin lunged at him but Guy was quick enough to roll away and Robin landed on the underside of the hide. His knees hit the hide with a sickening squishy thud and his trousers were soaked instantly with the hide's blood. Guy staggered back up to his feet, feeling lighter now that the hide was off of him. But he could barely hold up his sword between the weighty pull of the chains and the new gash on his left shoulder; he had not been quick enough in the roll to avoid more spilled blood.

Robin stood up, facing the King. "What would you have me do, Your Majesty?"

"Finish him!"

Robin saluted King Richard, but his resolve diminished. He was tired. He didn't want to hate Guy anymore. He looked over at Marian and saw her crying into Edwena's arms. She couldn't contain herself. He didn't want her to suffer. Morgaine and Guy were her friends and she did love him. So long ago they were all childhood playmates. Guy eyed Robin warily. He could see that Robin was conflicted about something. He looked over to where Robin was looking — at Marian.

"Finish him!" the King demanded again.

Guy took his chance, declaring with labored breathing, "You know she loves you. Do you think you are doing what is best? For her sake?"

Robin scowled. He didn't think he was. But he loved his King, too, and felt conflicted. For he did not see the rightness or the good in killing Guy.

Guy took Robin's hesitation as an opportunity to look upon his love, proclaiming with great earnestness, "Morgaine, I love you with all my heart and I will live and die protecting you."

With tears in her eyes, Morgaine nodded and uttered, "And I love you with all my heart."

With a motion from the King, two guards approached the family and Guy left the fight with Robin to attack the approaching guards. "NO!" Guy screamed and swung his sword. But as his sword came up to cut at the one, the other stabbed him in the side.

He staggered, and fell. He shouted at Richard, "My body may fall this day but never my soul...for I am the Stag King."

Roderick's mind whirled. The Chancellor stammered, "That title has not been invoked since the time of Uther Pendragon." Guy stared defiantly at him. He seethed and he spat, "You must have royal blood."

Guy coughed blood, "You know I do."

The King was in disbelief. "This is blasphemous. It's a myth."

Guy smirked, "It is true."

But before anything more could be said, Morgaine was at Guy's side and the King had to endure yet another assault to his senses.

Though Morgaine had watched in horror as the men fought, her legs would not move. But with the falling of her beloved, she parted the guards with a searing energy that knocked them down, their heads reeling in pain. She closed the gap in seconds and fell at her husband's side taking his head in her lap.

Guy forced his words through a pain-racked body. "Get me to Avalon. My sacrifice must not be in vain."

Before the guards could understand what was happening, Evelyn and Gareth rushed to Morgaine's side and together they focused on Avalon. Evelyn and Morgaine commanded the ethers to transport them, and the family vanished before the entire eyes of the court. They never heard Richard screaming, "Nooooo!"

The family felt the swirl of the whirlwind around them. When they adjusted their eyes, they found themselves in the Apple Orchard with Rainer and Juwelin in deep concentration, holding the space around them. Evelyn and Morgaine looked at each other, almost astonished that they managed to pull off such a feat. Instantly, though, Morgaine's attention was on Guy. He was dying. Morgaine could not bear to lose him.

Hearing her thoughts Guy whispered, "You will never lose me. Kiss me."

They kissed. Though they were in the Apple Orchard, Morgaine felt summer barley tickling her palms. She felt the breeze and saw the scythe, knowing that one cycle had come to its completion. She heard the Goddess ringing in her ears, "In a love so deep, so complete, the Dying God is compelled to return into Me." In placing her lips upon her beloved Guy, she felt a drawing in to her being. His spirit went into her. They joined as the Lady and Lord incarnate. Guy's body fell away from Morgaine. Morgaine looked around blinking, disoriented. Evelyn and Gareth looked on with concern while the expressions of Rainer and Juwelin were unclear. It was apparent that something quite rare had transpired in that kiss, and everyone could see that there seemed to be two beings looking out from Morgaine's eyes.

Morgaine spoke, her voice strange, deep and far away, "We must bury the body here. We must give back to the Goddess Her Champion, Her Stag King, to complete the circle. Together, They can protect Avalon."

As if on cue, the rest of the Guardians appeared. They prayed and then began to dig. The Earth opened up easily. The Guardians removed the torc from Guy's neck and then gently eased the body that was Guy into the ground.

As Morgaine threw a bit of soil on the body, she had the oddest expression on her face; it looked as if she was smirking like Guy would. "I really enjoyed that body." Suddenly she was crying.

Evelyn sat down next to Morgaine, trying to comfort her daughter. The Two-Who-Became-One looked penetratingly into Evelyn's eyes, "Faie blood. Use my blood to protect Avalon."

Evelyn looked frightened. It was not an expression Morgaine ever remembered seeing in her mother.

"Not mine. Guy's. You are the only one who can bring down the mists and break the bond between Avalon and Glastonbury. It is why I died."

Evelyn nodded, recognizing that it was hard for these two to express themselves in one body. She had never heard of such a thing occurring.

Rainer came to be with them. He had overheard. "They are right. We must act to save Avalon."

Gareth interjected, "We also need to protect the people of Glastonbury."

Suddenly, Morgaine redirected everyone's focus by exclaiming, "Where's my daughter?"

Rainer and Gareth had to help steady the Two-Who-Became-One as she rose to her feet. Guy was not used to being inside his woman's body in this way and he was very disoriented. The now-merged couple focused on walking, one step in front of the other. It got easier as they agreed to give themselves over to the Lady, allowing themselves to move as one. They reached the castle, walked the steps, and headed for their room. Meggie was on the floor playing with Rhiannon. They both looked up as Rhiannon's mother walked to them with Evelyn, Gareth, Rainer, and Juwelin looking on.

Morgaine squatted before her daughter and held out her hands but Rhiannon paused as she reached out for her mother. Something was different. She took her mother's face in her tiny hands, asking, "How do you bof fit in dar?"

CHAPTER 63

Escape from London

KING RICHARD, SO vexed by his glory having been stolen from him, demanded, "Burn it down. Burn down the heretics' town — all except the Tor. Show them that only the Church survives." He then turned on Marian. "And you! What are those tears for?"

Edwena had been watching and slightly bumped Marian, gesturing that Marian was to answer. "Me, Your Highness?" Marian questioned through her tears.

The King glared at her.

Thinking quickly, she responded, "This is all so upsetting. I didn't want to lose my husband."

"I think you are league with them. You lived with them."

Marian did not know how to answer. Moving her head back and forth slightly with her mouth open as if to deny his accusation but afraid to actually say anything, Marian was simply in shock with all that had just taken place. She was relieved that her husband had not killed Guy. She was relieved that the family got away and that her husband was alive. And she was in overwhelming grief to see her childhood friend, Guy, die.

"Guards, take the Lady Marian away!"

Robin stood in shock at his King's command. "Your Majesty…" Robin bowed low.

"Yes Lord Robin, you have something to say?"

"My wife, she is a good Christian. Please, she is just an emotional woman. She has done no wrong."

"Robin, she must be questioned. Those witches just vanished. Marian may know something."

Marian shook her head. Surely she did not. She cried out to her husband, "Robin!" She sobbed as the guards bore her away, two others barring the way with spears crossed as a warning to Robin not to interfere.

"Lord of Locksley, prepare for battle." The King's voice was commanding.

Robin turned to the King, bowed, and backed his way out the door. But he didn't prepare for battle. He wasn't going to Glastonbury. While the King was otherwise occupied, Robin stole down into the dungeon.

"Now you just sit tight, missy," one of the guards was saying as he closed the door.

Before he turned the key, Robin knocked him out with the hilt of his sword to the man's head. The other guard came at him and, with the dagger in his other hand, he cut the man's throat. For when it came down to it, Robin realized that he could not allow the love of his life to suffer. Nor could he live without her. He would kill to protect her. He didn't want to admit it, but Guy had the right sentiment for he, too, would live and die protecting his wife. Their love was more important than the King's law. He opened the door and Marian leapt into his arms.

"Robin, you came for me!"

"Marian, my darling, I love you. I will always come for you. Now let's get out of here."

As an outlaw, Robin was used to being sneaky. And so sneak they did, winding their way through the castle halls. With all the commotion of preparations to storm Glastonbury, no one managed to make their way to the dungeon until it was too late. The alarm was called shortly after the pair made it out of the castle. Together, Robin and Marian travelled to and disappeared into Sherwood Forest.

CHAPTER 64

Attack on Glastonbury

EVELYN HAD RETREATED into herself, concentrating fully on the task at hand to undo what she had done when she was Morgaine the First centuries ago. She stood in the Apple Orchard willing her mind to meld with her ancestor and her spirit. An eerie mist began to gather around her, and she listened to its instructions.

It was less than a fortnight later when soldiers marched on Glastonbury. It had been hardly enough time to prepare. So many did not want to leave their homes. They thought that surely the soldiers would only destroy the castle. But Gareth was not convinced of that. He pleaded with his people to empty Glastonbury. But when so many would not, he could not leave them to fend for themselves.

The Duke of Glastonbury called out to his people, "The future may judge me, but whether they deem me to be a hero or a villain, I did not stand by and do nothing. I made my choice to stand against a tyrannical king and to stand for a person's right to see God in one's own way, and I can live and die with that. For those who cannot, who will not leave, I will stand with you and fight by your side."

There were monks and nuns in the crowd amongst the multitude of various spiritual persuasions. They somehow all knew this sanctuary was coming to an end but they couldn't bear to part with this piece of paradise. And so remnants of Glastonbury stood their ground to protect those who chose to flee, to live another day.

Morgaine pet Merryweather as she saddled up Midnight, "No, little Love. You stay here with Rhiannon. I will ride into battle with Midnight." The horses touched cheeks as Morgaine, clad in armor slightly too big for her, prepared to help her father. The two beings were still working out how to be as one merged person. It was all so new, but duty called. Guy felt a strong pull to be out in front to stand with Morgaine's father.

Juwelin came up to Morgaine, but addressed her as if she were Guy, "I want to be with you. I want to fight at your side."

Morgaine squatted down to look Juwelin in the eyes, speaking as Guy. "I know you do. I am very grateful. Still, we must keep you safe. You are studying to be the next Merlin and this community will need your skills more than ever to keep them safe. Please understand; we have every intention of returning. We do not wish to die."

With tears in his eyes, Juwelin nodded and stated, "I understand, Morguy. I will stay here and wait for your return. Then we shall continue our studies together. All the books are already in Avalon Forest."

"There is a good lad. Morguy, eh? Hmm. It fits. Thank you. We needed a name that would make sense to us." The two hugged and Morguy kissed Juwelin on the forehead before saddling up. As Morguy rode off, Two-Who-Became-One caught sight of Ink circling around and then landing on her human's shoulder. She cawed mournfully, smelling death on the way. Juwelin petted Ink, whispering to her, "I know."

Midnight did not understand why his human's mate was mounting him but he sensed something was different. This female human, though still maintaining her own voice, was talking to him with the inflection and tone that his human used. And so when Evelyn, who came back to the castle to collect the rest of her belongings and bear them off to Avalon Forest, walked up to Midnight, whispering, "Be sure to bring them back alive," Midnight somehow knew that he was carrying two beings, despite there being only a small female rider on his back.

Rainer searched the throngs for his lover. He knew he would be staying behind to protect those remaining near the Lady of the Lake as she prepared to bring down the mists around Avalon. He also realized that Aelred would be going with the rest of the castle guards to protect the Duke. Too many helmets. He called out from his mind, "Aelred, my love, look up."

There! A tall muscular man looked up and was drawn to look around. That man then heard a whistle. It was a signal he knew was meant for him. Aelred broke away from the other guards and headed toward the sound. He found his lover standing at the corner of a wall. Rainer tilted his head as an indication for privacy, and the two men slid around the wall. Aelred removed his helmet and put it on the ground. They embraced and kissed each other fiercely. Rainer pulled at his brunette's hair and let his fingers tangle in the softness of it.

Aelred pulled away slightly to look Rainer in the eyes, his voice only slightly quivering, "Will I come back to you?"

Rainer wrinkled his nose in an effort to quell his concern, stating with passion in his voice, "You'd better!"

The two lovers kissed again and held each other for a moment longer. Then Aelred picked up his helmet and, with his other hand, put his fingers to his slightly bowed forehead, extending them out to Rainer. It was a goodbye of sorts, a way for Aelred to let Rainer know that he revered him and honored him. It was his way of demonstrating that his love for Rainer was undying. Rainer then touched his forehead with his fingers and extended them out toward Aelred, letting Aelred know the same. Aelred then turned and walked away to rejoin the castle guards who were now on their way to the field between the castle and the Lake. As Rainer watched his lover walk away, tears slid down his cheeks, for he had already foreseen his man dying in battle as so many soldiers do protecting their leader. He wanted to believe it was an honorable death. Still, it was a death and he mourned the loss of his sweet man.

Gareth and Morguy rode out ahead of the village, with the guards and armed townspeople behind them. Gareth and Morguy had begged Taharqa to stay behind and protect their family. Taharqa led Evelyn, Meggie, who was carrying Rhiannon, Gwenhwyfar and her children, and the other townspeople who were not joining the fight, to the relative safety of Avalon Forest past the Apple Orchard. Evelyn then stopped, as did Rainer. The other Guardians came from the forest and stopped at the edge of the Lake behind Evelyn. They kept a respectful distance and watched as Evelyn stood rigid at the edge of the Lake, her silvery-blue gown sweeping around her as she summoned the mists. She did not want to complete the spell however, until her beloved returned to her. She was not ready to lose him. She prayed that this fog she was creating would deter the King's soldiers from entering Avalon Forest.

The villagers, though some did possess a bit of skill with the sword, were not soldiers. They were not hardened by holy war; they were merely men, women and a few boys devoted to protecting their home. It was a slaughter. Morguy fought deftly, but in this slight body Morguy realized they were losing. Suddenly, Morguy felt the excruciating sting of an arrow and collapsed forward. Midnight, feeling his slight mistress slumping over, raced away from danger. Midnight felt the presence of both his master and his mate, and would not allow them to die. With Morguy leaving the field, those who could run away quickly did. So many were cut down as they raced for Avalon Forest, now shrouded in mist. Others ran toward Glastonbury Abbey, praying God would protect them. Gareth remained, pinned under his steed. As luck would have it, he was truly pinned and appeared dead to the soldiers coming through, stabbing all the wounded.

But the soldiers lost their stomach for pursuit of the retreating townspeople who were fleeing this way and that into the forests. Instead, they focused their efforts on Glastonbury. The King said he wanted Glastonbury burned so that is what they did.

Rufus was enlisted and allowed to march with the foot soldiers. As quickly as he could, he broke free of the fighting and ran away into town. He had no intention of dying on some battlefield. He stormed the castle in search of his sons. The place looked deserted. Even the dragon tapestry was gone. He called out to them, but they were not there and so did not answer. He screamed curses at Gwenhwyfar. But she was not there and so did not hear him. The only other souls who appeared to be in the castle were the King's men lighting the place on fire. He ran to the wing where he and his family had stayed during the wedding, but the room was barren of belongings. And as some semblance of justice would have it, Rufus found himself trapped in a burning castle. He attempted to flee by climbing up into a turret. But nothing would save him now.

Glastonbury burned. The castle was aflame. Even the bricks ignited. There were explosions as the bricks popped from the heat. Was it just the heat from the fire? That would probably be unlikely, though who would be the wiser? Nonetheless, as the magic fled from the structure, so many bricks shattered as if releasing all the pent up energy of maintaining glamour all those centuries. The castle burned to the ground leaving only rubble; shimmering Camelot was in ruin. While the structure was in flames some of the soldiers thought they saw relics burning in the fire. These soldiers screamed as though the vision was the cause of their agony.

"Burning! It is Camelot that is burning!"

"The Round Table is burning!"

"The Grail; the Holy Grail is burning!"

"The Lady of the Lake is burning!"

"The Mistress of Excalibur is burning!"

When these soldiers returned days later to tell King Richard, in their grief and madness what they saw, Richard had them killed, forbidding anyone from writing down this account.

CHAPTER 65

What Remains

MANY WILD STORIES would continue circulating across England in the coming months before King Richard had them all suppressed, including seeing Lord Guy of Avalon on his black stallion on the battlefield wearing a horse's hide. Others swore it was Morgaine covered in raven feathers. Her body was never found. Neither was Guy's. Rumors spread that when Glastonbury Castle burned, Morgaine the Sorceress was seen atop a turret, burning and screaming curses. Unfortunately, as Evelyn had foreseen, the Avalons' story would not be told, and the family would be forgotten. The Lady of the Lake would vanish from the outside world.

But that was not important in the moment. What was important was tending to the incoming wounded and the protection of Avalon.

Gareth, along with a few other villagers, staggered back into Avalon Forest.

Evelyn saw her husband limping heavily with the help of two villagers, and she rushed to his side, embracing him. "Oh, my love, you have returned to me! I saw too many variables and did not see you in them until you just walked through the fog."

"It was a narrow escape, Beloved. We must fortify the protective circle around this forest. All is lost out there."

Upon seeing Gareth coming in, Rainer had walked to up the Duke and Duchess. He regarded Gareth, and Gareth could see upon his face the question to which Rainer already knew the answer; still, his pained look needed confirmation. Gareth shook his head and brought Rainer into an embrace.

Rainer trembled with grief. He knew his lover, sweet Aelred, was dead; still, knowing it was vastly different than experiencing the hard truth of it. The weight of the loss crushed his heart; it hurt more than he imagined it could. Evelyn came from behind and cradled her dear friend so that Rainer was sandwiched between the pair.

After several moments, Evelyn squeezed Rainer's torso, whispering, "Come. We must finish this."

There was much sobbing among the villagers. So many were missing or dead but there was a sense of urgency to protect what was remaining. The King's men were burning Glastonbury. How long before they turned on the forests and burned them as well?

Evelyn stopped at the fallen tree where Gwenhwyfar was nursing her childhood friend. Gwenhwyfar had just finished removing the arrow and was now stitching the wound. Evelyn touched both Gwenhwyfar's and Morguy's heads. They looked up and smiled weakly at her. As she could tell Morguy would survive the wound, she continued past them to the shore.

Morguy winced as the needle penetrated her skin. She watched her friend working without looking at the wound that missed her heart. Suddenly, she looked sad as a memory of the ocean came unbidden; Guy remembering watching his wife swimming in the water and Will remarking on her undulating form. "We won't see Nichole and Will again. Or the children."

Gwenhwyfar shook her head, letting the tears fall.

Evelyn reached the shore again. The fog was thick but she heard the soldiers' shouts in the distance. They must not reach this side of the shore. She called upon the mists to descend once again upon Avalon. She reversed what she did when she was Morgaine the First. Standing at Guy's grave, she called upon his body, the body of the Stag King. "Guy, you knew what needed to be done and your sacrifice was not in vain," she whispered, "Your blood will protect the realm." She brought her mind in alignment with the Elements. Her breath was slow and she was centered. All of her focus was on protecting the remnants of Avalon and its inhabitants. Blood of the Stag King, the Sacrificial King. The blood that mingled with the Land, giving it nutrients, sustenance. She envisioned the Sacrificial King's blood penetrating the Land; drop by drop, it infused itself with the Land. As the Land was soaked in this offering, Evelyn called upon the Dragon's Breath to shroud the Land, protect the Land. Moisture collected and brought down the mists upon the Land. The fog that she had created before thickened until it became a barrier.

Those on the outside of Avalon bore witness to a mysterious thick fog, tinged red, settling in, swallowing the Lake, the Apple Orchard, and Avalon Forest.

Evelyn sighed heavily as she came out of her trance. She gazed at Rainer and Juwelin who had been present to assist her spell work. She stated mournfully, "Another cycle coming full circle. I have to believe it was right to bring Avalon back into the world as I am now drawing down the mists to shroud it again. It will be centuries before the world will see Avalon again."

It was weeks before the strange fog lifted; but when it did, the land looked barren. Where there was once a huge apple orchard with a wide hilly forest behind it, there were only hills and grass. At the edge of the Lake, only one old apple tree remained. A sentinel that both beckoned and barred the way. The landscape had an eeriness to it; one could swear that whispers were heard on the wind, as if there were ghosts going about their day. It would be decades before Glastonbury was slowly repopulated.

Evelyn emerged from the mists into Avalon, followed by Rainer and Juwelin, with Ink flying low, cawing. Evelyn came back to the fallen tree where Morguy and Gwenhwyfar were. Now the whole coven was gathered together, plus Juwelin. They formed a circle, breathing slowly together. The fog lifted around them, so that from their perspective, it was a sunny day and they were in a glade of Avalon Forest. The mists held the barrier and their world was now separate from the outer world. It would continue to slide away from England and join with the Realm of the Faie.

Evelyn turned, laid her hand on her wounded daughter, yet addressing her son-in-law, "Guy, what story did you think you were walking into when you left Nottingham and came to us?"

Morguy smiled tenderly, "A love story."

Evelyn's weary face showed a hint of merriness. "Indeed. And if you had to choose again knowing what you know now, would you make the same choice?"

Morguy was thoughtful in speaking to his High Priestess, "Lady, I was a man of the sword. The path I left was one in which I would die alone, having lived a life devoid of meaning. I would die a thousand deaths if it meant being with my one true love."

"And you live on."

The Two-Who-Became-One hugged her body tightly, shining with an inner bliss, saying confidently, "Yes, we do."

Beyond land, title, or name, love is what remains.
Beyond strife, fear, struggle, love conquers all.

Epilogue

Sitting alone in disgrace in his self-imposed prison at Nottingham Castle, Prince John received word that Glastonbury had burned. Surely that would mean Guy and Morgaine were dead. Now he had lost three people he cared about — William, Guy, and Morgaine. As he sat in self-pity, the form of Morgaine suddenly appeared before him. John was in awe and fear but did not call out to his guards. Instead, he tried to summon a causal tone. It was not overly convincing. "Ah, my pretty pet! Where did you come from?"

Morguy ignored John's question, stating instead, "My seed shall endure long after you are dead. My bloodline will flourish while yours will end in strife. We will germinate under the light of the moon and you will not see how our numbers grow. And centuries from now, when the waters rise and wash away the numbers of man, it is we, who cling closest to the Land, who will remain."

Before John could dare speak, Morguy vanished. John shook all over. He actually felt grief, such an unfamiliar sensation. Grief from what, he was unsure. But he knew he had lost something he could never regain.

About the Author

ARIANNA ALEXSANDRA COLLINS, Poet, Priestess, Naturalist, lives in Ashfield, Massachusetts with her Beloved, John P. Buryiak, and their two kitties, Bree and Madeline. She is devoted to her town and serves on several committees and can often be found walking the back roads or hiking through forest and field, leading wild edible walks. Through her business, Offerings for Community Building, Arianna provides services in event planning, networking and promotion. This is Arianna's first novel.

Made in the USA
Columbia, SC
09 June 2017